She walked to
the bed . . .

and stood looking down at him. She couldn't keep a little smile from coming to her lips. He no longer looked deathly ill, just slightly pale. With his face relaxed in sleep, he seemed younger, more handsome. When he was awake, there was a fierceness in his expression, a power, that kept one from noticing his good looks.

Idly Victoria traced the curve of his mustache with her index finger. She wondered what it would feel like to kiss him. Did the mustache tickle? It didn't feel wiry, as she had expected. In fact, it was almost soft. His lips twitched, and her eyes went to them. She remembered the way they had closed around her finger, his tongue licking the moisture from her skin.

Something hot and sharp curled through her abdomen. She shouldn't have thoughts like this about Slater. About any man, really. But especially Slater. He disliked her. She disliked him. Didn't she?

Dear Reader:

You are about to become part of an exciting new venture from Harlequin—*historical romances*.

Each month you'll find two new historical romances written by bestselling authors as well as some talented and award-winning newcomers.

Whether you're looking for an adventure, suspense, intrigue or simply the fulfilling passions of day-to-day living, you'll find it in these compelling, sensual love stories. From the American West to the courts of kings, Harlequin's historical romances make the past come alive.

We hope you enjoy our books, and we need your input to assure that they're the best they can possibly be. Please send your comments and suggestions to me at the address below.

Karen Solem
Editorial Director
Harlequin Historical Romances
P.O. Box 7372
Grand Central Station
New York, N.Y. 10017

Satan's Angel

Kristin James

Harlequin Books

TORONTO • NEW YORK • LONDON
AMSTERDAM • PARIS • SYDNEY • HAMBURG
STOCKHOLM • ATHENS • TOKYO • MILAN

Harlequin Historical first edition July 1988

ISBN 0-373-28601-5

KRISTIN JAMES,

a former attorney, is married to a family counselor, and they have a young daughter. Her family and her writing keep her busy, but when she does have free time she loves to read. In addition to *Satan's Angel* and a number of contemporary romances, she has written several historicals under another name.

To Dorothy Garlock,
for all her help and support

Prologue

Inside the bank it was as quiet as the grave. The only sound was the ticking of the clock. Slater wasn't one for talking, and the others were too scared to.

The sheriff sweated profusely under the weight of the long duster he wore to conceal his shotgun. The deputy behind the counter, dressed like a teller, shifted from one foot to the other, his gaze going first to the window, then to the large clock on the wall. The other deputy, seated behind the desk, fidgeted with the heavy pistol in his lap.

Only Slater was still and cool. He was used to it, Sheriff Clayton guessed, unable to refrain from casting a bitter, envious glance at him. No doubt a Texas Ranger like Captain Slater had stood waiting for Death to ride in and meet him many times before. It wasn't true for the sheriff and deputies of the little town of Santa Clara, who were more used to jailing rowdy drunks than capturing the notorious Brody gang.

The sheriff glanced at the clock for the fourth time in two minutes. "Gettin' awful late, ain't it? Almost closin' time."

Slater didn't even waste a look at the clock. "Brody likes to wait until closing. He figures it means more money and more distraction."

Sheriff Clayton wet his lips, then turned away, hoping Slater hadn't noticed the nervous gesture. His heart was thumping a mile a minute, and his nerves were wound up as tight as a watch spring. He wondered if Slater felt even a twinge of fear or excitement. He couldn't tell from the man's face.

In fact, had he but known the signs, he would have seen the anticipation in Slater—the tight set of his jaw and the rigid stance, the clenching of his hand. There was eagerness and excitement in him, and there was fear—but it was less fear of possible death than fear that his information would prove to be false, or that Brody would change his mind and decide not to rob the bank today. Slater had been waiting for two years for this.

He had tracked Brody and tricked him. He had offered good money for information. He'd chased down every lead. But he had never been able to locate Brody's hideout or set a trap for him. Brody was crafty and elusive, and it galled Slater that he, the best tracker in the Rangers, had been bested by Brody every time.

But his time had finally come. Slater knew it in his bones. When Dave Vance had come to him three days ago, saying Brody was planning to rob the First State Bank in Santa Clara, Slater had known the man spoke the truth. Vance had claimed he'd played cards with Brody in a saloon in Austin; everything he had said about Brody rang true. Slater had gotten close enough to Brody once to see him, and the informant's description was accurate. Moreover, what he had said about the plans for the robbery fit Brody's usual pattern. Brody liked to ride with six men, and he was short one. For some reason he had trusted Vance and invited him to join them.

Dave Vance was a petty thief, but he was more interested in the reward for Brody's capture than in the cash split he would take from the bank, so he had come to Slater.

This time he would get him, Slater promised himself.

He stiffened, sensing the difference in the town more than hearing or seeing anything. He moved to the window, peered out, then stepped back quickly.

"Get ready. They're coming."

Seven men rode into town on the west road, then turned onto Main Street and headed north. They moved quickly, quietly, steadily, and there was something frightening in the concentration and silence of their movements. They were dusty from the road; Sam Brody didn't believe in wearing dusters—they impeded his gun hand.

Their clothes were dark and nondescript, as were their horses. But a close observer would have noticed that the mounts were all prime horseflesh, and that the men were fully armed, with rifles strapped to their saddles and revolvers holstered to their thighs.

They rode in two rows of three, with Brody in front on the left. It was where he always rode, for his gun hand was his left one. He was silent, and he barely turned his head, but his gaze went everywhere, missing nothing. A feeling of danger stirred in him, different from the usual jitters, faint and indefinable.

The men pulled up in front of the bank, and even as they stopped, Brody was sliding from his horse. Another thing he believed in was moving quickly, and he was always the first one in. The others dismounted behind him. Brody reached for the doorknob. As he pushed it open, the danger-feeling sizzled up his backbone. He caught a movement out of the corner of his eye—the new man, Vance, sidling away from the others toward the alley. Metal glinted in the room he was about to enter.

It all came together in a rush, more an instinct than a thought. Brody jumped back. "It's a trap!"

He dived off the sidewalk just as the pane of glass in the bank door shattered under a hail of shotgun pellets. A shard of glass sliced open Brody's arm, and another cut his cheek, but he noticed neither the pain nor the blood. The only thought in his mind was to get to his horse.

The animals shifted nervously at the blast of gunfire, but it was a sound they were accustomed to, and they stood their ground. Four of the men, still beside their mounts, swung back into their saddles. The man right behind Brody was not so lucky. He turned and ran down the steps, but the next blast of gunfire from the bank caught him, and he fell.

Brody hit the dirt and came up in a crouching run, pulling his gun and twisting to return the fire from the bank as he ran. A bullet buzzed past his ear, and another grazed his thigh with a red-hot sting. He heard an oath from one of his men and a gasp of pain, and then the thunder of hooves as they raced away.

On the sidewalk, Stanton, who had been shot, staggered up, firing and cursing profusely. He went down again, his face a mass of blood. Brody grabbed the reins of his horse, but the rattle of gunfire was too much for the creature, and it twisted, then reared. Brody yanked down hard on the reins and grabbed the saddle horn. The horse squealed and jerked under the impact of a bullet, then bolted. Brody clung desperately to the saddle and was dragged along for a few yards. There was another shot, and his horse fell hard to its knees.

Brody was flung to the ground, and his Colt flew from his hand. He crawled across the ground to his horse, reaching for the rifle on his saddle and pulling it free. The street had fallen silent. Brody whirled toward the bank, intending to rest the gun on the barrier of his dead mount and continue the fight, but as he turned, a man came flying off the sidewalk at him.

He was too late. Brody knew it even as he raised the rifle. The other man kicked the rifle aside and stuck a Colt revolver in Brody's face.

Brody froze, waiting for the blast of death.

But the other man just stood, staring down at him with cold green eyes like glass. His lips drew back over his teeth in something like a smile, and he said, "I'm Slater, and I finally got you, you son of a bitch."

Chapter One

Everyone knew that the two girls were the light of Ed Stafford's life. He cherished them both, though in different ways, for no two young women could have been more unalike than Victoria and Amy.

Victoria, his daughter, was as wild as the west wind, headstrong, willful and utterly competent. She was an excellent rider and could handle a gun with the best of them, and there was no one except the foreman and Ed himself who knew more about the ranch's workings. Ed had no qualms about leaving his land in Victoria's hands when he died—provided, of course, that she hadn't already gotten herself killed pulling some damn-fool stunt.

On the other hand, Amy, his niece, was a sweet, biddable girl, shy around anyone outside the family and never one to get into scrapes. She had been raised with Victoria and, like her, had learned how to ride well—indeed, she was very fond of the horses, and most other animals, as well. But she had no interest in the running of the ranch. She hated figuring and had never so much as picked up one of the big black accounts books in Ed's office; branding the calves made her sick; and she wouldn't even touch a gun. While Victoria liked to ride with her father and the men, learning every aspect of the business, Amy preferred simply to ride for pleasure, looking at the world around her, or to stay home tending a sick animal or sitting in the swing beneath the big live oak tree, swaying and dreaming.

Even in looks the girls were opposites. Amy was small and delicate, with a sweet, heart-shaped face, pale blue eyes, and fine, white-blond hair, as lovely and ethereal as a fairy princess. Victoria, nineteen to Amy's twenty years, looked far more the woman. Her carriage was straight and tall, her figure voluptuous, with full breasts and a waist so narrow it beckoned a man's hands. Her hair was as black as midnight, thick and silky, and her eyes were a vivid, startling blue. Victoria was beautiful, but not in the sweetly feminine way Amy was. Her features were vibrant and compelling, from the crow-black slash of her eyebrows to her sensually full mouth.

Ed Stafford smiled down the length of the breakfast table at the two young women, thinking how fortunate he was to have such fine daughters—for that was how he had thought of Amy since the day she had been brought to his house, pale and trembling, fifteen years ago. Her mother had been Stafford's sister. She, her husband and the rest of their children had been killed in an Indian raid on their farm, and only little Amy, whom her mother had hidden in the root cellar, had escaped death. The neighbor who had found Amy two days later, hungry, weeping and speechless, had remembered the name of her mother's brother and brought her to him. The Staffords had taken Amy to their hearts, and she had returned their love in full measure.

"I'm going to miss you two," Stafford said, his manner joking, but his voice tinged with real regret. "Why'd I ever agree to let you go to San Antonio, anyway?"

"Because you're a wonderful man," Victoria replied with that flashing smile that had melted more hearts than her father's.

Amy smiled too, and added with a childlike modesty, "And because you said you'd be glad to have us out of your hair during the roundup."

Victoria chuckled. "She has you there, Daddy."

"Well, I should at least have decided to escort you there myself, instead of entrusting you to that softheaded Mrs. Childers."

"Mrs. Childers is a perfectly proper chaperone."

"You can be perfectly proper and still have fluff for brains, which is what I think that woman has."

Victoria stifled a laugh. "What could happen to us between here and San Antonio? We'll be on the stagecoach practically the whole time. Amy and I could go by ourselves without a bit of trouble.''

Her father snorted. ''With you along, I-hate to think what could happen between here and San Antonio.''

Amy smiled and said nothing. Victoria and her father often engaged in this sort of affectionate bickering, but she never entered into it. She just listened, hearing what was communicated by the tones of their voices more than what was said in words.

Victoria made a face at her father and rose from the table. ''Well, if you'll excuse me, I'd better see to the packing, or we won't even reach the stagecoach stop, let alone San Antonio.''

Her father nodded, and Victoria left the room. As she climbed the stairs to the second floor, she could hear the rising babble of excited voices, two in rapid Spanish and another in Irish-accented English. It was obvious that the housekeeper, Mary Doherty, was already engaged in a wrangle with the Mexican maids.

Victoria found the three women standing beside the bed in her room, surrounded by open trunks, carpetbags, and a profusion of dresses, petticoats, shoes and lacy underthings. They were all talking heatedly in their respective tongues and waving their hands about.

''Mrs. Doherty, what is going on here?''

The small, gray-haired Irishwoman swung around to face Victoria, relief showing on her face. ''The saints be praised, ye're here. It's the divil's own work, explainin' to these haythens—''

''Now, Mrs. Doherty...''

''Sure, an' there's not a smidgin o' understandin' in 'em.''

Victoria suppressed a smile. It was no use pointing out to Mrs. Doherty that Elena and Dorotea understood well enough everyone's English except Mrs. Doherty's heavily accented speech. The housekeeper was convinced that the two girls knew what she was saying and only pretended to misunderstand when it suited them. They got along well enough in the ordinary course of things, communicating in a bizarre garble of English, Spanish, Gaelic and hand gestures. It was only when tempers grew short that the voices became too rapid, the accents too thick, the gestures too wild, and their system of communication broke down completely.

"What's the problem?" Victoria asked, and was immediately hit with a spate of outraged words that she could make neither heads nor tails of. She threw up her hands. "Wait! Stop! ¡Silencio!" She drew a breath. Resolving quarrels, especially about "women's work," was not her strong suit, and it was an effort for her to be patient. "Now. Mrs. Doherty. You first."

"I came in to check on 'em, and look what I found 'em packin'." She pointed to the open leather trunk, where Victoria's riding skirt lay folded on top. The housekeeper waggled her finger, her face flushing with displeasure. "Them horrid, haythen ridin' trousers. Ye canna be meanin' to take them with ye to the city."

Victoria's jaw set. "I can be meaning to, and I am." She nodded at the other two women. "Go ahead and pack them."

"Tory, child, think! 'Tisn't daycent for a girl like you to be flittin' about in—in pants!"

"They're not pants. It's just a split skirt. When I'm off the horse, it looks like any other skirt."

"Any other skirt without petticoats! Faith, an' that's not the worst of it—ye sit a horse like a man when ye wear it. If yer poor mither, God rest her soul, could see ye wearin'—"

"She wouldn't be able to stop me, either," Victoria said mulishly. This was an argument she had had repeatedly with her housekeeper.

"An' what'll ye be needin' a ridin' skirt for in the city, anyway? Ye'll not be ridin' all over there like ye do here."

"Well, I might get a chance to ride, and I'm not going to risk having to turn it down because I don't have my riding clothes. I'm taking my boots, too."

Mrs. Doherty's lips thinned. It was obvious that she wouldn't win this argument, and it galled her. "Ye're a hoyden, an' it's glad I am that yer poor mither's not alive to see ye ruinin' your name."

Victoria glowered. She regarded herself as a grown woman and was sure that she could handle the ranch, the men and almost anything else that came along, but when Mrs. Doherty scolded her she felt like a child again, stubborn, angry and proud. "Amy wears exactly the same kind of riding skirt as I do, and I never hear you say anything to her about it."

The other woman's face softened, and she made a dismissive gesture. "Ah, that one—she's different. She was touched by the fairies."

Victoria would have liked to make a biting retort, but she couldn't. Mrs. Doherty always excused Amy; everyone who was close to her did. But Victoria herself was Amy's first and foremost defender. She had taken Amy under her wing when she had first come to them, so scared she couldn't talk, and had been her protector ever since. It was Victoria who had wrapped her arms around Amy when she awoke at night, screaming and crying from dreams she couldn't remember. It was Victoria who had held Amy's hand when they walked to school. And after Victoria had bloodied Ben Hartwell's nose for saying Amy was crazy, no one had ever said a word about Amy where Victoria could hear it. Whatever it took to save Amy from hurt, Victoria did.

Victoria sighed. "You're right. She's special." She straightened her shoulders and looked Mrs. Doherty in the eye. "But I'm a grown woman now, and you know I'm going to do what I want. I have since I was sixteen."

Mrs. Doherty's mouth twitched in a movement of combined irritation and amusement. "Sure, now, and before that, too."

Victoria smiled. "You're right. Now, this isn't getting us packed any sooner, is it?"

The housekeeper nodded her agreement, and the two of them pitched in to complete the packing.

When they were done, there were two hump-backed leather trunks full of their clothes, as well as another pair of carpet bags, stuffed to bursting. The two ranch hands who carried the trunks down groaned at the sight of the luggage.

"Sure 'nough, now, Miss Victoria, are you just goin' for a visit, or are you movin' in with 'em down there?"

"It's not all mine!" Victoria protested, chuckling. "And besides, you can't go to a wedding with only a couple of dresses."

"With what you got in here, I reckon you'll cast a shade over that bride."

"Don't be ridiculous." Victoria followed them down the stairs, laughing and joking with them. She always got along well with the men on the ranch. They knew they could be easy and friendly around her, but they also respected her knowledge and skills, and when she gave an order, none of them would think of not following it.

While the trunks were being loaded onto the back of the wagon, Victoria went in search of Amy. Time meant very little to Amy, and schedules even less. She could still be looking at the horses when they were supposed to be leaving for the station.

A quick glance told Victoria that Amy wasn't in her favorite spot, the swing under the live oak tree, so she headed toward the barnyard. She went first to the corral, thinking Amy was probably saying farewell to her mare, Cotton. Victoria stayed for a moment to caress the nose of her own gelding, then went inside the barn to the stall where they kept the motherless calf that Amy had been feeding by hand. Next she climbed up the ladder to the loft.

There she found Amy, sitting cross-legged on the floor, a pile of mewling, crawling kittens in her lap. One brave little ball of fluff had climbed up her arm and sat perched on her shoulder; another lay cupped in her hand. Her fine blond hair was pulling loose from its pins, and several strands straggled down around her face. There was a streak of dirt across her skirt.

Victoria sighed. She felt equal urges to scold Amy and to pull her close and hug her. "Amy."

Amy looked up and smiled, and all desire to scold flew from Victoria's head. Amy was different from other people; the same rules simply didn't apply. There were those who said that Amy was strange, even "touched." But if Amy was "touched," it was, as Mrs. Doherty said, by the fairies. She was special. There was a childlike joy to her that rubbed off on everyone around her, and she loved with intensity. There was always hope and kindness in her heart. She was attuned to any sort of hurt or unhappiness, and she was quick to offer her warm sympathy. Victoria couldn't count the number of times that Amy had quietly slipped her hand into hers, or given her a hug and a smile at just the moment when she was feeling the lowest. Just as Amy took in any stray or wounded animal and gave it suc-cor, she also opened her heart to any person in need of help.

It didn't matter that Amy didn't quite fit in with the rest of the world. It didn't matter that she was hopeless with figures, chores and decision-making, or that she was unconscious of time and unable to make small talk. Victoria or her father would always take care of those things for Amy. Amy's gift to the world was simply her presence.

"Hi," Amy said softly and extended the kitten in her hand toward Victoria. "Look, Tory. Isn't he beautiful?"

"Yes. Very beautiful." Victoria smiled and squatted down beside Amy, taking the little creature. The kitten mewed and settled into her palm, beginning a rumbling purr so strong its tiny body quivered. Victoria chuckled.

"I named him Thunder."

"How appropriate."

"And the white one's Lightning." Amy picked up another kitten and rubbed it against her cheek. Her face was alight with pleasure.

"Sweetheart, it's time to go. You need to come back to the house and get ready."

"I know. That's why I came to say goodbye to the kittens." Amy sighed and set each kitten down gently on the floor, gig-gling at the way they immediately tried to crawl back into her lap.

Victoria helped hold the kittens away, and Amy rose lithely. She looked down at them, and regret touched her face for a moment. "They'll be so old when I get back, I'll hardly know them."

Victoria took her cousin's hand. "Don't you want to go, Amy?" It had worried her that Amy might not enjoy being in San Antonio, even though she had wanted to go. What if she missed the ranch and the people she knew. What if San Anto-nio was so big and bustling that it frightened her?

Amy looked at her, her pale blue eyes lighting up. "Oh, yes, I want to go. It will be fun, won't it? I want to see the wed-ding. Daphne will look like a princess in her wedding gown. Don't you think so?"

Daphne Henderson, the bride-to-be, had gone to finishing school in San Antonio with Victoria. Though Amy had remained at home the three years Victoria had boarded at school, she had met Daphne when Victoria's friend had visited her on the ranch. Amy had liked the warmhearted girl very much, and she had been pleased and proud when Daphne had invited her to the wedding along with Victoria.

Amy's face fell a little. "Don't you want me to go, Tory?"

"Of course I want you to go. It'll be lots more fun with you along. I was just afraid that you might get lonely for the ranch and the animals."

"And Uncle Edward."

"Yes. Or that you might get scared in a new place."

Amy considered the thought. "I'll miss the ranch and everybody. But I won't be scared, not with you along. And I'll be back soon." Again the smile that was like the sun breaking through the clouds flashed across her face. "I think it'll be wonderful to see all those new things!"

"Then we'd better hurry. I expect Daddy's already pacing up and down the porch, waiting for us."

They climbed down from the loft and hurried out of the barn and across the yard to the house. Ed Stafford, while not actually pacing the porch, was standing there pulling out his pocket watch and glancing at it with an air of impatience. Amy and Victoria darted past him into the house and up the stairs. Victoria put Amy's hair back in order, and they changed into their traveling clothes, plain brown dresses that would not easily show the dust stirred up by the stagecoach.

Dressing for a party or church or any formal occasion was typically a complex process that required the help of another person and consumed a large amount of time, for then they had to wear laced-up corsets made of whalebone and a half-cage "bustle" in the back to produce a fashionable silhouette. But in daily life on the ranch and for ease in traveling, they wore much simpler dresses without the stifling corsets and awkward bustle, so they were able to change quickly and run back downstairs before Ed Stafford started sending up messages that they were going to miss the stage.

They hurried out onto the porch, tying their bonnets as they went, and Stafford helped them up into the wagon. It was a two-hour ride from the ranch into town, but it didn't dampen the young women's spirits. They were still chatting and laughing by the time the wagon pulled up in front of Adelaide Childers' house in town. It was a small white house fronted by a jumbled flower garden that was indicative of Mrs. Childers' personality.

As soon as they stopped, the front screen door flew open, and a middle-aged woman ran out onto the porch. "Oh, my gracious me, Colonel Stafford—" Victoria's father had been a colonel in the Confederate Army during the War, and many people in town still addressed him by his title. "I am *so* embarrassed. You're right on time, and here I am, not even ready yet. You must think I'm the silliest thing." One hand fluttered to her chest, and she smiled coyly, as though her silliness were a charming quality that Stafford would doubtless appreciate.

Victoria bit her lower lip to keep from grinning. It was quite apparent that the Widow Childers had her cap set for Ed Stafford. Victoria was sure that that was the reason Mrs. Childers had been so happy to chaperone his daughter and niece to the wedding in San Antonio. Unfortunately for Adelaide Childers, Mr. Stafford found little appeal in fluttery stupidity. It had galled him to have to accept the favor of Mrs. Childers' chaperonage, but he had been unable to find anyone else and was too busy with the spring roundup to go with the girls himself.

Stafford sighed and climbed down from the wagon, forcing a polite smile onto his lips. "Good morning, Mrs. Childers. There's still time before the stage arrives. Perhaps Victoria could give you a hand."

It was his daughter's turn to sigh this time, but she climbed down from the wagon, followed by Amy, and went into the house. The inside of Mrs. Childers' house looked as if a cyclone had hit it, but Victoria managed to get everything straightened away, and a trunk and a carpetbag packed in a matter of minutes.

Ed carried the trunk out to the wagon, and Victoria followed with the soft bag. Mrs. Childers tied on her bonnet and wasted several minutes searching for the key to her front door before she could lock it.

By the time they arrived at the stagecoach office, there was barely time for Stafford to purchase the tickets and kiss Amy and Victoria goodbye before they had to climb into the coach. Their luggage was strapped on top, the driver and shotgun rider climbed up onto the high seat and the coach pulled away. Amy leaned out the window, waving to her uncle, and Victoria squeezed against her for a last look at her father.

It was only when they could no longer see Mr. Stafford that Victoria and Amy settled down and took stock of the other passengers. The two young women and their chaperone sat on one bench seat; opposite them sat a portly middle-aged man in a dark suit, and next to him was a short man as wizened as the other man was fleshy. Under Amy's and Victoria's regard, both men doffed their hats and said "Afternoon, ladies," almost in chorus.

The short man seemed to see the humor in himself and his companion, for he smiled briefly. As the coach rocked along, there was little else to do than talk, and soon the short man struck up a conversation. He introduced himself as a businessman from Austin, and that led to the other man's saying that he was a legislator returning to the Capitol. Victoria started to introduce Amy and herself, but Mrs. Childers was cognizant of her duty, despite her general silliness, and she hurried to introduce the girls and point out that she was the young ladies' chaperone.

Before long, Mrs. Childers and the legislator were chatting away like old friends. The other man settled himself against the back of the seat, bracing his legs against the bumps, and went to sleep.

Victoria leaned over to Amy and whispered in her ear, "I think Mrs. Childers may have found a new quarry."

Amy's lips twitched into a grin, but then she looked back out the window. "Isn't it wonderful?" she asked Victoria, her pale cheeks pink with excitement.

"What?"

"Everything." She made a gesture toward the land through which the stagecoach rolled.

Victoria smiled. Any trip was interesting, of course, but she and her father had come this way several times when she was attending school in San Antonio, and the landscape was familiar to her. But she realized how rarely Amy had traveled away from home. She had never accompanied them to San Antonio when Stafford took Victoria to finishing school, and Victoria doubted that Amy had gone anyplace other than to Austin on

a few shopping trips. Victoria had never thought about how
little of the world Amy had seen. She had always assumed that,
shy and gentle as she was, Amy was happier in the shelter of
their home. But seeing Amy's enthusiastic interest, Victoria
began to wonder if Amy hadn't been deprived. It made her
doubly glad that her father had decided to let Amy come along
this time.

Amy, on the other hand, was enjoying the spring landscape
without regretting that she hadn't left the ranch many times
before. She was happy on the ranch and had never felt sorry
that she so rarely left it.

She remembered almost nothing of her childhood before she
came to her uncle's ranch. There was only a vague, dreamy
memory of a tall, dark man with a rumbling voice and of being
held in his arms, her head against his chest, feeling the rise and
fall of his breath against her cheek and the steady thump of his
heartbeat, and smelling the scent of man and sweat and horse.
She had no recall whatsoever of what had happened to the rest
of her family, and she had made no effort to remember; everyone said it was just as well she didn't. The first thing she really
knew was coming to the Stafford ranch. Her uncle had taken
her into his arms and held her, and so had Victoria, and she had
known instinctively that she would be safe with them. It was
always that way with Amy; she rarely thought, she simply felt.

The ranch was her home, her place; Victoria and Uncle Edward, her protectors. She had loved it there, and because she
took pleasure in simple things, she didn't grow bored; each and
every day held something new and fascinating. So when Victoria or her uncle had gone somewhere without her, she had felt
nothing worse than loneliness that they weren't there; she
hadn't wished that she could go, too. Even now, in the excitement of traveling and seeing different places, she felt no regret. She had been happy then; she was happy now.

Amy knew that her easy contentment was one of the things
that led people to say that she was stupid. She guessed they were
right in saying she wasn't bright. Certainly she didn't have
Victoria's quick wit, or her fascination with the why and
wherefore of everything. She didn't like figures, and she quickly
lost interest in books. Those things seemed to be what made
people intelligent. However, she was happy being the way she

was and saw no reason to try to change—even if she could have
done such a thing. Once she had heard Uncle Edward say that
Amy didn't think with her head, but with her heart. That was
true, she knew, and she couldn't imagine being any other way.

It was nightfall when they reached Austin, so they spent the
night at the Avenue Hotel on Congress Avenue. Amy had been
in the city a few times before, but she was still awed and amazed
by it. She was fascinated by the long horse-drawn trolley cars
and the crowds of people; she was awed by the state capitol
building. There was so much noise and movement, so many
large buildings, that it was almost overwhelming. Victoria told
her that San Antonio was even larger and more fascinating, but
Amy found that hard to imagine.

So did Mrs. Childers, who babbled on and on about the
modernity and beauty of Austin and "the Colonel's" kindness in sending them to places like this until Victoria wanted to
scream. She was beginning to wonder how she would manage
to endure their chaperone's interminable chatter for a whole
month.

Early the next morning they caught the stagecoach to San
Antonio. Victoria was thankful that at least at this hour Mrs.
Childers was a trifle more subdued. The stagecoach was full of
passengers today, and the two girls were squeezed between the
wall of the coach and Mrs. Childers. There was another businessman on this coach, as well as a newspaper reporter who had
obtained a job in San Antonio, a salesman, and a man whose
attire, weathered skin and callused hands proclaimed him to be
a cowhand.

The ride was even rougher and dustier than it had been the
day before, and with all the bodies stuffed into the vehicle, it
was soon hot. It was a distinct relief when the coach pulled into
its first rest stop two hours later in Santa Clara. But then Mrs.
Childers met with disaster.

She was stepping off the coach, her head turned back to ad-
monish the girls to be careful, when her foot tangled in her
long, trailing skirt, and she stumbled, one leg twisting behind
the other. Victoria grabbed at her, but she wasn't quick enough
to save her, and the older woman tumbled to the ground,
shrieking as she fell.

"Mrs. Childers!" Victoria nimbly jumped down to the ground and knelt beside her. "Are you all right? Did you hurt yourself?"

Mrs. Childers' face was contorted with pain, and a small groan escaped her. "I—I think there's something wrong with my leg."

Victoria glanced up at the other passengers, who stood gaping at them. "Send for a doctor. Quickly."

The cowhand hustled into the way station, calling for the manager. Victoria turned to Amy. Her cousin's face was white, her eyes wide and scared. She couldn't bear to see any creature in pain. "Amy, love, why don't you go inside? I'll stay here with Mrs. Childers." Victoria cast a look of appeal at the older businessman, and he took the hint, reaching out to take Amy's arm and leading her gently across the yard into the building.

They waited for what seemed an eternity. Now and then Mrs. Childers whimpered, and tears ran down her cheeks. She shook her head. "Oh, dear. Oh, dear. What a silly thing to do."

Victoria patted her hand and tried to reassure her, although she wasn't feeling very hopeful about the injury. She suspected Mrs. Childers had broken her leg.

The cowhand returned with the doctor, who brusquely ordered the rest of the passengers away. He introduced himself to Victoria as Dr. Bauer and, after one look at her calm face, told her that she could stay. Victoria stood beside Mrs. Childers, shielding her chaperone with her wide skirts as best she could, while the doctor turned up the woman's skirt and petticoats and examined her leg. Mrs. Childers yelped in pain.

The doctor sighed and informed them that the leg was indeed broken. He proceeded to set it there in the station yard. Mrs. Childers' modesty, even in the midst of pain, would not allow another man besides a doctor to view her naked leg and rucked-up skirts, so Victoria volunteered to help. She was used to the rough medicine of the ranch, where a doctor was usually several hours away. From the time she had been a child, she had tended wounds and illnesses, and she had a strong stomach and a rudimentary knowledge of medicine. The doctor found her quick and competent. It surprised him, but only a little; this hard country didn't breed weaklings, men or women.

Victoria held Mrs. Childers down with all her weight and strength, and the doctor straightened the woman's leg, pushing the snapped bone back into place. Mrs. Childers heaved against Victoria's restraint, crying out. Then her eyes rolled back in her head, and she fainted. After that, the process was easier. Victoria was able to release Mrs. Childers and help the doctor position the leg and the splints for binding.

When at last Mrs. Childers' leg was firmly wrapped in place, the men carried her on a makeshift stretcher down to the hotel. By this time she was conscious again and alternately bemoaning her clumsiness and deploring the spectacle she was creating by being borne through the streets like a piece of furniture.

They reached the hotel, and while Victoria checked them in, the men negotiated the stretcher up the stairs and through the hall to Mrs. Childers' room. Finally she was settled on her bed, and everyone left but Victoria and Amy.

"Oh, this is terrible! Terrible," Mrs. Childers wailed. "What will your father say?"

"I'm sure he will say that he's very sorry this happened to you."

"He'll be furious with me. I was so stupid."

Victoria was inclined to think that her father would believe Mrs. Childers had broken her leg through some sort of silly behavior, knowing how Ed Stafford felt about the woman, but she saw no reason to add to her load of remorse by telling her so.

"You couldn't help it," Amy said softly, coming around to the side of the bed and picking up one of Mrs. Childers' hands. "It's not your fault you fell. It was an accident. I broke my finger one time, and Uncle Edward wasn't at all angry."

Even in the depths of her despair and self-castigation, Mrs. Childers couldn't help but smile at Amy. Though Amy hated the sight of pain or blood and avoided it whenever she could, she was good with a recovering patient. Her gentleness and quiet patience were exactly what was needed to soothe the restlessness and discomfort of bedrest.

"Amy's right. It was an accident."

"But what an awful time for it! What are we going to do? There's the wedding in San Antonio, and here we are stuck in this place. I don't even know where we are."

"Santa Clara. At least it's big enough to have an adequate hotel. Don't worry about the wedding. It's almost a month away. We have plenty of time to get there. We can stay here until you're feeling better."

"But we can't just live here. I'm tied to this bed. You and Amy will be without a chaperone." Mrs. Childers looked horrified. "Why, already you've had to deal with that man at the desk, and you will have to eat in the dining room. Well, perhaps you could have your food brought up to the room on trays. But, in any case, you'll be on your own!"

Victoria suppressed a smile at the woman's horror. She had certainly done harder things in her life than signing a hotel register. It had been rather interesting, actually; she'd never registered at a hotel before, for she had always traveled with her father. And though she would never have wished anything so awful on Mrs. Childers, she was looking forward to these next few days on their own. Victoria was used to doing things for herself, and she hadn't liked the idea of a chaperone hanging over her for the next month.

"We'll manage. I'm sure nothing too bad will happen to us," Victoria replied lightly. "Now, you must stop thinking about this and get some rest. Amy and I will go and send Daddy a telegram about what's happened."

"Oh, dear, yes, you must let him know. He'll send someone to take care of you girls."

Unfortunately, Victoria was sure that was exactly what her father would do. For a moment she contemplated not sending the telegram for a day or two. After all, she was capable of taking care of herself and Amy. But even though Ed Stafford knew that, he wouldn't flout propriety by allowing them to go unchaperoned, and he would be hopping mad at her for not telling him. With a sigh, she decided that she'd better send the telegram straight away. At least she'd have her freedom for a day or two. She and Amy could explore the town, eat out in public by themselves, and do whatever else took their fancy.

The girls put their bonnets back on and went downstairs. The desk clerk gave them directions to the Western Union office, across the town square and just past the sheriff's office. Amy and Victoria sauntered down the street, taking their time and looking around them. Victoria might have to send her father a telegram, but that didn't mean she had to *hurry* about doing it.

They crossed the street and stepped up onto the wooden sidewalk that ran past the sheriff's office. Just as they did so, the door of the sheriff's office opened, and three men emerged. One of them was the sheriff. Another was also clearly a lawman, though he wore no uniform. There was a silver star in a circle pinned to his vest. He had a pair of lethal Colt .45 Peacemakers strapped to his thighs, and in his hand he carried a carbine. His other hand was curled tightly around the arm of the third man, who was just as clearly a criminal. His hands hung down in front of him, a heavy iron manacle on each wrist, connected by a length of chain.

Amy and Victoria stopped abruptly. The lawman and the prisoner turned their heads quickly at the sound of the women's shoes on the wooden planks, and Victoria felt the piercing gaze of two sets of eyes. One was a cold, clear green, like the color of leaves under frost. The other was as flat and black as death. For once in her life, Victoria felt a chill of fear; she'd never seen any two men who looked meaner.

Chapter Two

For a long moment, the four of them simply stared at each other. Victoria stiffened her back against the unaccustomed tingle of fear. There was no way she was going to let *them* see that she was intimidated by the mere sight of a criminal—even if he was the coldest, meanest, most vicious-looking man she'd ever seen.

The outlaw's clothes were dirty, as if he'd lived in them for several days, and one sleeve was torn and stained with dried blood. The front of his shirt was likewise splotched with blood. Several days' growth of beard roughened his jaw, and a red cut slashed one cheek. His black hair was long and shaggy. His skin was weathered, his face as hard and unmoving as granite. And his eyes—Victoria had never seen eyes that black or that cold. It was certainly no surprise that he was in chains.

The lawman with him was little better. He was shaven and clean, at least, but he had the same air of toughness, the same hard set to his face. All her life, Victoria had known rough men; it took that sort of man to tame the harsh land of Texas. But never before had she faced a man who was dangerous. And this man, star or no star, was dangerous.

The lawman's cool green eyes flickered over her, and suddenly Victoria was very aware of the fact that she was wearing a plain, travel-stained brown dress and bonnet. She must look like a Quaker, she thought, and wished she had changed her clothes. Men had always told her that she was beautiful, and it seemed unfair that at this moment she should look so ordinary.

Something of her chagrin must have shown on her face, for the barest trace of a smile touched the man's lips, and his eyes warmed a little. Color rushed to Victoria's cheeks. What was she thinking of! Why should she care what this man thought, or how she looked to him? She didn't even know him. She didn't want to know him. He looked like the kind of man you would walk out of your way to avoid.

But she couldn't help noticing that his face was handsome, his lips firm and finely cut beneath a rakish mustache, or that his shoulders were broad and powerful. And she couldn't keep her eyes from straying to the long, smooth line of his legs and his narrow hips, accentuated by the wide leather gun belt he wore.

It wasn't at all like her. Her breath came a little faster, and her fingers curled into her hands. For once in her life, Victoria was uncertain.

Then Amy moved beside her, startling them all. "Amy!" Victoria reached out to grab her arm, but it was too late; Amy was already past her, walking straight up to the men.

Amy had never viewed the world as others viewed it, and she didn't now. She did not see, as Victoria did, an outlaw in the grasp of the law. She saw only a man who was dirty, tired and in pain, whose cheek and arm were cut, and whose arms were weighted down by the heavy iron bands around his wrists, which had been rubbed raw by the manacles. Amy's heart went out to him.

"You poor thing." She reached out and took his hand, sliding the manacle up his arm to expose the broken skin where it had rubbed. She felt in her pocket, removed her handkerchief and wrapped it gently around his wrist to protect it from the rough friction of the metal.

Sam Brody stood utterly still. In his whole life he'd never seen a woman as beautiful as the one before him, all delicate pink and gold and white. She made him think of the painted angels that he'd seen as a child in St. Louis Cathedral when he'd slipped inside on a cold winter's night to get warm—before the priest or nuns saw him and chased him away.

She had stunned him by picking up his hand. Her flesh was soft and warm, her touch gentler than anything he'd ever felt. He'd known the hands of many whores, but no lady had ever touched him, and no woman's fingers had been tender on his flesh. Amy looked up into his face, her pale blue eyes huge and serious. "This will keep it from rubbing so."

Brody was stabbed with pure longing. He wanted her. Wanted her in a way he'd never known before, with his whole being. "Don't you know who I am?" he asked, his voice roughened with desire and the knowledge that she was as far away from him as the moon.

She smiled a little. "No. I'm sorry."

He was pierced by the sweetness of her words and voice, as if she had reached down inside him and laid her warm finger on the scars of his soul.

Slater was startled when Amy left Victoria and walked up to Brody. He had seen her beside the other woman, but he had barely noticed her, for he was too distracted by the vivid beauty of her companion to give this pale girl more than a glance. When she took Brody's hand, he was able to do nothing but stare for a long moment, transfixed by the sight of an obviously well-bred girl daring to talk to and even touch Sam Brody.

When Brody spoke, it broke Slater's trance, and he jerked Amy's hand away. "What the hell do you think you're doing? Get away from him."

The girl glanced up at him with wide, innocent eyes, not angered, just surprised and questioning. Brody's lips drew back from his teeth in a feral snarl. Slater released Brody's arm and lifted his rifle to hold it ready in both hands. But it was not from Brody that the attack came. It was from the other woman, the black-haired beauty with the vivid blue eyes.

She threw herself between Slater and the blond girl, as though to protect her. Her eyes were flaming. "Get your hands off her! How dare you!" Her voice was vibrant and rich, even though it was quivering with fury.

Slater's loins tightened involuntarily, and his response to her irritated him. This was no time to be thinking below the waist, with Sam Brody beside him and these two women creating confusion. "Who the hell are you?" he snapped. "Get out of here, and take her with you."

"Amy's not hurting you. There's no need to yell at her," Victoria retorted. She, too, was confused and more than a little irritated by the strange effect this man had on her, and it was a relief to be able to vent some of her feelings in healthy anger.

"No need? Lady, she's interfering with my prisoner. Do you know who this is?"

"No, and I don't care. You have no right—"

"I have every right. I'm transporting this prisoner to Austin on the noon stage. You and this girl are interfering with that. What's the matter with her, anyway? Is she crazy? This is Sam Brody, for God's sake!"

Had he not cast the slur on Amy, Victoria might have subsided. Frankly, she couldn't understand what had impelled Amy to take care of this criminal's arm, and she didn't like it. She wanted to pull Amy away. But when Slater questioned Amy's sanity, all Victoria's protective instincts rushed up inside her.

"No, she's not crazy! She's simply a decent person who can't stand to see another human being hurt. She's not an animal who doesn't care whether someone's bleeding or not!"

Slater's mouth tightened, and he moved forward. "Meaning I am?"

"If the shoe fits . . ."

Slater was aware of an almost overwhelming urge to grab this woman by the shoulders and shake her. What was the matter with her? She was as crazy as the other one, but so beautiful you didn't care.

"Who the hell are you?" Could Brody somehow have arranged for this bizarre distraction in order to escape? Slater cast a sideways glance at his prisoner, but Brody was just standing there, letting the blonde wind another handkerchief around his other wrist and staring at her as if he'd never seen a woman before.

"Stop swearing at me! You have no right to swear at me."

"I beg your pardon." Slater's voice dripped with sarcasm. "I didn't realize I was addressing a lady. I thought I was talking to a termagant who consorts with criminals."

"How dare you!" Victoria thought with real pleasure about slapping him. She couldn't think of anyone, ever, who had infuriated her so completely and quickly. The man was a crude, suspicious, overbearing—well, she couldn't think of a word bad enough. "It's obvious that you wouldn't recognize a lady. You can't possibly ever have been in the company of one. No gentleman would strike a lady."

"I didn't hit her!" Slater retorted indignantly. "I pulled her hand away from my prisoner!"

Slater's and Victoria's angry voices spiraled, but Brody heard them only as a meaningless buzz of noise in the background. He was aware of nothing except the smooth glide of Amy's fingers over his skin as she wrapped his wrist. He stood perfectly still, afraid that she might stop if he made any move at all. She was so beautiful, so gentle and good. How could she not be scared of him? How could she remain there doctoring him when every movement she made brought her into contact with his chains? Surely she must realize what he was, if not who. Yet she stood within his reach as innocently and trustingly as a child. He wanted to touch her face, but he held back, unwilling to break the fragile beauty of the moment.

So entranced was he by Amy's ministrations that at first he paid no attention to the rest of the street. He should have; it was part of the plan that he had drilled into his gang. But he didn't even glance around. So he didn't see a man in the next block leave the post he'd been idly leaning against and go inside the saloon, returning moments later with three other men. Nor did he see the four men mount up and start down the street, leading a riderless horse.

But when they suddenly spurred their horses forward, pulling their pistols from their holsters as they went, some sixth sense warned Brody, reminding him of his plan and his men. He looked back and saw them an instant before the sudden pounding of hooves penetrated the consciousness of the sheriff and Slater. Just as Slater spun around, Brody dived off the sidewalk onto the dirt street, curling an arm around Amy as he did so and taking her with him. He didn't think; he just reacted—there was no way he would let this woman get shot.

When Slater whirled and saw the men riding at them, hell-bent-for-leather, he, too, knew what was happening. Normally he would have jumped for the nearest cover and started firing. But this time there was the woman. She was standing beside him, staring in amazement at the approaching men, even as the first gunfire spurted out. Slater grabbed her arm and flung her to the sidewalk. He rolled and came up on his knees firing the rifle.

The street was in turmoil as people screamed and ran for cover, and the gunfire was deafening. The sheriff drew his gun, falling with a cry of pain even as he raised it to fire. The horses danced nervously, and the riderless horse reared, whinnying. Brody jumped to his feet, yanking Amy up with him. She was stunned, the wind knocked out of her by their fall. Brody grasped the reins of the plunging horse and brought him down sharply. Instinct rather than reason impelling him, he grabbed Amy and threw her up onto the horse. He was hampered by the manacles and chain between his wrists, but she was small and unresisting. He swung up after her.

Slater made his way, shooting, to the porch post. Victoria, aware now of what was going on, knew enough to crawl after him, keeping low to the sidewalk. A bullet thudded into Slater's left arm, but in the heat of the battle, he didn't feel the pain. He cursed vividly as he fired, furious that he hadn't seen the raid coming, that he'd let himself be distracted. He'd be damned if he would let Brody get away now, when he'd finally captured him!

When Brody jumped to his feet, Slater swung his carbine toward him. But Victoria, too, saw the outlaw rise, carrying Amy with him.

"No!" Victoria screamed, reaching out and knocking Slater's gun up so that it fired harmlessly into the air.

"Damn it!" Slater brushed her aside, but she came right back, grappling with him for the gun.

"No! No! You'll hit Amy!"

He flung Victoria away again, using his full strength this time, and she reeled back, hitting the wall of the sheriff's office. But it was too late—the gang was already riding away. Slater jumped to his feet and ran out into the street. He raised the carbine, sighted and fired. One of the men jumped and swayed in his saddle, but he kept on riding. It was not Brody.

Slater slammed his gun to the ground, cursing vividly. Behind him Victoria struggled to her feet and stared down the street after the quickly disappearing gang, her face as white as paper.

"Oh, my God. Amy. We have to go after them!"

Slater whirled, frustration and fury boiling in him, so angry he didn't even notice the blood oozing from his arm. "What the hell is the matter with you? You're as crazy as she is! Or maybe you're a friend of Brody's. Is that it?" He strode up to her, his green eyes shooting icy rage, his voice vicious. "She's his woman, and you're—what, one of the other men's sluts? Or maybe you're Brody's, too."

"What! How dare you imply that I'm—" Victoria bit back the words. "This is insane. You're insane. Why are you standing here slandering me? You should be chasing them." She stabbed her finger in the direction the gang had taken. "But I can see that it would be useless to expect you to do something that competent. You're obviously unable to handle the situation. After all, you just managed to lose your prisoner and allowed him to kidnap my cousin, too!" Victoria whirled, calling, "Sheriff? You're—"

She stopped abruptly. The sheriff lay on the sidewalk, blood staining the wooden planks around him. "He's been hit!"

Victoria and Slater reached the sheriff simultaneously. Victoria ripped off a long ruffle from her petticoat and pressed it against the sheriff's bloodstained stomach. The man's skin was gray, and he lay unmoving. Slater laid his fingers against the sheriff's pulse.

He sighed. "He's gone."

"What?" Victoria stared at the sheriff. Her stomach flip-flopped, and she thought she might be sick. It wasn't the first time she had seen a dead person. Her mother had died when she was twelve, and Victoria had been standing beside her bed, holding her hand. And three years ago, one of the ranch hands had been thrown and trampled by a horse he was attempting to break. But never before had she seen one man die at the hands of another.

She swallowed hard and glanced over at Slater. He was squatting down beside the sheriff, and his eyes were closed, his head propped against his hand. It penetrated Victoria's consciousness that he looked peculiarly sallow. He swayed and had to brace his hand against the supporting post to keep from overbalancing.

Automatically Victoria reached out to steady him, and it was then that she noticed his arm. Slater's sleeve was soaked with raw, red blood, and there was a dark hole on his upper arm. "Good Lord," she breathed. "You were shot, too."

Slater nodded. He felt suddenly light-headed, and he slipped down to a sitting position, leaning back against the post. "Damn."

"Don't you ever do anything but curse?" Victoria ripped another ruffle from her petticoat, noting that her fingers were bloodless and shaking. She wadded the strip up and pressed it against his arm.

Slater winced and let out a grunt of pain. "Easy, will you?"

"It has to be tight to stop the bleeding."

Victoria looked around her for the first time. In the heat of the moment, she hadn't noticed it, but several people had emerged from the nearby stores and offices and now stood in a ring around Victoria and Slater, staring, drawn by the drama and blood, yet seemingly afraid to come too close.

"Somebody get the doctor!" Victoria snapped, irritated by the blank stares. "Can't you see he needs help?"

As if her words had broken the spell the crowd was under, the people began to move. Two men came forward.

"Luther's already run for the doc."

"Are you all right, ma'am?"

Victoria grimaced. "Of course I am." What was the matter with these people? Couldn't they see that she wasn't the one who was wounded? She didn't know that her face was ghostly white and her eyes huge. Nor did she realize that the men took her cool competence for shock that would momentarily be followed by screaming hysterics. She was accustomed to dealing with people who expected her to be calm and in charge.

She turned back to Slater. His eyes were open, and they didn't yet have the dull glaze that forewarned of a loss of consciousness. "Are you hit anywhere else?"

Slater shook his head. "Till just a minute ago, I'd forgotten I was hit there."

"Most people would be aware that they were bleeding," Victoria responded tartly.

Slater's lips twitched up into something resembling a grin. "You're a hard one."

Victoria's eyebrows rose in an expression of disdain. "I'm as hard as I have to be. Most women are."

He shook his head slightly. "Not like you."

"Well, I'm not a member of that criminal's gang, if that's what you're trying to imply again."

"I'm not." Slater had spoken before in the heat of anger, but he knew that what he had said wasn't true. It had been obvious that she hadn't expected the gang to come riding in; after all, he had had to pull her down to keep her from getting shot. She was also shaken by the sight of the sheriff's dead body and his own blood, despite her calm efficiency. She had a cool head, but she wasn't indifferent or inured to bloodshed. And she had urged him to follow Brody's gang. She wanted him to get the other girl back. Besides, she had too much "quality" to belong to Brody or one of his men. Slater was still confused about her, but he was sure she wasn't in cahoots with Sam Brody.

The crowd around them grew with each passing moment. A man muscled his way through the onlookers to Victoria and Slater. He stopped short and stared at the sheriff's still body. "Oh, my. Oh, my." He looked vaguely around him, then back at the sheriff. He sat down heavily on the steps and rested his head in his hands. Victoria studied him. He was young, probably no more than twenty-two or -three, and badly shaken. He wore the badge of a deputy sheriff.

Victoria's heart sank. She had hoped that the deputy would follow the gang that had taken Amy, but it was obvious that he was not a person to take charge. And the lawman beside her was shot. He couldn't lead a posse.

What was she to do? She had to get Amy back, and quickly. It made her shake inside even to think of what those men would do to her sweet, innocent cousin. She remembered how terrified Amy had been when she first came to live with them. She was repulsed and frightened by any sort of violence. Even angry voices raised in a quarrel were enough to send Amy scurrying away. She would be horribly frightened. By the time they got through with her, even if they didn't kill her, Amy might be a mindless wreck.

Victoria shivered, and her hand trembled on the bandage she was holding. Slater's eyes darted to her face. He reached out with his good hand and took hold of her arm. "Are you going to faint?"

Victoria shook her head. "No."

She looked at him. Her eyes were huge, and a deep, fath-
omless blue, the kind of eyes that could pull a man's heart right
out of him. She appeared scared to death, and Slater found
himself wanting to put his arm around her and promise that he
would make everything all right. Good God, he thought. In the
space of a few minutes he'd gone from wanting to throttle her
to wanting to reassure her. Loss of blood must really be making him weak.

"I just realized," Victoria told him, "that you're my only
hope for finding Amy. And you're wounded. You can't go after them."

"The hell I can't. I got shot in the arm, that's all. It's not
even my gun hand."

Victoria cocked a disbelieving eyebrow, but before she could
express her opinion of his ability to ride in his condition, there
was a rustling in the crowd behind her, and she turned to see the
doctor elbowing his way toward them. He knelt quickly beside
the sheriff and felt for a pulse that he didn't really expect to
find. Then he turned to Slater and Victoria.

When he saw Victoria, his eyebrows rose. "You again?"
Victoria nodded. She still held the bandage on Slater's arm. The
doctor gently removed her hand, then peeled off the blood-
soaked cloth. "It looks like you did a decent job of stemming
the bleeding." He ripped away the sleeve and examined Slater's arm. "No sign of an exit. I'll have to go in and get the
bullet out."

"Damn." Slater released a breath. Victoria could see the
beads of sweat beginning to form on his forehead and upper lip.
He might have forgotten his wound in the heat of battle, but he
was doubtless fully aware of it now.

"You'll have to come to my office. I'll ask some of these men
to carry you."

Slater shook his head. "My arm's shot, not my legs. I can
walk there."

"Don't be a fool. You don't have to be a hero."

"No hero. Being carried will jostle me more than walking."

"You have a point there—if you can make it to the office
without passing out."

"I'll get there. Just help me up."

The doctor gripped Slater under his right arm and lifted, and Slater stood up. His color turned even paler.

"I'll help." Victoria stood up also. "You can lean on me. I'm strong."

"So I noticed." Slater curled his arm around her shoulders. She fitted very naturally there.

Dr. Bauer's office was three blocks away, and Slater felt every step of it. At first his arm was around Victoria more for balance than support, but by the time they reached the door of the office, he was leaning heavily against her, his fingers digging into her flesh. Victoria suspected she would have bruises on her arm the next morning.

She glanced up at his face. It was drawn with pain and covered by a sheen of perspiration. She looked at his arm; the wound was bleeding again.

Together she and the doctor helped Slater into the office and onto the operating table in the back room. Slater lay back with a sigh. Dr. Bauer turned toward Victoria. "Since you're here, you might as well help."

Victoria nodded. She wanted some work—anything—to keep her mind off what might be happening to Amy.

"Swab off the wound while I prepare the chloroform." He gestured toward the washbowl and pitcher on the other side of the room.

Victoria found a washcloth, poured water into the bowl and returned to the table to clean Slater's arm. He had been lying in a half-conscious state, but he came to with an oath when Victoria touched his arm. He glared at her. "What are you still doing here?"

"Helping Dr. Bauer," Victoria replied with a falsely sweet smile. "He knew you'd be such an ornery patient it would take more than one person to handle you."

"Why'd the doc say 'You again?' when he saw you?"

"What? Oh. Because we met earlier today. My cousin..." Her voice faltered almost imperceptibly on the word. "My cousin and I and our chaperone were on the stage to San Antonio, but my chaperone fell as she was getting off and broke her leg. I helped the doctor set it."

Slater winced as Victoria cleaned the wound, and his words came out a trifle unevenly. "Sounds like you're a dangerous

woman to be around.'' His breath hissed between his teeth.
''Ouch! Damn, lady, what are you trying to do?''

''Clean you up a little. I'm sure that's quite a task.''

She had a slicing tongue on her, Slater thought. A man would
be a fool to want her, even with those huge blue eyes and that
China-doll skin. Thank God he was in no shape to make a fool
of himself right now.

The doctor returned, carrying a small bottle and a pad of
cotton. Slater narrowed his eyes suspiciously. ''What's that?''

''Chloroform. So you won't feel the pain.''

''No. I don't want to be knocked out.''

''Captain Slater, be reasonable. I have to probe for that bullet. It's buried in your arm. If you're conscious, there will be a
great deal of pain.''

''They dug a bullet out of my leg after Shiloh, and I didn't
have nothing to kill the pain but a few slugs of Tennessee sour
mash. I survived that.''

Dr. Bauer looked pained. ''I'm afraid I don't recommend
Tennessee sour mash as an anesthetic.''

''I've had chloroform, too. It'll knock me out for hours, and
when I wake up, I'll be sick as a dog. It will put me out of
commission too long.''

''Exactly what do you think you would do in those hours?''
Dr. Bauer asked in the tone of one humoring a madman.

''Find Sam Brody.''

The doctor stared, then glanced at Victoria. She shrugged.

''But, Captain Slater, that is unthinkable. You've been shot.''

''It's happened to me before.''

''Obviously. Whatever the medical practices you have been
used to, here you will receive the best in modern care. I promise you, I have a light hand and will render you unconscious for
the shortest possible time.'' Dr. Bauer placed the pad over the
bottle and upended it. Slater reached out his free hand for the
bottle. Dr. Bauer gave Victoria a significant look. ''Miss Stafford, I require your assistance.''

Victoria nodded and came around the table to grab Slater's
arm with both hands. She leaned on it with her full strength,
pressing it back down to the table. Dr. Bauer stepped in nimbly and placed the pad over Slater's nose and mouth, muffling
Slater's roar.

Slater's eyes blinked, and the strength went out of his arm. The last thing he saw before he slid into darkness was Victoria's face, dominated by vivid blue eyes. "Beautiful," he mumbled, and closed his eyes.

Dr. Bauer stepped back. "I've given him a light dosage, so we must work quickly. Please hold his arm still to make sure he doesn't twitch in his sleep."

He picked up a scalpel and a pair of long tweezers and began to explore the wound. Victoria held the injured arm firmly and watched the doctor find and neatly extract the dented bullet. Triumphantly, he held it up, then dropped it into a pan.

They both looked down at the sleeping man on the table.

"They say Captain Slater is one of the best there is," the doctor commented.

"The best what?"

Dr. Bauer looked nonplussed by the question. "Why, one of the best Texas Rangers, I suppose. But, I forget, you are not from here. You know nothing about the excitement this Slater has caused in our little town."

Victoria shook her head. "Something to do with Sam Brody, I presume."

"That's right. You know who Brody is?"

"I imagine everyone in Texas does. He's robbed banks and stagecoaches for years, but they've never been able to catch him."

"Yes. Well, this Captain Slater has been after him for years. And he captured him the day before yesterday. Right here in Santa Clara." The doctor beamed, proud of the town's sudden rise to fame.

The doctor seemed inclined to talk more about the exciting events of the past few days, but Victoria washed up and made her escape as soon as she could. She had no use for the doctor's stories right now. She had to learn what was being done to find Amy.

She supposed she should hurry back to the hotel and tell Mrs. Childers what had happened. After all the time they had been gone, the woman was probably frantic with worry. But Victoria didn't have the time to waste. Instead, she returned to the sheriff's office.

Inside she found the young deputy she had seen earlier, an older deputy who seemed equally ineffectual, and several of the men from the town, discussing the possibility of a posse. When she entered, the men turned to look at her, and all conversation stopped.

"Please, go ahead," she told them. "I want to hear what you plan to do to find Amy."

"Who?"

"My cousin. The woman who was kidnapped."

"Oh." Several pairs of eyes shifted away from her.

Finally one of the older men said, "Ma'am, I'm real sorry about your cousin. We'll do our best to find her."

"I'm sure you will. What are your plans?"

The man looked a little taken aback. "Uh, I know you aren't from around here...."

"No. We were traveling on the stage to San Antonio."

"But maybe we could get in touch with your father. Or an uncle who could—"

"I plan to send a telegram to my father as soon as I'm through here. He'll come immediately, of course, and he'll do everything he can to help you find Amy. But it will take him a day to ride here, and we have to do something immediately. The colder that gang's trail gets, the harder it will be to find Amy."

"Well, yes, ma'am, of course we're planning on setting out right away. Just as soon as we talk to the Ranger."

"Captain Slater? He's out cold and will be for some time."

"He's one of the best." Victoria decided that was a phrase she could grow tired of easily. "We'll be better off getting his advice before we do anything. We're all agreed on that."

Victoria looked around the room. It was just as she had feared when she first saw the young deputy. With the sheriff dead and Slater laid up with a gunshot wound, there was no leadership for a posse. This bunch would never be able to find Brody's gang, let alone bring them in.

She would simply have to do it herself.

Chapter Three

When Brody had flung Amy to the ground, she had been stunned. A split second later, the guns had opened fire, roaring above and around her, and she had frozen in terror. Brody's warm weight over her seemed like a safe shelter, and she'd curled up beneath him, almost mindless with fright. Amy always hated the sound of guns, but this sudden explosion was far worse than ordinary gunshots. It went on and on, and there were screams and shouts and horses stamping and whinnying. It was like the nightmares she had had as a child, scary and senseless, filled with violence, noise and confusion. She wanted to scream, but her throat closed up, and she couldn't. The fear was like a blackness wrapping itself around her.

Then the man's weight was off her, and she was exposed to the danger. She couldn't move, couldn't think, could only lie there in blank terror. He loomed above her for an instant, dark and large, but somehow he wasn't frightening. What was frightening was that he had taken away her protection.

He bent down and jerked her up with him into the midst of the confusion. He tossed her onto a horse and climbed up after her. Amy didn't struggle; the thought never entered her mind. She was too confused, too numb with horror and fear. She was afraid not only of the present battle, but of a battle from years in the past. She wasn't just the woman she was now, but a little girl, too, cowering in the cellar, hearing the unintelligible cries of Comanches, the oaths of her father, and the deafening gunfire of three people shooting from inside the small cabin. And the screams. She heard the screams.

Brody's arms went around her taut body, holding her on the horse and bracing her against his hard chest. They raced away from the noise and confusion, and Amy clung tightly to the front of his shirt, burying her face against him.

The gunfire receded, and soon there was only the thunder of hooves, and an occasional shouted word. Slowly Amy's body began to relax. But she didn't try to move, nor did she release her death grip on Brody's shirt. There was something infinitely soothing about leaning against him, smelling the tart masculine odor of horse, sweat and tobacco, feeling his strength enfolding her, hearing the steady rhythm of his heart beneath her ear. It made her think of her childhood, one of the few memories she had. It had been raining, and she had been riding like this, cradled in a large, dark man's arms. *Daddy.* That had been warmth and safety. That had been love.

Amy snuggled into him instinctively, seeking shelter, and gradually the blind panic began to recede. She realized, with a kind of amazement, that she had been stolen from Victoria by this man. She didn't know who he was, or why on earth he would have taken her.

She was a woman of unusual naïveté, even in a time when innocence was the feminine ideal. From the day she had been brought to the Stafford ranch, she had been cosseted and protected from anything that was strong, blunt, or crude. To her family, the ranch hands, and even the townspeople, she had remained a child—too fey, too delicate, too *different*, to be treated as a woman. She had rarely been away from the warm cocoon of the ranch and the town of Bennett, and so she had never run into any other attitude. Even the rough young men never tried anything with her. She was too strange, they said, *not all there*. At dances, only the old men asked her to dance, and they did so with the same air as when they danced with a child, avuncular and sexless. Men didn't flirt with Amy, didn't smile at her with a certain knowledge in their eyes, didn't turn their heads to watch her walk by. Amy had seen men do that with Victoria, of course, but she had never connected that sort of thing with herself.

She knew too much about animals not to realize how their young came into being, and she had wondered how such things applied to humans. But when she had asked Mrs. Donnelly about it, the housekeeper had stared at her with such horror that Amy knew she had again said something bizarre and wrong, something no normal person would talk about. So she had quickly shut her mouth and left the kitchen, and she had been careful not to speak of such things again. And, though she had been curious at times about what went on between a man and a woman, she had absorbed the accepted view of herself as abnormal too well to even think of such things happening to her. And never would she have dreamed that that act, vague as it was in her mind, might be forced upon a woman.

So Amy was not racked, as Victoria was, with visions of Brody and his gang raping her. She only wondered why he would want her with him.

At the moment Brody was wondering much the same thing. He had acted on impulse, weighing nothing in the split second in which he had made his decision, knowing only that he could not let this woman go. But now his mind was working, and he knew it had been a foolish thing to do. She would slow them down. She was a tiny thing, delicate as a bird. She couldn't ride as hard and as long over the rough terrain of the Texas hill country as they would have to.

It was foolhardy to have a woman along in this situation, even crazier to have an unwilling one. She would weep; she would struggle; she would beg and plead. She would do everything she could to slow them down, praying that her menfolk would catch up with her.

And they would be after her. Father, brother, husband—no man would let this woman be taken from him. They'd come after him with blood in their eyes. No lawman or posse could pursue him with the tenacity and eagerness of avenging relatives. Even if this woman had no men to protect her, taking her would at least stir up the townspeople and ensure that he and his men would be followed.

If he was smart, he'd put her down right now, leave her on the road for the posse to find. That would take a lot of the fire out of their pursuit. It would slow them down, too, and maybe even reduce their number, for some of the men would have to take her back to Santa Clara.

That was what he'd do—if he was smart.

And he knew he wasn't about to do it. Cool reason didn't stand a chance against the sweet warmth that filled his chest as he held her. His arms curved around her protectively, and she cuddled into him as naturally as if she belonged there. She must be angry or scared, or both, but there was nothing to show it in the way she leaned against him, her hands curled into his shirt. It was almost as if she knew she was his.

Brody's arms tightened around her. She *was* his. And there wasn't any sheriff, any Ranger, any bunch of townspeople, who could separate her from him. Maybe he'd be dead in two days. But that was always a possibility, had been since he was a kid in the cribs of New Orleans, and, at least, until it happened, this woman, this princess, belonged to him.

He was reluctant even to let her out of his arms. But he knew that that was going beyond the bounds of foolishness. Frank Landers had been shot in the fracas in town, and he'd tumbled from his mount. His riderless horse had run with them as they tore out of town, and Purdon had managed to grab the reins. Slight as this woman was, she was still an extra burden for his horse, and it made sense to put her up on the free mount.

Brody sighed and reined in, signaling his men to stop. They had ridden hard since they'd left Santa Clara, and they were grateful for the chance to rest and regroup.

"I'm going to put you down now," Brody said softly in Amy's ear, and she looked up at him and nodded. He leaned out of the saddle, letting her slide to the ground. He knew it was fanciful, but it seemed almost as if she were reluctant to go.

Amy looked around her, pushing her windblown hair back from her face. Besides the man who had carried her, there were three men and four horses. The horses were lathered with sweat from the hard run. The men were a hard-looking bunch, dusty, weather-beaten and unshaven. One of them clutched his shoulder, and Amy could see the red staining his fingers.

The men stared at her, and Amy moved uneasily beneath their gaze. For the first time the fear of a real physical threat shivered through her. She still didn't know why they had taken her, but now she sensed that her situation was dangerous. She looked back up over her shoulder and watched the man who had carried her dismount. He came up to stand beside her, and Amy edged toward him.

She felt no fear of him. From the beginning she had been unafraid of this fierce-looking stranger, hadn't even seen the danger in his hard face and cold eyes. She had felt pity at first, then the security of his protection as they fled the gun battle. There had always been someone to take care of her. Now she put her trust in this outlaw who had held her, his body between her and the bullets.

"Hey, Brody." One of the men sauntered forward, leering at Amy. Even the touch of his gaze made her skin crawl, and Amy shivered, moving so close to Brody that her arm was against his. "Always thinkin', aren't ya? Not only gettin' outta town, but bringin' a woman with us to enjoy."

Brody moved in front of Amy. He had no weapon, but his eyes were so black and hard that the other man fell back a step. "She's mine."

His voice was flat, the words falling like rocks into their midst. There wasn't a man there who had any interest in disputing them.

"You understand, Purdon?"

Purdon writhed inside with humiliation. He hated backing down in front of the other men. He tried a little grin. "Why, sure, Brody, sure. Just funnin' ya' a little."

"Don't." Normally Brody would have given Purdon that way out. He knew how to handle the volatile men who rode with him; it was one of the reasons for his gang's success. But right now he wasn't cool enough to manipulate Purdon as he usually did. He was too filled with the red rage that had come upon him when Purdon looked at his woman. Never before had he felt such a fierce sense of possession about a woman, but he knew he'd kill any man who touched Amy.

Purdon swallowed and shrugged. His capitulation ate at him like acid, but he wasn't fool enough to go up against Brody. "Sure," he said again and turned away.

Brody relaxed. He nodded toward the man who was holding his shoulder. "You get hit, Jimmy?"

The man nodded. "It went clean through, though."

"Good. At least we don't have to dig it out." Brody went over to look at the wound. The young man paled when Brody pulled his shirt away, and Brody brusquely ordered him to sit down on a rock. He examined the injury; it was still oozing blood, and he knew that riding wouldn't help it any.

Brody started to tear off one of his own sleeves to bind the wound, but Amy tapped softly on his arm. He glanced up, surprised, and found her holding out a long piece of white cotton cloth. He realized that it must be a ruffle from her petticoat. He couldn't understand her. She was bound to know that she'd be better off if one of them was dead, or at least slowed down. So why had she offered help to Jimmy?

Brody took the cloth from her and tore it in half. He folded one half into a compact pad and placed it over the wound. Then he wound the other strip around Jimmy's shoulder and chest to hold the pad in place. Brody doubted it would hold well. Still, it was better than nothing.

"Can you ride?"

The young man nodded. He hated the thought of it. The jostling would make his shoulder burn. But the alternative, being caught by the posse, was a powerful incentive to keep up.

"Good. Now let's get these off, quick." Brody held up his hands, showing the manacles and chain.

But they lacked the tools to knock the manacles apart, and the butt of a gun wouldn't do it. Finally Brody had to settle for spreading the chain taut across a rock and letting one of the men shoot it in two. Amy's heart was in her throat as she watched. It looked dangerous, and the last thing she wanted was to be left with these men without her protector around. She closed her eyes. The loud report of the gun made her jump. Opening her eyes tentatively, she breathed a sigh of relief when she saw the black-haired man rising from where he had knelt.

"All right. Let's go." Brody didn't like the weight of the manacles, and the dangling chains were a bother, but at least he could move his hands freely now. They couldn't waste any more time; he'd get the manacles off when they reached the hideout.

One of the men handed Brody a revolver, and he tucked it into his belt. He turned to Amy. "You're going with us," he told her, his voice harsh. He had to make her ride with them, even if it meant frightening her into it.

Amy nodded. She couldn't imagine what else she would do. They had left the road, and she had no idea in which direction the town lay. She had no water, food, or a mount. If Victoria were here, she would doubtless be able to make it on her own, but Amy knew she couldn't.

Brody looked down at her. Her eyes were huge and blue, full of trust as she gazed up at him. He felt as though he could drown in those eyes. How could she look at him like that?

Her bonnet had been knocked off during the escape, and it hung down her back, dangling by the ribbons still tied under her chin. Her fine hair had straggled loose in the wind and hung in disarray. Brody couldn't resist reaching out to touch it. It was as soft as corn silk beneath his fingers. He smoothed it back from her face. He wanted to sink his hands into it and rub it against his cheek.

Amy recognized the look of hunger in his eyes. It took her breath away. He was staring at her the way men looked at Victoria, only franker, harder. No man had ever gazed at her like that. It made her feel hot all over. It was strange and a little scary—and exciting.

Brody forced himself to pull the bonnet up onto her head, covering the shining temptation of her hair. The color rose in Amy's face, and she turned her eyes down as she retied the bow under her chin.

"I'm going to put you up on Frank's horse." Brody nodded toward the animal. Belatedly he thought to ask, "Can you ride?"

"Oh, yes." That was one thing Amy knew she could do as well as anyone else.

Brody doubted that. All his men rode good horseflesh; he saw to it. Landers's mount was a far cry from the gentle mare Amy probably rode at home. But he would keep a close eye on her; if he had to, he'd lead her horse and let Amy hold on to the saddle horn.

The men mounted. Amy walked calmly up to the bay that Landers had ridden. She reached up and stroked its nose, speaking softly to it. Brody came up behind her, and she turned and smiled. "What's his name?"

"Who?"

Her smile broadened. "The horse."

Brody lifted an eyebrow. What the hell was she doing wondering about a horse's name at a time like this? Yet he couldn't help but grin a little. "I don't know. He probably doesn't have one."

"But he has to have a name. I'll think of one for him."

"All right." Brody thought about bending down and kissing her on her pert little nose. On her eyes and cheeks and chin and sweet, sweet mouth. He wet his lips and glanced away.

Amy's soft voice pulled him back. "Uh, I need a leg up."

"What? Oh." He cupped his hands for her to use as a step as she climbed into the saddle. He wasn't used to riding with women.

She placed her left foot in his hands, grasped the saddle horn and swung lightly up. She took up the reins competently and turned to look at Brody. He mounted his own horse, and they started off, Amy riding beside him.

Victoria hurried to the telegraph office to cable her father. Once that was done, she pondered her next move. As she had told the men in the sheriff's office, it would waste precious time to wait for her father.

She had to do something now. The only problem was, she didn't know what. She could get a horse and ride back to Austin, where she could probably hire men to track Brody down, but that, too, would eat up valuable time. Or she could follow the gang herself. She had no doubt that she could handle the riding that would be involved, and she was an excellent shot. But tracking was something she was inexperienced in. Moreover, however good she was with a gun, she had never used one on a human. And she was only one person. There had been at least four men in that gang—and who knew how many more had been waiting to join them outside of town? She wouldn't have a chance of subduing them.

Still, what other choice did she have?

Except Slater. He had said he would ride after Brody as soon as the doctor removed the bullet. What if he'd really meant it? What if he could do it? He had lost a lot of blood, and he would be weak and in pain. But he was whipcord tough; she had felt the lean strength in his body as they walked down the street. She had also sensed his bulldog determination. He was, after all, a Texas Ranger, and they didn't come any tougher than that. If any man could do it, it would be Slater. He might not be as quick or as skilled as he would be under normal circumstances, but he would still do a darn sight better than either she or the town's posse could do alone. At least Slater would be able to direct them.

But it would be a while before he was able to sit a horse, and in the meantime, she had a lot to do. First on the list was the matter of a horse. Victoria had no intention of being left behind when Slater and the posse rode out.

She went first to the livery stable, where she examined the animals carefully. The owner of the stable had only one horse, a paint gelding, that Victoria thought had the strength and stamina to last on the rough journey ahead. The owner wanted an exorbitant amount for the animal, but she wasn't in a position to walk away from the deal, so after a minimum of bargaining, she purchased the horse, along with a saddle and bridle.

Fortunately, since that took most of the money her father had given her and Amy for the month in San Antonio, she didn't have much left to buy—only a bedroll, the minimal food and supplies she would need on the trail, and a rifle. There was a pistol in her bag at the hotel, for Victoria had lived too long on the ranch to feel completely secure without a firearm within reach. But she would need a rifle, as well, if she expected to go up against Brody's gang.

She returned to the hotel with her purchases and found her bedridden chaperone in a panic over the length of time Amy and Victoria had been gone. Naturally Victoria's story only increased the woman's hysteria. Victoria didn't waste time listening to Mrs. Childers' wails and entreaties, or arguing with her over the merits of chasing down the outlaws. She just pulled her pistol and riding clothes out of her bags, loaded the guns, and neatly rolled up the ammunition and supplies in the bedroll. Now she would be ready whenever Slater could leave; all she had to do was change into her riding skirt and blouse.

For a moment she paused and held the royal-blue blouse in front of her. She smiled. The color set off her complexion well and turned her eyes a vivid blue; it was far more complementary to her than the dull brown of her traveling dress. She caught the direction of her thoughts and grimaced at her reflection. What a thing to be thinking of! This was no time for feminine vanity. She had to be all action now, with the same kind of competence and toughness that Slater would expect from a man, or she would endanger their mission.

Victoria laid the blouse aside. She had better see how Slater was doing. He might be coming around already.

There were several people loitering in front of the doctor's office, and Victoria wondered sinkingly if the doctor might turn her away as a mere curiosity-seeker as well. But he seemed to have accepted her as his assistant, for he opened the door to her cheerfully.

"Come to see our patient, eh?" he asked, looking amused. "Well, I wish you more success with him than I've had."

"He's awake?"

"Oh, yes." Dr. Bauer pulled a droll face. "Very much so. And he's asked about you." He didn't add in what terms.

But Victoria didn't need clarification. She was certain nothing the Ranger had had to say about her had been favorable. He had taken a dislike to her from the moment they met. "Good. I need to talk to him."

She walked past the doctor into the back room where they had taken Slater before. He was there, but not on the table, as she had expected. He was standing, but seemed a little wobbly, with one hand braced against the wall. He looked as washed out as a man as tanned as he was could look, and a fierce frown creased his forehead. His eyes focused on her with an effort, and the frown deepened.

"You." The tone of his voice implied anything but joy at the sight of her.

"Yes. You're up."

"Very perceptive." His tongue stumbled a little over the word. He wet his lips. "Yes, I'm up, and relieved of the contents of my stomach, as well." His eyes were accusing. "Thanks to you and that sawbones."

"Please. Don't be so effusive in your gratitude. I wouldn't expect any thanks for saving your hide."

"Lord." He brought a hand to his head. "The way you and Bauer talk, you'd think a bullet in the arm was one step away from the Grim Reaper. You didn't save my life, lady. You just put a bandage on me and helped that quack out there set off the siege of Vicksburg in my brain."

Victoria pressed her lips together tightly. Only the fact that she desperately needed Slater's help kept her from letting him have a few choice words. This man must be the rudest and most ungrateful wretch in the world! When she could trust herself to speak again, she ignored his comments and said only, "Did you mean it when you said you were going after Brody?"

"Of course I meant it."

"Naturally," Dr. Bauer said from the doorway. "The man's quite mad. I've been trying to tell him there's no need for him to leap on his horse and chase the outlaws. The townspeople will get up a posse."

Slater gave a snort that indicated his opinion of such a posse. "Yeah. That's why I have to leave before they manage to obliterate Brody's trail."

"I'm afraid he's right," Victoria added. "I've talked to the deputies and the other men. I don't think they'll be any use in catching Sam Brody."

Slater glanced at her, startled, then mockingly inclined his head toward her.

Dr. Bauer stared at her, shocked. "You can't mean that you think he should go after Brody's gang!"

"Normally, no. He's lost blood, he's in pain, and he's still feeling the effects of the chloroform."

The doctor nodded emphatically, reassured.

"But—"

"But?"

"But there's no one else to go. No one else here can do it. And somebody has to go after them! Someone has to get Amy back. Her life is at stake. And there's no one else to do it but him!"

The doctor looked from Victoria to Slater. Slater gazed back without expression. "She's right, you know. I'm the only choice."

"But you're in no condition to ride a horse!"

"That's right," Victoria agreed. "That's why I'm going with him."

"What!" The two men chorused and whirled to stare at her with identically dumbfounded expressions.

"Miss Stafford, you can't be serious."

"You're crazy."

Victoria gazed levelly back at them.

"You *are* serious."

"Damn."

Victoria was used to similar reactions from men who didn't know her. She was also used to handling them, which often meant riding over them roughshod. "When will you be ready to leave?" she asked Slater. "Tomorrow morning?"

"I'm leaving as soon as I can get a saddle on my horse. Not that it's any of your business."

Victoria found it hard to believe he would be able to ride out so soon, wobbly as he still was from the anesthesia, but she kept her opinion to herself. No need to do battle on two fronts. "All right. I'll change into my riding clothes right away."

"Don't bother. You're not going."

"I am."

"You're not!" Slater roared, then pressed both hands against his aching head. "Damnation. What did I ever do to deserve you?"

"Of course she's not going," Dr. Bauer reassured him soothingly. "Not as long as you'll be reasonable, too. A day or two of rest, and then you can lead the posse out."

"I can't wait a day or two," Slater growled between clenched teeth, each word distinct and grating. "Can't either of you understand? I am riding out today, and I'm riding alone."

"You must take some men with you! There were several of those gunmen, I understand."

"I haven't met a man in this town that I want backing me up. Either one of those deputies would just slow me down and probably make some damn-fool mistake that would get me killed. I'm better off alone. I'm used to operating that way."

"I'm sure people are usually happy to leave you alone," Victoria put in crisply. "But not this time. I won't entrust my cousin's safety to a man who can't use one arm or walk a straight line."

"I don't have to walk. I plan to ride. The chloroform will wear off soon, and in the meantime all I have to do is stick on my horse. I think I can manage that."

"Um-hmm. I'm sure you'll manage to saddle and bridle your horse with one working hand, too. Not to mention build a camp fire, control your horse if you have to use your gun—even roll up your bedroll or pull off your boots."

"I'll sleep with my boots on."

"No doubt you'll die in them, too. Very admirable, I'm sure, but in this instance, I'd rather you didn't. I need you, unfortunately."

"Well, I don't need you. Now get out of my way and let me leave, if you want that blasted girl back so much."

Victoria stood aside to let Slater pass into the outer office, but fell in right behind him. He turned and glared at her. Victoria gave him her blandest stare.

"You're staying here."

Victoria merely shook her head.

Slater's eyes turned a fierce green, and for a moment color stained his sallow cheeks. "Damn it, the last thing I need is a woman slowing me down. You'll do nothing but hamper me. I'll wind up having to protect you, as well. If you want to help your cousin, stay here."

"I won't hamper you. I've ridden since I was three years old. And judging from the way you look, I can go a lot farther and faster than you can. I have supplies, a good horse, two guns, and plenty of ammunition. I'm an excellent shot, and I've slept out on the trail frequently. Most of all, I have two working hands."

"Good. Then you keep them busy right here in Santa Clara. There must be someone who needs a busybody messing in his life. I don't. Goodbye."

He stormed through the office and out the front door, marring his impressive exit only slightly by weaving. He closed the door behind him with a deadly quietness. Victoria gazed after him, her eyes narrowed.

The doctor sighed. "Well, you did your best, I'm sure. At first I couldn't understand why you would make such a ridiculous statement, but then I realized, of course, that you were trying to make him realize how absurd—"

"I meant exactly what I said." Victoria started toward the door, giving the doctor only a brief backward glance. "I still do. Mr. Slater may think he's going alone, but he's in for a surprise."

The front door closed just as quietly after her, and only the doctor was left to stare, openmouthed, at the empty room.

Victoria didn't waste any time before returning to her hotel room. Even though she presumed it would take Slater a while to leave, she didn't want to take any chances. She *had* to go with him.

She quickly ripped off the clothes she had been wearing and changed into her riding outfit. She left enough money for Mrs. Childers' meals for the next couple of days; after that, her father would be here to take care of the woman's expenses. She divided the rest of her money, tucking some inside one of her stockings beneath the garter and the rest into a small leather bag, which she wore looped around and behind her belt. When she was dressed, she hurried downstairs to arrange with the desk clerk for a local woman to come to sit with Mrs. Childers during the day. Her last task was to go back upstairs and explain to her chaperone that she was leaving.

Predictably, the woman responded with agitated commands not to leave the hotel, mingled with dire warnings of what would happen if she did. Victoria did her best to reassure her, but in the end she simply left, carrying her neatly packed bedroll, rifle, ammunition belt and riding hat.

Slater was leading his horse out of the stables just as she arrived. He stopped abruptly. "What are you doing here? I thought I made myself clear."

"You did." Victoria shrugged, setting down her burdens. "But I have to remind you that the roads are free to travel. You don't own them."

Slater watched her walk over to one of the stalls and lead a horse out. He had thought she was lovely in the dull brown dress she had worn earlier, but he realized now that he hadn't had a notion of her full beauty. The narrow riding skirt revealed the shape of her hips and long legs, and the wide leather belt cinched her waist into nothingness. Her blouse, tucked into the belt, was drawn tightly across her full breasts, and its deep blue color emphasized the vivid hue of her eyes. Slater was sure she knew exactly the effect this outfit had on a man and was wearing it for just that reason. Well, not this time.

"But I can choose who I travel with, and it's not going to be you."

Again Victoria shrugged. She threw a folded blanket over the horse and swung the saddle up on top of it. "That's up to you. If you don't want the help..."

"Exactly what do you think you're going to do?" Slater would have died rather than admit that she saddled the horse far better and more quickly than he had with his one hand. Nor was he about to admit that watching her move made desire twist in his gut.

"Follow you."

"No."

"No?" Victoria glanced at him with a smile as she put the bridle over the horse's head. Carefully she checked the buckles she had fastened, tightened the girth a little and adjusted the stirrups. "How do you plan to stop me? Arrest me? Shoot me?"

"I'm not waiting for you. I'm not looking after you. I'm not bringing you back here. Do you understand? You are not with me. You're on your own."

Victoria looked amused. "I think I'll be able to manage."

The laughter in her eyes galled Slater, and he swung quickly up into his saddle. It was too sudden a movement for his still-swimming head, and for a moment, black dots danced in front of his eyes. He gripped the saddle horn tightly, picturing himself tumbling ignominiously out of his saddle right in front of her. The faintness faded, and he tapped his horse sharply with his heels.

Behind him, Victoria mounted and rode out. They trotted out of town in single file, with Victoria riding ten feet behind.

Chapter Four

Brody led Amy and his men northwest through the broken, scrubby countryside, staying well away from the route to Austin. Once, they picked their way up the middle of a shallow, rocky creek so that they left no hoofprints, but other than that Brody did little to hide their trail.

When Purdon questioned him about it, he shrugged, and answered, "Slater might have been hit, but I don't think he was killed. He's a tough son—" Brody stopped and glanced at Amy. "He's tough. He'll be after us. He knows we'll head into the hill country, so there's no point trying to make it look like we went anywhere else. When we get closer to the hideout, we'll throw him off."

Purdon's eyes narrowed. What was the matter with Brody all of a sudden? Brody had stopped on a cuss word because of that girl. Purdon couldn't fathom it. Brody had never been soft about women before, but this little piece of fluff had made him lose his head. Purdon didn't like it. He regarded himself as Brody's right-hand man. After all, he was the one who had regrouped the men after the fiasco at the bank and who had remembered Brody's plan for escape if one of them was captured. He was the one who had managed to bring off the rescue. But instead of thanking him, Brody had humiliated him in front of the other men—because of the girl.

Purdon looked at Amy. He wondered when Brody would come to his senses. He smiled tightly. Probably the first time Brody got between her legs. She didn't look like much, just a pale little thing who'd probably whine and cry the whole time

a man was pumping her. After tonight Brody would likely leave
her where she lay. Purdon wanted to see that. It would be some
balm for his wounded pride. His grin grew broader. In fact, if
Brody got disgusted enough, he might turn her over to Purdon, and then he'd make sure she paid for his having to back
down.

Brody caught Purdon watching Amy, and that same jealous
sense of possession swept over him. He'd see that son of a bitch
in hell before he'd let him touch Amy. Just his looking at her
was a desecration.

He didn't like any of the men looking at her. But he knew it
was hard not to. She rode the horse astride, which made her
skirt and petticoats bunch and ride up, exposing her shapely
calves in their thin white stockings. Brody himself spent too
much time gazing at those legs. He wanted to slide his hand up
her leg, feeling the glide of the thin cloth under his hand and the
firm curve of her flesh beneath that. He wanted to slide the
garter off and roll down the stocking, his hand on her warm
flesh.

Brody shifted in his saddle. He would drive himself crazy this
way. He'd find out soon enough how her leg felt, how all of her
felt. There was no point in torturing himself about it now. But
he found it difficult to stop. He'd never felt this way about a
woman before, the hunger running all through him, filling not
only his loins but his chest and head and every part of him.

He glanced over at Amy, wondering if she could sense his
lecherous thoughts. She didn't look as though she did. She just
rode along easily, glancing around as if enjoying the scenery.
He needn't have worried about her being able to handle Landers's horse. Nor was she tired, despite her appearance of
frailty. She seemed unafraid, unaware of the fact that he and
the others kept staring at her.

In that, he was only partially right. Amy wasn't particularly
afraid. She possessed an ability to live in the moment, without
worrying about the future or the past. She enjoyed riding, and
she enjoyed looking at the scenery. She knew, with a complete, deep trust, that Victoria and Uncle Edward would find
her, and in the meantime, she felt safe in the protection of the
dark man beside her.

But though she wasn't afraid, she was not unaware of Brody's eyes on her. The others watched her, too, but they didn't matter. It was his black eyes that caused the strange melting sensation inside her. It was to his hands on the reins that her eyes were drawn, and it was about his firm lips that she thought.

He had looked at her as a woman. Not as a child, or as someone who was "touched." Not as Ed Stafford's crazy niece. For the first time, Amy felt like a woman. Feelings stirred in her, dark and ripe. She wondered what happened between a man and woman. Kissing—she knew that much. She'd heard other girls giggling about it. How would it feel to be kissed by a man? Not *a* man. *This* man. Surely the rough growth of beard would scratch her, but his lips . . .

Amy sneaked a glance at Brody. His mouth was firm, even hard. Would it be soft when it touched hers? No, not when, if. She didn't *know* that he wanted to kiss her, after all. She only assumed that. But perhaps that was why he had taken her with him, because he saw her as a woman, because he wanted her as men wanted Victoria. Because he wanted to kiss her.

Unconsciously, she worried at her lower lip with her teeth. But there must be more to it than kissing. What did he do with his arms while he kissed her? What did she do? Did they stand or sit? There was more, much more, she was sure, all the things she had wondered about that no one would tell her, not even Victoria. They thought she shouldn't know, that it would never apply to her, because she wasn't normal.

But this man didn't see that. He didn't know. And he wanted her.

They crossed a shallow river, and soon after that, dusk fell. Their pace slowed in the waning light, and finally Brody signaled to them to stop. Amy slid down from her horse with a sigh of relief. Much as she liked to ride, it had been a long, tiring afternoon, and after riding without the protection of her split riding skirt, the insides of her legs were sore. She sat down on the ground and pulled her skirts up to her knee to examine her stockings. They were rubbed clear through in more than one place. Amy sighed and shook her head.

"Mrs. Donnelly will be cross. She says I'm always ruining my stockings."

She glanced up to find the dark man looking at her with a strange expression on his face. She realized that she had said something wrong; she was always doing that. Now he would figure out that she wasn't normal, and he would no longer look at her as a woman. Quickly Amy scrambled to her feet, shaking out her skirts.

"I'm sorry."

He frowned. "For what?"

She shrugged. "For whatever I did."

His smile seemed startled out of him. She didn't think it was something he did much. "That covers a lot of territory."

Brody didn't know what to make of her. She was so beautiful and feminine that he ached with desire, yet she was as innocent as a child. She couldn't be married and still be that innocent. But how was it possible that someone like her hadn't been snatched up by a man long before now? He took her left hand, lifting it up to look at it.

It startled Amy when he took her hand. His fingers and palm were callused, rough against her skin, and the very roughness made her skin tingle. She felt the color rising in her face.

"You aren't married," he commented, and his thumb began to circle her palm.

Amy giggled a little at the idea and shook her head. The hypnotic movement of his thumb made her feel strange and jumpy inside. Then his thumb touched a sore spot, and she winced a little.

Brody froze. "What's the matter?"

She shook her head. "Nothing. I'm not used to riding without gloves. The reins are starting a blister."

He turned her hand palm up. There were two small red spots where the leather reins had rubbed her tender skin. He disliked the thought of anything hurting her or marring her lovely flesh. "I don't have any gloves for you."

"I'll be all right. It'll just take a while to work up a callus."

"No. I'll think of something." Reluctantly Brody released her hand and stepped back, turning toward his men.

Jimmy was on the ground, leaning back against a large rock, his eyes closed. He had no interest in anything except rest. Purdon and Grimes were standing, watching Brody and Amy. Purdon looked as sour as if he'd bitten into a crabapple.

"I hope if she ain't for our enjoyment, at least she can cook us some dinner," Purdon commented.

"She'll do whatever *I* tell her."

"But I can't. I've never cooked over an open fire," Amy blurted out. Was that why he had brought her? To cook and do chores? If so, he might abandon her, and that idea terrified her. Alone on foot in this vast, harsh land, she could easily die before Victoria found her. Amy searched nervously for something she *could* do that might convince him to let her go with him. "But I'm good with horses. I can help with them."

She turned and unbuckled the saddle, then reached up to pull it off the horse. It was a heavy saddle, and she staggered under its weight. Brody caught her and took the saddle. Amy looked up at him, her eyes wide, afraid she had just disproved her worth by not being able to take off the saddle well. "I really can do it. I just need to stand on a rock or something. And there must be other things I can do."

There was a barely muffled snort of laughter from Grimes, and Purdon cackled. "I gotta hand it to ya', Brody. You sure can pick 'em. Not only pretty, but stupid, too. That's the kind of woman to have."

Amy blushed and looked down. She should have kept her mouth shut. She'd made another mistake. Why was it that she didn't know the ordinary things that everyone else seemed to?

"Shut up!" Brody's voice cracked through the night air like a bullwhip. He walked toward the other man, each step slow and deadly. "Maybe I didn't make myself clear this afternoon. She's *mine*, and that means there's nothing for you to say about her."

He stopped inches away from Purdon, and his black eyes bored into the other man's. It was like looking into the barrel of a Colt, and braver men than Purdon had broken and run under Brody's gaze. Purdon swallowed and backed up a step. "I didn't mean nothin'. You know I didn't."

"Yeah." Brody's voice was barely more than a whisper. "I know." He moved back. "I think the best thing is to take care of the horses, then eat and get some rest."

"Sure," Grimes was quick to add, and Jimmy nodded. The men removed the saddles and bridles from the horses and hobbled them to graze for the night. Grimes pulled a supply of beef jerky out of his saddlebags and distributed it.

Brody brought some of the jerky and a canteen of water over to Amy. He motioned toward one of the many large rocks in the area. "Let's sit down."

Amy was quick to obey his suggestion. The raw threat in his voice earlier had made her fear him for the first time. She tucked her feet up under her on the rock and waited. Brody sat down beside her and handed her a strip of the hard, salty meat.

"You don't have to cook," he told her. He saw the touch of fear in her eyes that had not been there before, and it unsettled him. He felt a need to reassure her, but he didn't know how. He was mean as a rattlesnake, that was something everybody knew; he didn't know how to convince her otherwise. "We can't risk a camp fire. It would lead them right to us, like a beacon. So we don't cook."

"Oh. I see. I didn't realize." Amy's voice dropped, and she looked down at her hands. "I didn't think. He's right. I'm not very bright."

Brody frowned, angry that anything Purdon had said had made her downcast. "Purdon's an idiot. He's angry 'cause I took him down earlier. He didn't mean anything by it. He was just trying to get back at me."

Amy smiled a little, her good humor quick to return, as always. "Then he's even more stupid than me."

Brody glanced at her, startled, then grinned. "You ain't dumb, lady." He gazed at her for a moment. "You're just different. What's wrong with that? Who'd want to be like most the people in this world, anyway?"

"That's a sad way to think."

"Is it?" He reached out and ran his forefinger down her smooth cheek. His skin was dark against hers, and he was suddenly aware of how dirt-stained he was. That was the way he was inside, too, he thought. If he touched her life, he'd leave a streak of black on her soul.

The thought bothered him, and he dropped his hand. Amy bit off a hunk of the tough meat and chewed, watching Brody's profile in the pale wash of the moonlight. He didn't speak to her like other people did, even Victoria and Uncle Edward, as if she couldn't understand anything. He talked as if she were normal.

They sat for a moment in silence, eating and drinking warm water from the canteen. After a while Amy grew bold enough to say, "I don't know who you are."

"What? Oh. I'm Brody."

"Brody what?"

"Sam Brody."

"Sam. That's a nice name." Amy smiled.

He felt a funny sad twist in his chest. He couldn't remember the last time someone had called him Sam.

"Oh! I'm sorry." Amy looked embarrassed. "That's not right, is it, to call you by your first name?"

He chuckled. "You think you should call me Mr. Brody?"

"I guess."

He shook his head. "Call me Brody or Sam. No mister."

"Then I shall call you Sam. I like Sam." She held out her hand. "My name is Amy Wallace."

He took her hand. "Amy."

The dangling chain from his manacle brushed against her. Amy tapped it. "This must bother you. I'm sorry you couldn't get it off."

"I can live with it until we get back home."

Amy's face brightened. "I have an idea." She turned up the bottom of her skirt, exposing the ruffle of her petticoat. Part of it had already been torn off, and she ripped another section from it, then tore that piece in two. She slid the ruffle through the top link of the chain, wrapped the cloth around his arm, and tied it. The metal links no longer dangled.

"There. Does that feel better?"

"Yeah."

She smiled and repeated the procedure on the other arm. Brody watched her. "Why do you do these things?"

Amy glanced up from her work. "What things?"

He gestured with his free hand toward the chain. "Helping kinds of things. Tying up the chain so it won't get in my way. Ripping up your petticoat for Jimmy's wound." He paused. "This morning, when you wrapped my wrists."

Amy looked perplexed. "I did it because your wrists were hurt. And that boy was bleeding." She couldn't understand why he asked. "Don't you want these chains tied up?"

"Of course. Just like I wanted your help this morning. It's only—well, most people wouldn't have."

"I know. I could tell Victoria was upset with me."

"Who's Victoria?"

"My cousin. I've lived with her and my uncle ever since I can remember. She's the woman who was with me this morning."

"I didn't notice her much."

Amy stared. "But she's beautiful!"

"Is she?"

"Oh, yes."

"Not as beautiful as you."

At his words, a glow started in Amy's stomach and spread outward. Could he really think she was more beautiful than Victoria? She shook her head, smiling, and her cheeks turned rosy. "No. She's the most beautiful woman I've ever seen."

"Then you ought to look in a mirror." Brody sat and watched her. She had taken off her bonnet, and the moonlight glittered on her pale hair. Her skin was smooth and white, her eyes huge dark pools. She seemed embarrassed, yet pleased at his words. Brody didn't understand why. She must have heard the same things a thousand times from men. She was so lovely it made him hurt.

Brody cupped her cheek, and Amy shivered at his touch. He frightened her, he knew, and he wished, for just a moment, that he was a different kind of man, the kind whose touch Amy would welcome, not shy away from. He stroked his thumb across her smooth skin. It was like caressing the petals of a rose. He wanted to touch her all over. He wanted to take down her hair and sift it through his fingers. He wanted to explore her with his mouth and tongue.

He thought of how her eyes would widen with fright if he laid her back on the ground, how she would shake and cry if he unfastened her clothes and rolled on top of her. He thought of the rest of the men across the camp from them, watching and listening as he took her. Witnessing her humiliation.

Brody stood up abruptly. "We better get to sleep. We'll ride early in the morning."

He spread out the thin blanket that he kept tied in a roll behind his saddle. Amy watched him uncertainly. She didn't know
what she was supposed to do. The other three men were
watching her, and it made her uneasy.

Brody nodded toward the empty land behind them. "You
might want to go out there behind those rocks, but don't go far.
I don't want to have to come after you."

Amy stared, fear clutching at her lungs. "You mean to sleep?
By myself?"

She looked so taken aback that Brody couldn't suppress a
chuckle. "No. To take care of—you know, woman things."

"Oh. Thank you." She stood up and started in the direction
he'd indicated.

"Amy."

"Yes?" She turned.

"You sleep here. Next to me."

Amy nodded. She was glad. She would have been scared to
death by herself. She hurried off behind the rocks, grateful that
Brody had suggested it. She had been embarrassed to ask.

When she returned, Amy saw that Brody was already lying
on the blanket on his side, his revolver within easy reach. She
wondered what sleeping next to him meant. She knew that an
unmarried man and woman never slept together. So it was then
that it must happen, the kissing and things that led to babies.
Did Sam expect to do those things to her? Would it be awful—
or exciting?

She knelt beside the blanket and folded her hands.

"What are you doing?"

Amy lifted her head, surprised. "Praying. I do it every
night." Praying was one of the things she enjoyed most. Her
God was a warm and gentle presence, and she worshiped him
with a simple, happy faith. She loved the songs in church, and
she loved talking to God at night. She knew He understood her
thoughts and the feelings in her heart, though she couldn't express them right to other people. She knew He loved her without doubt, pity, or reservation, and there was no fear in talking
to Him. "You'll let me, won't you?" she asked, worry touching her face.

"Sure." His voice sounded hoarse.

Brody watched her. She was the essence of purity, kneeling there with her head bowed. He knew that he would dirty her, corrupt her. Hurt her. He guessed it was an indication of exactly how low he was that looking at her in that saintly pose made him swell and pulse with desire. God, he wanted her. He ached to taste her sweat and hear her moan with pleasure. He yearned to watch that purity melt into womanly hunger, to look at the lady she was in the day and know that at night in his arms, for him, she was as hot and wild as the loosest woman.

But that kind of response didn't come from forcing a woman.

Brody rolled onto his back, throwing his arm across his eyes. He heard the rustle of Amy's skirts as she lay down on the blanket beside him. He didn't move or look at her; he couldn't.

"Good night, Sam," she said shyly.

"Good night."

Slater turned his horse onto the road to Austin, the direction in which he had seen Brody and his gang disappear. His wound burned, and his head pounded, and when his horse first started moving, he thought he might have to stop and empty his guts again beside the road. But after a few minutes his stomach settled down, and though the pain in his head and arm didn't go away, he was able to concentrate on his task—or he would have been, if that blasted woman hadn't been following him. He turned around every few minutes, and there she was, still riding along easily behind him.

He had to admit that she had good taste in horseflesh. The horse she'd bought was the only decent one in the livery stable. She sat in the saddle like someone who'd been born to it, too. But he still couldn't let her accompany him. The last thing he needed on this trip was a woman, even if she could ride. She was crazy. Why wasn't there a man looking after her? Perhaps he'd finally given up on trying to control her. Slater could understand how a man might reach that point.

He did his best to ignore Victoria. Most of the time he managed it, keeping his eyes on the sides of the road to find the tracks where the gang had turned off it. But he couldn't keep himself from craning around to look back at her now and then.

Victoria was amazed at how well Slater did. She knew he must feel terrible, but he never stopped or failed to keep up his meticulous search of the roadway. Finally, after about thirty minutes, he turned his horse off the road. When Victoria followed him, she saw that the tracks of several horses left the road there, too. Excitement flared in her. Maybe Slater really would be able to find Brody's gang. If they could trail the gang to its hideout, she'd be able to lead her father and his men to it. She hated the thought of her cousin remaining with that scum so long, but she was realistic enough to know that she and a one-armed, weakened man couldn't rescue Amy.

Slater moved faster now, since the hoofprints they were following were the only ones there and easy enough to spot. Again Victoria was impressed. Slater was tough, all right. She knew how trotting must jar his injured arm.

He didn't stop until dusk fell and he was no longer able to see the prints well. When he reined in and dismounted, Victoria pulled to a halt her usual distance behind him. She unfastened the saddle and bridle and pulled them from her horse, then hobbled him for the night. About thirty yards away from her, she could see Slater struggling to carry out the same tasks one-handed. Victoria smiled to herself. He was certainly stubborn! Well, he'd find out that she was, too. She wasn't about to help him until he asked for it.

Slater watched Victoria out of the corner of his eye. His head felt twice its size, and his arm was just as bad. He couldn't do anything that wasn't clumsy, and it irritated him to see Victoria competently performing the same tasks he was fumbling over. He leaned against a large flat rock. He was as weak as a kitten and sweating far too much for the things he had just done. He uncapped one of his two canteens and drank from it. He would have liked to have poured it all over his head, but he knew better than to waste the water. The water was warm from the sun, but it tasted delicious.

He pulled a stick of jerky from his saddlebags and sank down to the ground to eat it, leaning back against the rock. He wasn't really hungry, but he knew he had to keep up his strength. He would need every bit of it to track and capture someone like Brody, especially with one arm out of commission.

Slater glanced in Victoria's direction. It had become completely dark now, and he could see little of her except the shadow of a movement now and then. That irritated him, too. Why did she stay out there by herself? Any normal woman would have been scared by now and come over here seeking his protection. Slater looked down at his arm, and a wry smile twisted his mouth. Maybe she didn't consider him much protection, the shape he was in.

He continued to eat his salty food while his mind worried over the problem of the woman who was following him. He didn't like the fact that he couldn't see her. What if someone sneaked up on her in the night? What if she woke up and was scared? It went against all his instincts to let a lady fend for herself. He'd led a rough life the past few years, but he'd been reared to be a gentleman. Besides, defending others was his work, his life. It was his sworn duty—and the oath he'd taken hadn't made an exception for ornery females. He felt guilty for not making camp beside her, where he could protect her.

On the other hand, he had sworn that she would be on her own if she followed him. He had to stick to his threat. If she spent a night by herself, maybe tomorrow she would be willing to return to Santa Clara. But if he took pity on her and moved over there, she would think she had won and would insist on accompanying him the next morning. Then what would he do? He couldn't take a woman with him on a manhunt for one of the most dangerous criminals in Texas!

Slater's thoughts went around and around like a lion in a cage, and with every passing minute he grew more irritable. He saw a glow in the area where Victoria was, and a moment later, it flickered into a fire. *That*, he thought, was the last straw. He pushed himself up to his feet and marched over to her.

Victoria heard the crunch of his boots and realized that Slater was coming toward her. It surprised her. She hadn't expected such an early capitulation. She was relieved, however; much as she hated to admit it, she felt nervous sitting alone in this vast emptiness. She had slept outdoors many times—on roundups, on a cattle drive, on a camping trip to the springs on the northwest quarter—but she had never been alone. Her father had been there, or the foreman and several ranch hands. She found it a little eerie sitting under the black arch of the sky with nothing but a horse for company. That had been the main reason she had made the camp fire. She didn't need it for the warmth or to cook a meal; she had the small bundle of cold food the hotel restaurant had sent with her. But the fire would keep away wild animals. And it was comforting.

She continued to brush out her hair as if she had never felt a twinge of uneasiness, prepared to accept Slater's surrender graciously. She was startled, therefore, when he stepped into the ring of firelight and kicked dirt over the fire, dousing it.

"What do you think you're doing?" Victoria jumped up, furious and dismayed—more by the depth of her disappointment that he wasn't coming there to stay with her than by his action. "It took a lot of work to build that fire!"

Victoria's hair swung as she moved, falling softly around her shoulders and down to her waist. It was thick, and as black as the night. Slater wanted to touch it; he'd wanted to all the way over, as he watched her brush it out in the firelight. That fact increased his exasperation.

"What I'm doing," he repeated her words bitingly, "is making sure you don't provide a signal for Brody to find us by."

"Brody! He's long gone."

"Maybe. But he's crafty. He might decide to circle back and jump me before I can find him. I don't want to take the risk just so you can keep your feet toasty."

"I wasn't 'keeping my feet toasty'!"

"No? Then you won't miss the fire, will you?"

Victoria clenched her teeth. She had no answer for him, and that was more infuriating than anything else. She wrapped her arms around her knees and stared down at them.

Slater lingered uncertainly. He'd accomplished what he'd come for, and now he didn't know what to do.

"Well?" Victoria asked in an icy tone. "What are you standing here for? Shouldn't you return to your camp?"

Slater began to turn away, then stopped, sighing. "What can I say to get you to go back to Santa Clara?"

"It's a little late, I'm afraid."

"You can start first thing tomorrow morning. Look, I'll make camp here beside you, and at dawn you can—"

"Oh. You mean in return for your precious presence to-night, I have to agree to get back to my sewing and let you do the real work?"

He stared, momentarily flummoxed. "I didn't say anything about sewing."

"But that's what you meant, wasn't it? I'm not good enough to do anything difficult. I should stick to women's work."

"I didn't say that, although I don't know what you have against 'women's work.'"

"You would if you'd ever done it. It's boring. I wasn't raised to sit and twiddle my thumbs while others did my work for me."

"It's not your work. It's mine."

"If Amy is involved, it's my concern."

"If you want to help her, stay out of it. If you come, you'll get in my way."

"I can help you. I saw you struggling with your saddle. I know I'm not a lawman or a tracker, but I can follow orders, and—"

"If you could follow orders, you would have gone back to town hours ago."

"You have to have some help! You can't do it alone. One wounded man against, what? Five desperate outlaws? It's absurd."

"I know what I'm doing."

"So do I. You're assuring yourself of failure."

"I'll get Brody."

"When? In a few months? A year? That won't do Amy much good."

Slater sighed and rubbed his hand wearily over his face. The irritation that had motivated him earlier had drained away, leaving him exhausted. "Look, you're not doing anyone any good with this, least of all yourself. Don't you know what it will do to your reputation to spend several nights alone with me?"

"I suspect it will ruin it."

"Don't you care?"

Victoria shrugged. "Other things are more important to me. I wouldn't give a flip for what other people said about me if I could get Amy back."

"Damnation! Why can't you leave it alone? How can I do my job if I have to worry about you?"

"You don't have to worry about me. That's what I've been telling you. I can take care of myself. And I can help you!"

"Go back."

"No."

They glared at each other. Finally Slater made an exasperated noise and stalked away. Let her spend the night fending for herself. Maybe tomorrow morning she'd be more willing to see reason. He returned to his camp, wrapped himself in his blanket and lay down on the ground. There were some pebbles beneath him, but he was too tired to clear them away. He thought about Victoria all alone in the dark. And his last thought before he sank into sleep was that he felt lower than a snake.

It took Victoria quite a bit more time to go to sleep than it had Slater. The ground was hard, and she felt every bump and rock. She looked up at the stars and thought about the variety of wildlife that lived in the area. The night sounds seemed strange, and she kept looking around to see the source of this rustling or that snap. But she wasn't about to run to Slater like a scared child, even if it meant waiting out the night, sleepless.

She fell asleep finally, but her rest was fitful. She tossed and turned, plagued by bad dreams, and awakened more than once, heart pounding, wondering where she was. It was a relief when dawn finally came and she could get up. She glanced over at Slater's camp, now visible in the pale gold light of early morning. She smiled smugly when she saw that he was still rolled up in a blanket, asleep.

She got ready quickly. There wasn't much to do. She didn't need to dress, having slept in her clothes. She braided her hair and left it hanging down her back. It was the only way to keep it neat, outdoors. She ate the remainder of the bread the restaurant had sent with her and washed it down with water from the canteen. Then she rolled her blanket neatly, stuffing it with her supplies, and tied it. She was ready to go.

Again she looked toward Slater's camp. He was still asleep. Victoria sighed. No doubt he was exhausted. If only he would let her help, she could get his horse ready and let him sleep a few extra minutes.

Victoria glanced at the brightening sky. She couldn't let him sleep the day away. They had already lost precious hours yesterday. Victoria untied the hobble on her horse and put on the saddle and bridle. She tied her bedroll behind the saddle and slung her canteens and cartridge belts over the saddle horn. Then she mounted and rode over to Slater's camp.

"Slater." She called to him from a few feet away and again closer up. He responded only by turning from his front onto his back. Well, at least he was alive. But he didn't awaken, even when she walked up and stood right over him. Victoria looked down at him. His face was flushed and his hair damp. Sweat had gathered on his forehead. Victoria dropped to her knees beside him and laid a hand on his forehead.

Dear God. He was burning up!

Chapter Five

Amy lay curled on her side with her back against Brody. His arm was thrown across her, his hand cupped naturally around one of her breasts. When he awoke, he lay still for a moment, savoring the feel of her. Her breast was as soft as down, the bud of her nipple hard against his palm. He dragged his thumb across her nipple, and it tightened under his touch. Brody smiled and nuzzled her soft, sweet-smelling hair. Asleep, she didn't fear him; she responded to him. His thumb circled her nipple gently, and the response of the fleshy nub turned him hard and hot. He buried his lips in her hair, kissing the back of her neck.

She stirred and mumbled something in her sleep, and Brody stopped reluctantly. He wasn't doing himself any good this way, and he didn't want her to wake up to find him mauling her. He drew his head back, but he didn't remove his arm. Maybe if she woke up and found them lying together, entwined so naturally, it would help her grow used to him, make her fear him less. He closed his eyes and feigned sleep.

Amy's eyes fluttered open. It took her longer than Brody to adjust to the world. At first she was aware only of the warmth of Brody's legs and a strange, pleasant tingling between her legs. She liked the sensation, and she squeezed her thighs together, snuggling back into the warmth. Brody had to bite his lip to keep from groaning.

She became fully conscious, recognizing the warmth as a man's hard body down the length of her back. His arm was around her, his hand on her breast. Amy flushed all over. She was lying with Sam Brody on the ground, and his hand was on her in a place where no one had ever touched her. Her breasts were full, her nipples puckered and sensitive. His arm was heavy across her body, but it felt nice, too. And his hand on her breast felt—well, not nice exactly, but exciting. She sensed that the touch of his hand was somehow connected with the tingling between her legs. A mysterious moisture had formed there, too. It all felt strange and delightful, but somehow incomplete. Amy knew she wanted more, but she didn't know what it was.

She moved restlessly, and Brody rolled away from her. She turned to look over her shoulder and saw him sitting up, awake. Amy missed the feel of his body. She sat up, too, watching him. He stretched and looked at her.

Amy was beautiful, even waking up. Her hair had worked free from its pins and tumbled in a tangle around her shoulders, but its unkempt state didn't detract from her loveliness. Rather, it made Brody's fingers itch to sink into it. If they were alone, if she wouldn't scream and struggle, he would unbutton her dress and push it back from her shoulders. He would untie the laces of her camisole and bare her breasts to the pale light of dawn. He would study her like a work of art, and then he would bend down and take one rosy, pebbled nipple into his mouth....

Brody jerked his head away and swallowed. This was no time for such thoughts. He could do nothing about it now, and he was only killing himself dreaming of it. Tonight, he told himself. Tonight he would take his pleasure with her, regardless of her fear or unwillingness. That was, after all, why she was here. She was his, and after a time she would learn to accept it. And if she didn't, well, he would have eased his own hunger. It was crazy not to. She was completely in his power.

Brody stood up and walked away. Amy watched him, wondering if she had made him angry.

They saddled up and rode out as soon as they could, not even pausing to eat. Before they left, Brody had Amy rip another strip from her petticoat, and he wound the cotton cloth lightly around her palms to protect them from blisters.

They rode hard. Jimmy looked pale, but he kept up. Brody didn't talk, and his silence scared Amy. Her stomach began to growl, but she said nothing.

They came to another river, and there they dismounted and ate a quick meal while they stretched their muscles, which had grown cramped from riding. They followed the river downstream to find a good fording place. On the other side, Brody reined in and faced the other men.

"We'll split up here, make it harder for them to track us. Purdon, you and Grimes take Jimmy into Austin. Go to Doc Benson. He's a drunk, but he knows what he's doing, and he doesn't ask any questions. Hang around a few days. There aren't any pictures of you on posters, and I doubt Slater got a good look at you yesterday. You shouldn't be recognized."

"Why you want us to stay in Austin?" Purdon's eyes slid to Amy. He had a pretty good idea why Brody wanted them out of the way for a while, and he didn't like it.

"I want you to look around, listen, see if you can find out where Dave Vance is."

A vicious light flared in Purdon's eyes. "That son of a bitch traitor. I'll kill him. Real slow."

"No." Brody's voice made Amy shiver. "Just find him. I want to take care of him myself."

Purdon grinned. That was more like Brody. "All right. You're the boss."

"That's right." Brody turned his horse away from the others. "Meet you back at the place."

Amy watched him, frozen with terror. Did he mean to leave her with these men? He had said nothing about her.

Brody glanced back. Amy was just sitting there, her eyes big, staring at him. "Amy." The word was stern. Did she dare go against him? "You're coming with me."

Relief spread across her face, and she smiled sunnily, nudging her horse forward. She wanted to come with him, Brody realized, and he had to struggle not to grin back at her.

The others turned downstream, and Brody and Amy cut away in a northwesterly direction. It lifted Amy's spirits considerably not to have the other men with them, and she hummed as they rode along.

"Look at that hawk!" She pointed up at the bird drifting in lazy circles over the rolling land.

Brody looked where she pointed. A hawk was something he saw all the time; he usually paid little attention. But this time he noticed the grace and serenity of the hawk's movements. He glanced at Amy. She was gazing all around her.

"I've never been in this part of the country before," she said. "The hills are beautiful."

She was right, Brody thought, though he would never have put it into words. All he knew was that he liked it here, that the sight of the land soothed him. There was something grand and wild about the broken land, with its rolling hills and harsh granite bluffs. Near the creeks and rivers, the trees were thick— cedars, mesquites, huge spreading live oaks and pecans—but away from the water, they turned sparse and scrubby. The country was always primitively beautiful, but it was in its glory then, in early spring, when the wildflowers spilled in masses down the hillsides and across the flatland, vividly blue and red and yellow.

When they stopped later for a brief rest, Amy walked through the bluebonnets and finally sat down in their midst. She smiled back at him, and he felt again that strange, sweet-sad warmth inside him that she had brought out before. He wanted to enfold her in his arms and squeeze her so tightly that neither one of them could breathe.

They picked their way up a creek until they came to a rocky shelf stretching northward. Brody stopped and looked at the expanse of rough land, then continued forward through the stream. When he left the creek, he turned south. Amy followed him, puzzled.

"Aren't we going back the way we came?"

"Yeah. We're doubling back."

"But why?"

He glanced at her, wondering if she was trying to plan a way to escape, but her face was innocently curious. "To throw Slater off. He'll figure we went up the creek to hide our tracks, and he'll follow along, looking for where the prints come out of the water. But when he sees that shelf of rock, he'll suspect I came out there, so the hoofprints wouldn't show. He'll take that shelf until it ends, but he won't be able to find any prints. If he comes back to the creek and starts up it again looking for our tracks, he won't expect us to head south. But just in case, I'll make sure he doesn't see our trail."

He came to a halt and dismounted, broke a branch off a mesquite bush and retraced their path to the creek. He walked back to Amy, brushing out their tracks with the leafy branch as he went. He tossed the branch aside and remounted. Amy stared at him, amazed.

"You're awfully clever. I would never have thought of that. I don't think even Tory would have."

Brody chuckled at her expression and shook his head. He wasn't about to admit that her compliment pleased him. "I've just been hunted often enough that I figured out some tricks."

They rode for a while, Amy's forehead creased in thought. "But if we ride back the way we came, won't we run smack into the posse?"

"We'll go west soon. When we get far enough away, we'll lie low for a few days. Give Slater enough time to lose us, then head back to my place."

"You own some land?"

A wry smile touched his mouth. "No. I just found it. It's a place to hide out."

"Oh. I see. Someplace nobody can find."

"Right."

"I have a place like that. It's in a tree down by the creek. 'Course, Tory knows about it, but not my uncle or Mrs. Donnelly."

"Why do you need a place nobody can find?"

Amy shrugged. "For when Tory's Aunt Margaret comes to visit. I go there a lot then."

Brody smiled.

"Sometimes I like to be alone. Just to look around and listen to things. You know."

"Yeah."

It was very strange, he thought, to be riding along talking like this to a woman he had abducted. But, then, everything had been strange from the moment he met her. She amazed him in so many ways that he couldn't even think of them all. She looked as fragile as glass, yet she had ridden hard for two days without tiring and had slept on the ground without a com-

plaint. She hadn't whined or cried. She had enough courage for
two men. It seemed she was about as fragile as a piece of iron.

Yet there was nothing tough about her, nothing rough. She
was gentle, soft and unfailingly kind. She was remarkably
cheerful, talking and admiring the view as if they were out for
a pleasant Sunday afternoon ride. She displayed a naïveté
Brody had never encountered before, and at times she appeared slow-witted, but she was quick enough to catch on to
things when he explained them to her. Strangest of all, even
though he had kidnapped her, even though she must realize that
he would take her forcibly, she acted as if she *liked* him. She
chatted with him and warmed him with her smile; she had tied
up his chains so they wouldn't annoy him; she had beamed and
ridden forward eagerly when he told her to come with him.

She was an angel. But she was also womanly and sensual,
with none of the marble coldness of a saint. When he looked at
her, he felt good. He wanted her as a chilled man sought the
fire. He had to have her. He *would* have her. But it made his
guts twist to think of hurting her.

They returned to the river they had crossed earlier, but didn't
ford it. Instead they traveled upstream along the bank. Once
they heard the sound of voices, and Brody led her quickly away
from the river. When it grew dark they made camp in the nat-
ural shelter of the trees. Brody unsaddled the horses and hobbled them, and they ate. Then he laid out the blanket for them
to sleep on. Amy moved to help him, involuntarily wincing as
she stood up.

"What's the matter?"

"Oh." She shrugged and sat down on the ground, pulling up
her skirt to show him the inside of her calves, where her flesh
was reddened beneath her torn stockings.

Just the sight of her legs set up a tumult in Brody's loins, but
he ignored it as he squatted down beside her, his concern for her
overriding his lust. "You'll get blisters soon."

She nodded. "I don't usually ride like this. I have a skirt
that's split, you know, like full trousers. It keeps my legs from
getting rubbed."

He couldn't keep from reaching out and touching her leg.
She didn't draw away, just looked at him trustingly. Brody

gnawed his lower lip. He ached to slide his hand up her leg. Her skin was like satin.

"We'll have to do something." His tone was rough. He pulled his hand away. "I—I'll get you something else to wear."

"How?"

He shook his head. "Never mind. I just will." He looked straight into her eyes. "I won't let anything hurt you."

Amy smiled softly. "I know."

A sweet ache pierced him. He knew he wouldn't force her, no matter what he'd promised himself this morning, no matter how much he wanted her. He couldn't. It would be like cutting out his own heart to see the trust in her eyes turn to fear and disgust.

He moved away. "Go ahead and lie down. Get some sleep."

"Aren't you going to bed?"

"Later. I'll sit up for a minute."

He sat down a few feet away from her, his arms linked around his knees. He watched her curl up on her side, her head resting on her arm.

"Are you going to look at the stars?" she asked. "I love to look at them. They're so sparkly and tiny, and the sky's so big. They should be lost up there, but they aren't." She yawned. "But I'm too tired to watch them tonight."

Her eyes closed. He could see her body melt into sleep, but it didn't cool the fire in his blood. Brody sighed and lay down quietly beside her. Amy rolled over and snuggled against him. He pressed his lips against her hair, and his arm stole around her. It was a distinct form of hell to lie like this with her. It was also the sweetest thing he'd ever known.

He closed his eyes, but it was a long time before sleep came to him.

Slater had a fever. That sometimes happened with a wound, Victoria knew. She sat back on her heels, thinking. He needed medical attention, but she couldn't get him on his horse and back to Santa Clara. He was too sick. It was going to be up to her to get him well.

She sighed. She hadn't planned on this. It wasn't that she wasn't capable of doctoring a sick man. She'd done it often enough on the ranch. She had handled everything from a knife wound to croup. But not out in the open, and not without supplies.

Still, Victoria wasn't one to sit worrying about things she couldn't control. She would do the best with what she had. She pulled out her handkerchief and soaked it with water from her canteen. Gently she smoothed it across Slater's face. He mumbled something, and his tongue came out to moisten his lips. His eyelids fluttered open.

He looked at her for a moment in vague confusion. Then his eyes cleared. "Damn."

"Really, Mr. Slater. Even when you're sick, the first word out of your mouth is a curse." She summoned up irritation in her voice to hide her worry.

He smiled faintly. "Sorry. I'm afraid it's been too long since I was in the presence of ladies."

"I'm sure that's true." She wiped his face again. "Here. Try drinking a little water." Victoria put a hand behind Slater's neck and helped him lift his head, holding the canteen to his lips. He sipped from it, then sank back.

"It's hot as—" he began, then glanced at Victoria "—as Hades out here."

Victoria looked up at the sky. "It's your fever. It's early morning still. But soon the sun will be high, and it will be hot. That won't help your fever. Could you ride a short distance? There's a big live oak less than a hundred yards from here, and you could lie down in its shade."

He nodded weakly. "Sure."

"Stay there for a bit, and let me saddle your horse first." Victoria hopped up and walked over to Slater's horse. The animal eyed her warily and sidled away, but its hobble kept it from moving far, and Victoria's firm, sure hand soon settled it down. She put on the bridle and saddle, unhobbled the animal and led it back to Slater.

She knelt beside him. "All right. Let's try it."

He opened his eyes. They were glazed, but he nodded and pushed himself up onto his elbows. He paused, looking a little amazed at his lack of strength. Then he pushed up to a sitting position. From there, however, he couldn't make it up without help, so Victoria put both hands on his good arm and pulled.

Slater got to his feet. He walked to his horse, one arm around Victoria's shoulders.

"We seem to be making a habit of this," he joked, but the shortness of his breath drained the humor from his words.

"I'd just as soon we quit," Victoria retorted tartly. "You're too heavy for me to be carting you around."

When they reached his horse, he wrapped his hand around the saddle horn for support and leaned against the animal. "My gun," he said, wiping his forehead against his sleeve. "Need my gun."

What a time to be worrying about his gun, Victoria thought irritably, but she turned around to look for it. The double holster was lying on the ground above the blanket. She retrieved it and looped it over the saddle horn. "There. I trust you can ride a few yards without strapping it on."

He nodded. "I can get to it better here."

Victoria could see that simply getting up and walking to the horse had tired Slater. His face was even more flushed than before.

"Are you ready to mount?"

Slater rested his forehead against his horse's neck for a moment. "Come on, Old Jack," he whispered to the animal. "Don't get feisty on me today." He gripped the saddle horn, put his foot into the stirrup and pushed himself up. He was less than graceful, but he made it. Old Jack shifted restlessly, but didn't dance or shy, as he often did.

Victoria rolled up Slater's blanket, grabbed his canteen and saddlebags, and hurried back to her horse. She didn't take time to strap on the bags or blanket, just hooked them over her saddle horn. She mounted quickly, and they set off on the short journey.

Victoria glanced at her companion several times as they rode. He was drenched with sweat, and his color was too high, but at least he was able to stick in the saddle. He had been right yesterday when he said he could ride, no matter what. For a moment she considered taking him back to town, but she knew that was impossible. He would never make it.

When they reached the live oak tree, Victoria slid off her horse and spread out Slater's blanket in the shade. Out of the corner of her eye, she saw a movement, and she spun around. Slater was dismounting.

"No, wait!" she cried, rushing over to him.

She reached him just as his foot hit the ground and his leg buckled. She threw her arms around him, but he was too heavy for her, and they both toppled over, hitting the ground with a thud. Victoria would have scolded him for trying to do everything by himself, but his weight had knocked the wind out of her.

Slater's skin felt as if it were on fire. The effort of mounting and riding had made his temperature shoot up. All thought of scolding him flew out of her head. She squirmed out from beneath him and rolled him onto his back. He looked at her, his eyes glittering with fever. Victoria had the uneasy feeling that he no longer recognized her.

"Beautiful," he mumbled.

"What?"

He wet his parched lips. "Come on. Let's go upstairs."

He was out of his head.

"All right." She managed a shaky smile. "But you have to stand up."

He nodded and rolled unsteadily to his feet. Victoria put her arm around his waist, and they weaved their way to the blanket. Victoria ran to get the canteen and soaked her handkerchief again. She washed off Slater's face, and he turned gratefully toward the water. She tried to lift his head and let him drink, but this time he didn't help, and she could raise his head only a little. She brought the canteen to his lips, but it seemed as if as much water spilled as got into his mouth.

He moved restlessly, mumbling, and Victoria washed his face again, sliding the cloth down the column of his neck. She unbuttoned his shirt and pushed the sides apart. His shirt was as wet as if he'd dipped it in water, and his skin was slick with sweat. The golden-brown hairs on his chest curled damply. Victoria felt an unaccustomed tightness in her own chest, and her breathing was suddenly shallower and faster. She had taken care of sick men before, but somehow it wasn't the same with Slater.

His chest was hard and ridged with muscle, his skin smooth and bronzed. A long white scar curled down across his rib cage.

She reached out and traced it with her forefinger. Slater moved restively, and she snatched her hand back. Whatever was she thinking of! There was no reason to touch him like that. And there was no reason for the funny feeling in her abdomen when she looked at his bare chest. She'd seen other men without their shirts—her father and some of the ranch hands.

Her eyes went back to Slater. None of the men she'd seen had looked like him, so lean and hard and elemental. Her gaze moved up to his face. His lids shuttered his eyes, but she could well remember their piercing green. They had cut right through her. His lashes were long and dark against his cheeks, giving him a vulnerable look at odds with the hard line of his jaw, roughened now with stubble. His mouth was full and wide, his lips dry from the fever and slightly open.

Victoria dampened her finger and drew it across his lips. They closed on her finger, capturing the moisture, and she felt his tongue against her skin. Her stomach quivered, and she pulled her hand back. He groaned softly. Again she moistened his lips with her finger, and his tongue flickered over her flesh like fire. Victoria swallowed. An ache started low in her abdomen.

She wet the piece of cloth again and swept it down Slater's throat and chest. Her hand slowed as it moved over his chest, almost turning into a caress. Slater moved his head. "Opal," he uttered in a hoarse whisper. "Don't, sugar. Have to leave."

Victoria's hand stopped in midmotion. Her eyebrows rose. It didn't take much imagination to guess where his feverish mind was. She turned away and wrung out the handkerchief. It was warm from his body. Her breath was shaky. Earlier, he had called her beautiful. She wondered if he had meant it, or if it had been the fever talking. Had he even been seeing her when he said it? Or Opal?

She laid the cloth out on a rock, then went back to Slater and tried to get him to drink. She was a little more successful this time, but when she laid his head back down, leaning over him, suddenly his hand snaked up her body. She gasped and froze. He cupped her breast and squeezed gently.

"Come on, sugar. Been on the road...six weeks." He smiled in response to something only he heard and saw. "Sure." His hand caressed her breast.

Victoria closed her eyes. No man had ever touched her so intimately. He was out of his head, so she couldn't really get mad at him. But he ought to move away. Still, she stayed for a moment longer, unable to move. The touch of his fingers sent such strange feelings washing over her. It made her head light and her knees weak, and the ache inside her spread.

Though she was not as naive as Amy, Victoria had little experience with men other than the kiss or two that Riley Landman's son had stolen from her at dances. There were very few men who would try to trifle with the daughter of as wealthy and important a rancher as Edward Stafford, and if they did, Victoria was quite capable of setting them straight. Victoria found most of the local boys foolish and young, and Dave Landman's pecks on her lips had never aroused enough interest in her to permit anything further.

But Slater's touch was something altogether different. His hand on her breast set off a yearning, a desire to explore and discover. She looked at his lips, full and sensual beneath his thick, curving moustache, and wondered what it would be like to kiss him. His kisses wouldn't be like Dave's, she suspected.

Victoria jumped to her feet. This was insane. Amy was in the hands of an outlaw, and Slater was ill. This was no time for such thoughts. Anyway, even if Slater weren't ill, he was the last man she should want to have kiss her. He had made it clear that he couldn't stand her, and she didn't like him, either. He was rude and rough, and he opposed her at every turn. If he did kiss her, she would slap him. His kiss wouldn't be nice or respectful or gentlemanly. Or boring.

Victoria made a noise of disgust and walked over to the horses. She had to stop thinking like this and keep her mind on their situation. Both their lives depended on it. The first problem was water. The water in one canteen was gone. Each horse had carried two canteens, so that left them with three, but at the rate she was using water on Slater, that supply wouldn't last long. Before the day was done, they would need more.

She could ride ahead and try to find water. She felt sure she would reach it soon. By her calculations they were headed toward the Blanco River, and she didn't think they were far from it. She could find the river or some smaller tributary, refill the canteens and return to Slater. The problem was Slater.

How could she leave him lying here defenseless? He would be easy prey for any predator, animal or human, that chanced to come along. Out of his head as he was, he could do himself harm. He might stumble off God knew where, or try to get on his horse and fall. Or what if something happened to her, and she was unable to get back to him? He would be left alone here to die.

But the fact remained that if she didn't get water, eventually he would die anyway.

Victoria sighed. Thinking about her troubles took her mind off her unladylike thoughts, but it wasn't bringing her any ease. She decided to put off the decision. Right now she would just worry about taking care of Slater.

She removed the saddles and supplies from the horses and let them graze. Then she picked up a fresh canteen and returned to Slater. He was still out of his head, mumbling, tossing and turning. She bathed his face and chest again, sternly keeping her touch—and her thoughts—impersonal.

All morning and into the afternoon she continued to watch him, washing him down and forcing him to drink. It was the only thing she could do to combat the fever. She felt so helpless. If only she had brought medical supplies! It had been foolish of her not to ask Dr. Bauer for something, considering the fact that Slater had been wounded. She should have guessed that this might happen.

Slater was restless, unable to lie still, and sometimes he talked, though usually she couldn't understand what he said. After a while he got the chills and began to shiver. Victoria wrapped both blankets around him, but still he shuddered uncontrollably. Finally she lay down beside him and wrapped her arms around him, holding him close so that her body heat would penetrate him. His arms were tight around her. His body was like a furnace, enveloping her with heat. Yet, strangely, it wasn't unpleasant.

Victoria wasn't overly concerned with proprieties; she wouldn't have ridden with Slater if she had been. But she had never had any reason to flout convention; socially her life had been much the same as that of any young woman of her class and age. She had never held a man except for the times she'd hugged her own father; certainly she'd never lain down beside one. But she found that there was something very warm and comforting—and breathtakingly exciting—about it. His lean body was tight against hers all the way up and down, the contours of his body so hard, so different from hers. He was muscled and tough, and, even as sick as he was, she felt protected within the circle of his arms. His intense heat permeated her body; his sweat dampened her blouse and skin. She wanted, for the first time she could ever remember, to lean her head against that hard chest and surrender her problems to him. Yet she felt an equal need to give comfort and healing, to strengthen him with her strength. And tangled in among those emotions were other, fiercer physical feelings, stirrings that she had never known before and that made her shiver despite the heat.

She knew she should have been relieved when he rolled away from her, kicking off his covers, hot once more, but instead she was aware of a faint sense of disappointment. She sat up and continued her watch.

Once or twice he opened his eyes and was lucid again, and she took hope. But soon he returned to his incoherent mutterings and uneasy movements. He didn't seem to be improving. She didn't know how long it would take for the fever to break. By the middle of the afternoon, Victoria knew that she would have to leave him and search for water. She had emptied almost three canteens already.

Victoria left Slater with the holster and pistols above his head, as he had slept with them last night, hoping that instinct at least would impel him to reach for them if he were in danger. There was no point in explaining to him where she was going, so she left him lying there, his eyes closed, and rode quickly north.

She had torn a ruffle from her petticoat and ripped it into short strips and she tied these strips to trees and bushes periodically. She wasn't familiar with the area, and she wanted to make sure that she could find her way back to Slater as quickly as possible.

It was less than an hour before she came upon a creek, and she uttered a small prayer of relief. She wouldn't have to be away from Slater long, and with the creek this close, she would be able to come again tomorrow. She drank from the clear stream. She had led Slater's horse with her, so that both the horses could have water when she found it, and now she let them loose to drink downstream while she filled the canteens upstream.

She stayed only as long as was necessary to water the horses, then hastened back to Slater. The white strips of cloth were easy to spot, and she traveled quickly. She drew closer to the place where she had left him. Soon she could see the top of the live oak tree beyond a small rise that was piled with slabs of rock. As she started to climb the rise, Slater's horse suddenly whickered and came to a stop, pulling away nervously. Victoria kept a tight grip on the reins, so that he didn't get away from her, but her own horse balked and pranced, too. Victoria's stomach went cold. There was something wrong. The horses had scented danger.

Victoria pulled her rifle from its holster and slid off her horse. After tying the reins of both animals firmly around the largest branch of a mesquite, she started silently up the rise on foot. Whatever was ahead, it would be better to sneak up and get a view of it instead of charging in on her horse.

She tiptoed as quietly as she could, using the rocks for cover. She edged around a larger boulder, and for the first time she could see Slater. He lay asleep on the ground, oblivious to everything around him. Now and then his limbs twitched, or he rolled over onto his side, but he had no idea that, standing on a large boulder, only feet away from him, was a cougar.

Victoria's heart leaped into her throat. Silently she raised the rifle to her shoulder and sighted down the barrel at the powerful cat, grateful that he was upwind and hadn't caught her scent. He drew back on his haunches, and Victoria went taut all over. Carefully she squeezed the trigger just as he began his leap.

The bullet caught him, and he screamed with pain, crashing to the ground. At the sound Slater sat straight up, scrabbling for his pistol and looking for the danger. Victoria hurried forward, her gun still trained on the animal. The cougar twitched a few times and went still. She had killed it with one shot. Victoria relaxed with a sigh and glanced over at Slater. He had his pistol out and aimed at the animal on the ground, though his hand wavered with fatigue. His eyes were hot, but clear, and she knew that for the moment, at least, he was aware of who and where he was.

He looked at her, and his hand dropped. He gave her a weak grin. "Damn. You're right. You can shoot."

"It's a good thing for you I can." Victoria tried to match his light tone. She prodded the animal with her gun to make sure it was dead, then turned back to Slater. "How are you feeling?"

"Like a wet washrag." He flopped back onto the blanket.

"Mmm. You kind of look like one, too." She squatted down beside him and laid her hand on his forehead. He felt cooler. She smiled. It was then that she noticed her hand was shaking.

She swallowed and stood up. She was beginning to tremble all over in the aftermath of the excitement. She looked down at Slater. His eyes were already closed, and he had slipped back into sleep. Victoria walked over to a rock a good distance away from the slain cat and sat down, her elbows on her knees and her head in her hands. It was some time before she stood up and began to move again.

The horses balked at returning to the camp, even though Victoria dragged the slain cougar out of sight. Its scent was still there, and that spooked the animals. Victoria tethered them some distance away. She returned to Slater's side, bringing the full canteens and her rifle and ammunition.

Through the rest of the afternoon, she continued to bathe Slater's head and torso with water and urge him to drink from the canteen. Her back began to ache from bending over him, but she kept at it, horribly aware that there was nothing else she could do.

When it grew dusk, she built a fire. Despite Slater's fears about Brody turning the tables on them, she wasn't about to go through the night without a fire, not after her experience with the cougar. The fire would keep away wild animals, and at the moment they were of more concern to her than the outlaw.

Victoria took out a twist of beef jerky and ate it for supper. She had tried to get Slater to take a bite, but he had steadfastly refused it. She wished she had a strengthening meat broth to feed him. She wished for a lot more than that, actually—medicine, water nearby, a doctor to give her advice. Victoria had tended wounds and nursed people through illnesses, but she'd never been completely alone when she did it. There had been a doctor in town who could be sent for, and her father and Mrs. Donnelly had been close by, along with ranch hands and maids to help her.

Victoria glanced over her shoulder at Slater. Earlier his temperature had dropped, and he had slept more peacefully. But now it was back up, and he was moving fitfully. She wondered what she would do if he grew worse in the night. It would be impossible to get him onto his horse. She couldn't leave him and ride for help. Would she have to sit here and watch him die, bit by bit?

Victoria set her jaw. She refused to sit here like a ninny and worry over the things she couldn't change. She had tended lots of fevers, and the person had always gotten better. She was capable of handling Slater's illness, even in the middle of nowhere.

She heard the jingle of metal, and Victoria's head snapped up. She peered through the gathering gloom all around them. She jumped, and her heart began to pound wildly. A tall, dark shape was moving toward her from the south. Victoria snatched up her rifle and moved behind the fire, so that she wouldn't be silhouetted against the light. She held the rifle ready, waiting, her senses alive to the slightest sound or movement.

The figure came closer and resolved into a man on a horse. Victoria raised her rifle to her shoulder and waited. The rider stopped several feet away from them. He held his hands up in the air, palms open, to show that he held no weapon.

"Hello, ma'am." It was a young man's voice, and cheerful, considering that he was facing a gun.

"Hello."

"It's all right. I'm not going to hurt you. Saw your camp fire and thought I'd get acquainted." His gaze went to Slater. "Looks like you could use some help. What's the matter with him?"

"Fever," Victoria replied shortly. She didn't know what to do. The man didn't appear to be a threat. Maybe he would help her. On the other hand, he could be trying to lull her so that she'd let down her guard. "Who are you?"

"Dennis Miles. Mind if I get down?"

"Go ahead."

He slid off the horse and came closer to the fire, still keeping his hands up. He looked to be in his twenties, with a boyish, clean-shaven face. Victoria relaxed a little. He certainly didn't look like a desperado. He was staring at her in a slightly stunned way that she was quite familiar with and would normally have found amusing.

"Can I put my hands down now?"

She glanced at his waist. He wasn't wearing a gun belt. His rifle was still on his saddle. She nodded. "All right."

"This is pretty lonely country for ya'll to be in. Did ya get lost?"

"No."

Miles nodded toward Slater. "That your husband? When'd he take sick?"

"Last night." Victoria answered the easier question, slipping by the first one. She could well imagine what he'd think if she told him Slater wasn't her husband.

The young man ambled over to Slater and stared down at him. "He looks powerful sick." He turned back. "You know, our house ain't no more'n an hour or so from here. If he could make it there, my Ma would be happy to have you stay a spell."

Victoria relaxed even further at the mention of his mother. Surely someone bent on harm wouldn't invite her to his mother's house. She lowered her rifle.

"She could help you," Miles went on eagerly. "She's real good at physickin' folks."

Relief swept through Victoria. "Thank you," she said, a smile breaking across her face like sunshine. "You're very kind to invite us into your home. I'd be most grateful for your mother's help."

Chapter Six

Brody jerked awake. It took him a second to realize what had awakened him. The warmth of Amy's body was no longer against his back. He whirled around. Amy's side of the blanket was empty. She was gone.

A feeling of deep betrayal stabbed through him. She had tricked him, lulled him with her seeming innocence, and when he had come to trust her, she had run. Brody jumped to his feet, furious, yanked on his boots and grabbed his gun belt. He started toward his horse, buckling on the belt, and it was then that he realized both their horses were still there.

The fury in him eased. She wouldn't have left on foot, not in this wild country. He glanced around. There was no sign of her. He walked back slowly to the blanket. She hadn't run away. She must have gone off to where she could be private; she was a modest woman. He let out his breath slowly. He hadn't realized until then that he had been holding it in, or that his muscles were clenched tightly.

He adjusted his boots and tucked his shirt into his trousers. He finished buckling the gun belt and tied the holster around his thigh. Then he sat down on the blanket and waited.

Amy didn't return. Suspicion began to blossom in him again. She shouldn't be taking this long. Could she have decided to set out on foot? It seemed crazy. More likely something had happened to her.

He leaped to his feet and looked for signs of her. He saw her small, shallow footprints in the dust, leading into the trees, and he followed them. His heart hammered harder in his chest with each step. He imagined Amy stumbling and twisting her ankle, falling down, unable to walk. He imagined a rattlesnake striking her, or wild animals attacking her. He sped up until he was trotting.

He emerged from the trees into a clearing. It was blanketed with wildflowers. In the middle of it Amy sat cross-legged, perfectly still, leaning forward intently.

He stopped, going limp with relief. Then irritation spurted up in him. What the hell was she doing? She'd scared him to death. He started forward, opening his mouth to call her name, but Amy turned, saw him and held her forefinger to her lips for silence.

Frowning, he moved forward cautiously. When he drew near enough, Amy took his hand, tugging at it to pull him down beside her. She smiled into his eyes and pointed in front of her. Less than two feet away, poised on the head of a bluebonnet, was a huge black-and-yellow butterfly. Was that what she was looking at? The reason she'd motioned to him to be quiet? He glanced back at her, and she smiled.

Stretching up, Amy whispered in his ear, "Isn't it beautiful?"

He gaped at her, astonished. She was his prisoner, yet she had sneaked away from him to watch a butterfly.

Brody turned his eyes back to the butterfly. It clung to the flower, its velvety yellow wings beating. The butterfly reminded him of Amy: beautiful and fragile, vulnerable to the roughness of the world. He could crush it in an instant. He could crush her.

Brody looked at Amy. She was so beautiful and sweet that it made him hurt. Watching her, he could feel something giving way inside him, breaking up and dissolving. He wanted to enfold her in his arms and hold her so tightly that she could hardly breathe. He had to blink the moisture out of his eyes.

The butterfly rose from the flower and floated away. Amy watched it, entranced, and when it was out of sight, she turned to Brody, her smile sunny. "Wasn't it lovely? Doesn't it make you happy?"

"Yes." He wasn't sure whether he was happy or scared or what. This woman made him feel soft and crazy inside.

Brody stood up and reached down a hand to Amy. She took it and rose lithely to her feet. To his surprise, she didn't release his hand as soon as she was up, but kept hold of it as they started back toward the camp. He wasn't sure what to do. He wasn't used to holding a woman's hand. Whores had taken his hand to lead him to their rooms, but he couldn't remember his hand being held in simple friendship or affection. At least, not since he was a boy, when his mother had sometimes clasped his hand as they walked through the Quarter.

He wanted to grip her hand so tightly that she couldn't get away, but he was scared of hurting or frightening her. He thought she was like a shy little animal that might bolt at the first hint of restraint, so he let her hand lie loosely in his, hoping that she wouldn't pull it away. She didn't, seemingly content.

"I like to look at things. Do you?" she asked.

"I don't know. I never thought about it."

"Most people don't. At least, not as much as me. Do you think it's silly?"

"No."

She turned a pleased face up to him. "I'm glad. You like me, don't you?"

The question took him aback, and he blinked. "Of course. I'm sure most people do."

Amy shrugged. "I don't know. Not like you. It's different. You don't act like I'm stupid or crazy. I know I'm a mess." She glanced down ruefully at her dress, dusty and askew, with leaves clinging to it. She knew her hair was half down and sticking out all over the place. "But you haven't scolded me once."

"Why would I scold you?"

"Mrs. Donnelly usually does."

"Who is this Mrs. Donnelly who's so mean?"

"She's our housekeeper. She's not mean, really. But she talks to me like I'm a child." Her sunny smile nearly took his breath away. "You don't. I'm glad. I like being with you."

"You aren't a child." He was acutely aware of that.

"I know. But most people think I am."

They strolled along in silence for a while. Brody wasn't eager to reach their camp, not with her hand in his so trustingly.

"Why do you live with your cousin and your uncle?" he asked her. He found that he was curious about everything to do with her.

A frown marred her forehead. "Because my parents died a long time ago, when I was a little girl. Comanches killed them. I don't remember it. I don't remember them." She paused. "They say I was there, too, that a man found me later, hiding in the root cellar." She shook her head. "I can't remember anything before Uncle Edward's. They say that's why I'm strange, 'cause I saw them killed. I don't know."

Pity stirred in Brody. It was a new and strange emotion to him. He didn't know what to do about it. "I—I'm sorry."

"Thank you. But you needn't be. I don't feel bad about it."

"Yeah." He understood her even less now. With that background, how could she not have been terrified by him and the violent way he had ridden off with her? How could she not be scared that he would hurt her?

They reached the horses and their supplies. Reluctantly, Brody let go of her hand so that he could pack.

"Could I help?" Amy asked tentatively.

"Sure." It surprised him that she wanted to, but he guessed that by this time he shouldn't be surprised by anything Amy did. He left her to roll up the blankets while he tended to the horses. When they were through, they mounted and rode west along the river.

After a couple of hours they topped a rise, and Brody stopped. A small house nestled at the base of the hill, close to the river. Brody watched the place carefully.

"Are we going down there?" Amy asked, surprised. She had the impression that Sam steered clear of people.

"Yeah. I know the folks who live there. We can get real food and something for you to wear to protect your legs."

"And a brush?" Amy asked eagerly. "Could I have a brush for my hair?"

He nodded. It made his loins knot just to think about her brushing out the long, silky golden strands. He'd see if Beatriz had a ribbon for it, too. He wanted to give Amy a pretty bauble, something to decorate herself with.

"Oh, thank you." Her face glowed.

The slightest thing made her happy. Brody wanted to catch her in his arms and hold her close. Instead, he looked back down at the quiet farm below them. He could see no sign that anything was out of the ordinary, or that anyone was there besides Raul and his wife. There was only the tiny house, laundry flapping on a line behind it, and the corral beside it.

Brody started down the hill, Amy following him. As they drew near the house, a woman came out onto the porch, shading her eyes to see them. A smile lit her face, and she hurried off the porch toward them.

"Brody!" she cried in a softly accented voice. She turned to call in the direction of the corral. *"Raul, rapidamente. ¡Brody está aquí!"*

Brody dismounted, smiling. "Beatriz! It's good to see you. You're more beautiful than ever."

Amy felt a sharp stab of a very unpleasant emotion. She noticed how pretty the dark woman was, with loads of thick black hair and dark, vivacious eyes. She wondered exactly what her relationship was to Sam Brody.

Beatriz grinned, obviously pleased by Sam's remark, but swatted playfully at him. "Flatterer." She glanced up at Amy curiously, but said nothing.

"Amy." Brody came around, holding up his arms to help her down from the horse. Amy needed no help, but she took it anyway. He set her down beside him. "I want you to meet Señora Garcia. Beatriz, this is Amy Wallace."

"Señorita." Beatriz smiled at her a little shyly. "I am happy to welcome you to my house."

"Thank you, *Señora*. I'm pleased to meet you."

Just then an older man hurried around the corner of the house from the corral. "Brody!" he exclaimed, and broke into a trot. "It is you. *Dios*, it's been a long time!"

"Raul!" Brody and the Mexican man embraced like long lost friends, then stepped back to look at one another.

"Do you come for a visit, or do you need another horse?"

"No, it's not a horse this time." Brody explained in an aside to Amy, "Raul is the best trainer of horseflesh in the state."

"In the state?" The man looked hurt. "No, no, my friend. All the way to California, I am the best."

"And modest."

Raul laughed. "Come. Come into my house. You have eaten?"

"Not real food."

"Then you must eat. Beatriz, let us feed these hungry people." The two men made their way into the house, joking and laughing. Amy watched them go. She hadn't seen Brody like this before, relaxed and cheerful. He certainly hadn't been this friendly with the men who rode with him.

Amy glanced at Beatriz and found the woman studying her intently. Amy offered her a tentative smile. She hoped she wouldn't do something wrong in front of Brody's friends. She would hate to embarrass him. Beatriz started toward the house, and Amy fell in beside her.

"Raul and Brody, they know each other a long time," Beatriz said as they walked. "Since before Raul and I married."

Amy was swept with relief at the woman's words. Beatriz was married to the other man, which meant there was nothing between her and Sam. "Really?"

"Yes. They worked together when Brody was a boy. My Raul taught Brody how to ride."

They entered the house, and Beatriz put a pot of beans on the fire. Brody went to Amy and took her by the arm. He stood very close, staring down at her with hard, intense eyes.

"You are not to say anything to these people," he whispered.

Amy frowned, puzzled. "How can I not say anything?"

"About how you came to be with me. They won't help you. They can't."

She was even more puzzled by his last words. "I'm sorry. I don't understand. I thought we came here for help—for supplies and clothes and all." She pressed her lips together to stop their trembling.

Brody's brows rose, and a reluctant grin crossed his face. "Well, yes, of course. Raul will give us those things—and a hairbrush, too." His voice turned teasing. Amy smiled, glad that she hadn't displeased him. Brody cleared his throat. It was damned difficult now to recapture any sternness. "I meant help against me."

"Against you?" Amy stared.

"Getting away from me."

"But I don't want to get away from you."

Sam had to clench his teeth to keep from smiling idiotically. He wondered if she had any idea what her words did to him, how warmth and passion flooded him at the idea that she didn't want to leave him.

"Where would I go?" Amy continued prosaically.

"Back home."

"Oh." Strangely enough, the prospect of going home didn't fill her with as much happiness as she would have expected. She wanted to be with Victoria, of course. But she was enjoying the trip with Brody now that his men were gone. She would miss him when she had to leave. "But Victoria will find me eventually, and until then I'd rather be with you."

"They won't find you. I'll make sure of that." He paused. "You're staying with me."

He didn't know Victoria, or he wouldn't say that, Amy thought. No doubt he thought Victoria was just another silly girl like her. But she said nothing. It gave her a pleasant, warm feeling to know that Sam wanted her to remain with him, and she didn't wish to dispute his words.

Brody wished he could somehow soften what he had said. He hated to frighten her. But Amy had to realize that she was his, and that there was no point in trying to escape him. He smoothed his palm across her cheek, hoping to comfort her. She leaned into his hand like a cat, and her eyes closed in sensual pleasure. Heat flashed through Brody at her gesture. He wanted to move his hand all over her and see that same expression on her face.

He pulled away reluctantly, and Amy opened her eyes. She looked regretful. Brody stepped back, then turned and rejoined Raul. Amy wished she could stay with Brody, but she realized that he and his old friend must want to talk privately. So she went to the fireplace, where Beatriz sat, stirring the pot.

"May I help you?"

"Yes, of course. That would be nice. If you would watch the beans, I will make tortillas."

Amy nodded and sat down on the low stool near the fireplace. She pulled the crane holding the pot out of the fire and stirred the beans, then shoved the metal rod with its burden back over the heat. Beatriz knelt on the floor, stirring a mixture of cornmeal and water until it was thick. She began to pat out the round, flat tortillas on the slab of stone before her. Amy watched with interest. She had eaten tortillas before, but she had never watched them being made.

"Could I try that?" she asked shyly.

"Of course."

Amy knelt on the floor beside Beatriz, and Beatriz showed her how to do it, laughing with her at her mistakes and smiling when she succeeded. Beatriz leaned closer to her. "I am glad you are with Brody. You will be good for him."

"I will?" Amy looked up from her task. "Why?"

"You are a good-hearted woman. You like to laugh. You will make him happy."

Amy glanced over at Brody. She thought she would like to make him happy. "Sam is in trouble, isn't he? That's why he had those chains on."

"Yes. He's wanted by every lawman and bounty hunter in the state."

"Why? He's not a bad man."

"I haven't seen the bad in him. I don't think you will, either. With you, he is gentle. But they say he can be hard. They say he is a killer."

"Sam?" Amy's brow wrinkled. She found that hard to believe, and yet . . . she had seen the cold violence in him when he spoke to Purdon.

Beatriz nodded. "Raul is as much his friend as any man. But he would never dare to cross Brody." She paused, then smiled at Amy. "But when a man like that loves you, you need have fear of no one. He will keep you safe."

"Yes. I know he will."

Across the room, Raul and Sam sat talking, watching the women by the hearth. Raul glanced from the blond girl to his friend, studying the expression on Brody's face. "She is very pretty."

"Yeah."

"You've never brought a woman here before."

"No."

"She is special, no?"

Brody shrugged. It was a sign of weakness to let a woman mean so much to him, and Brody never revealed weakness. "She was handy, and she looked good, so I took her."

Raul nodded, but amusement lifted the corners of his mouth. He knew how it felt when you tumbled head over heels for a woman, and Brody had that look about him, however much his friend might wish to hide it. Brody watched every move the girl made—and he watched as if he'd never seen anything that lovely or graceful before.

"A woman slows you down when you're on the run," Raul commented.

"Not this one." Pride settled over Brody's features. "She can ride hard and fast, and she never complains."

Raul grinned. "If that is true, then don't let her go. I never met a woman who didn't complain."

"She's different."

"I can see." But Raul was looking at Brody, not Amy. "Well, let's go out in the back and take off those chains."

The two men went outside. They were gone for a long time, and when they returned, Brody looked different. His manacles were gone, and he was dressed in clean clothes. The stubble was gone from his face, and his hair was slicked back and wet. Amy stared at him, her mouth dropping open in astonishment.

"Oh, my," she murmured. "Isn't he handsome?"

Beatriz's glance flew from Amy to Brody and back, and she hid a smile. Handsome wasn't a word she would have used to describe Brody. There were scars on his face where he'd been cut in fights; his nose had been broken; and the sun and wind had weathered his skin. Brody had sexual appeal; Beatriz herself had felt a tug of attraction to him. But it was the pull of raw power and danger, of the untamed animal. It wasn't the appeal of good looks.

Amy obviously saw him with different eyes.

Brody looked everywhere but at Amy. He felt silly and nervous. When Raul had offered him a razor, soap and a change of clothes, he had jumped at the chance to clean up. He knew his eagerness sprang from a desire to look good to Amy, and he had called himself all kinds of a fool for doing it. He'd never worried before what a woman thought of his looks. But now it mattered, and, having made the effort, he discovered that he was scared Amy wouldn't find him any more attractive than before.

Amy glanced down at herself. It was terrible that she should be so unkempt when Sam looked so good. What would he think of her? She turned to Beatriz. "Where did he clean up? Could I, too?"

"Of course you can. There's a spot in the river that's perfect for bathing. You can go right after lunch. I'll lend you the lavender soap Brody bought for me last year in Austin." She heaved a giant sigh of pleasure. "It smells heavenly."

Amy had always used scented soap to bathe in, and she was used to doing so in a tub indoors. But right now the thought of bathing in the river with lavender-smelling soap seemed like the height of luxury. "Thank you. I would love it."

All through lunch, Brody and Amy kept sneaking little glances at each other. Beatriz found it hard not to giggle. She had never thought to see Brody so smitten with a woman—nor an obviously genteel woman so taken with him.

When they were through eating and cleaning up the dishes, Amy hurried down to the river to wash. Beatriz went with her to show her the way, then stood guard with a pistol. It was unlikely that a stranger would chance by, but there was always the possibility of a water moccasin or a wild animal.

Amy stripped without shyness in front of Beatriz. She was used to dressing and undressing around Victoria. She walked out into the water, which was a little chilly, despite having been warmed all morning by the sun, and ducked down into it. She worked up a lather with the sweet-smelling soap and washed her hair and body, then submerged herself to let the current wash away the white foam. It was marvelous to be clean again. She wondered if Sam would be as impressed with her new appearance as she had been with his.

She came out of the water and took the towel Beatriz held out to her. After she had dried her body, she dressed in the blouse and skirt Beatriz loaned her. The blouse was of bleached muslin, a little rough to the touch. Its cut was plain, with a wide, scooped neckline that pulled together and tied with a drawstring, but it was decorated gaily with bright embroidered flowers. The skirt was a vivid blue, full-skirted in a Mexican style, with a broad ruffle around the bottom. It was shorter than the skirts Amy was used to wearing, reaching only to her ankles instead of sweeping the ground.

Amy sat on a large rock with Beatriz, and they chatted while Amy combed through her hair with Beatriz's wide-toothed comb. It took a long time, for her hair was hip-length and badly tangled in places, and Beatriz had to help her work through some of the worst tangles.

Finally they returned to the house. Raul and Sam were leaning against the corral fence, watching the horses and talking, and they turned at the women's approach. Brody's hands tightened unconsciously on a wooden slat of the fence. Amy was beautiful in the colorful blouse and skirt. Her slim ankles were enticingly visible, and the simple, wide neckline cut across the tops of her breasts. Her hair hung loose down her back like a golden waterfall. Beatriz was talking animatedly, gesturing widely with her hands, and Amy listened, smiling, her eyes alight with interest.

She was an angel, Brody thought, a beauty too rare and good for him. It made him swell with desire just to look at her, even though he knew he was an animal to want to despoil anything so precious and pure.

Raul had urged him to spend the night at their house, offering Brody and Amy their bed, but the thought of sleeping with Amy in a soft feather bed was too much for him. He would never be able to keep his hands off her. It was far better that they lie on the hard ground, not cocooned together beneath a quilt and surrounded by softness. He had refused Raul's generosity.

Brody came forward, his hands jammed into his pockets. He wanted to tell her how beautiful she was, but he figured she didn't want to hear that from him. Instead, he said, "It's time for us to leave."

Amy sighed inwardly, disappointed that he had made no comment on her new appearance. But she said nothing, just went inside to change into the riding clothes Beatriz had found for her.

Raul and Sam saddled the horses and loaded the supplies while Amy got ready. Sam was standing with the horses, waiting for her, when she walked out of the house. He sucked in his breath. This outfit did even worse things to his nerves than what she had worn before. The only one to blame was himself; he had come up with the idea of dressing Amy like a man in a shirt and denim trousers to keep her legs from being rubbed raw. The problem was that the clothes didn't make Amy look in the least like a boy. True, the full glory of her hair was braided and pinned up under a man's hat, and Raul's old shirt was so large on her that it concealed the curves of her breasts. But the trousers, which had once belonged to a boy who had helped Raul with the horses, were a trifle tight. They fit Amy snugly, outlining the shape of her legs and cupping her rounded derriere. Sam had never seen a woman in anything but skirts before, and looking at Amy, he understood why trousers were forbidden to respectable women.

Amy glanced at Sam and then away, blushing. She felt strange in the trousers, almost naked. Yet the trousers were wonderfully freeing, as well. It was nice to take longer steps and not to have the weight of skirts and petticoats, and it was far easier to swing up into the saddle.

She smiled at Sam. "Thank you."

He shook his head, unable to say anything.

Beatriz had given Amy the skirt and blouse too, and when Amy had protested that she couldn't take so much from the other woman, Beatriz had smiled and told her that Brody had amply compensated them for everything. Pleased that Sam wanted to give her the skirt and blouse as well as the riding outfit, Amy wrapped them up and stowed them in one of her saddlebags.

They mounted and rode out of the yard, Brody leading the way. Amy looked back at Beatriz and Raul and waved gaily. She had enjoyed their company, but it was even nicer being alone with Sam again. She nudged her horse forward to ride beside him. She thought about Victoria. She hoped that it would be a long time before Victoria caught up with them.

Victoria and Dennis Miles helped Slater to his feet and up onto his horse. Then the small group started out for Dennis's home.

"Are you sure you'll be able to find your way back in the dark?" Victoria asked Miles doubtfully. With nothing but a crescent moon and stars for light, the night was dark, and Victoria could see only a few feet in front of her.

Miles grinned. "I know this country like the back of my hand. I was born and raised here."

"Oh. Good."

Miles began to talk about his mother, who he was sure would be glad of feminine company, living all alone out here with Dennis and his younger brother. He went on to talk about their small piece of land, lying along the Blanco River, and about the visitors they had from time to time. "Mostly people heading west, up the river. We like havin' 'em stop in, on account of that way we hear all the news."

Victoria soon realized that it was going to be no problem keeping a conversation going with this young man. He was obviously hungry for someone to talk to. Victoria listened with half her attention while she kept an eye on Slater. He was slumped in the saddle, his head hanging. He held the reins, but his hands were also curled around the saddle horn. Victoria wondered if he was asleep or lost in his fever. Slater swayed in the saddle, and Victoria edged her horse closer to his. She was afraid he wouldn't be able to stay mounted much longer.

He began to list to the right, and Victoria reached out and grabbed his arm, holding him in the saddle. "Mr. Miles!"

"Oh, call me Den, ma'am, everybody does."

"I need your help."

He turned and saw her predicament. He guided his horse to the other side of Slater and pulled him upright. But Slater still swayed dangerously, and the reins slipped from his fingers.

"Maybe we ought to leave him here," Miles suggested. "I can take you up to the house, and my brother and me'll fix up a litter and come back for him. It'd be a lot easier on him, I reckon."

"No." Victoria shook her head decisively. "I can't leave him out here alone. I did that this afternoon, and a cougar almost got him. At night it would be even more dangerous. I could stay with him...." She mused over the thought. "But that would take a lot of time, and it would be a bother for you." Victoria pulled her horse to a stop. "I think the best thing is for me to ride with him."

Dennis Miles looked doubtful, but Victoria dismounted and gave him the reins. She picked up the reins Slater had dropped and removed his feet from the stirrups. Then she put her own foot into the stirrup and swung up into the saddle behind him. It wasn't an easy matter. Miles had to help her wiggle Slater forward so that she could fit. But Slater was too big and long. His legs dangled down over hers, and she could see only by peering around him. Victoria put her arms around him, holding the reins in front of him. Fortunately, he leaned back into her, so that she was able to take the brunt of his weight against her torso. Even so, it put a strain on her muscles, and she knew that if anything should startle the horse and make him jump or run, she wouldn't be able to keep either of them in the saddle.

They started out again at the same slow pace. Slater's body was like a furnace. Victoria's arms started to ache from the effort of keeping him straight, and the weight of his legs over hers was making them numb. But she gritted her teeth and kept her arms tight around him.

Despite the discomfort, she couldn't help but be aware of the intimate way her legs cupped his body and her breasts pressed against his back. She remembered his hand on her breast earlier that afternoon, and she was glad for the darkness that concealed the heat in her face. The movement of the horse beneath them rubbed his body against hers, and the friction set up a warm ache between her legs. She could feel dampness gathering there.

She spread one hand out flat on his chest. He had been so hot that she hadn't rebuttoned his shirt, and it hung open. Her hand lay on his bare skin. It was smooth, except for the prickle of his chest hair. She felt his muscles jump beneath her touch, and he made a noise. Victoria imagined moving her hand lower, onto his stomach, imagined circling the shallow well of his navel. She curled her hand up tightly, her fingernails digging into her palm.

Where in the world had she come by such thoughts? She could never remember feeling this way before. It was perverse; the man was sick! Did it take only this, the touch of a man's hot flesh, the feel of his body against hers, to arouse the lust inside her? Her Aunt Margaret had always told her that her willful, independent ways would lead to no good. Was this what her aunt had feared? Was this why she had scolded Victoria for her improper behavior?

Victoria leaned her forehead against Slater's back, closing her eyes as if to blot out her wayward thoughts. It didn't help. She was too aware of his firm flesh beneath his shirt. Even the scent of his sweat was somehow exciting. She wondered if other women had feelings like this. Probably not; she usually did and said and wanted things other women didn't.

At her finishing school in San Antonio, the girls had often whispered about men and what went on in the marriage bed. They had come up with all kinds of conflicting information. Victoria remembered that Sally Ann Carter had told them that a man and a woman took off all their clothes to make babies, and the other girls had blushed, giggling, and accused her of lying. Victoria had thought Sally Ann was wrong, too. Sally Ann generally was. Victoria couldn't see why anyone would want to embarrass herself by taking off her clothes in front of a man—or see a naked man, for that matter.

But now, thinking of the excitement that had risen in her when she had opened Slater's shirt and seen his bare chest, she wondered if Sally might not have been right, after all. Perhaps it wouldn't be so embarrassing to see a man's naked body, or to have him look at her that way. She thought of undressing in front of Slater, and it brought a shivery feeling, part fear and part eagerness.

Victoria shifted unconsciously in the saddle. Her movements rubbed her body against his, increasing the heat between her legs. When she realized what she was doing and why, she was shocked. Was she unnatural? Wanton? Or was this why no one wanted men and women to be alone together? Because such feelings were so easily aroused?

She was jolted from her thoughts by Dennis Miles saying cheerfully, "Here we are. This is home." He jumped down from his horse. "Ma! Nathan! I brought visitors!"

Gratefully Victoria relaxed her cramped arms and dropped the reins. She gazed at the two-story frame house in front of them. It was weather-beaten, the paint long faded from it, and its lines were plain, but it looked heavenly to her at the moment. A large man, younger than Dennis, but greatly resembling him, emerged from the house, and right behind him came a middle-aged woman. Her iron-gray hair was done up in a tight knot at the back of her head, every hair in place, and her clothes, though as faded as the house, were neat and clean. It was obvious where her sons had gotten their size, for she was a large woman, taller even than Victoria, and she looked strong. Her eyes were a pale blue against the tan of her skin, and they were bright with interest and curiosity. Victoria suspected that she was a mother whose children had never gotten away with anything.

The two brothers hauled Slater out of the saddle and carried him into the house with ease. Victoria got down wearily, and Mrs. Miles put a bracing arm around her waist. "There now, you poor thing. I bet you're tired as can be. You'd best go on up and rest. I'll bring you a nice hot dinner."

"Thank you. I'm not hungry. But I would be grateful for some sleep. Do you think—I hate to impose, but if—" Victoria hesitated. She had started to call him Mr. Slater, which would dispel the notion that he was her husband. But, looking at Mrs. Miles, she found she didn't have the nerve. Mrs. Miles would consider her a scarlet woman; she might even refuse to let them stay the night in her house. So Victoria continued. "—If my husband could have a bowl of broth, I think it would help him."

"Why, sure thing. I got a pot of nice hot soup simmerin' on the fire. I'll dish up a bowl and bring it straight up to him."

Mrs. Miles hustled Victoria inside and directed her up the narrow staircase to the first door on the right. Victoria wearily climbed the stairs, meeting Dennis and Nathan coming down. They tipped their hats to her, grinning identically, and clumped down the stairs. As Victoria reached the top she could hear Dennis's voice below, exclaiming, "Isn't she beautiful, Ma?" and his mother's replying more calmly, "Yeah, she's pretty, all right."

Victoria smiled a little and went into the bedroom where Dennis and Nathan had put Slater. It was a small room under the eaves, with only one little window. But Victoria couldn't have cared less about its size or appearance. All that mattered was the bed in the middle of the room where Slater lay. He would be much more comfortable here, and soon she would get some strengthening soup down him. Before long, he would start feeling better; she was sure of it.

Victoria went to the bed and tugged off Slater's boots, setting them on the floor beside the bed. She moved to the head of the bed and looked down on him. He was sleeping, his face flushed. She hoped the ride hadn't sapped him of too much energy. She laid her hand across his forehead. It wasn't necessary—she knew already that he was too hot—but somehow she had to. She smoothed her hand across his skin and pushed his hair back from his brow.

As she gazed down on him, she noticed the silver star that was his badge. She wondered if Dennis had seen it; he hadn't said anything. Slater's shirt had hung open, probably covering the star attached to his leather vest. She frowned. If the Mileses knew he was a Texas Ranger, it might make them more eager to help him. But they were friendly and helpful anyway, and knowing that he was a Ranger might make them suspicious of her marital status. After all, why would a Ranger be carting his wife around the countryside with him while he was chasing a criminal? Mrs. Miles didn't look like the sort to regard lightly the idea of an unmarried woman traveling with a man. Victoria didn't want to offend the woman who was offering them such kind hospitality—nor did she want to risk having that hospitality revoked.

She unfastened the badge and slipped it into one of Slater's empty boots. Then she went to the washstand, poured water into the washbowl and returned with the bowl and a rag to begin the task of washing Slater again.

A moment later, Mrs. Miles bustled into the room, carrying a tray. "There, now, poor man," she said, with a sympathetic look, and set the tray down on the dresser. "I brung him some soup, but I'm afraid it's too hot just yet to eat. 'Sides, he looks too tuckered out to eat anything. Den tells me he's sufferin' from a fever."

"Yes, he is."

"Well, let's see what we can do for him. I'm pretty good at doctorin' folks."

"So your son told me. I'd be very grateful for any help."

Mrs. Miles felt his forehead and then the back of his neck. She glanced at Slater's arm. "What happened to him there?"

"I think that's why he's got the fever. His wound has pus in it. I cleaned it once today, but I didn't have anything to put on it."

Mrs. Miles unwrapped the bandage and examined Slater's wound. It was red and inflamed, and yellowish pus oozed from it. The older woman's eyes narrowed, and she looked up at Victoria. "Why, that's a gunshot wound."

Heat rose in Victoria's cheeks. She hadn't thought about the wound when she decided not to tell them Slater was a lawman. She glanced away nervously. Would it be better to tell the truth and face the consequences? She was so tired; it was hard to think straight. "I—some men tried to rob us, and my husband fired at them. They ran away, but one of them hit my husband in the arm."

"I see." She studied Victoria for a moment, then returned her attention to the wound. "Well, he was lucky the fella wasn't a better shot, I reckon." She picked up the cloth, wet it and began to carefully clean the wound. Slater cursed at the pain her probing caused, and his eyes flew open.

He blinked at Mrs. Miles. "Who the hell are you? Ow!" He cursed vividly.

"Slater!" Victoria tried to smile at Mrs. Miles. "I'm sorry. He's out of his head."

"That's all right. I've heard worse'n that, believe you me. My husband Joe, he could cuss a blue streak, God rest his soul. I'll run down and get some of my remedies."

She left and Slater slid back into sleep. Mrs. Miles returned with two bottles. One contained a powder, which she sprinkled on Slater's wound. She bound up the wound again with fresh bandages, then mixed a little of the liquid from the other bottle with water. She lifted Slater's head, and Victoria held the glass to his lips, coaxing him to drink in the soft, cajoling voice that she had found worked best that afternoon. His eyes opened hazily and closed again, but he slowly drank, wincing slightly at the taste. When he had finished, they fed him several sips of soup, until finally he sealed his lips and refused to eat any more. Mrs. Miles eased his head back onto the pillow. He gave a sigh and closed his eyes.

"You give him another dose of this in the middle of the night," Mrs. Miles told her. "Now I'll go back down and let you get some sleep. You look flat bushed."

"I am," Victoria admitted, unable to stifle a yawn.

She followed the older woman to the door and closed it behind her. Then she turned and went back to the bed. She crawled in on the far side, but it was a small bed, and she couldn't keep much distance between them. It seemed very strange to lie in a bed with a man beside her, no matter how little could happen with him sick. Slater seemed so big and masculine, taking up his half of the bed and sprawling over into hers. Victoria curled up on her side, looking at him. He was overwhelming, almost scary, yet she had to fight the urge to slide across the bed and snuggle up to him.

With a sigh, Victoria flopped over onto her other side and closed her eyes. She was too exhausted to stay awake, and she soon slept. But within a few hours, she woke up. The sheets around her were damp with Slater's sweat. His temperature must be awfully high. Victoria slid across the bed to his side and propped herself up on her elbow. She placed a hand on his forehead.

She couldn't believe it. She felt his neck, then his forehead again. He felt almost cool. This last spell, when he had sweated so much, must have broken the fever. Tears filled Victoria's eyes. She made a little noise that was part laugh and part sob, and rested her head against his shoulder. He'd pulled through.

Victoria sent up a silent prayer, then pressed her lips to Slater's forehead. She watched his sleeping face for a moment. She gave him another dose of the medicine, just to be safe, and lay back down beside him. Smiling, she hugged her joy to herself and slipped into a sleep that was at last deep and untroubled.

Chapter Seven

Brody and Amy traveled northwest from the Garcias's farm, pressing on until the last bit of light had faded from the sky. Brody built a fire when they camped, feeling safe enough now from Slater's pursuit. The other man should be far to the east, hunting for their trail.

He cooked a dinner of beans over the open fire, and they ate them with the tortillas that Beatriz had sent along. Afterward, they sat beside the fire, Brody idly poking it with a stick. Amy drew in a deep breath and leaned her head back, gazing at the brilliant stars overhead.

"Isn't it beautiful?"

He glanced up. "Yeah." Brody lay back and linked his arms behind his head. "You know, when I was a kid, I never noticed the stars. You don't, in the city. That was one of the things I liked when I came out here. I used to lie out on the ground looking at the sky for hours."

"Was that when you worked with Raul?"

Brody looked at her, surprised. "How did you know about that? Oh. Beatriz."

Amy nodded. "She told me that Raul taught you how to ride." Amy studied Brody's face, shadowy in the dim light. She was curious about him. "Tell me about you. Please."

"About me?" He gave a short laugh. "There's nothing you'd like to know."

"Yes, I would. Where are you from? How did you come here? Why are you running from that sheriff?"

He didn't want her to know about him. He could imagine her distaste when she heard the details of his sordid life. Yet, deep down he longed to tell her. Brody sighed. "I'm from New Orleans. My mother's name was Maida. I never knew my father. Maida didn't know who he was."

Amy frowned, puzzled. "How could she not—"

"She was a—" He paused, struggling for a way to explain it to this innocent woman. "She sold her body," he said finally, bitterly.

Amy looked even more confused. "She couldn't have been a slave!"

A bark of laughter escaped him. "No. Not the way you mean. Though she might as well have been. Once you get started down a road like that, you can't get off. I know." He paused. "What I meant was that she slept with men for money. That they used her and paid her."

She gazed at him, wide-eyed. "You mean, she stayed with a man as if they were married, only they weren't? And he gave her money for it?"

His lips twisted in something resembling a smile. "Not like she was married. There were different men every night. At first, when I was little, she lived in a big house with a lot of other women like her. They let me stay around as long as I didn't cause any trouble. I was kind of their pet. Most of them had gotten rid of their own kids, see. And when I got bigger, I'd run and fetch things for them, sweep the floors, do things like that. Later, when I was older, Maida had to leave the house. She wasn't pretty enough anymore. She aged fast. She started working in the cribs." Seeing Amy's puzzled look, he explained, "Those are the little, cheap rooms where women like her worked—women who walked the streets."

Brody closed his eyes, running a hand over his face as if he was very weary. Amy watched him. She didn't understand a lot of what he said, but she sensed the pain and bitterness beneath his story. His mother had been an embarrassment to him, but he had hurt for her, too.

"The men she had were rougher, and sometimes they'd hit her. I could tell that she hated her life. But I wasn't around much then. I couldn't live with her. All she had was a little room, and there was no place for me. I stayed out on the streets a lot. I did all kinds of things for money—picked pockets, begged, held horses for the men who visited the area, ran errands for some of the madams. I was tough, and I was fast, and I did pretty well for myself. But one day I went over to Maida's, and...this man, one of her customers, had beaten her up real bad."

Brody sat up abruptly and began breaking up the stick he had been holding earlier, tossing the pieces into the fire, his movements jerky. Distressed, Amy crept closer to him and laid her hand against his back, gently rubbing. He jackknifed his knees, wrapping his arms around them, and continued talking in a rush, his voice low and rough.

"It was weeks before she was completely healed. She was scared of this man, scared he'd come back and hurt her again. I told her I wouldn't let him, that I'd take care of her. So I hung around where she worked. But nothing happened, and I started not to stick so close to her. One evening I went to her crib, and as I walked up, I heard her screaming. I ran in, and there he was, hitting her. I jumped on him, trying to get him off, but I wasn't strong enough. I was just twelve, you see. I was in a rage, and I picked up a flatiron and hit him with it. I hit him a whole bunch of times." He shrugged. "I killed him."

"Oh, Sam."

"So I ran."

"But you couldn't be blamed. You were trying to protect your mother."

"He had a job and a family. She was a whore. No jury would have considered protecting her worth killing an upstanding citizen. They would have sent me to prison, at best. I jumped on the first ship out of the harbor that night. It went to Galveston. And that's how I came to Texas."

He lay back down. Amy lay down next to him. "Tell me more. How'd you meet Raul?"

He chuckled. "That was Razor Bill's doing. I stayed in Galveston at first. I stayed alive doing odd jobs, and when I couldn't get a job, I picked pockets, like I had in New Orleans. I fell in with a boy a couple of years older than me, and he taught me about robbing people with a gun. Didn't take as much time and trouble as picking a pocket. He suggested we go to San Antonio, so we took off. And after a year or so, we met

Razor Bill. That man knew horses. He could ride like the devil, too. Raul took care of his stock for him. Razor Bill kept a horse farm, and some of those horses were wild mustangs that he caught and broke. But most of them he stole. That's where I learned how to ride and shoot. Raul was a good friend to me. I saved his life once. Razor Bill and several of us got caught red-handed. They hanged him on the spot. I was lucky enough to get away, and I rode back to the ranch to warn Raul. He owes me. I owe him."

"Then what happened?"

"I left horse-thieving, but I got caught robbing a store, and they sent me to prison. I was about sixteen. I had thought I was tough before that, but I found out then what tough really was. Eventually I got out, and I needed money, so I held up a man. Hell, I thought he was an easy mark. He looked old and walked with a cane. But he whipped that cane up and knocked my gun clean out of my hand." Sam chuckled. "For a minute I figured I was finished. He'd either shoot me right there on the spot or take me to the sheriff."

"What happened?"

"He gave me a job."

"What?" Amy laughed.

"Yeah. Sounds crazy, doesn't it? There was never anybody like T. J. Moore. He believed in people, thought everybody had good inside them somewhere, just waiting to be brought out."

Amy looked at him warmly. "He was right about you, I think."

Brody gave her a startled look. "Maybe, for a while. As long as he was around. It was hard not to be good with him. He took me back to his ranch and put me to work punching cattle. I didn't know anything about it, but he taught me. He was like a father, only better." Brody's voice roughened. "One day somebody killed him. The man was a worm. He was a lieutenant in the army, and this was in '67, right after the War, when the Union army was running everything. He was stupid and arrogant, and he looked on himself as a conqueror. He thought everybody should back down from him just because he wore a blue uniform. Mr. Moore wouldn't. He didn't believe in backing down from anybody. One day, the lieutenant was drunk, and he got into an argument with Mr. Moore. He pulled a gun and shot T.J.''

Amy's eyes filled with tears. "Oh, Sam, I'm so sorry."

"I got the son of a bitch." Brody's voice was as cold and brittle as glass. "I knew the law wouldn't do anything to him. So I packed up my things and took one of Mr. Moore's rifles, and I went into town and shot him." He paused. "I was only sorry that I couldn't kill him more than once."

Amy touched his arm in sympathy. It was as hard as iron, the muscles tense. Sam stood up suddenly. T. J. Moore was someone he made it a point not to think about. And Amy's sweet kindness only made it worse. "That was seven years ago, and I've been on the run ever since. I reckon my soul's gotten blacker every year. I've killed five men. I've robbed so many banks and stagecoaches I've lost count. I've lived outside the law all my life, and I guess I'll go on doing so until somebody puts a hole through me."

"Don't say that!" Amy jumped to her feet. More softly, she continued, "Please. You don't have to die like that."

He turned, surprised by her concern. "That's what happens to people like me. Either that, or they get their necks stretched."

"No. You're not a bad man."

He gave a laugh that held little humor. "I don't understand you. I kidnapped you. How can you say I'm not bad? You think it's all right to grab a woman and carry her off?"

"Well, no . . ." Amy looked confused. "But I—I just don't think you're bad."

He came back to her suddenly and stopped so close that Amy could see the glitter in his dark eyes. He held himself rigidly, and he looked angry or in pain—or perhaps it was both. "Damn it! Are you a saint? Don't you ever get mad? You should hate me!"

His tone was scary, and tears welled up in Amy's eyes. "Why? I don't want to hate you."

Brody made an exasperated noise. "You ought to! Damn it, don't you know why I took you? Don't you know what I planned to do to you?"

Silently, Amy shook her head, not trusting herself to speak. She couldn't understand why he was so angry, but his tone sliced her to the quick.

"I saw you and I wanted you. I didn't give a damn about what you would feel. I was going to rape you!"

She looked at him blankly.

He whirled away, slamming his clenched fists against his thighs. "You don't even know what that means, do you?"

"No. I—I'm sorry." Her hands knotted together in frustrated confusion. Why couldn't she understand things like everybody else? She wanted it more than she ever had in her life.

"Oh, God." He laughed despairingly, plunging his hands into his hair and pressing them against his scalp as though he could hold in the crazy emotions bouncing around inside him. "Don't say that."

"What should I say?"

He walked back to her and grasped her arms, staring down into her eyes. "You're so beautiful. I never saw a woman as beautiful as you."

The tension left Amy. He wasn't angry with her anymore. She smiled. "There are lots of women prettier than me."

"I've never seen them." He paused, then drew a breath. "I'm bad, Amy. And you're so pure you can't even see it. You don't know what evil is."

"Yes, I do. Purdon was evil. He gave me the shivers."

"Yeah. He's evil. But he's the same kind of man as me."

"No." Amy shook her head firmly. "You're not like that."

"I am. I grabbed you because I wanted to have you. I wanted to take you."

Amy's breath shortened. She sensed now what he meant, though her understanding came more from the hungry look on his face than the meaning of his words. She moistened her lips and saw his eyes follow her movement. His grip on her arms tightened.

"Is that wrong? To—to want me?"

"I was going to force you. That's worse than what all those men did to my mother. At least they paid her. At least she had the choice, even if she hated what she chose."

"But you didn't force me, did you? You didn't hurt me. You didn't let your men hurt me."

"That wasn't from nobility. Nobody takes what's mine." He reached up and smoothed his hand over her cheek. "I haven't let you go. I won't. And I don't know sometimes if I'll be able to—" His hand trembled against her skin. "Amy, I want you so bad. I want to kiss you and touch you and—" He clamped down on his words.

Shyly, Amy placed her hand against his cheek. His skin was tough beneath her palm; she liked the feel of it, so different from her own. "I've never been kissed. I mean, not by a man. Not really. I think I'd like for you to."

She heard the change in his breathing, felt his skin suddenly flame with heat, and it made her own heart begin to hammer inside her chest. She waited, gazing up at him with anticipation and trust. Her look tore at him; he knew he wasn't worthy of it. Even his kiss would defile her. But he couldn't stop himself, not now. Her invitation had turned him to fire. He was a son of a bitch, he thought, but he bent his head and kissed her.

His lips met hers gently. Amy felt their warmth and their softness. His breath touched her face, and she tingled all over. Her hands came up unconsciously and curled into the front of his shirt. His arms slid around her, pulling her into him. He was hard and flat, all bone and muscle and sinew. His arms were like iron; she knew she could never break his grasp. But the idea didn't scare her. She had no desire to get away.

He kissed her harder, moving his lips over hers. Amy's arms went around his neck, and she went up on tiptoe, returning the pressure of his mouth. She liked this feeling. She'd never known anything like it. Everything inside her seemed to be jumping around, and her skin felt strangely hot, as if she were blushing, but it was far more exciting.

Brody made a noise, and his mouth widened, forcing her lips open. His tongue edged her lips farther apart, and Amy drew in her breath, startled. His tongue crept into her mouth, surprising her even further. She tried to draw back, for suddenly everything seemed too foreign, too fast, but Brody's hand came up and cupped the back of her neck, holding her head immobile. His grasp was harsh, but his tongue and lips were seductively soft. His tongue slid gently over her teeth and caressed the roof of her mouth, then twined around her tongue. Amy trembled and slowly relaxed, her surprise changing to pleasure.

When at last he broke their kiss, lifting his head and breathing in gulps of air, Amy leaned her head against his chest. She felt almost too weak to stand, as if the kiss had melted her bones. But it didn't matter, for his arms were hard around her, holding her up. She ran her tongue over her lips, tasting him on them. He kissed the top of her head, burying his face in her hair, and squeezed her hard. Then his arms loosened around her, and he stepped back.

Amy looked up at him, smiling in the shining way she had. "I liked that. Can we do it again?"

He groaned. "Amy, don't." She was so innocent that she didn't know what her sweet lips did to a man. She didn't understand how the passion was racing through him after only one kiss. If he kissed her again, he knew he would have to touch her, and then he wasn't sure that he would be able to stop. And he would have to stop. Making love to her wasn't something that could be rushed. She would stiffen and get scared, as she had tonight when his tongue went into her mouth. She needed to be coaxed and gentled, to be led gradually. It had to be good for her; it had to be right.

Sam Brody had never been an unkind lover; he had too much sympathy for the women who had to make a living as his mother had. But neither had he concerned himself with whether a woman enjoyed herself. He had paid them and that had been all there was to it.

But now he wanted, more than he could remember ever wanting anything, for Amy to find pleasure in his kisses and his touch. He wanted her to welcome him, to take him into her eagerly. With some amazement, he realized that he desired her heart as well as her body.

So he stepped back from her. "I can't. Not now. We—uh, need to get some sleep."

"Oh." The disappointment in Amy's voice almost made him sweep her back into his arms. "All right."

Amy spread out their blankets, and he banked the fire. They lay down, and Amy snuggled up next to him. "It's nice to sleep with you. Then I don't feel scared. Do you like it?"

Brody's throat was suddenly too tight to speak. He swallowed. His voice came out low, almost whispering. "Yeah. I like it."

Amy smiled and closed her eyes. She drifted easily into sleep; Sam could feel her relaxing against him. But he lay awake for a long time, staring at the stars, but not seeing them, aware of nothing but Amy's soft body against his side.

The next morning Victoria found that Slater's fever was still down. She got up and went downstairs for breakfast, not wanting to disturb his sleep.

Mrs. Miles and her two sons were sitting at the table, finishing their coffee, the remains of their breakfast in front of them. Dennis looked up and saw Victoria, and a broad smile crossed his face. His brother's smile was almost as big. Victoria couldn't imagine what they found so appealing about her, for after days on the trail and caring for Slater, she looked haggard and messy. She supposed that she should have been amused and heartened by their obvious admiration, but, frankly, she didn't feel in the mood to play flirting games with them, putting them off while not hurting their feelings. She remembered that they thought she was married to Slater and therefore they wouldn't make any advances toward her. That made her even gladder that she had gone along with Dennis's original assumption that she was married.

Mrs. Miles stood up, beaming at her. "Well, there you are. I hope you got a little sleep last night."

"Oh, yes, thank you."

"You look a lot perkier this morning."

Victoria smiled. "I feel much better. Slater's improved."

Mrs. Miles looked surprised, and Victoria realized that the older woman hadn't thought much of Slater's chances. "Has he? Well, now, isn't that wonderful? Here, come set down, and I'll get you some breakfast."

"Please don't go to any bother."

"It's no trouble at all. I left some sausage warming on the stove for you." She went to the stove and carried back an enameled iron plate, using her apron to carry the hot dish. She set it down in front of Victoria, and Nathan passed down the biscuits, butter and gravy.

Victoria ate heartily, finding that the combination of relief and the hard work she had done the past few days had made her hungry. The two men sat and watched her, sipping their coffee, while their mother cleared the table.

When Mrs. Miles had stacked the dishes in a large tub to soak, she turned and said, "I think I'll slip up and take a look at your husband, Mrs. Slater, if you don't mind."

"No, of course not. I'd appreciate it."

She left the kitchen. Victoria continued to eat, wishing that the two men would do something besides watch her.

"Your mother's medicine must have helped," she said. "Your finding us last night was a lifesaver, Mr. Miles. Thank you very much."

"Call me Dennis, ma'am. I'm glad I came along."

"Yeah. Wish I'd been there." Nathan's speech was a little slow, and Victoria had the impression that perhaps his mind was, as well.

"Maybe later Nathan and me can show you around the place."

Victoria suppressed a sigh. Perhaps the fact that they thought she was married wouldn't be enough to discourage their attentions. "Thank you, but I'll spend the day looking after Slater."

"Ma'll do that for you," Dennis offered.

"That's very kind of her, but I wouldn't want to burden her. Besides, I'd worry if I wasn't with him." Victoria smiled to take any sting out of her refusal.

Dennis frowned and sat back in his chair. For a moment the boyish cheerfulness disappeared from his face, and he looked older and harder. Victoria suspected that he wasn't used to being crossed. Then he smiled and shrugged. "Reckon we'll have to get to work, then. Come on, Nate."

He rose, clapping his brother on the shoulder, and the two of them left the kitchen. Shortly afterward, Mrs. Miles bustled back into the kitchen, beaming, and told Victoria that Slater did, indeed, look to be getting better. Victoria started to return to the bedroom to watch him, but Mrs. Miles stopped her.

"He'll be asleep for hours yet," she assured Victoria. "Fever like that leaves you weak as a kitten. Why don't you set on the porch and rock a while? You need to get away from tendin' him, or you'll make yourself sick. Say, maybe you'd like a nice, hot bath.''

Victoria hesitated. "Well, actually, it would be nice to take a bath." After two days on the trail and taking care of Slater, she felt grimy and sweaty. It would be heavenly to soak in a tub and wash the dust from her hair.

Mrs. Miles had her sons bring in the big washtub and fill it with water she heated over the fire. Mrs. Miles suggested that Victoria give her the dirty clothes she and Slater had on, and she would wash them, as it was her wash day. Victoria realized, embarrassed, that although she had brought another blouse, she had only the one riding skirt. Mrs. Miles would be bound to think that was odd, traveling with so few clothes. But she took it in stride, as she seemed to take everything, and merely lent Victoria a robe to wear until her clothes were dry.

Victoria went upstairs and changed into the robe. Mrs. Miles had already briskly stripped Slater's clothes off to wash them, for which she was thankful. It would have been highly embarrassing for her to have to disrobe him, even though he was unconscious.

She went downstairs, where Mrs. Miles was waiting for her. The woman took her clothes and went out the back door, leaving Victoria to her bath. Victoria pulled the door to the living area shut. She wished she could lock it, but there was no lock on it, so she had to content herself with securing the outside door. Surely Mrs. Miles had ordered her sons to stay out of the kitchen while Victoria was taking a bath, so no one would be walking in on her. Still, it made her a trifle uneasy to disrobe and bathe in a strange house.

Telling herself not to be foolish, Victoria took off the robe and hopped into the tub. It was much smaller than the elegant slipper tub she was used to at home, but the water was hot, and it felt wonderful. She leaned back against the side, letting the warmth soak into her. After all that had happened the past couple of days, it was marvelous simply to relax.

Suddenly, her eyes snapped open, and she sat up straight, looking around. She had the eeriest feeling of being watched. It was obvious that there was no one there, but she still had the feeling so strongly that she half expected to see a leering face peeking through the doorway. She waited stiffly, her arms crossed instinctively over her chest. Nothing happened. No one came in.

Victoria shook her head. She usually wasn't this skittish. It must be her fear for Amy, so great that it was overflowing into every corner of her life. She couldn't shake the uneasy feeling, and she finished bathing and washed her hair in record time. She found that she was reluctant to stand up and dry off, as though she would be exposing herself completely to someone, and she had to force herself to do it. She dressed in the robe Mrs. Miles had given her and rushed back upstairs.

Mrs. Miles had also lent her a skirt, which, of course, was far too big for her, but she wrapped a belt around the waist and managed to keep it up. When she was dressed, she sat down in the chair beside Slater's bed and combed out her wet hair. She toweled and brushed it over and over, moving her chair a little so that she was in line with the window, where the sun and the slight breeze would help the drying process.

"Beautiful."

Victoria's head jerked up, and she whirled toward the soft whisper. Slater's eyes were open, and he was watching her brush her hair. For the first time in a long time, he looked at her clearly, his gaze untainted by fever.

"Slater!" A blazing smile burst across her face. "You're awake."

"And what a sight to wake up to." She could barely hear him, his voice was so low.

The words pleased her out of all proportion, and Victoria sternly reminded herself that there was nothing she liked about the man. It shouldn't matter a whit to her if he thought she was beautiful. That probably wasn't even what he had said.

She went to the bed and bent over him. "How do you feel?"

"Like somebody poleaxed me." Victoria's long hair brushed the pillow and bed beside him. He took a strand gently between his fingers.

"Do you hurt anywhere?"

He shook his head. "Just my arm. And my head, a little. But I'm weak as a kitten. Where are we? I thought—" He looked puzzled and irritated, and his fingers released her hair. "Aren't we chasing Brody's gang?"

"We were until you came down with a fever."

Slater closed his eyes and rubbed a hand across his face in a weary gesture. "Yeah. I remember you helping me onto my horse, and we started riding. Did we ride here?"

"No. Just to the nearest shade tree. You weren't in any shape to ride. You were out of your head all day yesterday. Your fever didn't break until the middle of the night."

"Tell me how we got here."

Victoria told him briefly about Dennis Miles and how he had taken them back to his house. Slater was too exhausted to hear a long story. Already his eyelids were starting to drift closed. "Mrs. Miles put some soup on to heat for you. I'll get you a bowl. You need to eat before you go back to sleep."

"Then you'd better hurry."

Victoria smiled. Hearing him try to joke, weak as he was, made her feel funny inside, as if she could laugh and cry all at once. She left the room and trotted down the stairs. She knew her face was stamped with an idiotic grin, and her feet felt so light she thought she might float. Slater was going to be all right! He was awake and talking, and all he needed was time and care to regain his strength.

There was no one in the kitchen when she entered it, so she went to the cupboard and found a bowl. She pulled the pot out from the fire and dipped about half a bowlful of soup from it, searching for several chunks of meat. Then she hurried back up the stairs to feed Slater.

His eyes were closed when she entered, but they fluttered open at the sound of the door. He smiled faintly. "Can't seem to keep from drifting off," he said, his words slurred with exhaustion.

"I think you have reason enough. But you do need to wake up and eat."

Slater nodded and tried to sit up. Victoria set the bowl down on the dresser and went to help him, putting her hands behind his back and lifting. When her hands touched his skin, Slater stiffened, and suddenly Victoria was very aware of his naked chest and arms, and of the feel of his skin beneath her fingers. While he was feverish, she had become somewhat used to putting her hands on his bare skin, but now that he was conscious, it was different. Now he felt her touch. The thought made her uncomfortably warm and sent strange prickles all through her. Victoria stuffed the pillows behind him and stepped back quickly.

"I—I'm sorry. Mrs. Miles took your clothes to wash."

"It's all right. I can eat without a shirt." Slater studied her face, becomingly tinged with color at the moment. The lack of a shirt didn't bother him, though he had felt it all through him when she'd laid her hands on his back. What bothered him were the vague memories floating in his head, memories of being horribly hot, on fire, and of a woman's hands, cool and wet, moving deliciously over him. Had that been Victoria Stafford washing him? Her hands had been so soft and gentle, lingering on his burning flesh, that it seemed impossible that it could have been Victoria. It seemed more likely that she would have been cussing him out for failing her, rather than taking care of him. Even now, weak as he was, desire began to swell in him, as he thought about those hands.

He pushed himself up higher on the pillows, using his elbows, and tried to dismiss the thought from his mind. Victoria picked up the bowl of soup from the dresser and sat down next to him on the bed. She dipped the spoon into the soup and held it up to his lips, letting him sip from it. Slater started to protest that he could feed himself, but he stopped. Frankly, it was an effort even to hold up his head. Besides, it had been a long time since he'd been cosseted by a woman, and he found it a pleasant change—particularly when it was this woman. It was the last thing he would have expected from her.

The soup was good, and, as he ate, he realized how hungry he was. But soon he grew tired, and he turned his head away, sliding down on the pillows. His eyelids drifted closed of their own volition. Slater felt stupid for being so tired, yet he had no control over it. There was nothing he hated as much as being weak. Thank God that, if he'd had to depend on someone, it had been a woman like Victoria Stafford. That thought surprised him so much that it almost brought him back to consciousness, but he was too exhausted to think, and he let it go, sliding down into the darkness of sleep.

Victoria took the bowl downstairs and returned to Slater's room to sit with him. He slept on and off for the rest of the day, and Victoria kept watch in the chair beside his bed. She wished she had some sewing to keep her hands busy, or a book to occupy her mind. As it was, all she could do was worry.

With Slater apparently on his way to recovery, all the fear for Amy that she had pushed to the back of her mind returned in full force. She'd been with those men for over two whole days now! Victoria couldn't bear to think of what had happened to her. She pictured Amy, bleeding and broken, abandoned when they were through with her. Perhaps she was already dead.

A small noise of loathing and denial escaped her lips at the thought, and Slater woke up. He saw the fear on her face, and it surprised him. He hadn't seen fear in her, even when bullets were flying all around them, or when she was helping the doctor clean his bloody arm. "What is it?" he asked, his voice still low, but a little stronger than before.

Victoria shook her head, embarrassed that she had awakened her patient and that she had let Slater, of all people, see her doubt and anguish. "Nothing. I'm sorry I woke you. Go back to sleep."

He frowned. "What is it? Tell me."

"Nothing, really. I was just thinking about Amy and wondering what's happened to her. How we'll ever find her."

Tears sparkled in her blue eyes, turning them even brighter and more vivid. It wrenched Slater's gut to see the tears, and that surprised him. He had thought himself immune to a woman's tears. "Don't worry. I'll find her. I'll get her back for you. It's a promise."

Victoria swallowed down the sobs that threatened to rise in her throat. She would not break down in front of him. The last thing a sick man needed was someone weeping and wailing all over him. Despair never made anyone feel better. She blinked and summoned up a sketch of a smile.

"Of course you will. I'm giving way to weakness."

"You're tired. You have been taking care of me all by yourself."

"Mrs. Miles helped me."

"How long has it been?"

"Since you've been feverish? This is the second day."

"We didn't get very far, did we?"

She shook her head. That wasn't a good way for him to think. "Since you're awake, how about more soup?"

He grimaced, but allowed her to help him up and feed him. When he was done, he slid back down in the bed and let Victoria tuck in the sheets around him. Her clean, flowery scent teased at his nostrils, and he fell asleep smiling.

Once more Victoria curled up in the chair, and this time she dozed off, too. She came to with a start and found herself face to face with Slater, who was sitting up on the side of the bed. He was the color of paper. Victoria came to her feet, concerned.

"What is it? What's the matter? What are you doing?"

"Watching you sleep. I started to get up, but I couldn't quite make it."

"Of course not. Don't be foolish. Lie back down."

"Where are my guns?"

"What?"

"My guns. The Peacemakers and the carbine."

"What a thing to be thinking of now. The carbine's downstairs, and I brought your gun belt up to the room with us."

"Where is it? I want it."

"For heaven's sake." Victoria rolled her eyes. "Are you planning to shoot me?"

The ghost of a smile touched his lips. "Not unless you drive me to it. Which is not entirely unlikely."

Victoria sighed and crossed over to the dresser. She couldn't imagine why he had to see his guns, but as long as it would keep him quiet . . .

She came back to the bed, holding out the gun belt. "I can't understand why you want them. We're in a house, with people around. We're safe."

He shrugged. "I've found it's not wise to assume you're safe in any situation. I like to be able to reach my guns." He took each revolver from its holster and checked the chambers.

Victoria watched, one eyebrow raised. "Did you think I'd stolen your ammunition?"

"I wouldn't put anything past you. But I always check. It's safer. I've stayed alive this long by not leaving room for mistakes."

He buckled the belt and hung it over the bedpost above his head. "Damn. I feel like I've been out breaking horses all day."

"It'll take a while for you to regain your strength."

He shot her a sideways glance. "If you're going to try to make me eat more of that soup, forget it."

Victoria chuckled. "All right. If you don't want to get well . . ."

He snorted and lay down. Victoria looked at him blandly. He sighed. "All right. Get the damn stuff."

"Well, at least you've recovered your usual vocabulary," Victoria said primly as she started out the door, and she heard him snort again behind her. The little exchange with him raised her spirits, and she went down to the kitchen humming. She dipped up more soup while she answered Mrs. Miles's questions about Slater's condition. Mrs. Miles offered to take over the chore of watching him, but Victoria refused. She didn't want to turn the task over to someone else. She supposed it was because at least it gave her something to do.

She returned to Slater's room, but she found him asleep, and she set the bowl aside. He needed to rest more than anything. She walked to the bed and stood looking down at him. She couldn't keep a little smile from coming to her lips. He no longer looked deathly ill, just slightly pale. With his face relaxed in sleep, he seemed younger, more handsome. When he was awake, there was a fierceness in his expression, a power, that kept one from noticing his good looks. Idly, Victoria traced the curve of his mustache with her index finger. She wondered what it would feel like to kiss him. Did the mustache tickle? It didn't feel wiry, as she had expected. In fact it was almost soft. His lips twitched, and her eyes went to them. She remembered how they had felt against her fingers when she had dampened them. She remembered the way they had closed around her fingers, his tongue licking the moisture from her skin.

Something hot and sharp curled through her abdomen. She shouldn't have thoughts like this about Slater. About any man, really. But especially Slater. He disliked her. She disliked him. Didn't she?

She was no longer sure. They had disagreed about almost everything before he fell ill, and she suspected that as soon as he was well, they would disagree again. Still, she felt a closeness to him, a bond that had been forged during the long hours when she had struggled to save him. She had worked and worried and even prayed for him. And she had sensed that they were pulling together, paired in an intense effort. She hardly knew him, yet because of what had happened, Victoria was connected to him in a way she wasn't connected to men she had known all her life.

She moved to the window and stared out for a time, thinking. Finally she returned to the chair. Slater slept through the rest of the afternoon, waking late in the day and eating the bowl of soup despite its coldness.

Mrs. Miles brought up their clean clothes. Victoria laid Slater's shirt and trousers over the footboard of the bed and changed out of Mrs. Miles's skirt into her own. She felt much more comfortable in her own clothes.

The tantalizing odors of dinner began to rise from the floor below. Victoria was hungry, and felt a trifle edgy, too, from being in the room all day. She glanced at Slater to make sure he was sound asleep, then went downstairs. Mrs. Miles was putting supper on the table, and the two men were washing up. They turned at her entrance and smiled.

"I'm glad you decided to eat with us. Mr. Slater'll be fine for a while without you."

"That's right. You worry about him too much." Dennis came closer, drying off his hands. His eyes swept down her, and Victoria was shocked at the positively licentious expression in his eyes. She glanced nervously at his mother, wondering if she had noticed. She was glad that the woman was here. She was also glad that Slater was on the mend and they wouldn't have to stay here much longer.

Nathan joined his brother. "Be dark soon," he said, apropos of nothing that Victoria could determine, convincing her more than ever that he was not quite right in the head.

But his mother seemed to understand him, for she shook her head firmly. "After dinner, Nate."

"Yes, ma'am."

Victoria guessed he must have been promised some kind of treat after it got dark, but she didn't inquire. Dennis's look had made her uneasy, and she would just as soon not get involved with anything concerning either brother.

Everyone was strangely quiet throughout supper, even Mrs. Miles. Victoria's unease grew. She didn't know what was wrong, but she sensed that something was, something...

secret. She wished that she hadn't decided to come downstairs for supper. She should have stayed in the room with Slater and eaten from a tray, as she had earlier.

After supper she helped Mrs. Miles with the dishes, but she was glad when the chore was finished and she could escape to her room. She left the kitchen and crossed the living room. Mrs. Miles followed right behind her. Victoria noticed that only Nathan was in the room. She glanced around and caught sight of Dennis disappearing up the stairs. She gave Nathan and his mother a halfhearted smile.

"I'll go up to my room now. Thank you for supper."

Mrs. Miles shook her head. "No."

"What?" Victoria looked at her, puzzled.

"I said no, you can't go to your room."

"Why not?" She couldn't understand what the woman was talking about. It was such a strange thing to say, and her tone was peremptory, almost commanding, not at all the hearty, friendly way Mrs. Miles usually talked.

"'Cause Den's got something to do up there."

Victoria waited. The woman said no more. They stared at each other. Victoria realized that Mrs. Miles looked different, too. The smile that had been so constantly on her lips was gone, and without it her mouth was a hard, straight line. Her eyes were hard, too.

The vague sense of unease that Victoria had felt all evening burst into full flower. There was something wrong here. Victoria whirled and started for the stairs, instinctively running toward Slater. Mrs. Miles clamped a hand around Victoria's arm and jerked her to a halt.

Victoria turned. "What's the matter with you? I'm going to see Slater." She tugged in vain against the other woman's grip. Mrs. Miles was bigger and stronger than she was. "Let me go!"

"I said you ain't goin' up there."

Above their heads a gun suddenly blasted. Victoria froze, staring into Mrs. Miles's eyes. "Slater!" She began to struggle furiously. "Slater!"

Chapter Eight

Victoria fought wildly, clawing and kicking at her captor, her only thought to get upstairs to help Slater. Mrs. Miles held on with both hands and called to Nathan for help. The man wrapped his arms around Victoria from behind, lifting her off her feet, and walked back with her to the far side of the room. Victoria's arms and legs flailed ineffectually, and she screamed with frustration and rage.

"Put me down! What have you done to Slater? Let me go! Slater!"

"He's dead," Mrs. Miles told her dispassionately. "Be thankful the boys wanted you, or you'd be the same."

It was her tone, even more than her words, that chilled Victoria. There was no heat, no anger, in her, only a businesslike calm.

"What do you mean?" Victoria stopped struggling and stared at the other woman in shock.

"Den and Nate wanted to have you, so we're lettin' you live. We got no use for your husband, 'cept for his horse and things. So he'll go the way of the others."

"Others?" Victoria could barely get the word out.

"Sure. Den told you we get a lotta visitors, and we're always happy to take 'em in." A cold smile curved her lips at her own humor.

"You kill them? You kill the people to whom you offer hospitality?"

Mrs. Miles's smile broadened. "Only when I figure they can't be traced to this house. It was clear from that gunshot wound in your fella's arm that you two are on the wrong side of the law, so I don't reckon anybody much'll be missin' you. I don't like to put us in danger. That's why I was hopin' he'd die natural-like, from the fever. You'd have gone along with the boys easier, too. Now it'll take you a while to calm down and face up to what you have to do."

"Ya mean we gotta wait, Ma?" Nathan asked plaintively.

His mother grimaced. "I didn't say that, boy. Soon as Den comes down and has his turn with her, then you can."

"Ah, Ma! Why does he always get his pick? You let him have that fancy Mexican saddle last month, too. He's your favorite. You always let him have everythin'."

"You hush up! That ain't the truth, and you know it. Den asked for it first, that's how come I let him have it. An' he saw this girl first, too. He'd been hankering for her for hours 'fore you ever even saw her."

Victoria stared at Mrs. Miles in horror, unable to speak. She couldn't believe that this woman, so friendly and ingratiating before, was now calmly talking about giving Victoria to her sons.

"Do you mean—" Victoria gasped when at last she was able to recover her voice "—do you mean to let them rape me?"

Mrs. Miles gave a dry, mirthless laugh. "Happens to all of us, honey."

"But how can you? You're a woman, too! You're their mother!"

She shrugged, obviously unmoved by Victoria's plight. "They want you real bad. I practically had to peel 'em away from the peephole this morning when you was bathin'. An' if they want it, I get it for 'em. See, I like to keep my boys happy. I'd do a lot worse than to keep 'em home and content."

Victoria shuddered, appalled. This woman was evil through and through. How could she have thought her kind and generous? How could she have let herself be so deceived! There must have been signs that the Miles family was not what it seemed, but she had failed to see them. She had been foolishly trusting, and Victoria knew that in part it had been because she had felt helpless out there in the open with Slater sick. She had been scared, and glad to have an older woman shoulder the re-

sponsibility. She had wanted to believe in Mrs. Miles, and that
had made it awfully easy to do so.

Mrs. Miles saw Victoria's involuntary shudder, and she
chuckled. "Don't worry. We ain't gonna kill you, even when
the boys tire of you. I reckon a pretty thing like you will draw
the men. Practically any man passin' by will want to spend the
night when he sees you."

Victoria straightened, and her eyes flashed fire. A cold rage
swept through her, wiping out her fear. "If you think I'll go
along with this, you're sadly mistaken. There are worse things
than dying."

"And my Den knows how to do most of 'em. You'll go
along, sooner or later."

"You'd better think again. You'll regret this day as long as
you live."

"Brave words, missy."

"It's a lot more than words. That man up there, the one you
killed? He's a Texas Ranger. They won't rest until they find the
people who killed him. Maybe nobody's caught on to you before now, but you've never had the whole of the Texas Rangers looking for you."

"Sure." Nathan snorted. "Sure he's a Ranger. And I'm
Stonewall Jackson."

"Well," a soft voice drawled from the direction of the stairs,
"I never realized General Jackson was so ugly and stupid."

Everyone turned toward the voice in astonishment. Slater
stood halfway down the stairs, leaning against the rail. His face
was washed-out, and one hand gripped the banister tightly. But
in the other hand, one of his Colts was leveled at Mrs. Miles.

"Slater!" Victoria gasped, astonishment mingling with the
relief in her voice.

He smiled. "What's the matter, darlin'? Surely you didn't
think I couldn't take a worm like that, even if I'd been on my
deathbed."

"I should have realized," Victoria replied a little breathlessly.

"Now," Slater went on, "unless you want to see your Ma's
blood all over this floor, boy, I suggest you let go of Miss Stafford."

"Ma?" Nathan's voice quavered a little, like a child's, and he looked over at his mother.

Mrs. Miles looked into Slater's eyes. "Do it, son."

"Wise decision."

Nathan's arms relaxed, and Victoria scooted away. Slater's carbine had been set in the corner of the room, and she hurried to pick it up, carefully staying out of Slater's line of fire. She checked to make sure it was loaded, then aimed the gun at Nathan. No matter how miraculously Slater had been able to outshoot Dennis Miles, she knew he was too weak to hold Nathan and his mother at bay for long single-handedly. He might slide to the floor in a faint at any moment.

"Good girl," Slater softly praised Victoria's move. She was a woman who knew what to do and how to do it, and she didn't waste time having hysterics.

"Where's Dennis?" Mrs. Miles asked, and her eyes were dark pits of fear.

"If he's the one you sent up to my room with a gun, he's lying on the floor with a bullet between his eyes," Slater replied bluntly.

"No! No!" she shrieked, and her face contorted. "Not my boy. Not Denny!" Suddenly she moved, startling them all. She ran to the gun rack on the wall and jerked down a rifle. She whirled and lifted it to her shoulder, aiming at Slater.

For an instant Victoria was too surprised to move, her responses numbed by the shocks she had received this evening. But she saw Slater's hesitation. Instinctively she fired. Mrs. Miles screamed and fell, her finger jerking on the trigger. The rifle blasted a hole in the stairs below where Slater stood, and fragments of wood flew. The sound was deafening.

Stunned, the other three occupants of the room stared at the inert form on the floor.

"Lord." Slater's voice was so low that Victoria could barely hear it. He looked at her. "You saved my life. I couldn't pull the trigger for a second—I've never shot a woman."

Victoria's eyes were huge; the blood had left her face. "Neither have I," she whispered.

He came down the steps and put his arm around her shoulders. Victoria leaned against him gratefully. She felt sick to her stomach. She didn't think she would ever forget that woman's crazed face as she leveled the gun, or the burst of red across her chest before she crashed to the floor.

She had killed a person. Victoria began to shiver. Slater's arm tightened around her, and his lips brushed her hair. "It'll be okay."

"Ma?" For the first time, Nathan spoke. He sounded lost and scared. "Ma?"

He walked over to where his mother lay and dropped down on the floor beside her. "Ma? No. You can't leave me. Ma, don't leave me!" He began to cry and bent over her, clutching her lifeless body. "What'll I do now? What'll I do?"

Slater made a noise of pity and disgust. He walked over and picked up the gun from Mrs. Miles's slack fingers, then turned and went outside. Victoria watched him hurl it out into the yard. He didn't have enough strength left in him to throw it far. He sat down on the front steps, his elbows on his knees, and stared at the ground.

Victoria followed him. She was numb and yet somehow jittery at the same time. "Slater? Are you all right?"

He looked up at her. His sharp green eyes were a bright contrast to his drawn face. "Yeah. I'll get by. How about you? Are you okay? Did they hurt you?"

"No." She paused. She wanted to burst into tears, but she was determined not to. That was the last thing Slater needed, especially in his weakened condition. She had sworn that she would help him, not hinder him. She had spent most of her life proving to her father and everyone else that she was as good, as tough, as strong as any man, and she had learned well how to hide any sign of weakness. She did so now, pushing back her tears and concentrating on the practical. "What are we going to do?"

Slater glanced up, surprised. She was a cool one, all right. She had just killed a person for the first time, yet except for that momentary lapse when she had leaned against him, trembling, she showed no signs of falling apart. He couldn't help but admire her courage.

He shrugged. "Ride, I reckon. I don't relish spending the night here, do you?"

"No," Victoria admitted. If it was just her, she knew she would jump on her horse and ride as fast and as far as she could. "But what about you? How can you stay on a horse?"

"Don't worry about me. I'll stick."

"You aren't in any condition to ride."

"I said I'd do it," he snapped and pulled himself up by the railing. "I'll go and get our things."

"Don't be silly. I'll do it."

He shook his head. "You don't want to see what's in that room."

"I'm sure that's true. But I can do it anyway. There's no sense in your wasting your strength climbing up and down the stairs."

He gave her a doubtful look, then said, "All right. Go ahead."

Victoria knew he expected her to run back down the stairs, screaming, or maybe sink into a maidenly faint. She was determined not to. She already felt the burden of having gotten them into this mess; she'd been too trusting, not tough or sharp enough. She refused to give Slater further proof of her inability to handle a rough situation.

It was almost more than she could do not to run, however, when she eased through the open doorway into their bedroom and saw Dennis's body lying on the floor. She crept into the room. Her heart was pounding, as if he might jump up from where he lay and grab her. There was no chance of that. She could see the dark hole in his forehead between his eyes; she could see the glassy stare of death. Her gorge rose. It was even worse, somehow, than when she had shot Mrs. Miles. That had been in the heat of action, an instinctive defense. This was just gazing on the cold, hard face of death.

Victoria swallowed hard, and, keeping her eyes averted, scooped up their belongings from the dresser. Slater's holster and second revolver still hung from the bedpost on the opposite corner of the bed. Victoria couldn't bring herself to walk around Miles's body to get them, so she crawled across the bed and snatched them from the post. Then she picked up Slater's boots from the foot of the bed and fled back downstairs.

Slater glanced up at her approach, and she could see the surprise and respect on his face. "Damn, lady," he said softly. "Doesn't anything faze you?"

"A lot of things," she responded tartly. "I just don't let myself give in to them."

"Remind me not to expect you to cry at my funeral." His voice was dry.

"You think I ought to cry for him? The man who was going to blast you to kingdom come and force me to—to submit to his brother and him? No, thank you. I don't cry for scum."

Slater reached out and took her hand. "I'm sorry. I had no right to say that. You have more courage than most men." Maybe the way she acted wasn't very feminine, but the last thing he needed was a weeping, frightened female. Right now he had to rely on her courage and strength—and that was probably the reason he had sniped at her. He was angry at himself for failing. He had told Victoria that she couldn't come with him because she would slow him down and put him in danger. But, in truth, he was the one who had slowed them down. He'd put them out of commission for so long with his illness that it was unlikely they'd find Brody's trail again. Instead of him protecting her, it had been Victoria who had saved his life—twice over. Worst of all, he still had to depend on her; he was so damnably weak. Slater wasn't accustomed to relying on anyone other than himself, and he thoroughly disliked it.

Victoria turned away. She didn't know how to act when Slater complimented her. She wanted to cry again, but she couldn't, not when he'd just said how strong she was. The best thing to do was to concentrate on the business at hand. "What are we going to do about Nathan?" She nodded toward the house, where Nathan still knelt beside his mother's body, weeping.

Slater sighed. "Hell if I know. I guess I ought to take him in. He was in on it." He looked through the open front door at the pitiful scene. He shook his head. "But he's not much of a danger to anybody without his mother and brother around. If I take him in, by the time I get back, Brody's trail will be stone cold." He reached out and grasped the porch post and pulled himself to a standing position. He swayed for only an instant before he steadied himself. "Seeing as how you saved my life, the least I can do is find your cousin. Leave Nathan to bury his dead. Let's ride.''

"Oh, Sam, it's beautiful!" Amy exclaimed, pulling her horse to a stop. They had traveled most of the day, going west and north, deeper into the hill country. They saw no other people—or even a house or barn in the distance. It was lonely, isolated country, but Amy liked it. Finally they had crossed the Colorado River, and Sam had led them up one of its smaller tributaries. They had come around a curve in the stream, and there before them was a small waterfall, splashing down a rocky ledge into a pool. It was a lovely, secluded spot, shaded by trees and protected by a bluff.

Amy jumped down from her horse and stood gazing at the sparkling waterfall, enraptured by its beauty. She looked up at Sam and smiled. "Thank you for bringing me here. I've never seen anything like it. I mean, not so beautiful or so high. What's it called?"

Brody shrugged as he swung off his horse. "I don't know. I just came upon it one time. I don't know if anyone else even knows about it."

"Then I'll name it." She went forward, a slender figure in her boy's trousers, and reached out to touch the mist drifting from the falls. "Look how it sparkles in the sun! I'll name it Crystal Falls." She glanced back over her shoulder at Brody, her face glowing. "That would suit, wouldn't it?"

"Perfect." He couldn't have cared less what it was named, but his heart lurched inside his chest when she looked at him like that. She was the most beautiful creature he had ever seen. He wanted to hold her and caress her and say all kinds of soft, loving things he'd never said before. But he felt clumsy and unsure, and he was scared he might frighten her, so he hung back, watching her.

Amy stood at the edge of the pool, laughing, her eyes closed, letting the mist cover her. Brody watched the gentle spray gradually dampen her clothes until her shirt molded itself to her small, firm breasts. He imagined sliding his hands under the too-big shirt and up over her satiny skin to cup her breasts. He imagined moving his hand down her abdomen to the juncture of her legs, so clearly delineated by the masculine clothing she wore. He began to sweat, just thinking about it, and his fingers itched to touch her. He knew she didn't have the first idea how she affected him.

She turned back to him, her face beaded with water from the spray. Sam wanted to lick off the drops with his tongue. He wiped his palms nervously down his trouser legs.

"Is the pool deep?" she asked, wiping the moisture from her face with her hands. Her lashes clung together in wet spikes, giving her eyes a starry look.

He shook his head. "No. Not much. I can stand up in it."

"Good. Can we go in?"

His heart began to hammer. "If you want."

"I'd like that. I want to stand under the falls and feel it pouring down on me."

"All right." The blood thundered through his veins as he thought of her slim, white body standing under the glittering stream of water.

"Now?"

"If you want." It was difficult to keep his voice level. "But we'll be camping here for several days, if you want to wait."

"Oh, no, I'd like to do it now. Then I can do it again later." She sat down on a nearby rock and began to pull off her boots.

Brody wondered if she would undress in front of him with equal lack of concern. But when she had pulled off her boots and heavy socks, she glanced up at him, and a blush stained her cheeks. She looked away.

"I—uh, I'll take care of the horses while you're doing that." He took the reins and led their mounts down the stream and around the curve so that they were out of sight. He unsaddled and hobbled them, but his mind was not on what he was doing, but on Amy by the pool.

He thought about going back and watching her bathe. He could do it without her knowing. He wanted to. But it would be a violation of her trust in him, even if she wasn't aware of it, and he felt a curious queasiness at that idea. He wondered if he was developing a conscience at this late date. It seemed unlikely. Still, he found himself staying away, taking his time about caring for the horses. Then he sat down on a rock and smoked one of the small cigars he'd gotten from Raul, watching the horses grazing peacefully beside the stream.

He'd just get all stirred up if he crept back to spy on her bathing, Sam told himself. That wouldn't serve any purpose. His body grew heated enough envisioning Amy's naked form; it would be sheer torture to actually see her. He had sworn not to take her without her consent, but watching her cavorting in the water would make that promise hard as hell to keep. It was far better that he stay where he was.

He had finished his cigar and was grinding it out on the rock when he heard the tiny rattle of pebbles on the ground behind him, and he whirled. Amy came around the formation of granite rock that hid the falls from view. She had dressed again in her boy's clothes, but they were damp and clinging from her still-wet body. Her hair was loose and pushed back from her face, hanging wetly down her back. Her face glistened with moisture. The desire that clawed at his gut was sudden and fierce. God, he wanted her! He ached to take her, to taste her, to pour himself into her. It took all his willpower to stay seated and smile at her.

"You through? Too cold?"

She smiled. "Yes, but I loved it. It's so clear and clean, and that spray touches you like—" She shook her head. "I can't describe it."

"I know."

"I thought you might want to try it, too, before it gets dark."

"It's nice in the dark, too." His voice came out rusty. He was thinking of going into the pool with Amy at night, the moonlight gleaming on the silver stream of water and on Amy's white flesh.

"I never thought of that. It sounds like fun. But I think I'd be scared at night, alone."

"Maybe you wouldn't do it alone."

Amy's eyes widened, and she sucked in her breath. Did he mean they would both take off their clothes and go naked into the water together? The thought made her loins hot and achy. She came a step closer and stopped. She wanted Sam to kiss her. She wanted a lot more than that. She wasn't sure what it was that she wished would happen, but the thought of being naked in front of Sam filled her with excitement and embarrassment.

"Sam, why did you kiss me last night?"

Desire forked through him like lightning. "Because I wanted you."

"Why did you stop?"

He cleared his throat, but his voice was still hoarse when he spoke, "Because you—I need to go slow with you. I don't want to rush you. You're—innocent."

Her teeth worried at her lower lip. Brody's eyes couldn't move from her mouth. "Do you mean because I'm stupid?"

"No!" He jumped up and went to her, though he'd told himself he wouldn't. "You aren't stupid. I told you that before. Don't you believe me?"

She gazed up at him, her eyes huge and lambent. Brody felt as if her eyes were sucking him in. "Yes. I believe you. But what do you mean, then?"

"I mean that you're untouched. Pure." He trailed his hand down the side of her face and neck to her shoulder. Then he moved it back up, spreading his fingers out on her soft flesh. His thumb caressed her chin and traced the line of her lips. "I don't want to spoil that. I don't want to hurt you or scare you."

"You don't scare me. I trust you."

"I'm not sure I trust myself."

Amy looked at him quizzically. "I don't understand."

Brody's eyes were riveted to her lips, watching the slow progress of his thumb over them, feeling their texture against his skin. He remembered the taste of her lips last night. "How could you understand?" he murmured. "You're too good to see the wicked things inside me."

There was a part of him that wanted to seize her, crush her to him and kiss her. There was a part of him that desired only to rip off the tantalizing shirt and trousers and thrust into her until he reached blissful satisfaction, no matter how it hurt Amy. That was the part of him that raged and burned, that took what he wanted and damned the consequences, that fought anything that got in his way. It had long been the biggest part of him.

But there was something else in him now that could contain that part, hold him down so that he didn't hurt Amy. He didn't know what that other thing was, but it hungered after the sweetness and joy of Amy even more than he hungered after her body. It was warm and soothing, as though the light that glowed in Amy had crept inside him, too.

He bent and touched his lips lightly to hers, savoring the softness of her mouth and the flutter of her breath against his lips. It was Amy who pressed up into him, her arms sliding naturally around his neck, her mouth seeking his. It took only that encouragement for him to kiss her deeply. Sam's tongue came into Amy's mouth, reexploring what he had discovered the evening before. But this time Amy's tongue moved timidly to meet his, touching, then retreating, and finally coming back again to twine around his.

Brody's breath shuddered out at the innocent seduction of her action. His arms wrapped around her tightly, molding her against him. His skin was suddenly searing. He ached to grind his mouth into hers, crushing and possessing, but he held back, letting their tongues flirt. He was determined not to push or frighten her with the full force of his passion.

Because of his gentleness, Amy was emboldened to try more—to taste his mouth as he had tasted hers, to let her body move against him, to work her lips over his, seeking new sensations. His breath turned harsh and uneven, and the sound of it quickened Amy's pulse. She had never felt anything remotely like this. Her blood raced through her veins, and her heart hammered. She wanted to kiss Sam again and again, kiss him so deeply that she melted into him. She wanted so much— a thousand things she didn't even know the names of. Her fingers dug into Sam's shoulders, and she clung to him, trembling.

When she increased the pressure of her mouth, it was too much for him. Brody shuddered, and his mouth devoured hers, searching and greedy, pulling from her the sweetness he hungered for. He broke their kiss only to change the slant of his mouth and kiss her again and again. Kissing her was like dying and being reborn, all at once, over and over.

Brody sank to his knees, pulling Amy with him. One hand went behind her head, gripping her tightly as though she might slip out of his grasp. Her hair, damp and soft, was like silk in his hand; he wanted to bury himself in it. He wanted to bury himself in her. His breath rasped through his lungs. Fire exploded in his head and coursed through his body. He wanted her so much that he trembled from the force of it.

His hands slid down to her buttocks, digging in and lifting her up into him so that his throbbing, insistent maleness pushed against the soft, shallow cup of her pelvis. He rubbed her against him, groaning at the almost painful pleasure it brought him.

He kissed her face, and his mouth trailed down onto the soft flesh of her throat, nipping, then laving and soothing. Amy's head lolled back, exposing her throat to his mouth, and her hands roamed over his arms and back, her fingers clenching at each new frisson of pleasure. She lay limp in his arms, stunned by the new sensations sweeping through her body. She couldn't begin to understand and sort them, but she didn't try. She simply let them take her.

Brody found her ear and worried the lobe with his teeth; he traced its convolutions with his tongue and probed inside. Pleasure sizzled down her to the growing, pulsing knot of warmth deep in her abdomen, and she trembled and moaned.

The sound almost broke him. He tumbled back to the ground with her, kissing her deeply, desperately. He had to have her, had to be inside her. His legs wrapped around Amy, imprisoning her against his unmistakable desire, and they rolled across the ground. As they moved mindlessly, their mouths locked together, Brody jerked the buttons of her shirt from their holes and shoved the fabric apart.

He sat up slowly, straddling her, and gazed down at her. She wore a chemise beneath the shirt, a simple white cotton thing with a row of eyelet embroidery across the neckline. It laced up the front with pink ribbon, tied at the top in a small bow. The swell of her breasts showed above the ruffle, soft and quivering. The circles of her nipples were dark beneath the thin cotton.

"Amy." His voice was almost reverent as he reached out and slowly pulled the bow loose. His fingers inched down the center of the garment, slipping the thin ribbon free from its eyelets. When he reached the bottom, he opened the chemise, exposing her to his view. She was slender and pale, her waist impossibly narrow. Her breasts were small, but perfectly formed, high and taut. The nipples rose up from them, rosy and pebbled. The touch of the air against her nipples made them tighten, but his eyes on her made them harder still. He could imagine how they would look when his tongue had teased them into hard points, the deep red of raspberries and glistening with moisture.

Brody's eyes were black and intense, glowing with the passion that thrummed through him. "You are so beautiful."

Amy stared back up at him, her eyes wide and wondering. She should feel embarrassed, she knew—and perhaps she did, a little. But far more than that, she felt a fierce pride in the way he looked at her. He thought she was beautiful; he enjoyed gazing at her naked body. It stirred her own desire to be naked before him. She could feel her nipples growing tight and pointy as he watched her, and that deepened the ache between her legs. She was growing moist there, too, and she knew that it was part of that pleasurable ache.

Brody ran his tongue across his lips. He reached down and cupped her breasts in his hands. Amy drew in her breath sharply, but she didn't flinch. He squeezed her breasts lightly, then ran his thumbs around her nipples. Amy caught her lower lip between her teeth.

Brody was as hot as a furnace, his manhood stiff and pounding. He'd never wanted anything, never *needed* anything, as much as he wanted and needed to take Amy now. Everything inside him screamed to make love to her. He thought of taking her nipples into his mouth, of rolling them between his lips. He imagined opening her trousers and sliding his hand inside, finding her soft, damp heat. He thought of shoving himself deep inside her, of moving with her tight around him. He wanted to take her fast and hard. He yearned to possess her so completely that she would never be anyone's but his.

He bent and touched the tip of his tongue to her nipple. The air hissed through Amy's teeth, and she jerked in surprise. He circled the nipple slowly with his tongue, then lazily flicked it until the small button was hard and engorged. Amy moved her hips beneath him restlessly, further inflaming his desire. Sam stretched out on her full length, pressing into her. His mouth went to her other nipple, laving it with the same slow care. He pulled her nipple into his mouth and sucked at it, and Amy arched up, almost whimpering at the unexpected delight. Her fingers dug into his hair.

He caressed the bud with his lips and tongue, pulling and pressing. Amy moaned out his name, turning her head restlessly, and her legs struggled to unlock his and move apart.

A tremendous heat burned between her legs, and she felt empty and aching. She didn't know what she wanted, only that she was unfulfilled, unsatisfied, and that only Brody could give her what she wanted. She wanted to wrap her legs around him and pull him to her, and it frustrated her that he would not let her move. She bucked up against him, wriggling.

Her unconscious movements aroused him almost past bearing. Brody was aware of little except the thick, pulsing ache of his desire. Only her body could bring him ease. His hand moved down to the buttons of her trousers. The buttons were metal and flat, difficult to undo, and the trembling of his fingers made the process even harder. Sam growled with frustration and sat up, grabbing the material with his other hand to rip it apart.

Suddenly he saw himself as clearly as a picture, as someone who walked in upon the scene would see him—straddling Amy's helpless body, his breath rasping, growling, about to tear her clothes from her body. He was an animal. She was a delicate, innocent girl, and he was about to rip off her clothes and thrust into her as though she were a whore. He was about to hurt and humiliate her, all because of his own savage, elemental desire.

Brody swore and flung himself away from her. Desire clawed at his gut. He wanted her so much it was a physical pain. But he forced himself to walk away. He leaned against an outcropping of rock, crossing his arms tightly across his chest as though to imprison the raging beast inside him.

Amy sat up, confused. She didn't understand what had happened, why Sam had left her so abruptly. Had she made a mistake? She shivered, feeling suddenly cold, and pulled the sides of her shirt together. Her nakedness embarrassed her now, and she hastened to lace up her chemise and button the shirt.

"I'm sorry," she said in a small voice.

"God, no," he groaned. "You have nothing to be sorry for. I was the one who acted like an animal. I apologize."

The words were wrenched from him. But Amy didn't know how rare a thing an apology from Sam Brody was, and she took no satisfaction in it. She knew only that he had stopped doing what she enjoyed so much, and she didn't understand why.

Brody breathed deeply, struggling for control over his rampaging lust. He had to go slowly, he reminded himself. He must not hurt her. Must not rush her. He had to be gentle with her, far gentler than he had ever been.

He straightened. He forced his hands to return to his sides. But he didn't look at her; he couldn't do that, or he might throw himself on her again. "All right. Let's set up camp."

He gathered up their gear and walked back toward the falls, still without looking at her. Amy frowned, her eyes troubled. No matter what he'd said, she suspected that it must have been her fault. She disliked the empty, dissatisfied way she felt. She wished Sam would come back and start kissing her again. She wished he would tell her what was wrong.

She sighed and stood up. She didn't know how to make those things happen. Normally she would have been content to wait and let the matter work out as it would. Amy wasn't one to try to change life. But not this time. She didn't want to wait. She wanted to be in Sam's arms again.

She strolled back to the falls, her forehead creased in thought. Somehow, she vowed to herself, somehow she would get Sam to kiss her again.

Chapter Nine

Victoria and Slater were eager to put as much distance as they could between themselves and the sick evil in the Mileses' house. They simply followed the river upstream, because Victoria couldn't retrace their path to the camp where Dennis Miles had found them. They said little. Neither of them wanted to talk. Slater felt embarrassingly weak, and there seemed to be a hundred hammers banging in his head. Victoria was still numb with shock.

After an hour or so, they stopped and camped for the night. Slater fell asleep instantly, but Victoria could not. She lay awake, hearing every noise. At least there was some comfort in being able to look over and see Slater sleeping only a few feet from her. When she finally did fall asleep, it was shallow, and she woke often.

The next morning Slater was better. The night's rest had returned some of his strength, and his head no longer throbbed. He was still in poor condition to ride, but at least Victoria no longer had to worry about whether he could stay in the saddle.

They saddled up, crossed the river and started upstream again. Slater stayed close to the bank, searching for hoofprints. Twice he found prints in the muddy ground at the water's edge, but there weren't enough for the number of men they were seeking, so they continued searching.

Finally Slater stopped and dismounted. Victoria watched him as he squatted down to examine a set of hoofprints. He straightened and turned to her, the bright glitter of triumph in his eyes.

"What?" she asked eagerly, hope rising in her chest. "What is it?"

"At least four horses crossed here, maybe five. The tracks are too jumbled to be certain."

"It's Brody?"

He nodded. "Unless another group that size rode through in the last few days. It's our best chance."

"Then let's go."

They followed the tracks, riding faster now. Their pace still seemed exasperatingly slow to Victoria, whose desire was to race after Amy as fast as she could. But the trail was old, and difficult to follow on the hard, dry ground away from the river. Often the tracks vanished altogether, and then they rode in the most likely direction, constantly sweeping the ground for another clue to the gang's passing.

In order to make up time, they kept their stops to a minimum, usually pausing only to give their horses a chance to rest or drink. Victoria watched Slater, wondering when he would finally give up and stop for the day. With every passing mile he looked more exhausted and his face lost a little more color. But he continued to ride.

He didn't stop until it grew dark. When Victoria finished unsaddling her horse and turned around, she saw that Slater was sitting on the ground, leaning back against a rock, already asleep. She shook her head, torn between admiration and sympathy. He was a tough one all right—but if he wasn't careful, he just might push himself into a relapse.

She took care of his horse, knowing that it was an indication of how bone-weary Slater was that he had left the animal still burdened with a saddle. Then she laid a fire and lit it. There were coffee beans in Slater's supplies, and Victoria decided to make some coffee; she needed something to spark her up after this day. She ground up the beans in a battered tin cup that was Texas Ranger issue, using the butt of her revolver as a pestle, and boiled the coffee in a shallow tin pan, also part of Slater's gear. She drank it for dessert after her meal of beef jerky and water. It was hot and fragrant, if a little too strong, and she drank it slowly, sitting cross-legged on the ground and watching Slater sleep.

He looked vulnerable and peaceful. There was something about him; she didn't know what it was. But it warmed her to watch him sleep. She thought about him lying on the blanket in his fever, his shirt open, sweat glistening on his brown skin, and suddenly she felt an entirely different kind of heat.

Victoria set down the cup and pulled her knees up, wrapping her arms around her jackknifed legs. She had kept her eyes on him most of the day today. At the time, she had thought she was watching him to judge whether he was too tired to ride. But now, when she thought about it, all she could remember was the way his legs had gripped the horse, muscles taut and smooth beneath the material of his trousers, the way his body had rocked with the movement of the animal. She had noticed the muscles of his back beneath his shirt and his hands on the reins. His hands were big, the palms wide and the fingers long and big-jointed. The backs were lightly sprinkled with brown hairs that gleamed golden in the sun.

She wiped her suddenly sweaty palms against her legs. She suspected that Aunt Margaret would classify her thoughts as lustful, especially if she knew that Victoria kept imagining his hands sliding down her arms, curving over her bottom, covering her breasts. Victoria pulled her legs up tighter, dropping her head onto her knees. She was crazy to think about Slater like this. He was the last man who would ever want her. He thought she was cold, hard, and unfeminine.

She wondered if that was why she thought about him. Perhaps only a man who didn't pursue her could arouse her interest. Or maybe only a man tough enough to go after Sam Brody with a bullet wound in his arm, a man with the grit to get out of his sickbed and ride all day. Victoria thought of his wide shoulders and his lean, powerful body. She remembered the feel of it against hers, hard and strong. She remembered his hand cupping her breast when he was crazy with fever. What was it like to lie with a man like that?

Victoria had never thought much about sex before. But now she did. What would it feel like to have Slater make love to her? What would he do? Would she enjoy it?

She'd never know. A man like Slater wasn't for her, even if he had the slightest interest in her. Which he didn't. If she gave herself to a man, he would be the marrying kind, the sort who'd settle down and work the ranch with her. He'd be a man who wanted to build something and to leave his mark on the land, just as she did. He wouldn't be a roving lawman who'd probably die young and leave behind nothing but a pair of Colt .45 Peacemakers.

And maybe that was what made him so intriguing—knowing that he wasn't for her. He was forbidden.

Victoria smiled to herself at her fancifulness. She was making Slater sound exotic and wild. Alluring. But he was only a trail-roughened man who could shoot better than most and was too stubborn to give up.

She stood up and spread out her blanket near the fire. The movement woke Slater up. He looked at her hazily for a moment; then his eyes cleared, and he smiled wryly.

"Sorry to give out on you like that."

"I'm sure you're very tired. You did too much today."

He shrugged. "The strength'll come back eventually. It always does."

"Would you like something to eat?" He nodded and took the beef jerky she offered him.

He ate slowly, watching Victoria smooth out the blanket. Her movements were graceful and efficient, and he liked the way the narrow riding skirt outlined her hips and legs.

Slater wasn't sure where he stood with her. The last clear memory he had before the fever was of arguing with Victoria and stomping off, leaving her at her own campsite. Practically every word they had spoken to each other had been in disagreement. But she had taken care of him through his fever, and she had saved him from Mrs. Miles's bullet. He owed his life to her, twice over. Something had happened during his fever; they had become allies. He hadn't thought even once today about sending her back. And there was something softer about Victoria now when she spoke to him.

He had had to depend on her, and that was a rare thing. Instinctively, he trusted her. That was rare, too.

He wished he could better remember what had happened while he was sick. His mind was full of hazy memories, and he couldn't distinguish between what had been real and what had been only feverish imagining. He had seen a girl he'd known when he'd been stationed at a Ranger camp near El Paso. What

had her name been? Obviously that hadn't been real, though
it had seemed so at the time. He had thought he was talking to
her, touching her, and she had caressed his naked body. But
those caresses were all mixed up with the coolness of a wet cloth
on his skin. Had that been Victoria?

And there was the memory of riding his horse with a woman
up behind him. He had been sweating, on fire. Her breasts had
pressed against his back, and her legs had curved erotically
around him, cradling him against her femininity. His body
stirred at the thought. It must have been a dream, and yet he
sensed that the woman was Victoria, just as somehow the
prostitute he had seen was Victoria, too.

Then there had been that damned cat. That was a nightmare
if he'd ever had one—opening his eyes to see a cougar leaping
at him from a rock. It had crumpled to the ground in mid-leap,
spurting blood, and Victoria had walked up with a rifle in her
hands. A dream, it must have been a dream. But it had seemed
so vivid, so heart-stoppingly real.

"Did I dream the cougar, or did that happen?" he asked
abruptly, startling Victoria.

"What?" She twisted back to look at him. "The cougar? He
was as real as they come. I'd say seven feet from the tip of his
tail to his nose."

"He *was* springing at me?" Victoria nodded. "And you shot
him?" She nodded again. "You weren't lying when you said
you could shoot."

"My father taught me how when I was a little girl. I'd have
to rest the barrel of the rifle on a fence or a rock. He wanted me
to be able to protect myself."

Slater smiled faintly. "Well, I'm glad." So that much had
been real. Did it mean the rest of it was, too? "I—I don't remember much about the past couple of days."

"You were out of your head with fever most of the time."

"Did we ride somewhere? It's all hazy."

"You rode a little way over to a shade tree when you first had
the fever. Then, when Dennis Miles led us back to his house, we
had to ride again. But you were weaving, so I had to hold you
in the saddle."

Then she *had* ridden behind him. The arms around his chest,
the soft body against his, had been real; they had been Vic-

toria's. Desire stirred in him. That in itself was surprising. He
didn't know where he got the energy to feel anything but exhaustion. "You're something, you know that?"

"Why do you say that?"

"Last time I remember, you and I were fighting like cats and
dogs. But you took care of me when I was sick."

Victoria looked at him quizzically. "What did you expect me
to do? Leave you out here to die by yourself?"

He shrugged. "I guess what I'm trying to say is thank you."

"Anybody would have done the same."

"Not anybody *could* have. You're one tough lady."

Victoria had seen the look he was wearing now before, a
mingling of respect and amazement. She preferred it to other
men's looks of lust or lovesick awe, which she'd also seen before. But this time it bothered her. Usually when a man started
looking at her like that, he stopped seeing her as a woman.

That was crazy, she told herself. What did she want, to be a
silly, simpering girl just so Slater would think she was pretty
and feminine? It didn't matter what Slater thought.

There was a moment of silence, then Slater said softly,
"Aren't you going to say 'I told you so'?"

"About what?"

"The value of having you along on this trip. Remember? You
told me I couldn't do it alone."

"Oh. Yes. Well..." Victoria picked up a dried twig and began to poke holes in the dirt with it. "I wasn't as valuable as I
thought. I put us in that mess back there."

"At the Mileses' house?"

"Yeah."

"It wasn't your fault they were murderers and thieves."

"I never even doubted them."

"They were convincing. At least, Mama was. When she came
up to my room to see how I was, she seemed like a warm, jolly,
motherly sort. I didn't see through her. I didn't dream what was
going on until that kid walked through the door with his revolver out."

"You were suspicious enough to hang your holster on the
bedpost."

"Habit. I've learned how dangerous it is to be far from your
gun when you're a Ranger. It was pure luck that I was able to

get to it before he put a hole in me. He was too cocky, and he thought I was asleep. He stopped to admire my boots—probably wondering how they'd fit him. I was able to slip out the .45 before he got down to business."

"But I should have been more on my guard. I was so glad to have somebody help me. I was scared you were going to die. It was a relief to turn the responsibility over to an older woman."

"And that makes you feel ashamed? Guilty?"

Victoria nodded.

"Hell, honey, everybody gets scared. When I woke up and saw Miles slipping into my room with a gun in his hand, my heart started pounding like a cannon."

Victoria glanced at him, surprised. "You always seem so cool—when Brody's men rode in and took him, when the doctor cut the bullet out of your arm, when you came downstairs, holding your pistol on Mrs. Miles. I've never seen a man face death like you do. So calm and matter-of-fact."

"You're pretty cool yourself."

"Sometimes." She snapped the twig in two and tossed it into the fire.

Slater reached out and touched her hand. "It's all right to be a little weak. When you reach the point where you aren't, you aren't human anymore."

His hand was warm and rough, and her skin tingled where he touched her. Victoria's breath became uneven. There was a kindness in his voice that she hadn't heard before. She remembered his arm around her, strengthening her, when she shook in the aftermath of shooting Mrs. Miles. She wanted to lean against him again and feel the security of his lean, tough body. It was an effort not to. "Thank you."

He shrugged. "Just telling the truth. No reason for you to feel bad."

Slater liked the feel of her hand in his, soft and slender, yet with an underlying strength. He was disappointed when she let go.

He drank a cup of the coffee she had made; then they banked the fire and lay down to sleep. Slater pillowed his head on his arm and looked across at Victoria. The embers cast a glow over her features, turning her creamy skin golden. Her eyes were closed, the long lashes lying dark against her cheeks. She was a beautiful woman. Slater thought that if he felt any better, it wouldn't be easy to lie this close to her.

He thought about the days ahead, and they no longer seemed a dismal prospect. As long as he could keep her out of the way when the shooting started, Victoria wouldn't be a problem. She wouldn't hold him back. In fact, she'd proven herself to be quite a help. And her company would make the long hours on the trail far less lonely. He hated to admit it, but the truth was that he actually looked forward to tomorrow. He closed his eyes and fell asleep smiling.

The next few days were a combination of heaven and hell for Brody. He had never felt as happy and at peace. But he had never been as tormented, either, as sweating and aching with unsatisfied lust.

They were as safe by the falls as they could be anywhere except the hideout, and he was able to relax, to sit with Amy and enjoy her beauty and enthusiasm. She loved nature; she was attuned to everything around her. She climbed into a tree to show him a bird's nest. She pulled him to the creek to watch the shimmering flash of fish or a turtle sunning on a rock. She gathered wildflowers and held them up to him so he could observe the tiny, delicate patterns.

Brody had never before viewed the birds or animals as anything except prospective food or potential enemies. He had never lain on his back and watched the gliding circles of a hawk in the sky, or giggled over a line of baby quail following their mother like little soldiers. He hadn't paid attention to the joyous bursts of color that were the wildflowers, or to the peculiar rosy beauty of the granite rocks, flecked with glitter. Now, with Amy, he did.

He sat with her for an hour, laughing at the antics of a pair of mating birds. He rigged up a fishing pole out of a mesquite branch and sat beside the creek, lazily waiting for a bite and watching Amy jump from rock to rock through the water, her skirts pulled up to her knees to keep them from getting wet. He lay with her on a flat rock, gazing down at a busy prairie dog town. She had an elemental, uncomplicated enjoyment of life that he slowly learned to share. Here, with her, it was hard to remember that there was any other kind of life.

Because they would be there for several days, Brody built a small lean-to out of branches. It was a cozy, leafy home that sheltered them at night and during the mild rain that fell one day. Amy watched him build it and pelted him with questions. He answered them patiently, explaining every step in the process. He didn't mind her questions or the explanations; it was pleasant just to hear her voice and to have her look at him so attentively. But to Amy, used as she was to Victoria protecting her and to others believing that she was too stupid to learn anything, Brody's attitude seemed the height of kindness and patience.

They talked about horses and people they had known. Their conversation wasn't profound, just easy and slow and colored with affection.

Neither of them had ever been as happy.

But as sweet as their life was, Sam couldn't escape the pangs of desire. He wanted Amy constantly. When he followed her across the rocks in the stream, he couldn't keep his eyes off her slender legs. When they sat together talking, he gazed at the line of her jaw and throat and thought about planting kisses there. When they lay side by side in the evening, studying the stars, she was so close that he could feel the warmth of her body, and he wanted to roll over, pinning her beneath him, and kiss her.

He couldn't think straight around her. He wanted to touch her and kiss her. He wanted to stroke her silver-gold hair and wrap it around him, to bury his face in its fragrant silkiness. He wanted to slowly remove each piece of her clothing and explore her body with his mouth. The fire in him never died, just grew hotter and hotter every moment that he was around her.

Amy did nothing to help him. Now that they were no longer riding, she took to wearing the skirt and blouse that Beatriz had given her. The skirt was short, ending just above her ankles, and when she walked he could see flashes of her bare legs. The scooped neck of the blouse left the smooth white skin of her upper chest and shoulders bare to his gaze. She didn't wear her chemise, because its straps would have shown above the low, wide neckline, and without the undergarment, the dark circles of her nipples showed through the material. Whenever her nipples tightened, he could see them pressing against the cloth. The sight was almost as provocative as her bare breasts. The blouse veiled, yet hinted, and the combination set Brody's imagination afire. He couldn't keep his mind off her breasts and how easy it would be to slip his hand inside the blouse and caress their softness.

Whenever Amy leaned forward, he could see the creamy tops of her breasts, soft and rounded, gently trembling with her every movement. At night she snuggled up against him. She often reached out to take his hand as they walked, or laid her hand on his arm as she leaned close to whisper something. Her touches were never sexual. They could have been the touches of a sister or a friend. But to Brody, each one was like a hot brand on his skin.

Every night Amy unbraided her hair and brushed it, and the next morning she brushed it again and wove it back into its neat braid. Sam knew he should leave when she started; he would only end up sick with longing. But he could never summon the willpower to leave. She would run the brush slowly through her hair to the ends, letting it drift softly down. Over and over in smooth, long strokes, she brushed it, and the lazy rhythm stirred him almost as much as the sight of her hair floating loose around her shoulders. In the dawn, her hair glowed golden, like molten metal, and in the pale light of the moon, it was silvery white. He could imagine it in his hands or lying across his chest; he dreamed of burying his face in it. It was like gold, like silk, the kind of hair a man would die to touch. He knew that if he reached out and sank his fingers into her hair, she wouldn't move to stop him.

That was the hardest part—knowing that if he kissed or caressed her, or even began to take off her clothes, she would not stop him. She would blindly, trustingly, let him do what he wanted, not knowing until too late that he would invade her virgin body, that he would hurt her, soil her, frighten her. He had to be responsible for both of them, and it was not something Brody was used to being, even for himself.

There were times when he let the barrier down, when he forgot to guard her against him. One night he had an old familiar nightmare as he slept, and he woke up to Amy shaking his shoulder. "Sam! Sam! Wake up!"

He opened his eyes and stared at her for a moment before he remembered who she was and where he was. Then he threw his arms around her, pulling her down tightly against his chest and burying his face in the juncture of her neck and shoulder. He was slick with sweat, and his heart was hammering, but he felt warm and safe with her. No matter what had happened, no matter what horrors sometimes penetrated his sleeping world, right here, right now, there was only Amy.

She stroked his hair, whispering low, soothing words, until finally his hold relaxed. "What was it?" she asked. "What were you dreaming about?"

He wanted to shrug it off. It was embarrassing for a grown man to be so shaken by a nightmare. But somehow, with Amy, he could not pretend. "A man—a boy—that I shot. We were robbing the Richards Stage Line; it runs from Austin to Houston. It must have been four years ago. This kid was riding shotgun. We put a barricade in the road and ambushed the coach. I hollered to hand down their money box. The driver started to, but the fool boy went for his gun. I saw him doing it, saw him raising it. I yelled, 'No!' All I could think was that it was so stupid, so damn stupid. He had to be a hero. I shot him. I had to. He would have shot one of us."

"Oh, Sam." There were tears in Amy's voice, and she hugged him tightly. "I'm so sorry."

"I remember he looked so surprised, like he couldn't believe he was actually going to die, and he toppled off the stage onto the ground in front of me. He was a kid. Couldn't have been more than seventeen. I looked down at him, and he was so young." Sam squeezed her to him even more tightly. "Ever since then, I dream about him sometimes. I see him reaching for the gun, and I see that look on his face when I shot him. He just hangs there staring at me. And I wake up in a cold sweat."

Amy held him without saying anything, stroking his head and back. It was wrong to kill another human being; it was one of the things she believed in most strongly. Amy hated and feared violence. But this time she didn't think about that. She was aware only of Sam's pain and remorse. It reinforced her belief that he was a good man; a truly bad man would have felt no regret or guilt for what he had done, but Sam did.

Amy rocked him in her arms, laying her cheek against his hair. He nestled his face into her neck. He grew still, his muscles relaxed, and she knew he was calmer. They lay together for a moment longer. Amy kissed his hair. His skin was hot where it touched hers.

Amy smiled. She liked the way it felt when his flesh seared hers. She slid one hand slowly down his back, then up. His back was roped with muscles. He made a funny little sighing sound and kissed her neck. His breath tickled her skin, sending tingles through her. He kissed her neck again, his lips lingering. Amy twined her fingers through his hair, rubbing his scalp. Sam's mouth moved up, slowly traversing her throat until he reached her jaw.

"Oh, Amy." Her name was a sigh on his lips.

He rained kisses over her face, soft little kisses that brushed her eyes and cheeks and nose, returning again and again to her mouth. His hand moved slowly, caressingly, down her body, curving around her breast and gliding across her stomach down to her legs.

Gradually his kisses deepened. Their tongues met and tangled. The sweet warmth burst into passion. Sam hadn't planned to kiss her; he had done his best to avoid it for two days, trying to give her time to grow used to him. But the emotions of his nightmare and Amy's sympathy had swept away the careful guard he had set on himself. He had had to hold her, touch her, kiss her, desperate for the warmth in her. He was ravenous. Closeness was not enough; he wanted the supreme intimacy. Comfort and love were not enough; he had to have fire and ecstasy.

Sam's lips dug into hers, his mouth widening as though to take all of her in. His hand slipped inside the low, loose neck of her blouse and closed over one breast. He'd been fantasizing about doing that since she'd put the blouse on. His fantasies couldn't compare with the actual feel of her cool, smooth flesh beneath his hand, uniquely soft and yielding.

He traced the areola of her nipple with his forefinger, circling in to the center. The fleshy bud rose eagerly at his touch, and he responded by playing with it, first pulling and squeezing lightly, then rolling it between his finger and thumb, or teasing over it with a feather-soft touch. The thick, pebbly texture fascinated and aroused him, and its response to each touch set up an answering sensation deep in his own loins.

His hand went to her other breast, fondling and exploring it in the same way. Then his lips moved down her throat and chest to the quivering top of her breast. Sam cupped the globe, squeezing slightly, lifting it like a prized gift to his mouth, the nipple seductively poised in the center. He paused, his mouth inches from the succulent peak, and simply gazed at its perfect beauty and beckoning sexuality. Desire thundered through him, and he teased and aroused himself by holding back, delaying the pleasure. Finally he bent his head and took her nipple in his mouth.

He did it so slowly, so tantalizingly, that Amy moaned aloud in satisfaction when the wet suction of his mouth closed around her nipple. His tongue lashed the bud with firm, velvety strokes, then gentled into lazy circles. He laved and caressed and suckled; he attacked and soothed.

Passion was thick and molten in him, outreaching his reason. There was in him only one faint restraining force, an awareness that was not even conscious thought, that he had to take care with her, that he must go slowly. There must be no pain or fear for her, and it was only this deep inner commitment that leashed the elemental desire in him.

As his mouth loved her breasts, his hand slid down her body, caressing each line and curve. His fingers spread out over her abdomen, finding the sharp points of her pelvic bones beneath her skirt, and moved down onto her leg. But the thick folds of the skirt impeded him, and he impatiently bunched the material up in his hand. He found the flesh of her leg and moved under her rucked-up skirt. His fingers encountered the thin cotton of her undergarments, but slipped beneath it. Her thigh was soft under his fingers, but firm with muscles, too. His hand spread out, kneading her flesh, as it moved upward. Her skin was hot and incredibly soft. His fingertips touched dampness and then the prickly curls of hair that surrounded her womanhood. A groan escaped him.

Amy stiffened. She had been lying back, floating in a haze of physical pleasure, overwhelmed by the riot of exquisite sensations rippling through her. But when his hand touched her there, it was too startling, too different, and it jerked her out of her sensual daze. She tightened all over. "Sam?"

Sam went still. He couldn't speak.

"Sam?" she asked again.

His hand left her, curling up into a fist, and he rolled away. This time the groan he emitted was full of pain, not passion. "Oh, God. Amy. Amy, I'm sorry."

Amy sat up shakily. She didn't understand why he had left her, just as she hadn't understood it the other night. Was what they were doing wrong? "Sam, what's the matter? Did I do something wrong?"

"No. Of course not."

"Then why?"

"It's me." His voice was rough with disgust at himself. "I pushed you. I rushed you. I'm sorry. I won't do anything else."

Amy looked at him. He was turned away from her, so that all she could see was his back, taut and unbending. "But I—I liked what you were doing."

His breath came out in a rush. "God, sweetheart, don't."

"I don't understand."

How could she? She was too good, too pure. "I was about to take you. If I keep on, I will."

A shiver of excitement and apprehension darted through her. She wasn't quite sure what he meant. It seemed a little scary, yet she wanted it, too. "It's all right."

He laced his hands together tightly and forced himself to keep his back to her. It was all he could do not to whirl around and grab her and smother her with his lovemaking. But he knew he had frightened her; he'd gone too hard and too fast. "No. I wouldn't be able to stop."

"I don't want you to stop."

Her words affected him as much as if she'd drawn her hands down his bare flesh. He thought he would explode if he didn't have her. He hated himself for wanting to take her no matter what the consequences for her.

"Amy. You don't know. What I was starting to do scared you. If I went on, I would scare you more. You're innocent. I— it'll hurt you."

She frowned. "A lot?"

He had to smile a little. She sounded like a child, weighing whether climbing up a tree was worth a scraped knee. "I don't know. I never—" He shrugged. "I never had a virgin before. I've heard that it hurts."

"All women?"

"The first time."

"Only the first time?"

He nodded. "I guess."

"But all women do it, don't they? It couldn't be that bad.
I've hurt myself lots of times riding horses and things like that.
And then it'll be over, and it won't hurt again."

"You don't know what you're offering to me. I'd take advantage of you."

"How?"

"Damn it!" He whirled to face her. "You should have
gentleness. You need a soft bed and a good man, not the hard
ground and a worthless son of a bitch who'll bring you nothing but sorrow!"

They stared at each other in silence for a moment. He hadn't
realized it until he'd said it, but he knew it was the truth. He
had held back not only because he didn't want to frighten Amy
or hurt her. He didn't want to ruin her, and he knew that even
knowing his touch would blacken her.

"Don't say that about yourself!"

"It's the truth." Brody's face was bleak and hard. "We both
know it. I'm wicked. I'll hurt you. I'll ruin your life. I already
have. And if I make love to you, I'll make it even worse."

"No. No."

"It's the truth! Damn it, I can't let go of you, but I won't
stain you with my wickedness. I won't drag you down in the dirt
with me."

He whirled and walked away from her. Amy sat staring after him numbly.

Chapter Ten

It was slow work tracking Brody's gang, but Slater and Victoria pursued it doggedly. The trail was old and faint, very difficult to follow, and Victoria was often amazed that Slater could find any tracks at all. There were times when he lost them altogether, but each time, with what Victoria could only think was some sort of sixth sense, he would eventually pick up the trail again.

When she commented on the uncanny way he was able to find the right path, Slater smiled and said, "It's not that strange. Some of it's dumb luck. The rest is mostly persistence and patience." He shot her an amused, sideways glance. "Not an occupation suited to you, I gather."

Victoria raised an eyebrow. "Are you implying that I lack patience?" she asked with mock hauteur. She didn't know how to act with Slater. She wasn't sure what they were to each other—friends, strangers, enemies? Slater accepted her without argument now, and even indulged in friendly teasing.

"You've been fidgeting all day, like an ant on a hot rock."

"It's horribly slow."

His mouth quirked. "Mm-hmm."

Victoria grimaced. "I know. I know. Patience and persistence. Surely it must be more than that."

"A little more. I know Brody pretty well. I know in general where he's headed. I've been after him for a long time."

"How long?"

"Two years. He has a lot of tricks. He's as good at running and hiding as I am at following. Better, I guess, since he's managed to elude me."

"Why have you been after him for so long?"

He shrugged. "Stubbornness, I suppose. I don't have a particular grudge against him—except that he always stays ahead of me. I was working out of the Ranger camp at Copperas Cove the first time I went after him. He'd robbed a stagecoach line. He lost me slick as a whistle. It got my dander up. I thought I was something special at tracking. After that I spent a lot of my spare time trying to find him. I've set spies on him, paid informers, ridden after him in posses and by myself. He always gets away from me."

"You almost sound as if you admire him."

He glanced at her, startled. Then he gave a short laugh. "Maybe I do, in a way. I admire his skill. He's organized, he's fast, he's smart. He knows how to lead his men, and that's difficult, considering the caliber of men he deals with. He's not as bad as some. He doesn't kill for meanness."

"He kidnapped Amy." Victoria's words were sharp. "And we know what he'll do to her."

Slater's eyes were unreadable. "Some men will risk anything to have a certain woman. He's never done it before."

Victoria's eyes opened wide. "Are you suggesting that my cousin was somehow responsible for his taking her?"

"I didn't say responsible. But you don't go up to a rattlesnake and pet it. That's what she did with Brody."

"Amy has a warm, generous heart. She can't stand to see anyone hurt. She was being kind, and that makes what he did all the more vicious and reprehensible! I'd like to take a horsewhip to him."

"It's possible he won't hurt her."

"Won't hurt her! Why else would he have taken her?"

"Maybe as a hostage. He could have figured she'd be something I'd bargain for."

"That doesn't mean he won't hurt her while she's in his power."

"If he kills her, he won't have any advantage."

Victoria's hands tightened convulsively on the reins. "There are other things—oh, poor Amy! She's so defenseless."

Victoria's distress touched Slater. He wished there was some comfort he could offer her. "I think he might . . . keep her to himself."

Victoria's eyes shot fire. "Is that supposed to make me feel better?"

"It's better than the alternative."

"She's so innocent! If you only knew her. She's never even flirted with a man. She doesn't have the first idea what—she'll be so scared and hurt. I can't bear to think of her in pain."

"I told you, Brody doesn't kill out of meanness, and I never heard of him hurting women. Maybe he'll be gentle with her."

"A man like that wouldn't know the meaning of the word. And how could the—the violation of a woman possibly be gentle? Do you think it's permissible for him to rape her as long as he doesn't beat her, or give her to his men, too?" Heat rose in Victoria's face, part anger and part embarrassment. She'd never had a conversation with a man that touched on sex; she'd never before even said the word "rape" aloud. But she was too furious and distressed to be ladylike.

"I didn't say that! Damn it, you sure know how to twist a man's words. I was trying to reassure you, to give you some hope."

"Thank you, but I'm not a shrinking violet that has to be protected with false hope."

"It's not false hope. It's a reasonable assumption from what I know of Brody that he won't kill her or beat her or let his men abuse her. That doesn't mean that I think it's all right for him to take her against her will. But I don't want you fretting over the worst things that could happen to her. We'll get her back, and I'll get Brody. And he will pay for what he's done to your cousin, just like he'll pay for his other crimes."

"He couldn't possibly pay enough for hurting Amy. She's an angel. She's not at all like me."

He chuckled. "You mean you aren't an angel?"

She shot him a fulminating glance. "I know what you think of me. What most men think of me."

"Oh? And what's that?"

"First, until I open my mouth, they think I'm beautiful."

"You're modest, as well."

Victoria shrugged. "I'm honest. I can't claim any credit for
it. They say I look like my mother. Besides, it's never been
anything but a hindrance. Everyone assumes I'm an idiot because of the way I look." Her eyes met his challengingly. "Isn't
that what you thought when you saw me?"

Slater's mouth was suddenly dry. He remembered his first
sight of her in that dusty brown dress, blue eyes vivid in her
perfect face. He remembered the way his eyes had run down her
body to the swell of her rounded breasts and the narrow circle
of her waist. "Yeah. I thought you were beautiful." He cleared
his throat. "A man would have to be blind not to."

"But when they hear me talk and see me act the way I do,
they think I'm a harpy."

"Harpy?"

"Yes. They think I'm willful, domineering and difficult to
deal with."

Slater pressed his lips together. "I can't imagine why."

"Because I don't act like a simpering fool, which is what men
want."

"Not all men."

"No? I've never met one who didn't. There are two reasons
why men are interested in me: one is the way I look, and the
other is my father's ranch. They couldn't care less about what
I think or say or feel, except that it usually makes them angry."

"Is there something wrong in liking beauty?"

"No. But there's more to me than that."

Slater knew that for a fact. There was strength and courage
and skill in Victoria—and enough hardheadedness for two
people. But he had to be grateful for all those qualities; they'd
saved his life.

Victoria chuckled, but there was something a trifle wistful in
her face. "The rest of me is what makes men run for the hills."

"I doubt that."

"It's true. I scare men."

"Maybe some. There are other men who enjoy a challenge." Heat slithered through him at his words. He thought of
the challenge of taming Victoria, of wooing and winning her in
his bed. He thought of her strength beneath him, of her
toughness turning into soft pliancy for him.

He looked at her. Her eyes were huge, and so dark a blue they were almost purple. They were the kind of eyes that could make a man do almost anything. Slater glanced away. That kind of thinking was dangerous. Victoria Stafford was dangerous. She was beautiful, but she'd drive a man crazy, and she wasn't the kind you could take, then leave.

For once, Victoria was speechless. She wanted to ask him what he'd meant by his words, but she didn't have the courage. Was he a man who preferred a challenge? If any man did, he would. There was a strength in him that she'd never met in anyone else, even her own father. Slater was tough to the bone.

"Besides," Slater went on softly, "maybe you aren't as hard as you like to think."

"What does that mean?"

"I remember you said you didn't care about your reputation, about what people would say if you went off with me alone for several days."

"So?" Victoria turned her chilliest gaze on him.

"So why did Mrs. Miles call you my wife?"

Victoria colored a little. "No doubt she just presumed that was the case."

"Uh-huh. And how come you didn't set her straight?"

"It didn't seem important."

"I see. So unimportant that you took my star off and hid it in my boot. That *is* why you did it, isn't it—because they wouldn't think we were married if they knew I was a Ranger pursuing a felon?"

His voice was laced with amusement, and that irritated Victoria. Unfortunately, she couldn't think of much with which to defend herself. "I was afraid Mrs. Miles might turn us out if she knew the truth. That's all. I couldn't risk her doing that with you being so sick."

"Not because you're worried about people talking about you."

She shot him a fierce look. "They won't say anything to my face. At least, not more than once."

He chuckled. "I'm sure of that."

Victoria recalled how annoying he had been before he came down with the fever. As his health returned, apparently so did his ability to irritate her. She nudged her horse away from his.

She could sense his silent amusement, but she refused to give him the satisfaction of looking at him. She kept her head turned straight ahead and her lips clamped tightly together. They rode on in silence.

They crossed the Pedernales, and it was there, in the damp dirt beside the river, that Slater saw the multiple hoofprints diverge. "Damn. They've split up."

"What? Oh, no." Victoria dismounted and went to stand beside him, staring down at the two sets of tracks. "Which one will we follow?"

"My guess is the set of two. The men headed east, and Brody took Amy with him in that direction. He'd keep her with him, and why take another man along? Besides, look." He went down on one knee beside one of the prints. "These prints are shallower. Probably a lighter rider, like a small woman."

So they followed the set of hoofprints from two horses. It led northward. They often lost the prints, and sometimes it seemed as though only luck enabled them to pick them up again. As Slater pointed out gloomily, they couldn't even be sure it was the same horses, for two horses together were far more common than the set of five they had followed earlier. It was possible they were taking off after a false trail.

When it grew dark, they camped and started afresh the next morning. Almost immediately, they lost the trail they had been following. It stopped at the edge of a rocky creek that fed into the Colorado River. They crossed the creek and followed it up the other side. After a while they came upon a long, rocky shelf of land that would hold no footprints and Slater took it, knowing that this was a trick Brody had used before. But when the finger of flat rocks ended in dirt, there were no prints to be seen. Slater got off his horse and covered the ground inch by inch, ranging in ever-widening circles. There was no sign that a horse had been anywhere near there.

"He's done it again." Slater's voice was flat and devoid of emotion, hiding the rage that swirled in him.

"What?" Victoria frowned, watching him.

"He got clean away. I've lost him."

Victoria was surprised. She hadn't seen Slater grow discouraged before. "Don't worry. You'll find the trail again. You have every other time."

"No. This time it's different. I think we're finished."

Fear leaped in her stomach. "Don't say that. We will find it. We have to."

"Wishing's not the same as getting." Slater swung back up into the saddle. "Come on. We'll travel a little farther up the creek, then head back down."

They traveled both up the creek and down from their original point of crossing, but they found no sign of tracks in either direction. Victoria's fear grew by leaps and bounds. Slater had been so successful at finding whatever scrap of trail Brody had left that she had come to assume that he always would, no matter what. But now, suddenly, she saw all hope of finding Amy crumbling away right in front of her.

They searched until darkness fell and they were forced to make camp. The next morning they crossed back over the creek and traveled alongside it in either direction, hoping that Brody had doubled back. He could find no trace of the passage of even one horse. Finally, in mid-afternoon, Slater pulled to a halt in the shade of a large live oak and dismounted. Victoria followed him. He turned to her, his face impassive.

"I've lost him. The trail's gone. There's nothing to do but head back."

Victoria felt as if he had knocked the wind out of her. "No. We can't."

"We haven't got any other choice. Brody's gone."

"But what about the other times? You picked up the trail eventually."

"Victoria, I've looked for a day and a half without finding a clue. It's pointless to stay out any longer."

"But you can't just go home! You can't leave Amy out here with him!"

"What else can I do?" Slater's face was lined with weariness.

"Keep looking!"

"Where? How?" he barked. "I've checked every square foot of land up and down this river for miles."

"But he couldn't have vanished. There must be a sign of him somewhere."

"He outsmarted me again. Whatever his last trick was, it did the job. I'm sure he didn't disappear, but his trail did. He's gone."

"No!"

"There's nothing else we can do. We'll go to Austin. It's closer, and that's where I'm headquartered. You can send a telegram to your father from there."

"You're crazy! I'm not going to Austin. You may be a quitter, but I'm not!"

Slater's mouth tightened. "I'm not quitting. I'll find Brody."

"When?"

He turned away. Slater hated the look of betrayal and scorn in Victoria's eyes. She had trusted him, counted on him, and he had let her down. After what she'd done for him, he hadn't been able to give her what she wanted. He had failed, and the knowledge left a bitter taste in his mouth.

"When he robs his next bank?" Victoria continued acidly. "A few months? A year? Or maybe two, like you've already been waiting!"

"When I can get any information that will lead me to him."

Had she thought about it, Victoria would have been surprised at the depth of her feeling of betrayal. "I thought you were a special man, someone with courage. With strength and determination. Obviously I was wrong. You're weak. A coward. I'm more of a man than you are!"

Slater's eyes blazed, and he grabbed her wrist, jerking her closer. "That's a good thing, 'cause you sure as hell aren't much of a woman. You're a selfish, spoiled brat who thinks the rest of the world should bow down to her whims. Reason doesn't count with you. Logic means nothing. You don't give a damn about what's possible and what's not. All you care about is getting what you want."

"I care about saving a human being, that's what I care about!"

He uttered a harsh expletive. "And nobody else does, is that it? Just because I don't throw a temper tantrum, you think it's fine with me to have to give up? You think I don't mind leaving an innocent woman with a criminal like Brody! I mind. I mind like hell. It's why I spend my life doing what I do instead of sitting at home, having a family and raising cattle. But I'm not a baby. I don't cry for the moon. I don't fly into a rage when things turn against me.''

Victoria jerked ineffectively against his hold. "Let me go! Damn you! Give up if you want to. Go running to Austin. I'll look for Amy myself.''

He flung her arm away, turning aside with a growl. "Sure, lady, sure. Stay out here and get yourself lost. Starve to death running around in circles looking for tracks that don't exist. That'll do your cousin a hell of a lot of good.''

He strode away from her toward his horse, filled with fury and frustration. He would have liked to yell and pound something. He wanted to grab Victoria and shake her. What made it so hard, so damnably infuriating, was knowing that it had been his own weakness that had slowed them down. If he hadn't fallen ill, they would have been on the trail two days sooner, and it wouldn't have grown so faint and cold. Maybe then he could have found where Brody left them behind.

But Brody had defeated him again. He had failed, and Victoria despised him for it. He despised himself.

Victoria stared after Slater, torn between anger and misery. Why had she been so foolish as to get her hopes up? Why had she thought this man could accomplish so much? Why had she depended on him, when she knew the only person she could really depend on was herself?

She couldn't stay out here alone. Even as she had uttered the furious words, she had known they were absurd. If an expert like Slater couldn't find Brody's tracks, she would never be able to. It would be pointless. If Slater gave up, she would have to abandon her search, too. She thought of Amy, who depended on her, and it tore her heart to think that this time she had failed her cousin. She hated herself, and she hated Slater for making her abandon the search. It disgusted her that she had ever thought him handsome, that she had felt prickles of desire for him and actually wondered what his lips would feel like.

She walked to her horse and went through the ritual of checking the buckles and straps of her gear, just to give herself time to calm down. A few feet away, Slater fiddled about in much the same way.

When Victoria finally spoke her voice was quiet and calm, but as hard as rock. "You're right. I can't do it myself. I will ride to Austin with you and hire the best tracker there is."

Slater grimaced. "No, you won't, lady, 'cause the best tracker is me. And if I can't find Brody, there won't be anybody else in Austin who can. Give it up, and let me find him."

"Thank you. I don't have any desire to wait that long. I intend to get my cousin back, and soon."

Slater's fingers curled into his palm. He itched to take hold of Victoria and force that contemptuous calm from her voice. To think that he'd actually begun to like the woman! He'd even lain awake last night for an absurdly long time, thinking about kissing her, recalling the shape of her mouth and imagining its taste and texture. He might as well kiss a viper. It would be crazy to desire her; she'd lead a man around by the nose.

He picked up his reins and swung up into the saddle. Victoria did the same. Slater started in the direction of Austin, and Victoria followed, riding well away from him. Neither of them spoke.

Brody knew that his position with Amy was impossible. He burned with desire for her, yet he was determined not to touch her. And he couldn't bear to set her free. There was no way out for him.

After he had stopped his lovemaking that night, he had been careful not to touch or kiss her again. He'd done his best, in fact, not to even come too close to her. But nothing had eased his surging desires. Just seeing the sun glinting off her silver-gold hair, or watching her walk beside the creek, or hearing her hum to herself, was enough to send desire rocketing through him. There was nothing about her that didn't make him want her.

It seemed as if she took every opportunity to incite his passion. She brushed out her hair in front of him every morning and night, lingering over the silken, glittering strands until he could almost feel them between his fingertips. She sat close beside him as they talked or ate, and she touched him often—linking her fingers through his as they strolled, or giving him a playful pat on the cheek. Once he had awakened from the depths of a hot and lascivious dream to find Amy stroking his hair.

It had startled him so much to come from the fantasy of making love to her into the reality of her touching him that his hands had gone to her face to pull her down for a kiss before he realized what he was doing and moved away.

The worst time was late one afternoon, when he came back from hunting for their dinner. He made enough noise that he would have thought she heard him coming, but when he walked into their camp, he found her standing by the creek after her bath, wearing only her long pantaloons. Her breasts were bare, white and round and cherry-tipped, and water glistened on her skin.

Sam stopped, stunned. He was instantly, overwhelmingly on fire for her. He wanted to seize her and kiss her, to plunge his tongue deep into her mouth. He wanted to pull her down onto the ground and possess her. For a moment he couldn't move, couldn't think, could only stare and feel the emotions ripping through him like a tornado. His hands clenched and un-clenched. Finally he whirled and walked away.

There were times when he thought he was crazy not to take her. Amy had given him permission. She seemed to enjoy his kisses and caresses; she wanted him to make love to her. Yet he held back, denying himself what he desired more than any-thing in the world because he wasn't good enough for her, be-cause being loved by him would desecrate her. All the men he knew would have roared with laughter at the idea. Since when was Sam Brody a protector of the weak and innocent? Every-one in Texas knew he didn't have a conscience.

Except Amy.

That was the problem. She saw good in him. He couldn't bear to disillusion her, to see the light in her eyes die when she looked at him. He couldn't stand to take her and have her know the weak, wicked person he was. He didn't understand why, but somehow he knew that to make love to Amy would be to open up his soul to her. And there was nothing for her to see there except blackness. It scared him to death to think of her realiz-ing that. In fact, it frightened him worse than death, for that could only happen once, but this would be like dying again every time she looked at him.

So he continued to try to ignore the passions clamoring within him, to stay away from Amy and endure the frustration of the innocent lures she threw out. He was certain they were innocent; Amy couldn't have been trying to seduce him.

In that he was wrong. Amy was trying very hard to seduce him in her own inexperienced way. She was hampered by her lack of knowledge, but she observed Sam and saw when the spark of desire came into his eyes. Then she tried to do the same things every chance she got.

To her frustration, nothing seemed to work. She would have sworn that he desired her, that the things she did aroused his passion. Yet he maintained his cool reserve, not touching or kissing her, holding himself tightly away from her. Though it went against her basically shy nature, she realized that she would have to take things a step further. She had to be more direct.

One afternoon, when Sam was sitting on the bank of the creek, fishing, Amy sat down beside him, drawing her knees up and locking her arms around them. Sam turned his head and smiled at her. It was always a pleasure to have her beside him, no matter how hard it made it to keep his promise.

"Sam, would you answer a question?"

"Um-hum." He looked back at the water, moving his pole a little to give the minnow an attractive wiggle.

"Why does it hurt a woman? The first time—when a man, you know . . ."

His fishing pole almost went into the water. Sam glanced at her wildly, then looked straight ahead. He realized with astonishment that he, who had grown up in the bordellos of New Orleans, was embarrassed to discuss the subject of sex with Amy. He cleared his throat. "Sugar . . . I don't think . . ."

"Please, Sam." Amy leaned closer, putting her hand on his arm. "Nobody ever told me anything. They think I'm too slow. That I don't understand, and that I'll never need to know, anyway. Everybody thinks no man would want to be with me."

"That's crazy. Any man would want you."

"Will you tell me?"

Brody jerked the pole out of the water and laid it down on the bank. There was no hope of his being able to fish now.

Amy's words made the blood sizzle through his veins. "Amy... please. I'm no good. I told you the other night. I—"

"You'll ruin me? If I'm not pure, does that mean you wouldn't like me anymore? Wouldn't want me?"

"No! Of course not."

"Would I be bad if you made love to me?"

"No. You couldn't be bad."

"Then I don't understand. How will it ruin me?"

Her question perplexed him. He didn't know the answer. Amy couldn't be any less sweet or kind or enchanting just because a man had made love to her—even if that man was him. It wouldn't change Amy. Yet he knew that for him to possess her would dirty her. "I'm no good," he reiterated helplessly. "I'm no good for you."

"I think you'd be good for me." Amy reached out and laid her small hand against his cheek. He had shaved every day since they'd been camping there, and his skin was smooth beneath her touch. "I liked the things you did to me. I wish you'd do them again. I want to feel that way again."

Sam didn't say anything. He couldn't. His lungs were suddenly laboring to breathe. His skin was on fire. All Amy had to do was touch him and he was filled with passion. Just her soft, evocative words could turn him hard and pulsing.

He didn't move under her hand. Amy let her fingers glide over his cheekbone and down his nose, across his lips. It stirred her to touch him. She traced the curve of his mouth and smoothed her thumb over his chin. Her other hand came up, too, and moved in the same slow, tender way over his face. Sam's eyes closed, and his lips parted. Amy could glimpse his teeth and hear the rasp of his breath.

Feeling bold and daring, Amy leaned forward and placed her lips against his. She didn't know how to initiate a kiss, had only responded to Sam before, but she began to experiment, kissing first his upper lip, then his lower, finally settling her mouth onto his. Sam made a noise in his throat. Amy put her hands on his upper arms to balance herself. He was as taut as a bowstring beneath her fingers.

She sat back on her heels, uncertain what to do. Sam opened his eyes and looked at her. His face was flushed, his eyes bright. "Please," he said, and nothing more.

"Don't you want me?" Amy asked.

"More than anything."

"I've done everything I can think of to make you kiss me again. I thought it would make you want me, but you haven't done anything. Even when I kiss you . . ."

"You did those things on purpose? Putting your hands on me? Standing so close?"

Amy nodded, and her head dropped. She was unable to meet his eyes.

"All right." He drew a breath. "I'll tell you. There's a piece of skin there—where a man comes inside you." He could feel a flush rising in his face, but it wasn't entirely the heat of embarrassment. Even talking to Amy about the subject aroused him. "The first time, it tears. That's what hurts. That's what makes you no longer a virgin."

"Sam, if you made love to me—" she went on, ignoring his quick murmur of denial "—would you be gentle to me?"

"Of course I would."

"Do you think another man would be more gentle? Do you think another man would hurt me less?"

He hesitated. "Well, no, I don't guess so."

"In fact, another man might hurt me more, mightn't he? Maybe he wouldn't be as careful or thoughtful. He might not feel the same way about me that you do."

Sam frowned. "Any man would love you."

"No. No other man does. No other man's ever kissed me, or looked at me the way you do. Most men think I'm stupid and worthless."

"That's impossible."

"It's true. I'm twenty years old, and I've never had a beau, let alone a marriage proposal. And I've never felt this way about any other man, either. You're special. I know you wouldn't hurt me." She rested her cheek on her knees and gazed wide-eyed at him. "I'd like you to be the one."

She *had* been trying to seduce him. He could hardly believe it. "What about the time I came on you changing clothes? Did you know I was coming?"

Amy nodded again. "I'm sorry. Are you angry?"

"No. How could I be angry with you?" The idea that she wanted him enough to tease him into passion was too exciting, too stunning, for anger. "But that kind of thing could be dangerous."

Amy leaned forward and kissed him lightly. "How?" She kissed him again.

His mouth moved on hers as he kissed her back, and his hand came up to cup her neck. Amy could sense the tension thrumming through his body, feel it in the faint tremor of his hand.

He broke the kiss. "Like this, that's how." His chest rose and fell rapidly. "I'm not the kind of man you're used to. Sometime I'll let go, and I'll—"

Amy wrapped her arms around his neck. "That's what I want." She kissed the corners of his mouth. "Please." Her lips hovered less than an inch from his. "Make love to me."

With a groan, Sam put his arms around her, and they tumbled backward. His mouth sought hers blindly, and they rolled on the ground in a frenzy of kissing. He kissed her mouth, her face, her ears. His teeth teased at her earlobe; his tongue delved into her ear. He nibbled down the sensitive cord of her neck. Amy's fingers dug into his back and arms in a wordless plea, and she pressed her body up against him. His breath came out hot and ragged on her skin, and the feel of it made her nerves tingle.

Her nipples were pointed and hard; her breasts ached for his touch. She thought she would go crazy if he didn't touch them. Then, at last, he did. His hand moved around to her front and slowly down her body, curving over her breast and down her abdomen to her legs. Then, with the same exquisite slowness, it slid back up. He paused at her breast, and Amy's hand covered his, holding it there. Sam smiled against her throat. The fact that she wanted him to touch her made him feel proud and powerful and impossibly hard.

"Sweet," he murmured as his mouth moved over the soft expanse of her throat. "Sweet. Ah, Amy."

He pulled down her loose, wide-necked blouse, exposing the tops of her breasts inch by inch until at last he saw her nipples, deep rose and hardened. He lifted himself on his elbow and gazed at them. With his forefinger he circled one nipple and watched as it tightened. His manhood throbbed painfully at the sight. He felt as if he might burst. His head was sizzling with wild, erotic thoughts; there was no room there for reason any longer. He was pure emotion and need.

Sam bent and ran the tip of his tongue around her nipple. He dragged his tongue across the top of the bud, then lashed it with light, teasing strokes, and at every new touch, Amy's breath grew more uneven. He moved to the other nipple and caressed it in the same way, stoking her desire until Amy arched up, her breasts begging for his mouth. He fastened upon one nipple, pulling it into the hot, wet cave of his mouth. He sucked as his tongue continued its fiery dance.

Wild lights danced in Amy's head, shooting and cracking like sparks. She dug her fingers into his thick hair as though to keep him at her breast. As the tumult of sensations rose in her, she curled her fingers, tugging painfully at his hair. But the tiny pains were only a titillating counterpoint to the storm of pleasure raging through Sam. He nibbled at her breast, rolling the nipple between his lips and teasing it with his tongue.

He sat up abruptly, and Amy opened her eyes in surprise. She looked up at him, blinking, her mind too scattered to even phrase a question. Sam unbuttoned his shirt with fumbling haste and ripped it off, spreading it out on the ground beside him. Then he pulled Amy up into a sitting position and tugged her blouse off over her head. She understood then what he was doing. He wanted to undress her, and he had laid out his shirt as a protection for her from the hard dirt and scratchy grass.

She stood up and unfastened her skirt to help him. Sam sat back on his heels, watching as she opened the side of the skirt and let it fall to the ground. She wore no petticoats under it, only the long white cotton drawers, with their girlish ruffle around the hem. He wet his lips; his heart and lungs thundered like a freight train. Amy glanced down at him. Her cheeks were pink with heat, but she thought only a small part of it was embarrassment. She enjoyed his eyes on her. He gazed at her as if he could eat her up, and his expression turned her insides to hot wax, bringing the moisture of pleasure between her legs. No other man had ever seen her naked; she would have been humiliated if one had. But it wasn't shameful with Sam; it was exciting. She felt bold and powerful.

Amy untied the strings of her undergarment and pushed it down, letting it fall to the ground. She stepped out of it and stood before Sam, utterly naked. His eyes traversed her body slowly, taking in every inch of her smooth, alabaster flesh. He stared at her for so long that uncertainty began to creep into Amy's mind—did he find her unappealing?

But then he said, his voice filled with awe, "You are so beautiful. I've never seen anything as lovely as you."

He spread her skirt out on the ground below his shirt, then took Amy's hand and pulled her down. Amy lay back on the clothing, her eyes fixed on Sam. He was beautiful to her, as well. It was a primitive, masculine beauty, a thing of taut muscles and rough, tanned flesh, hard and enduring. There was a scar across one shoulder, and crisp dark hair dotted his chest, growing down in a V to his navel. Sweat gleamed in the sun on his shoulders and chest. He was lean; she could see the lines of his ribs and the overlapping slabs of muscles. Years of hardship showed on his face and body. But these things gave him strength and power, too, beautiful in their own way, just as a wild animal is beautiful.

Amy reached up and touched his shoulder. His skin was sleek, the muscle beneath it firm. Her fingertips slid across him, feeling the contrast between his flesh and the sharp collarbone underneath it. Sam sucked in his breath. Quickly, he divested himself of the rest of his clothes. Amy watched him, her eyes widening. She had never seen a man naked, and she was unprepared for the sight. She swallowed. He frightened her a little; he was so big, so powerful, so male. She didn't know what to do. He was overwhelming.

Sam sank down on his knees beside her. His eyes were glittering, and his features were sharp and intense. For an instant he seemed a stranger, harsh and frightening. Then he touched her face gently with his forefinger, and his touch reassured her. Curiosity and desire rose within her, battling her apprehension. Amy thought that he would stop now if she asked him to, no matter how much he wanted to go ahead. But she wouldn't ask him. She wanted too much to know, to experience the pleasures that beckoned her, to *belong* to him. She held out her arms to him.

Sam covered her, his long, hard body touching her everywhere. She could feel the prickle of his curling body hair against her soft skin, the curves and bulges of his muscles, his sharp pelvic bones, and, prodding her legs, the throbbing hardness of his manhood. He was heavy, but Amy enjoyed his weight on her. He kissed her, his mouth urgent and hungry. The sight of her, lying there naked before him, holding up her arms to him, had inflamed him past all reason. There was nothing that could stop him now, no thought of hurt or fear or his unworthiness of Amy. There was only desire, raging out of control.

He pressed her tightly to him, moving against her. The hair-roughened skin of his chest abraded her nipples. His shaft throbbed between their locked bodies. His mouth left hers and trailed down her body, loving her throat and chest and breasts, then moving onto her stomach. Amy moaned and moved restlessly beneath him, assaulted by a storm of pleasurable sensations. She ached for a satisfaction she could not name or explain.

Brody's hand slipped down to the juncture of her legs, and this time when he touched the curling red-blond hairs there, she did not jerk away or stiffen. Instead, her legs moved apart eagerly, and his fingers met the slick satin warmth of her femininity. He felt the shock of pleasure all through him. The damp proof of her desire pushed his own passion past the limits. He had to have her now.

He thrust his knee between her legs, moving them farther apart, opening her even more to his questing fingers. Amy whimpered and rubbed against his hand. He positioned himself between her legs and pushed into her slowly, a last remnant of reason making him try to hurt her as little as possible. Amy felt a tearing and a brief spasm of pain, and then he was inside her. She gasped at the sweet satisfaction of it, the fulfillment of his body wedded to hers, and she realized how empty she had been until now.

He began to move inside her. She gloved him with her tight heat, so that every thrust brought a friction so exquisite it bordered on pain. Amy matched his movements, racing toward a conclusion she didn't know, but wanted desperately. She thought she could feel no more, go no higher, but with every thrust he took her beyond where she had been before. He pushed her over the precipice, and she fell with a high, thin cry into an oblivion of sensual pleasure. Her body shook with the intensity of the sensations. Her ecstasy rocketed Sam to his own peak, and he shuddered and groaned, spilling his seed into her.

They lay together in the aftermath, their bodies sweaty and limp, intertwined. Amy was dazed by the sensual storm she had just gone through. She felt like giggling with happiness, but she was too lazy to even move or speak. She thought she would be content to lie there in Sam's arms forever, her body throbbing with the force of his passion.

Brody had never known such peace, such complete and utter fulfillment. Amy was his; she had given herself to him, and he had possessed her sweetness. He was still sure he was unworthy of her, but he wouldn't think about that. He could never let her go. She was part of him now, blood and bone. They could never be separated.

"I love you," Amy whispered.

Sam stroked a lazy hand down her body. He couldn't remember ever saying the words before, but now he did, his voice low and hoarse. "I love you."

Chapter Eleven

When they reached Austin, Slater took Victoria to the Avenue Hotel, and they parted. Normally he would not have thought of leaving an unescorted young lady to fend for herself, but Victoria's silence had been like a hair shirt, exacerbating his own bitter sense of guilt and failure. She had hardly spoken to him since their argument almost a day and a half before. The air had been as chilly between them as if a blue norther had blown in.

Her attitude infuriated Slater. There was nothing more he could do. Victoria was asking for the impossible. She was spoiled, selfish and unreasonable. But he couldn't lose the nagging feeling that he had failed her, that he hadn't been strong enough or smart enough to give her what she needed. He reminded himself that he owed Victoria nothing, that her cousin had gotten kidnapped through her own damn fault, and that if the two women hadn't been there distracting him, he might have been able to stop Brody's escape. But nothing could make him forget that Brody had outfoxed him again, or that Victoria's trust in him had been smashed. He *was* able, though, to work up a healthy resentment of Victoria and her high-handed ways. By the time they reached Austin, he was eager to drop her in front of her hotel and hurry on to Ranger headquarters.

Victoria was equally glad to be rid of Slater. Or so she told herself as she dismounted from her horse and tied it to the hitching post in front of the hotel. There was a lump of tears in her throat only because seeing the hotel reminded her of when she and Amy had been here a week ago. And watching Slater ride away left her with a gaping hole inside her only because it made her realize how little hope she had of getting Amy back.

She climbed the shallow steps and went inside. Eyes turned toward her, both on the street and inside the lobby. Much as she wished she could deny it, the stares made her uneasy.

Victoria went up to the desk clerk. "I'd like a room, please."

The clerk frowned. "I'm sorry, Miss, unescorted females aren't allowed in this hotel. You'd better try a place in the First Ward."

Victoria straightened, and her eyes flashed. "I beg your pardon?"

"You heard me, Miss, now move along."

"My name is Victoria Stafford. My father is Edward Stafford. How dare you treat me like a—a common—"

The clerk glanced significantly at Victoria's travel-stained clothes and windblown hair. Victoria knew that she hardly looked like a proper young lady. She wanted to scream at him. She wanted to burst into tears. Why had Slater ridden off without taking her inside the hotel! Blast him, anyway!

She forced herself to swallow her ire and smiled. This was obviously not a situation she would win with threats or anger. "I must look a mess. I've been traveling rather quickly. An emergency, you see. My father should be joining me soon. I would appreciate it if you could show me to a room now, as I'm rather tired."

The clerk wasn't entirely convinced, Victoria knew, but her smile had its usual effect, and her manner of speech assured him of her status in life. He handed over a room key and graciously allowed her to sign the guest register. His suspicions were renewed, however, when he offered help with her luggage and Victoria was forced to admit that she had none. But she already had the key in her hand, and she walked away before he could try to take it back.

The first order of the day was stabling her horse, and she saw to that immediately. Then she carried her small roll of belongings back to the hotel and slipped up the stairs to her room. It was a small room and quite ordinary, not nearly as attractive or comfortable as her own bedroom at home, but after days on the trail, it looked magnificent to her. She was dusty and weary, and she thought for a moment about taking a bath and lying down for a nap. But there were things she had to do; she couldn't afford to waste any time indulging herself. She had to notify her father of what had happened, as well as locate someone who would find Amy for her. So she just dusted off her clothes and did a quick washup at the basin.

She went down the stairs and asked at the desk where she might hire a man to track someone. The desk clerk looked at her as if he'd smelled something bad, and Victoria was sure he regretted his decision to allow her to stay at the hotel. "I'm sure I don't know, miss," he said finally.

Victoria gritted her teeth and asked him where the Western Union office was, a question that he was at least able to answer. She went there first. Since she had no idea where her father was now, she sent two telegrams, one home to the ranch and the other to the hotel in Santa Clara where Mrs. Childers was staying. She hoped someone at one of those places would know how to reach him.

She ate a quick lunch at one of the chophouses on Congress Avenue. There wasn't another woman in the place, and she was the recipient of several curious glances. It was obvious that the business center of Austin was a man's domain. The waiter was no more helpful about finding a tracker than the desk clerk had been. Victoria decided that the kind of man who could track criminals probably spent his time in a rougher part of town. When she had first checked into the hotel, the clerk had suggested she try the First Ward. Since his opinion of her had obviously been low, perhaps that was where she should go.

She asked the waiter where the First Ward was located. He looked at her askance, but replied that it was south toward the river and west of Congress. She paid for her meal and left the restaurant, then walked a couple of blocks southward and turned west off the main street. There were boarding houses, hotels, saloons and businesses, just as there had been on Congress. There were also homes. But it soon became obvious that the homes were small and run down, and that the saloons and boarding houses were seedier. The looks directed toward her were far bolder than those she'd received on Congress Avenue.

Victoria stopped in front of a yard where a sign advertised that Mrs. Gandy took in washing. A robust woman stood in the yard, busily scrubbing away over a large wooden tub. She was flushed from her exertions, and her salt-and-pepper hair had escaped from its high knot and plastered itself around her face. Victoria was glad to find a woman whom she could ask for directions, and she called out a hello. The woman looked up, and surprise touched her face. She came to the fence, wiping off her hands on her apron. She had washed the clothes of enough ladies to know one when she saw one, no matter what part of town the lady had strayed into.

"Miss, I think you must be lost," she told Victoria earnestly.

"No. I'm looking for someone. A tracker. Someone who can find a missing person."

Mrs. Gandy stared, intrigued, and Victoria went on to relate the whole story of Amy's kidnapping. When she was finished, Mrs. Gandy nodded her head sagely. "That's a terrible thing, him takin' your cousin like that. Well, there's not much goes on in this part of town that I don't know about. I reckon I can help you. Seems the man you're needin' would be Cam McBride. He's a bounty hunter, one of the best. 'Course, he's mean as a snake, not the kind of man you oughta be dealin' with."

"That doesn't matter. All I care about is whether he can find Brody."

The older woman shrugged. "Maybe. Nobody's caught him yet. But Cam's hot to get him. He got away from Cam years ago and gave him a scar Cam'll never forget." Mrs. Gandy drew a long, curving line across her cheek with her fingernail.

"Where could I find Mr. McBride?"

"Now, that I don't know. Hangin' around some saloon or other, I'd guess. Seems to be what men spend most of their time doin', don't it? Try Billy Carson's place. Or maybe Weichert's. But don't go in 'em, hear? Give a boy a penny and send 'im in to ask. They're no place for a lady like you to be seen in."

She gave Victoria directions to the saloons. Victoria went first to Weichert's. Glancing in, she decided that Mrs. Gandy was right about it being a place she didn't want to enter. It was narrow and dark, with a long, crude plank bar and a few tables and chairs. A woman sat at one of the tables, laughing and talking to a man. Her face was painted garishly, and her dress was low-cut. Victoria realized with some shock that she was looking at an actual woman of the streets. She stared so long that it finally caught the woman's attention, and she turned around and glared at Victoria.

Victoria backed away hastily. She found a dirty youngster playing in the street and gave him a penny to inquire inside about Cam McBride. She didn't find McBride at either Weichert's or Carson's, but she learned that he'd been seen at still another saloon, and it was there that she finally ran him to ground.

She asked a passing stranger to go into the saloon for her, and a few minutes later, a tall, thin man walked out of the building and stopped in front of her. He wore a pair of ivory-handled pistols in holsters at his thighs, and in one hand he carried a sawed-off shotgun. There was a long bowie knife strapped to his belt. He had a beard and mustache and long, unkempt hair, all sprinkled with gray. His eyes were the murky color of swamp water, and they gazed at the world with suspicion. His clothes looked as if they hadn't seen water in months. Over his shirt he wore a long, sleeveless vest made of pieced-together animal skins. A scar curled across the side of his face, disappearing into his beard.

Victoria knew he must be Cam McBride. Her skin crawled. She had no desire to do business with this man. Just one look into his cold, blank eyes was enough to make her run in the other direction.

She squared her shoulders. For Amy's sake, she had to deal with him. "Are you Cam McBride?" His only answer was the barest nod. "I've heard you might be able to do a job for me. I need someone to track down Sam Brody."

Life sprang into his muddy eyes at that name. "I been after Brody a long time. What ya' want him for?"

Victoria began her story again. McBride watched her, saying nothing. She wound down finally. There was a moment of silence. "Well?" Victoria prodded. "Can you do it?"

"Sure. I'll hunt Brody for ya'. If I get the girl back, ya' pay me, but Brody's mine."

Victoria felt as if a snake had slithered across her feet. Involuntarily she shivered. "I don't care about Brody. I just want my cousin back unharmed."

"An' what are ya' willin' ta pay?"

"Don't waste your money," a hard voice said right behind Victoria.

She jumped and whirled around, her heart pounding. Slater stood behind her, his green eyes glittering with anger.

"What are you doing sneaking up on me like that!" Victoria snapped.

"I didn't have to sneak. You were too busy cooking up your scheme with this slime."

McBride's eyes narrowed. "Who the hell ya' think ya' are, Slater, talkin' to me that way?"

"Well, I'm not a carrion-eating buzzard like you, that's for sure. I don't make a living murdering people."

"I never shot a man 'cept in self-defense," McBride hissed. "An' I never shot one that wasn't wanted dead or alive."

"Maybe. But you always shot them, didn't you? Did you ever bring one in alive?"

McBride's hand tightened around the stock of his shotgun, and for one frozen moment Victoria thought he might swing it up and fire at Slater. She must have let out a gasp, for McBride's eyes flickered to her. His fingers relaxed, and he nodded to her. "Anytime ya' wanna talk 'thout him around, let me know."

"Mr. McBride..." Victoria began, but the man turned and walked away without a backward glance. Victoria whirled toward Slater, seething. "Now see what you've done! Why did you light into him that way? If you aren't going to pursue Amy's abductor, the least you can do is let me find someone who will."

"I'll give you the benefit of the doubt," Slater said, tight-lipped. "I'll assume you have no idea what kind of a snake Cam McBride is."

"He is a tracker who was agreeing to find Amy for me until you barged in!"

"He's a yellow, back-shooting murderer, that's what he is. He's a bounty hunter, and he brings in men with a reward on their heads. Somehow they always seem to have tried to kill him, and he had to shoot them in self-defense. He kills men for money, as surely as any hired gunslinger.''

"But he's within the law."

"Sure. But as far as I'm concerned, he's not within the boundaries of common decency. He sure as hell isn't the kind of man you ought to have anything to do with."

"I'm not going to a church social with him! I'm hiring him to find Brody."

"Kill Brody, you mean."

"If that's what it takes. Frankly, I don't care about Brody's life. He stole Amy and has done God knows what to her, and it won't hurt me a bit to see him dead. Why all this tender concern about a criminal like Brody?"

"I'm an officer of the law. That means I believe in bringing in criminals and seeing that they stand trial for their crimes. It doesn't mean I believe in shooting them out of hand. McBride ambushes men. He shoots them from behind, or while they sleep. He doesn't give them a chance to surrender. And he won't care about your cousin's safety. If she gets caught in the crossfire, well, that'll be too bad. All he wants is to get Brody. He carries a grudge against him."

"So do you. So do I. So does half the state of Texas, probably."

Slater rocked back on his heels, crossing his arms in front of his chest, and studied her. "So you're determined to run out with him after your cousin. I wish you the best of luck. Maybe you'll come out of it sane and whole."

"I didn't say I was riding out with him. I will remain here and wait for my father. Mr. McBride will look for Brody and Amy."

"I see." An irritatingly amused smile curved his lips. "You aren't going to help him like you helped me."

"He doesn't need my help. He's not wounded, as you were."

"Yeah. I forgot. I'm sure that's the reason. Not because you'd be scared to spend even thirty minutes alone with him."

Victoria glanced away, a blush rising in her cheeks. Slater was right, of course; she wouldn't trust McBride as far as she could throw him. She gazed across the street while her mind raced to come up with an appropriate answer. "You don't have to like a man to hire him to chase down a—"

The words stopped in Victoria's throat. A man had stepped out of the small hotel across the way and now stood idly on the sidewalk, glancing around. He pulled a cigar out of his pocket and bit off the end, then lit it. Victoria knew that man. His face was imprinted on her mind with all the permanence of a daguerreotype.

"Victoria? What is it? What's the matter?" Slater moved closer, his hand coming out to steady her arm.

Victoria drew a shaky breath and forced herself to look at Slater. She didn't want to be caught staring. "Slater, there's a man across the street. Don't be obvious," she warned as he started to turn his head. "He's one of Brody's gang."

Slater went as still as she had. His eyes bored into her, silvery green in the bright wash of sunlight. "Are you serious?"

"Of course I am!"

"How can you be sure?"

"I saw him! I'll never forget standing there watching them ride down on us. And the man across the street is one of them!"

Casually, Slater turned to face the street. The man in front of the hotel looked faintly familiar. But he also looked like hundreds of other men Slater had seen in his life—hat, boots, and nondescript shirt and trousers, weathered skin, unshaven face, a general look of having lived hard. He could easily be a member of Brody's gang. He could also be a ranch hand in for a night on the town.

"I couldn't say I recognize him. But I didn't get a good look at the men."

"Well, I did, and, believe me, he was one of them."

Had it been another woman, Slater would have been disinclined to trust her judgment. She had, after all, been scared, and everything had happened quickly. But he knew Victoria would have kept a cool head, even in the midst of danger and surprise.

"All right. I'll follow him."

"I'll come with you."

Slater shot her a look of patent disbelief. "Don't be absurd."

"I'm not being absurd. I'm going with you."

"You're going back to your hotel to wait in your room until your father gets here to take charge of you."

"Nobody takes charge of me, including my father. And it doesn't make a lick of difference whether you want me to come. I'm going. I'm the one who knows what he looks like."

"I think I can recognize his face now, thank you."

"And," Victoria rolled on, as if Slater hadn't spoken, "I can identify the others, too. Don't you think he might meet them?"

"Maybe. But you won't."

The man in front of the hotel stepped out into the street and began to amble down it.

"I have to go after him." Slater wrapped his hand around Victoria's wrist and squeezed it none too gently. "If you go with me, he'll see us. In case you haven't noticed, you stick out like a sore thumb around here. Ladies don't stroll around this part of town."

"They don't know I'm a lady."

He rolled his eyes. "All they have to do is look at you to know that. Our friend would be bound to notice you sooner or later, and then he'd figure out we were going wherever he was. You'd give us away."

Much as it galled her, Victoria knew Slater was right. She had been attracting stares all afternoon. Mrs. Gandy had known immediately that she was a lady. She sighed. "All right."

"Good." Slater started away.

"But, Slater . . ." He turned back. "You'll let me know?"

"Yeah."

Victoria watched him walk away, then turned and started back toward her hotel in disappointment. She wished she could have gone with him. She wanted to follow that man and see if he met the others who had helped Brody escape. Was it possible that even Brody might be here in Austin? Victoria's heart began to race. After the gang had split up and Brody had managed to lose his pursuers, he and Amy could have turned and ridden to Austin to rejoin the others.

Her hopes spiraled. By following the gang member, Slater might find Amy soon, even tonight or tomorrow. As Victoria's eagerness grew, so did her desire to follow the men. She really should be there, she reasoned. She had recognized the man when Slater hadn't; Slater might not recognize the others in the gang, either. If Amy should be with them, Victoria would spot her immediately, but Slater probably wouldn't. He had only seen Amy that once, and he had been busy arguing with Victoria.

By the time she reached the end of the block, Victoria had decided that it would be for the best if she helped Slater follow Brody's man. What made it impossible was the fact that she looked like a lady. Victoria tried to remember what the woman she had seen in the saloon looked like. Hadn't there been a garish feather stuck in her hair? She remembered that the woman's dress had been indecently low-cut. She could change her hairstyle, but she certainly had no clothes that would suit. How could she acquire the sort of tawdry dress she needed?

She paused at the street corner and glanced down the side street. It must have been fate, she thought, for just then a woman emerged from a small tumbledown house and started up the street toward her. The woman wore a blue satin dress that shimmered as she walked. It was far too short, ending above her ankles, and its neckline was cut in a low V. It was cinched in tightly at the waist. Black lace ruffles adorned the hem and neckline, and her hands were encased in black lace gloves.

Victoria stood and waited for her. As the woman drew closer, she glanced at Victoria uncertainly, and when she was a few feet away from Victoria, she stepped out into the street as though to avoid her.

"Hello," Victoria said quickly, going toward the woman. "No, don't be frightened. I only want to ask you a favor. Well, not a favor, really, because I'll pay you for it."

The woman stared at her.

"I, well, this may sound a trifle strange, but I would like to buy your clothes."

"My clothes?" the woman repeated blankly.

"Yes. The dress and things you have on. I would like to purchase them from you."

"You're havin' fun with me, ain't you?"

"No. Truly. I swear to you, I'm not joking. I need a dress like yours, and I need it now."

"Well." The woman glanced around as though expecting someone to pop out and accuse her of something. "I reckon it'd be all right. Could you come back to my house? I cain't take it off in the street."

"Yes, of course." Victoria followed the woman down the street to her house. It didn't enter her mind that what she was doing could be dangerous. She had always been too capable of taking care of herself to worry about something happening to her. Certainly not in a city with people all around.

They reached the woman's battered house and went inside. An old woman sat in a chair, her chin on her chest, snoring. A baby played on the floor, and an older child watched it from the other side of the room.

Victoria's companion gestured toward the older girl. "This here's my daughter Hazel. My name's Gemma."

"How do you do? I'm Victoria Stafford."

Gemma looked at her for another long moment, then disappeared into another room, shaking her head. She returned moments later with the clothes. When Victoria asked if she could change into the dress now, Gemma gaped at her, but agreed.

Victoria went into the woman's tiny bedroom and quickly peeled off her clothes. She pulled on the blue dress, but she had to call Gemma to fasten the buttons up the back. Then, at Victoria's request, Gemma fixed her hair in an upswept tangle of curls that resembled her own and pinned a clip of paste jewels and a blue feather on one side.

Victoria looked at herself in the spotted mirror above the small chest. Her breasts swelled indecently above the top of her dress. The bodice was so tight it pushed them up; she could hardly breathe. Gemma's cheap shoes were a little too small; her feet would soon hurt. And more leg than she had ever shown anyone stuck out below the hem of the dress, clad in patterned black stockings that looked like sin itself.

Victoria sighed. Did she have the nerve to go out on the street looking like this?

Gemma looked at her doubtfully. "Honey, why you doin' this?"

"I—well, I'm trying to find someone."

"A man?"

"Yes. Maybe you could tell me where I'd be likely to find a man around here." Since she hadn't followed the outlaw with Slater, she would have to find him all over again.

"Well, I go to Charlie Coney's place in Mexico."

"Mexico?"

"Yeah—where the Mexicans live, west of the First Ward." She seemed amazed by Victoria's ignorance.

"I see."

"Charlie runs a big saloon, and two or three times a week he has fandangos—dances, you know. There's always lots of men, and all the girls go there. I mean, girls like me."

"That's where I'll go, then."

Gemma frowned. "Sometimes I carry a little Smith & Wesson with me, in my bag. Maybe you ought to take it, too."

"That would be wonderful." Victoria smiled. She had no doubt that she could protect herself now.

The woman brought the bag with the tiny gun inside. Then she rouged Victoria's lips and cheeks a little, so that she would blend in better with the other women. Victoria paid Gemma, adding more than she had asked for. There was something about the two women and children that made Victoria's heart ache.

Victoria left, and followed Gemma's directions to Charlie Coney's saloon. It was a harder thing to do than Victoria had bargained for. When the idea of exchanging clothes with a "scarlet woman" had occurred to her, she had thought of it only as acquiring a costume that would allow her to pass undetected through this part of town. She hadn't considered the embarrassment of walking along a public street in less clothes than she would normally have left her bedroom wearing.

Every man she passed gave her a long once-over, his eyes lingering on the expanse of her creamy bosom. It was all Victoria could do not to cover her cleavage with her hands. Her face felt puckered and strange beneath the makeup. She ducked down an empty side street and wiped most of it off, but her cheeks and lips were still stained unnaturally pink, and she smelled of the cheap perfume that scented the cosmetics.

When she arrived at the saloon, she stopped outside and peeked in. She saw a large room with walls and floors of rough, unpainted lumber. A bar ran most of the length of the room, and countless men stood at it. Spittoons dotted the floor, and smoke hung like a pall in the air. At one end, a Mexican band played zestily, though it was difficult to hear them over the noise of the crowd. Couples and even some single men danced energetically across the floor. The rest of the room was given over to tables and chairs occupied by men and a few women dressed like herself. Glasses of beer and hard liquor sat on the tables in front of them. Some of the men and women were kissing with an abandon that made Victoria blush.

She hesitated outside the door, her courage slipping at the sight of the rough, noisy crowd. Could she go in there and face those men? She reminded herself of Amy, helpless in the hands of men like these—and worse.

She drew a deep breath and stepped inside.

Brody glanced over at Amy from where he was cleaning the afternoon's catch. She was leaning over the fire to stir the beans. He watched the curve of her hips and the gentle sway of her breasts beneath her blouse. A smile touched his mouth. He enjoyed looking at her, just as he enjoyed the fire it always started in his loins. It was a sweet ache now, for he knew it would be satisfied.

If he called to her, he knew she would come to him, ignoring their supper and everything else. He found it the most amazing thing in the world, but Amy seemed to want him as much as he wanted her. Since they had first made love, they had lain together again and again. Nothing mattered—the time of day, the hardness of the ground, not even the fact that they were being hunted by Amy's family and the Texas Rangers— nothing except their love and desire for each other.

Amy straightened and turned. When she saw him watching her, she smiled. "Hello."

"Hello."

"The beans are almost done. Are you ready to broil the fish?"

He nodded and knelt at the water's edge to wash off his hands and knife. Amy came up behind him and began to massage his shoulders. Brody sighed, and every muscle in his shoulders went limp. "Mmm, that feels good."

"I'm glad."

She often rubbed his shoulders or back. She seemed to want to touch him. Brody had never been caressed with love before, and he absorbed it like the sunshine, hardly able to believe his good fortune. Every time she touched him, or smiled at him, or offered her sweet lips to him to kiss, he felt as though another dark, brittle piece of him broke off and fell away. He knew he wasn't a good man, but somehow Amy made him feel good.

"I've been thinking," Sam began slowly. "We ought to head for the hideout. It's been a week now. I think we've lost them."

"All right." Amy accepted his decision without complaint, as she always did. She trusted him implicitly. Her faith in him was almost a scary thing. Sometimes he wondered how he could ever live up to it. But he'd be damned if he didn't try.

He stood, wiping his wet hands off on his trouser legs. "I hate to leave here," he admitted, glancing around at the secluded area that had been their home for five days. It held memories that he knew he would never forget. He thought of the first time that he and Amy had made love, here on the ground. He thought of lying in the shade with her and lazily watching the turtles sunning themselves on the rocks. He thought of standing naked with her beneath the waterfall, the water spraying over them and Amy's skin slick beneath his hands.

"I do, too." Amy wrapped her arms around him from behind, leaning her head against his back. "It's been like a home of our own, hasn't it?"

"The hideout will be like that, too. You'll see. It's tight and secure. I have a house there, just a shack, really, but at least it has a bed."

Amy giggled. "That'll be nice. I think my backside is permanently bruised."

He smiled, reaching behind him to link his arm around her. "Then we'll leave tomorrow morning." Strangely, there was a sadness in him. In the past, he'd always been eager to return to the hideout and escape from the world. Now it was different. He had known a feeling of freedom here, of hope and joy. They couldn't stay, of course; they needed the protection of the hideout. But for the first time, it seemed less a refuge than a prison.

Chapter Twelve

Remembering the role she was supposed to play, Victoria sauntered across the saloon floor with what she hoped was a come-hither sway and sat down at an empty table. Almost immediately, two young men pulled back the other chairs at the table and plunked themselves down, grinning at her.

"Can we buy you a drink, Miss?"

Victoria smiled with relief. She knew she could handle these two. By her guess, they were young ranch hands in for a night on the town. She dealt with men like them every day and had danced with them at social events, and she'd always been able to keep them in line. "Sure, but why don't you boys call me Vicky?"

They beamed, and one of them went off to purchase her drink. The other asked her if she'd like to take a twirl around the floor. Victoria agreed readily. That would be the safest way to occupy her herself. Plus, it would give her a chance to see more of the people in the saloon. She danced two dances with the boy, who was energetic, if not terribly graceful, and all the time she looked around. By the time she sat down again, she was sure that the outlaws weren't there.

She sipped at the drink the boy had brought her, almost choking on the raw taste of the bourbon, and watched the entrance. The young men seemed happy to dance and talk with her. They paid her extravagant compliments and spoke in a free-and-easy manner that Victoria would never have allowed at home, but they did little more than hold her too close on the dance floor and nuzzle her neck or trail a hand across her shoulder and arm.

She spent over an hour with them before one of them worked up the courage to suggest that they go upstairs to one of the rooms that Charlie rented out. Victoria turned him down gently, and soon afterward they drifted away in search of more willing game.

Unfortunately, she wasn't alone long. Another man, older and harder than her two former swains, sat down beside her, scooting his chair closer to her. "I been watching you. Those pups aren't enough for a woman like you, are they?"

His gaze dropped suggestively to Victoria's breasts, and she had to fight the urge to tug up on the top of her dress.

"Actually, I'm waiting for someone."

"I know. I'm him."

Victoria smiled feebly. "No. You don't understand. I'm meeting a man here, and, uh, I'll be leaving with him."

"We could sneak out and be back before he ever gets here." He ran the tips of his fingers down her chest and delved into her cleavage.

Victoria couldn't repress a shudder. She grabbed the man's hand and pulled it from her dress. "Please. No. My, uh, friend, is a very jealous man."

"I suspect he has a lot of occasion to be, with a woman like you."

He draped one arm around her and bent his head to nuzzle her neck. He smelled of sweat and whiskey.

"No, please. You mustn't."

He made no answer, just nibbled and kissed her neck, working his way upward to her ear. His free hand came up to cover one breast. Victoria pushed it away, but his hand kept returning, touching her breasts and stomach, even sliding down her legs and trying to pull up her skirts. Victoria finally grabbed his hand with both of hers and held it forcibly away.

"What's the matter with you? You think you can tease me and up the price, huh? I'll tell you, girl, I wasn't born yesterday."

"You don't understand!" Victoria snapped. "I'm not trying to raise my price. I don't want you!"

His mouth inched closer to hers. "I bet I can change your mind."

"No!" She let go of his hand and shoved hard against his chest. He was as solid as a rock, and Victoria couldn't budge him. She turned her face away from his questing mouth, panicky now. He was far stronger than she was, and no one would come to her rescue in this place. No one would even notice that she was struggling!

She began to really fight him, hitting and scratching at his face and kicking out with her feet, but he continued, as though her struggles were only a minor nuisance. Suddenly he went still. He released her, his arms falling to his side. Victoria turned her face back to look at him, amazed by the sudden change in his attitude. Then she saw the reason for it.

The barrel of a long revolver was pressed against his temple. Victoria's eyes followed the revolver to the male hand holding it and up the arm to the man's face. She found herself staring into Slater's pale green eyes.

"Mister," he said quietly, "I think you're someplace you shouldn't be. This lady is waiting for me."

Her attacker's face was a sickly yellowish color. "Sorry. Didn't mean to poach."

"That's what I thought. Now, if you'll leave, it'll all be forgotten."

"Right."

Slater stepped back, but he kept the gun pointed straight at the other man. The man rose slowly and walked toward the front door of the saloon. By the time he reached it, he was almost running.

Victoria sighed with relief, her muscles turning to jelly. "Thank heavens you came along."

Slater holstered the gun and reached down to grasp her arms. He pulled her up so that his furious face was only inches away as his eyes bored into hers. "What the hell are you doing here?"

Victoria lifted her chin and tried to return his stare with a haughty one of her own. It was a little difficult, given the way she was dressed and what had just happened to her. "What does it look like?" she retorted, embarrassed when her voice had come out not defiant but shaky.

"Like you're trying to get yourself raped. That's what it looks like." He gave her shoulders a shake. "Damn it, Victoria, what if I hadn't come along? Do you realize what could have happened?"

"I have a pocket revolver in my bag."

"Wonderful. Victoria Stafford—arrested for murder in a saloon, dressed like a common prostitute. No doubt that would have made your family proud."

Victoria flushed, and a saving anger flowed into her, washing away the fear and humiliation of the past few minutes. "Let go of me."

"Gladly." Slater released her abruptly, letting her drop back into her chair. He stood towering over her, and Victoria had to bend back her head to see him. She felt at a distinct disadvantage.

"You're going back to your hotel."

"No."

"Yes—even if I have to throw you over my shoulder and carry you."

Victoria glared at him. She had no doubt that he would, and she was no match for him in a battle of strength. But she had her wits. "And leave the man you're following? I presume you have managed to follow him."

"Yes, I've managed to follow him," Slater mimicked her tone. "He's playing cards about three tables to your right."

"He might not be here when you get back from delivering me to my hotel."

Slater's mouth got tighter, if that was possible. "Then be a good girl and go home on your own."

Victoria smiled sweetly and was rewarded by the flare of anger in Slater's eyes. "I don't think so. I suggest that we work together."

"Impossible."

"First of all, why don't you sit down and stop looking so fierce? You're attracting attention. You wouldn't want our friend to notice you, now, would you?"

Slater's teeth clamped together so tightly that the muscles of his jaw jumped, but he pulled out a chair and plopped down in it. "Victoria, this is crazy. If you want me to catch the men who took your cousin, why are you doing everything you can to get in my way?"

"I'm not here to get in your way. I'm here to help." She heard his low growl of frustration, but plowed ahead anyway. "I can identify him, and also the other two. And, as I told you, I have a gun with me, so I could help you if things got rough."

"You would not help me. You'd be a hindrance. I'll have to watch out for you, not just myself."

"I think I've proved myself in that regard," Victoria said steadily, holding Slater's gaze until finally his eyes dropped.

"All right. I'll admit that you're better with a gun than I had guessed. But that doesn't mean you should place yourself in unnecessary danger. I don't need your help."

"Yes, you do. If nothing else, I'd give you an excuse to be here."

"What?"

"I mean, here you are, trying to look inconspicuous while you're waiting for that outlaw to do something. It could take a long time, and in the meantime you're sitting here with nothing to do. If he were to see you sitting for hours in the same place, just twiddling your thumbs, don't you think it might make him suspicious? But if you were talking and flirting with a woman of dubious character..."

Slater stared. "You never cease to amaze me. I thought it was the limit when you were determined to ride after Brody's gang. Then you decide to dress up like a—a lady of the night, so you can spy on an outlaw in a saloon. But this beats everything. You want me to pretend to make love to you in Charlie Coney's place."

Victoria colored. "Well, I didn't say actually—well, you know. But we could dance together, and we could sit here and pretend to drink and talk and...you know...."

"Yeah. I know." Slater's eyes went to her lips. She had removed most of the rouge, but the scrubbing had left her lips rosy and faintly bruised looking, as if she had been kissed hard. His gaze slid downward to the exposed white expanse of her chest. She appeared to be on the verge of popping out of the cheap blue dress at any moment. It was so tight that her nipples were visible against the satiny material. Her breasts were shoved upward, luscious, quivering white mounds, pressed together and almost spilling out of the neckline.

It wouldn't be any problem to kiss and caress her as if he wanted to persuade her into his bed. The problem would be stopping.

Victoria felt Slater's gaze all through her. She thought about him holding her as the other man had, thought about his lips nibbling at her neck, his hand caressing her breast. She was suddenly hot, her mouth dry and her hands sweaty.

Slater sighed. "Sometimes I wonder if you really have a father. I think you must be the Devil's spawn."

"Does that mean you agree to my plan?"

"I must be insane, but yes, I'll agree." He pointed a forefinger at her warningly. "As long as you agree to get out of sight if things get nasty."

"Like a good little woman?" Victoria simpered, the gleam in her eyes spoiling her imitation of a vapid girl. "Why, of course. What else would I do?"

Slater didn't believe her for a moment, but, as usual where she was concerned, there was nothing he could do. He couldn't force her to leave without calling attention to himself, and that was the last thing he wanted. Even if he did manage to haul her out of here without his quarry getting suspicious, the man might be gone by the time Slater returned.

He decided to accept defeat with as much grace as he could. "Let's dance." He grabbed Victoria's hand and led her out to the dance floor.

A waltz was playing, and Victoria was surprised to find that Slater guided her around the floor as gracefully as if they'd been in a ballroom. It was strange to stand so close to him as they moved to the music, to feel his hand on her waist and his other hand curled around hers, to be in his arms. Except for when she had held him while he shivered with feverish chills, she had never been this close to him. Her arm lay against his; her hand rested on his shoulder. She could feel the warmth of his body, the tightness of his muscles. His strength was intimidating, but the flutter in her stomach wasn't of fear. A woman wanted a strong man, she thought—both physically and mentally. Slater was the first man she'd met who was as strong as she was.

The thought flustered her. Slater was *not* a man to whom she could give her heart. It was ridiculous, impossible. He thought of her as a nuisance, an annoyance. To distract herself from her thoughts, Victoria tried to start up a conversation. "You dance well."

"You sound surprised."

"A little."

"Contrary to popular opinion, I was not born on a horse with a pistol in each hand."

Victoria smiled. "That's a relief to know. Where *were* you born?"

"In a bed in a house," he teased her, and his teeth flashed beneath the thick brush of his mustache. Victoria noticed that he had a wicked smile. She thought that under normal circumstances Slater would be what her friend Daphne termed a heartbreaker.

She dug her fingers into his shoulder, and his grin widened. "Stop. I yield. I grew up on a ranch in South Texas, not far from Corpus Christi. My mother actually managed to drill some etiquette into me—as well as a few dance lessons."

"Do your parents still live there?"

The amusement died out of his face. "No. They're both dead."

"I'm sorry."

He shrugged. "My father was killed in the war, and Mama was lonely without him. It's probably better that she went, too."

"Do you still have the ranch?"

"Yes. I tried living there after the war, but it didn't work out. I was too restless."

"So you just left it?"

He nodded.

"I can't imagine that."

"Why not?"

"Daddy's land is so much a part of my life. It will be mine after Daddy dies, and someday it will be my children's. It's like a trust, something that's given to you for a few years to love and take care of. I think I'd die if I had to move away from it, if I had no home."

"It's easier for some of us. The war changed me. I couldn't settle down." He paused, then said, "I was with Hood's Texans. Half my company was killed before the war was over. Some were boys I'd known all my life. Four of us joined up together. I was the only one who came out of it whole. You know, I've probably killed three times the number of men Sam Brody has."

He stopped abruptly and led her from the floor. Victoria went with him without protest, her heart pierced by sympathy. Slater seated her at a table, then walked over to the bar to buy a beer. Victoria glanced at the table where their quarry sat. He was engrossed in a card game. The pile of money in front of him was smaller than the other men's, and she had the impression that he was losing.

Slater sat down beside her and took a quaff of his beer. "Sorry to wax so melancholy."

"It's a sad thing. My father was in the war, but he never talks about it."

"It's not much to talk about." He smiled at her. "Come on, don't pull such a long face. We don't look much like a couple spooning."

Victoria smiled back. "Is that what you call it?"

"In this context, no. But what I *would* call it is something I can't say in front of you."

"I thought you were convinced I wasn't a lady."

"No. I'm convinced that you're insane. But no doubt genteelly so."

She giggled. Slater pulled his chair up against hers. He looped his arm around her shoulders, pulling her nearer and lowering his head until it almost touched hers. "Is this sufficiently loverlike?"

"Yes, I think so." Victoria's voice was stifled. She was inordinately aware of his nearness. She could smell the scent of his shaving soap and see the texture of his weather-roughened skin. He was so close that she could also see that his eyes were pure green, without a fleck of gold in them, and his golden brown lashes were thick, giving his eyes a heavy, slumberous look. His breath skimmed her face, and it sent shivers through her.

Sitting this way, Slater had little choice but to look straight down her dress at the swelling globes of her breasts. That dress ought to be illegal, he decided, at least on Victoria. He was surprised she hadn't been raped on her way over here. She was more temptation than most men could bear. Slater wasn't at all sure how much *he* could stand.

His hand itched to slip down and cup her breast in his palm. He thought about sliding his hand down the slick material of the dress, running it over her breasts and stomach and legs. He wondered what she wore beneath the dress—probably the demure white cotton of a lady. The thought was almost unbearably enticing. Lord, he was growing hard just sitting this close to her.

"He's leaving the table," Victoria whispered.

"What?" It took a moment for it to register on Slater that she was talking about the man from Brody's gang. "Oh. Where's he going?"

"He's coming this way." Victoria gazed earnestly up into his face. Her lips were only inches away. "Shouldn't we look convincing?"

"Yeah." He laid his hand against her cheek. His thumb brushed her velvety skin. "I'm going to kiss you. Don't draw back."

"I won't." Victoria's heart was hammering in her chest. She wouldn't have dreamed of drawing back from his kiss.

He lowered his head the short distance that separated them, and his lips touched hers. At first he just held his mouth against her lips, pretending to kiss her. Then he made an unintelligible noise, and his mouth moved against hers, soft and questing, gently initiating her into pleasure. For a moment Victoria simply sat stiffly. It was strange and disquieting to be kissing a man in the middle of a crowd of people. But as Slater's lips continued to work on hers, arousing a host of tingling sensations she had never before experienced, Victoria's hands crept up to encircle his neck.

Slater raised his head, releasing her mouth. "Where is he?"

"Who? What? Oh." Reluctantly Victoria turned her head. "There. At the bar. He's looking around and drinking a glass of beer." She moistened her lips. "Are we going to continue— I mean, pretend to—"

He answered her by kissing her again. His tongue traced her lips, startling her. She froze for a moment, but then, as he continued to trace the line between her lips with his tongue, she relaxed. Her lips parted, and his tongue probed inside. No man had tried to kiss her this way, and she was shocked. She was also pulsing with excitement. His tongue filled her mouth; it teased and stroked and explored. Great shivers of desire ran down through Victoria and burst in her abdomen. She pressed up into Slater, tightening her hold around his neck and pressing her lips against his. When at last his mouth left hers, she made a soft noise of protest at the loss.

Slater stared down at her, trying to collect his scattered thoughts. His chest rose and fell in deep, uneven breaths. Damn, but she was beautiful! Victoria's head was tilted back, her eyes closed. Her lips were a deep rose color, moist and softly swollen from his kisses. There was an expression of bemused pleasure, almost wonder, on her flawless features. She was the picture of a woman lost in the throes of sensual pleasure. His gut tightened. He wanted her far more than was safe.

Victoria's eyes fluttered open, and she gazed at him in puzzlement and regret. "Slater?"

It was time to stop playing with fire, he knew. He should draw back. Instead, he pulled her over onto his lap. His arm went behind her back to support her, and Victoria leaned against his chest.

"It'll be easier for me to keep an eye on him this way," Slater explained, but his hand stroked her cheek and his eyes gleamed down at her in a way that had little to do with practicality.

Victoria had seen desire in men's eyes before, but it had never been this raw or this fierce. And it had never sparked an answering fire inside her as Slater's desire now did. She raised her hand to his face. Lightly, her fingers traced the line of his cheekbone. He was so handsome. His skin was rough against her fingertips; touching it made her tingle. She ran her forefinger over the brush of his mustache; it was far softer than it looked. Victoria remembered the way it had felt when he kissed her. Her lips parted slightly; it was growing more difficult to breathe. Her finger slid down to his chiseled lips, following the curve of each one. She could feel Slater's chest rising and fall-

ing rapidly against her side, and she knew that he wasn't unaffected by her touch. Her finger brushed back across his lips.
She wanted to taste them again.

Slater's eyes were piercing, the bright green of sun-washed
leaves. They held her as his face moved slowly, steadily downward, until finally she closed her eyes and sighed with satisfaction as his mouth fastened on hers. His kiss was long and slow
and hard. His tongue played in her mouth. When Victoria's
tongue came forth to meet it, a shudder ran through him, and
his arm squeezed her more tightly to him. She could hear his
labored breath, and the sound sent tendrils of heat through her
body. Slater's mouth widened on hers, and he kissed her as
though he would consume her. His hand plunged into her hair,
destroying the artful curls that Gemma had put there. He
stroked the silken strands and bunched them in his hand,
wanting to caress and grab, all at the same time.

He left her mouth, trailing kisses like fire across her cheek
and up to her ear. He nibbled at its lobe and his tongue traced
its delicate whorls. Victoria moaned softly, and her hands
moved restlessly over the front of his shirt. Slater bent her back
over his arm, and Victoria let her head fall back, exposing the
long white column of her throat. His mouth moved vora-
ciously down it.

Neither of them remembered the man at the bar. In fact,
neither was aware of the roomful of people around them. They
could have been on the steps of the Capitol at noon for all they
knew, so wrapped up were they in a haze of hot, driving pleasure.

Slater's hand slipped down Victoria's neck and shoulders and
curved around her breast. Her nipple thrust out against the
soft, slick material of her dress, and his thumb circled it. His
mouth moved lower until it reached the quivering tops of her
breasts. He nuzzled into her cleavage. He ached to see her
breasts. He yearned to hold them in his hands, to kiss them, to
pull the nipples into his mouth and make them harden and
lengthen.

Victoria bent over Slater's head, her hands clenching in his
hair. She had never felt anything like his lips on her flesh. She
was dazed by the bombardment of her senses. Her skin was on
fire, and wild sparks shot out from wherever he kissed her. The

heat he created collected low in her abdomen, growing steadily, and the soft feminine place between her legs was suddenly moist and aching. It didn't seem proper to have that dampness there. But then, there was nothing proper about anything that she was doing right now. And she was enjoying it thoroughly.

This was the lust her Aunt Margaret had warned her about. The things she had thought and felt about Slater earlier and had termed lust paled in comparison. This was something wild and rampant. Dangerous. But danger had always had an allure for Victoria. She was rarely afraid—or, rather, if she was, it only made the pleasure more intense. And this was the most intense pleasure she had ever felt. It was dazing, overwhelming—but she wasn't about to cry "stop."

"Sweetheart," she heard Slater murmur against her heated skin. "Victoria. Victoria." His voice shook as he said her name in a way that started a throbbing between her legs.

"Slater," she answered breathlessly, burying her face in his hair and kissing him over and over. She wriggled on his lap, seeking to ease the ache.

Slater groaned, and his hands went to her hips, pushing her down hard and rubbing her against him. She was intensely aware of the hard length of flesh beneath her bottom, growing and pulsing. She realized what it must be, and she blushed. But despite her embarrassment, the empty ache low in her abdomen increased.

"I'm about to explode!" he muttered, and buried his face in the crook of her neck. His breath gusted against her skin; his hands trembled slightly on her hips. He waited, willing the storm of passion in him to subside. He couldn't make love to Victoria right here. They would have to go to— Good Lord, what was he thinking! He couldn't make love to her anywhere. His brain began to clear. Victoria was an unspoiled girl, a lady, not some tart. She was under his protection. Moreover, he had a job to do. How could he have so easily forgotten all reason and duty?

Slater groaned and lifted his head. "Oh, God. Victoria. I'm sorry."

"What?" She stared at him, aghast. "Are you stopping?"

Her face fell so ludicrously that Slater almost chuckled despite his own frustration. "Yes. I'm stopping. I was practically making love to you right here in a saloon." He turned to look at the bar. He spat out an expletive. "He's gone."

"Who?"

"The man we were supposed to be watching!" Slater's eyes began to search the room.

"Oh, no." Victoria remembered guiltily what they had set out to do, then had promptly forgotten in the heat of their kisses. She, too, began to look wildly around the room.

Finally, Slater spotted him and let out a breath of relief. "Thank God. There he is, talking to two men."

Victoria followed Slater's gaze. She stiffened. "Those are the other men in the gang."

"What? Are you sure?"

"I'm positive. I saw them clearly. Look, see how the younger one is favoring his arm? You shot one of them."

Slater smiled down at her. "You have a good eye."

"I told you so. Now maybe you'll believe me."

"It's not a question of not believing you." He continued to gaze into her eyes, and unconsciously his hand rubbed over her back. Victoria arched against him, like a cat being stroked, and her eyes fluttered closed. Slater drew in his breath sharply, and pulled his hand away. "Damn it." He put his hands at her waist and lifted her from his lap, plopping her back down in her own chair. "We can't continue this."

"I know." Victoria kept her eyes averted. He was right. However much his caresses made her tingle, or yearn for him to kiss her again in that ravenous way, she was fully aware of how foolish it was. He desired her, but desire wasn't enough. When they rescued Amy, he would return to his own life, and Victoria would return to hers. She would never see him again. It would be sheer folly to give her body or her heart to him. "But what will we do about—our act?"

"Sit together. Have a drink or two. Talk and laugh. Dance. Anything else is too dangerous."

Victoria nodded. She continued to stare down at the table in front of her, tracing a pattern in it with her fingernail. Slater fixed his eyes on their quarry. Neither of them noticed the disreputable-looking man who came up to their table until he spoke, "Well, well, well. If it ain't my old friend, Slater." Victoria and Slater turned to look at him. It was the bounty hunter Victoria had tried to hire earlier that day. He stood in front of their table.

Slater stared right through him. "You're playing a little fast and loose with the term 'friend,' McBride."

A sarcastic smile snaked across McBride's face. "You're sure unfriendly, Slater. What'd I ever do to you?"

"Your very existence is an affront to the concept of law and order."

"That's a funny way to look at it, seein' as how I catch crooks, same as you."

Victoria thought that the look Slater shot him would have frozen fire but McBride seemed unaffected. "Don't compare yourself to me, McBride."

McBride glanced around. "Seems funny, such a virtuous law-lovin' man like you sittin' around in a saloon. I woulda reckoned you'd be out tryin' to catch Brody. Seein' as how he gave you the slip and all. But instead, here you are, enjoying the pleasures of a drink and a pretty woman just like—" His eyes flickered over Victoria as he spoke. He stopped and stared at her. His eyebrows shot up. "Well, now, ain't this somethin'? That fancy young lady that was tryin' to hire me to find Brody is now a whore, working in Coney's Saloon. Don't often see a switch like that, and in such a short time, too."

Victoria glanced nervously at Slater. Slater was expression-less.

"Well, I guess you must have your reasons." McBride's eyes traveled around the room. "You wouldn't mind if I sat down with you a spell."

"Yes, I would." The two men gazed at each other for a moment, then McBride shrugged. He tipped his hat to Victoria and strolled away. Victoria watched him take a seat at a table near the door, his back to the wall. Crossing his arms, he watched Victoria and Slater.

Victoria turned to Slater. "He suspects something. What are we going to do?"

"Nothing we can do, except try to make sure that he doesn't catch on to which men we're watching."

"I wish I had never spoken to that man!"

Slater gave her an eloquent look, but said nothing. Victoria grimaced. "I didn't know what he would be like! I just wanted to find Amy."

"I didn't say anything."

"I know. But you thought it."

He shrugged. "There's no point in exchanging recriminations. All we can do is wait for Brody's men to leave, and follow them—without McBride following us. I'll be damned if I'll let that vulture come in and snatch Brody from us."

"You hate him worse than Brody, don't you?"

"I told you, Brody doesn't kill for pleasure. McBride does. One time I saw a corpse that McBride brought in. It was obvious that he didn't die easily or quickly—or in self-defense."

Victoria swallowed the gorge that rose in her at the picture Slater created. "I'm sorry."

"I said there's no point in apologies." He reached out and brushed his knuckles down her cheek. "But I wish you had believed me. Trusted me."

Something tightened painfully in her chest. "Slater..."

"I'll get him for you, Victoria. I swear it."

"I believe you."

"Good." For a moment she thought he was going to kiss her again, but he didn't.

The next three hours were some of the most difficult Slater had ever spent. He had to lean close to Victoria, his arm around her, laughing and talking, maintaining the appearance of a man enjoying the company of a loose woman. It was hard to be so close to her, to gaze at her beauty, and not bend down to kiss her again. He could remember far too well the taste of her mouth on his and the smooth swell of her breast in his palm. He wanted to taste her again, to touch her again. He couldn't keep his eyes off the deep décolleté of her gown. Half the time he could think of nothing but burying his face between her full, milk-white breasts.

Dancing with her was even worse, for then he had to hold her close to him. Her soft breasts pressed against his chest, and her thighs brushed his legs. His hand on her back too often strayed to her side or down to the curve of her buttock. He couldn't stop imagining her without clothes and with her hair down. He knew that she must feel the rigid proof of his hunger pressing into her abdomen.

After a time, one of the men disappeared upstairs with a woman. "Where's he going?" Victoria whispered anxiously. "Shouldn't we follow him?"

Slater shook his head. "No. He'll return. This is the only way out."

"What's up there?"

He glanced at her, and there was a flash of heat in his eyes that sent excitement rippling through her. "Rooms. With beds."

Victoria stared at him blankly for a moment before the meaning of his words sank in. "Oh." Pink tinged her cheeks. "You must think I'm awfully naive."

"You're a lady. Ladies don't know about dance halls and the rooms upstairs."

"I imagine they guess something about them when their husbands spend their time there," Victoria retorted tartly.

"That's something else you shouldn't know about."

She made a face, and Slater smiled. He liked talking with her—or at least he would have, if desire weren't clawing at his gut. Victoria was an engaging mixture of lady and hoyden, without the simpering dullness of so many women who'd been brought up "properly." She had fire and ginger, as well as beauty and refinement.

As he had predicted, the man returned, and shortly after that, all three of Brody's men started toward the front door. Slater grasped Victoria's arm and pulled her from her chair, bending his head to whisper, "Look like we're following that man going through the door right now. Our friends are leaving, and I want to fool McBride."

To his intense relief, Victoria didn't make a murmur of protest, but hurried toward the door with him, not once glancing back at their real quarry. When they reached the street outside, Slater hustled her around the corner of the building into a dark alleyway. They waited. After a moment McBride strode by, his eyes fixed on the man Slater had pretended to follow. Not long after, the three men they sought strolled by, weaving a little and laughing drunkenly.

Slater took Victoria's hand, and they hastened down the street after the men. They followed them out of "Mexico" into the streets of the First Ward, where they turned in at a shabby hotel. Victoria and Slater followed them inside.

Slater paid for a room, demanding one on the second floor overlooking the front entrance. They climbed the stairs to their room and went inside. It was dark, but Slater found an oil lamp and lit it. Victoria looked around the room.

"You should have left it dark," she commented dryly.

The room was small and dingy. There were no curtains, and the paint on the walls had long since faded to a nondescript color. Victoria's eyes went to the bed. It was narrow and lumpy. She swallowed. Until now she hadn't thought of the implications of their staying close to the outlaws. She glanced at Slater.

"Don't look at me like that." His smile was tight and brief. "The bed is yours. I'll sleep in the chair by the window."

"No. You won't be able to sleep in that."

"It doesn't matter. I've slept on worse. Besides, I have to wake up early in the morning to keep watch. I don't imagine our friends will get a bright and early start, but I can't take any chances."

"That's all the more reason you should get a good rest while you can. You take the bed, and I'll sleep in the chair. Then, in the morning, we can switch."

"No."

"Why not?"

"Contrary to your opinion, I was raised to be a gentleman."

"Slater, be reasonable."

"I am. This is what's reasonable. Unless you'd like to return to your hotel?"

"No! I couldn't possibly go back there this late at night, especially looking the way I do. They already think I'm rather shady. They only let me in because I said my father would be joining me."

"Then I suggest you lie down on that bed and let me get some sleep tonight."

"All right." Victoria turned down the bedspread. There was a yellowed sheet on top of the mattress, but there was no top sheet, only the bed cover. "Do you suppose these are clean enough to sleep on?"

"Depends on how tired you are, I guess." Slater flopped down in the chair. It was not soft and comfortable. "Could I have one of those pillows?"

"Of course."

Slater pulled off his boots, sighing with satisfaction as he stretched out his legs and wriggled his toes. Victoria had seen her father do exactly the same thing a thousand times. It was an endearingly familiar masculine gesture, but an intimate one, as well. She had seen Slater remove his boots before; she'd even taken them off herself when she'd put him to bed at the Mileses' house. But this was different. Then she hadn't been dressed as she was, and they hadn't been kissing as they had earlier this evening. Tonight, watching Slater kick off his boots started a warm, melting sensation in her abdomen.

Victoria picked up one of the pillows and handed it to him. He reached out to take it, and their eyes met. They both glanced away quickly. Victoria laced her fingers together and stared down at them.

"Uh, Slater. I—I can't sleep in these clothes. The dress is far too tight."

"Then take it off." He thought of the implications of her sleeping only a few feet away from him in nothing but her underthings, and the coil of desire in him wound tighter.

"I can't—in front of you."

Slater stood and ostentatiously turned his back. He heard the rustle of her net petticoats as she slipped them off. He could think of nothing but how she must look stripping off her clothes. She couldn't have worn anything under the top of that dress. When she unfastened it, her breasts would spill out, freed from their confinement. He thought of their ruby tips at last bared to his sight. He crossed his arms. How much more of this could he take?

"Slater?" Victoria's voice was tentative and tinged with embarrassment. "I hate to ask you, but there are some hooks in the back that I can't reach. Do you—would you mind?"

He pivoted slowly. She was standing beside the bed. She had taken off her shoes, stockings and black net petticoats, and those garments lay piled on the bed. Her dress was undone at the top and down as far as she could reach in the back, and the straps sagged off her shoulders. She held up the front of the dress with both hands, but her creamy shoulders and part of her back were bare.

Slater's mouth went dry. He walked over to her and stood for a moment, gazing down at her back. Her head was bent forward. Slater ached to kiss the nape of her neck. He reached down and unfastened the hooks, his hands clumsy. There was a tiny mole on one of her shoulder blades, and Slater thought about kissing that, too. He imagined that the woman who usually wore this dress had put the fastenings in the back so that her customers could have the pleasure of undoing them. But it was a painful pleasure for him to brush his fingertips against her skin, seeing it revealed inch by inch under his hands, and know that he would have to turn away and sleep in a chair, alone.

When he was done, Slater walked away quickly and pulled his boots back on. "I—uh, I think I'll take a stroll outside. Smoke a cigar. Then you can have some, uh, privacy."

"Thank you." Victoria's voice was muffled. She didn't turn to look at him. Her dress hung open, baring almost her entire back. Slater thought about running his hand down her spine. He hurried out of the room.

Victoria was grateful that Slater had left her alone. All the time he had been turned away, pointedly not watching her undress, she had imagined him watching her. The idea had made her nipples harden and her blood begin to race. Then, when he had undone the fastenings on her dress and she had felt his callused fingers against her flesh, it had been almost more than she could bear. She had wanted to turn to him and let her dress fall to the floor. She'd wanted to put her arms around his neck and ask him to kiss her. She thought he would have. Surely even Slater didn't have that much control.

It was better, far better, that he had left. She would be able to regain control of her wayward feelings.

Victoria undressed and took down her hair. She had no brush, so she just braided it in a clumsy plait to keep it from tangling further. She climbed into bed and pulled the covers up over her shoulders. She thought she wouldn't be able to sleep before Slater returned, but in the end the day proved to be too tiring for her.

She was asleep when Slater walked back into the room. He stood looking down at her. She lay on her side, facing him. Her face was slack with sleep, her lips parted slightly. Her thick, dark eyelashes cast long shadows on her cheeks in the flickering light of the kerosene lamp. She was so beautiful it made his heart ache. What was he going to do about her? She was invading his life at every turn. The scary thing was that he was beginning to become accustomed to it. He was beginning to *like* it.

Slater sighed and blew out the lamp. He sat down in the chair and pulled off his boots again. Then he arranged the pillow behind his head as comfortably as he could. He closed his eyes, but sleep wouldn't come. He kept thinking about Victoria curled up in the bed with next to nothing on. He gritted his teeth and shifted into another position. He could tell that this was going to be a long, sleepless night.

Chapter Thirteen

The pale light of dawn streamed in through the uncurtained window, awakening Slater. He sat up gingerly, his joints cracking and his muscles crying out in protest. He rose and walked to the window, rolling his neck to get out the kinks. The street was quiet, as he expected it to be.

He stretched and yawned. What a night. He'd been right in thinking that he wouldn't get much sleep. He had still been wriggling around in that chair, trying to get comfortable, at four o'clock this morning. He couldn't have gotten more than two hours' sleep, and it had left him feeling more like he'd been beaten than rested.

He glanced over at Victoria asleep in the bed. Her hair had come loose from the poorly done braid, and it lay in a dark cloud over the pillow. He knew it felt like silk to the touch. He imagined it spread across his bare chest, tangling in his chest hairs and caressing his nipples when she moved. Slater moistened his lips. His mouth was as parched as sand. There was no way he could make it through another day this way. He couldn't be closed up in a hotel room with Victoria, with the bed looming between them and her dressed in clothes that revealed more than they concealed. Nor could he take her with him from saloon to saloon tonight, following Brody's men, playing the role of her would-be lover so that they would fit in.

There were things that were more than duty could demand. Somehow he had to convince her to return to her hotel room and let him trail the three men by himself.

Victoria's eyes opened, and a startled look crossed her face. She sat up, and the bed cover slipped down. She grabbed for it with both hands and held it primly to her. She blushed. "Good—good morning."

"Good morning."

Slater looked sleepy and unkempt in his stocking feet, his shirttail hanging out on one side and his hair messed up. Victoria thought he looked rather endearing. She pulled up her knees and rested her chin on them. She had to stop thinking about how appealing he was. There was nothing but business between them. There could be nothing else.

"I'm going out for a while. Get dressed. When I come back, we need to talk."

"All right." She was glad to be alone for a few minutes, so that she could pull herself together. It was too easy to let her defenses down first thing in the morning.

When Slater left, Victoria rose and dressed quickly. There was little she could do for her hair except wind it up and secure it with the hairpins she'd removed last night. It looked sloppy and unkempt, but she decided that, considering the way she was dressed, it didn't really matter. When she had done all she could, she sat down on the side of the bed and waited for Slater to return.

He did so shortly, carrying with him a tray of coffee, two cups and a basket of sweet rolls. Victoria jumped up, beaming. "Oh, thank you. It smells delicious. I'm starving. I didn't eat supper last night."

"No doubt you were too busy acquiring a costume," Slater returned dryly.

Victoria didn't bother to dignify his remark with a reply. She simply dug into the rolls and coffee with gusto, licking the stickiness from her fingers with unself-conscious pleasure. Slater watched her pink tongue slide across the tips of her fingers, and again desire forked through him like lightning. He jumped up and strode to the window.

"Any sign of Brody's men?"

Slater shook his head. "Nah. I doubt they'll be up and around for hours yet."

"Would you like to sleep in the bed while I keep watch?"

"I'll be all right." He didn't add that he would get no sleep, even in the bed, as long as she was in the room. "Victoria . . . I want you to go back to your hotel."

Her brows drew together, as Slater had known they would. He supposed it was a sign of how badly off he was that even that familiar recalcitrant expression made him want to kiss her. "Why?"

"Because you don't belong here, that's why!" Slater snapped. He clenched his fist and slammed it against his leg, then swung away with a gusty sigh. "Ah, hell, I said that wrong. I meant to be calm and reasonable; I had it all worked out what to say."

"You mean how to trick me into leaving?"

"Not trick you. I just—it would be easier for me if you weren't with me. I don't need to pretend to be buying your favors in order to sit in a saloon and drink all night. Besides, there are saloons that no women, even a fallen one, enters. What would you do if Brody's men went into one of them? Lurk around outside waiting for me to come out? And I can't very well follow them during the day with you on my arm. We'd be conspicuous. It won't work."

Victoria knew that Slater was right. She would be more of a hindrance than a help to him. But she couldn't bear the thought of going back to her hotel room and just sitting, waiting for her father to arrive and take over. Frankly, she wasn't looking forward to seeing her father, either. He would be furious with her for taking off on her own with Slater, and they would be bound to have a huge argument.

She wanted to be here, in on the excitement of the chase. She wanted to participate. She wanted to be with Slater. "Couldn't we take turns watching them during the day? How will you manage all by yourself?"

"I'll do it. I've done it before."

"I could bring you food." Her eyes were huge blue pools of sadness. Slater's heart twisted within him, and he wondered if he was really as mean as he felt at this moment. "I'd like to help! I need to be there when you find Amy."

Slater came over and squatted down beside her. He took her hands in his. "What if I let you know when they leave town? You could go with me then."

"Could I?" Victoria's face brightened immediately.

"I don't see why not." There were lots of things he saw, but he ignored them. Much as he would have liked to deny it, he had enjoyed her company when they had been trailing Brody before. She was quick, sharp, and beautiful to look at. He had made the offer primarily to wipe out the unhappiness on Victoria's face, but he had to admit that he wanted her along.

After all, when they were outdoors, without the enclosed intimacy of a hotel room, he wouldn't feel such a sharp sexual yearning, he told himself. He hadn't been torn with desire when they were on the trail together before. "You'll figure out some way to go, anyway. I might as well keep you with me, where I know what you're doing.

"In fact," he went on, "you could help me. We'll have to leave very quickly. You could get together our horses and supplies while I stay with Brody's men. Here, I'll write down where my things are, and a note so they'll release them to you." He sat down, pulling a scrap of paper from his pocket, and began to scribble a note on it. "Then, when I see that they're about to leave, I'll send for you."

"Yes, I can do that." Victoria's brow wrinkled. "But it will take so long for you to send for me and then for me to come back here. We'll lose them. I have a better plan."

"I should have known."

"I'll get all our things. Then I'll check out of my hotel and come back here. We'll stable the horses close by, so we can leave as soon as we need to."

He gritted his teeth. Her plan made sense, but it meant they would spend another night together. "Victoria, I don't think that's such a good idea."

"Why not?"

"Consider what you're doing. Spending the night in a sleazy hotel room with a man is even more damaging to your reputation than everything else you've done."

"Slater, I've spent the night in the same bed with you. How can my reputation suffer any more than that?"

"What?" He stared, his word coming out as a croak.

"At the Miles's house, when you were sick, and they thought we were married."

"I was no danger to you then."

"Are you now?"

His eyes darkened. "I wouldn't rape you." He paused. "But after last night, I think I could persuade you."

"Oh! Of all the conceit!" Victoria planted her hands on her hips. His words had hit home—she had melted like butter under his kisses, as though she had no will of her own; she had wanted him to take her, and it had been Slater who had stopped. But that knowledge only exacerbated her anger. "As if I couldn't resist you. Let me tell you something, *Captain* Slater, I let you kiss me because we were pretending to be, well, you know . . ."

"Then you're one hell of an actress. Did you think that people could see you had your tongue in my mouth?"

Victoria's eyes flamed. "No gentleman would have brought up this subject at all."

"No lady would have been hanging around saloons dressed up like a tart."

Victoria would have liked to make a crackling retort. The problem was that she was running out of things to say. Everything he brought up had too much truth in it. She *had* dressed up like a tart; she *had* kissed him back with fervor. She *had* felt the kind of lust decent women didn't feel. Maybe she wasn't a lady; her aunt had always told her so. But it stung to learn that that was Slater's opinion of her.

Victoria pressed her lips together. She smoothed down the skirt of her too-clinging dress. "Since I have no desire to compromise your virtue, Captain Slater, I suggest that I rent a room of my own in this establishment. That should save both of us embarrassment, as well as time. Is that acceptable to you?"

Her face was stamped with hurt. Slater felt lower than a snake's belly. She started toward the door, but he reached out and grabbed her wrist. "Victoria, wait. Don't be angry. I'm sorry for what I said. I had no right."

"Everyone has a right to his opinion."

"That's not what I think of you. You're a lady. Your traveling with me, sleeping in this room, kissing me—none of it tarnishes my opinion of you."

"Because it couldn't be blacker than it already is?"

"No. Because I think you're a hell of a woman and a hell of a lady, even though you're also the most obstinate, bullheaded one I've ever met."

"Such high praise." Victoria couldn't stop a smile from quirking the corners of her mouth.

"I was angry at myself. I'm afraid I'll lose control if I have to spend another night with you. I couldn't sleep last night. I kept thinking about you sleeping over there. Every time I look at you in that dress, I want to hold you and touch you and kiss you. I loved your kiss. I loved your tongue in my mouth. I'd like to feel it right now." He bent and pressed his lips lightly against hers, then returned for another, longer kiss. "You have a beautiful mouth. Perfect." He groaned softly and rested his forehead against hers. "Please, Victoria, I'm no saint. Watching you sleep drove me crazy. I can't do it again."

Victoria swallowed. She was trembling all over from his words. He was right. They shouldn't spend the night in the same room. "I'll get another room, as I said."

"This hotel isn't a fitting place for you. The doors don't even lock."

"I'll get the room next door, so you can come to my rescue if I scream," she said lightly. "Now, don't try to persuade me otherwise." She stepped back and smiled. "I have lots of things to do this morning, and you need to get back to watching for Brody's men."

She smiled and walked out the door. Slater ran his tongue across his lips, tasting her on them. He went to the window and watched her walk across the street and out of sight. He'd never known another woman like Victoria Stafford. And, damn, but he wanted her.

Victoria did her errands with her usual efficiency. She returned to Gemma's house to exchange the clothes she wore for her own riding skirt, blouse and boots, then brought their horses and supplies to a livery stable just a block away from Slater's hotel. Last, she went to her own hotel. She retrieved her things from the room and, under the desk clerk's gimlet gaze, paid her bill and left.

She found it far easier to get a room at the inelegant hotel where she and Slater had spent the previous night. The clerk asked no questions, though he did direct a puzzled look at her attire. An extra dollar slipped to him got her the room next to Slater's, again without questions.

She went up to her room happily. Even if this hotel lacked the comfort and attractiveness of the Avenue Hotel, she was glad to be here. She was afraid that if she spent another night at the Avenue Hotel, her father would arrive and forbid her to go with Slater when he left again.

The rest of her day passed in a thoroughly boring manner. She spent most of her time looking out the window, and she saw Brody's men leave and Slater follow them. She chafed at having to stay in her room, but she knew that Slater was right. It would be better for both of them if he went by himself. She sat up for a long time, hoping that she would get a full account of the evening when Slater came back. But by twelve o'clock she gave up listening for his return and went to bed.

She knew nothing until Slater knocked on her door the following morning and brought in a tray of breakfast. They sat and ate companionably while he recounted following the men the night before from saloon to saloon, sampling the beer in each place.

"If they don't leave town soon," he said wryly, "my stomach and my head will both rebel."

Victoria smiled. He didn't look the worse for wear to her. "Is that all you accomplished?"

"No. I heard bits of their conversation. They've been asking around town about a man named Vance. He's the one who gave me the information about the Santa Clara bank robbery. Brody doubtless has revenge on his mind."

"You think he's going to hurt him?" Victoria's eyes widened. "Kill him?"

"Brody can't afford a breach of loyalty. He'd think he had to make an example of the man. Besides, he despises him. I saw the look he gave Vance when I arrested him."

Slater stayed with her the rest of the morning, and they talked and took turns keeping watch on the entrance. It was almost noon when Victoria saw Brody's cohorts leave the hotel.

"Slater, they're on their way out." He jumped up and came over to the window. "They're carrying their saddles. And they're wearing spurs this morning."

He raised his eyebrows. "Looks like they're about to take a ride." He turned to her. "Shall we go?"

The gang's horses were housed in the same stable as Slater's and Victoria's. Slater went in to saddle their horses, while Victoria loitered outside to see which way Brody's men rode off, and moments later, Slater emerged with their mounts and supplies. They swung up into their saddles and started after the gang, keeping a safe distance behind them, mingling with the other horses and carriages as they made their way through town. Neither of them looked back, so they didn't see that, some distance behind them, Cam McBride was also leaving town.

They rode north out of Austin on the road to Round Rock. There were other riders on the road now and then, but not the sort of traffic that there had been in Austin, so Slater and Victoria fell farther back, barely keeping the three men in sight. Before they reached Round Rock, the gang turned west, and Slater allowed them to pull even farther away, following their tracks on the little-traveled road.

Darkness fell, and Slater and Victoria made camp. They ate their cold dinner and soon rolled up in their blankets to sleep. Slater found that he had been mistaken to think that it would be easier to sleep close to Victoria out in the open than in the hotel room. There was some relief in knowing that she was fully clothed, and at least there was no bed, with all its sensual implications. But he still wanted her. He could see her face in the wash of moonlight, and he could remember in great detail how she had looked in that bed, her bare white shoulders peeking out above the cover and her hair a shining black waterfall over the pillow. She was only a few feet away from him. It required as much willpower as he possessed not to cross that small distance and take her in his arms. It shook him to realize exactly how much he wanted her, no matter what the circumstances.

The next morning they rode out again, following the men's tracks. Slater reflected bitterly that Victoria seemed to have no difficulty sleeping when she was around him, for she was as bright and beautiful as ever.

However, no matter how fresh and lovely Victoria looked to Slater's eyes, she had been anything but free from tension. She had done little the past two days except think about what had

happened between them—and how much more she had wanted
to happen.

Her desire surprised her. She had never felt even an inkling
of this feeling for a man before. She had assumed that desire
was something a woman felt only for the man she truly loved.
Yet she desired Slater, and she didn't love him. She couldn't
love him. He was completely wrong for her. He lived like a
gypsy and was always in danger. He had no ties to the land;
why, he had simply abandoned his home. He was maddening,
infuriating, conceited....

And strong. Brave. Quick, confident, skilled, smart. He
could laugh wryly at himself, unafflicted with the usual male
pomposity. He was even man enough to admit Victoria's abil-
ities. And his fingers on her skin were like fire. His mouth was
velvet, hot and aggressive. His hard body, pressed against her,
had aroused trembling, eager sensations she'd never known
before, but wanted desperately to feel again.

So her thoughts went, circling around in futile argument, half
of her wanting him and urging her to toss aside the consequences, the other half reminding her of all the reasons why she
couldn't love him. Victoria had never been so confused or
helpless, and she hated the feeling.

She was an unconventional woman, and there were moments when she told herself that she should take the physical
pleasure Slater could bring her and forget about love and marriage and living with him forever on the ranch. This might be
the only chance she would ever have to feel this way. She had
never felt this before, so it was possible, even likely, that Slater, rough and hard and oh, so masculine, was the only man
who could arouse her. Why not take the leap and let the consequences come as they would? What did it matter if he didn't
love her? What did it matter if there would be no future for
them? There was at least the present, and surely she would feel
no worse when Slater left her if she had slept with him than she
would if she hadn't.

But she balked at taking that final, irrevocable step. Somehow she knew that if she made love with Slater, she would never
be the same, that she would be utterly vulnerable to him. So,
despite her turmoil and the desire that ran hidden in her veins,
Victoria remained aloof.

It was close to noon the next day when the tracks they were following ended among the flat rocks at the base of a hill. Slater sighed in exasperation and dismounted to search the ground more closely. He saw nothing to indicate that the horses had climbed the hill. It was rocky and difficult, and he judged it more likely that they had skirted the base of it. But there was no sign of that, either.

Slater was beginning to curse vividly when he spied fresh horse droppings between a mesquite bush and the cliff. He rode around the bushes and saw that amid the large, jumbled boulders behind them was an opening in the cliff wall. He dismounted and tied Old Jack to one of the bushes, his heart starting to pound.

The opening in the rock wall was big enough for a horse to enter. Slater walked up to the entrance and peered in. He could see the ground in front of him for only a few feet. It sloped down gradually. Beyond that was sheer darkness. He turned back to Victoria, excitement lighting his face.

"I think we've found it. Damn, no wonder I've always lost him. Brody's hideout is a cave!"

The entrance to the hideout frightened Amy a little, and she hung back, looking suspiciously at the black hole in the side of the hill, but Brody stepped inside confidently. He pulled out a lantern from a niche in the rock beside the entrance and lit it, then motioned to her to follow him. "Come on. It's not as bad as it looks, as long as you stay with me."

"Is it a cave?" Amy asked, leading her horse in behind Brody and his mount.

"Yeah." Brody held up the lantern, and it cast an eerie, flickering light over the pale rock walls of the cavern. "I found it years ago. There are a lot of different offshoots. If you don't know where you're going you can get lost. Some of them are dangerous. But not this one."

"You stay inside here?" Amy's voice quivered a little, despite her best intentions.

Brody smiled, hearing the fear in her voice and the brave way she tried not to show it. "No. Not in the cave. It's a passage. There's a valley on the other side, where we come out."

Sam led her through the cave into a tunnellike passageway. They walked for some distance. Once they skirted a pile of rocks, which Brody explained he had dug out long ago when he was first exploring the cave. "That was when I found out this tunnel went on to the outside. Sometime, if you want, I'll take you into the main cavern. There're three passages that go down from it. I've never gone down one of them. It's a sheer drop-off. One of them goes down gradually enough that you can climb down it. And the third we went part way down on a rope. There are strange-looking rocks in the caverns below ground. There are pools of water, and columns that look wet, like melting ice. They hang from the roof, or come up from the floor. Some of them are bigger around than my arm."

"I'd like to see it," Amy answered, "as long as you're with me. Then I wouldn't be frightened."

They had been going at a more or less downward tilt most of the time they had been walking, but now they began to go up again. They crossed a narrow stream of icy water. Finally, ahead in the distance, Amy could see light. It became stronger as they drew nearer, so bright that it dazzled her eyes, accustomed now to the darkness. At last they squeezed through a jagged crack in the rock and emerged several feet up a sloping hill.

They climbed down, and Amy stopped to look around her. They stood in a very narrow valley, with steep limestone cliffs on either side. At midday it would be light, but by late afternoon, as it was now, much of the place stood in shadow. Mesquite bushes and cacti grew along the floor of the valley, and there were even a few small trees beside a tiny stream. Cactus and low, scraggly bushes clung here and there to the cliff walls. Two ramshackle huts stood against one rock wall, built of narrow, twisted mesquite branches lashed together. There was a circle of rocks in front of the huts, where it was obvious that fires had been built many times.

Brody glanced around as Amy did, looking at the valley with fresh eyes for the first time in years. He had grown accustomed to it long ago and valued it as a place of refuge. But now he saw it as Amy must, and he noticed how narrow it was, and how often it lay in shadow. For the first time, the close, high walls made him think of prison rather than protection.

The stream provided water, and they always had enough provisions stored to see them through several weeks. The horses could survive on the bushes and thin grass, and the huts provided shelter from the elements. But suddenly it seemed a meager existence. Brody had built a bed in one of the shacks, but its mattress was made of sacks stuffed with grasses and leaves, and they lay across a webbing of rope. In the dead of winter, the cold crept through the cracks in the shack's walls so fiercely that they often spent the nights in the relative warmth of the caves. In the summer, there was little shade from the heat, and no breeze.

Sam had never thought about its comfort or lack of it. It had just been a place to run to. A place where he couldn't be found. The gang traveled much of the time, and they were often in San Antonio or Austin or some other town, spending their money, or doing another job. But obviously he couldn't drag Amy with him from town to town like that, and he had expected that she would stay here at the hideout, waiting for him.

But now he saw that it was hardly a place for her to live. Even at the best of times, it was not the sort of home a lady like Amy was used to living in. There were no comforts, none of the little things that made life pleasant. Any sodbuster's wife in her shanty lived a better existence than Amy would here.

Sam glanced at Amy. She smiled and slid her arm around him. As always, he responded to her touch, warming with love. "Shall we look around?" she asked. "I'd like to see all of it."

"We will." No doubt she would see more of it in the course of time than she wanted. She wouldn't complain; he knew Amy. She would make the best of it, as she made the best of every bad situation, from sleeping outdoors to being kidnapped. But how could she be happy here for long?

He thought of riding away, leaving her here, when he and his men went out to waylay a stage or rob a bank. She would be here all alone. She could get sick, or a wild animal might come along. What if he got captured again, or shot, and couldn't come back to her? What would she do, stranded here all by herself? He couldn't just leave her. Yet it would be even more impossible to take her with him. He hated the thought of exposing Amy to violence and crime.

Brody realized suddenly how impossible the situation was. Lost in his haze of pleasure, he had pushed away any thought of the future. He'd been living in a dream world. But coming to the hideout had thrust him rudely into reality.

He wished he and Amy were still back at the falls. He wished they were almost anywhere but here. He thought of the small strongbox of gold buried beneath one of the pin oak trees, and he wondered if he could take it and run far enough away that the law wouldn't be after him. He wondered if it was possible for a man like him to start a new life. It didn't seem likely. But, then, when he looked at Amy's sweet face, it seemed as if anything might be possible.

He spent the afternoon with her, talking and teasing and aimlessly walking along the narrow stream. They gazed at each other and reached out to caress each other with the same kind of disbelieving wonder that they always felt. Sometimes the touches were sensual, but more often not. It was with awe and with love that they reached out, as though to reassure themselves that the sweetness they had found really existed. Amy expressed delight at the sight of the cabin's real bed, however primitive it might be, and, laughing, she drew Sam down upon it to test its softness. They made love on the crackling mattress, smiling and laughing as much as they panted and writhed. It was often sweet and gentle like this for them, though at other times their lovemaking was like a fast-rising storm.

Brody tried to put the idea of leaving the valley out of his mind, telling himself that there was plenty of time to decide that later. But all afternoon the canyon seemed to grow more and more oppressive. And he thought more about what he would do away from it. This had been his way of life for years; he didn't know how else he would live. The gold would get them through for a while, maybe buy them a piece of land. But it wouldn't last forever. He would need to build a home and a life for Amy. They might have children. The thought was astounding, overwhelming. It scared him, yet at the same time he ached inside to see it come true.

He knew horses. Perhaps he could do what Raul had done. T. J. Moore had taught him a lot about running cattle those few years when he hadn't lived as an outlaw. Maybe he could make a living like other men. Maybe he could be a husband. A father.

Once he would have missed the danger and the excitement if he stopped robbing. But not any longer. Amy filled all the empty spaces of his life. He had no need for the things that had driven him in the past. The idea of running away with Amy lured him like a siren's song.

Just after dark, Brody heard the sound of horses' hooves striking stone. He grabbed his rifle from where it stood propped against the wall of the hut, and he drew Amy back into the brush, away from the fire, raising the rifle. A light glowed from the entrance to the cave, growing brighter and brighter until finally a man stepped out of the entrance, holding a lantern aloft. It was Purdon.

Brody lowered his gun. Purdon and the other two men scrambled down to the floor of the valley, leading their horses. Brody walked out to meet them.

"I see you made it."

"Yeah." Purdon set down the lantern and began to unsaddle his horse.

"How was Austin?"

Purdon shrugged. "We found out about Dave Vance."

It took Brody a moment to remember who Vance was. "Oh. What about him?"

"He got his blood money and lit out. That's what old Blackie Morris heard. Folks say he went south, somewhere around San Marcos."

"Yeah?" When he had been captured, Sam had hungered for revenge on the man. Now he just felt indifferent.

"Yeah." Purdon turned, a frown creasing his forehead. "Is that all you got to say?"

"What do you want me to say?"

"When we goin' after him?"

Brody shrugged. "I don't know. I hadn't thought about it."

"What you plannin' to do to him?"

"I hadn't thought about that, either."

Purdon stared at him without saying anything. Amy emerged from the brush and came to stand behind Brody, seeking the comfort of his presence. The other men made her uneasy; the very air seemed to change when they were around.

Purdon looked surprised. "She still with you?"

Brody stiffened a little. "Yeah. Why?"

"You never brought a woman to the hideout before." Purdon turned his horse loose and came toward Brody. His face was hard and suspicious.

"I never wanted to before." Brody gazed back at him flatly, his expression making it plain that the matter wasn't open to discussion.

For a moment Amy thought that Purdon was going to object to her presence, but then he turned away and squatted down beside the fire, pulling out a plug of tobacco and breaking off a chew. The other men turned their horses loose and sauntered over to join them. Brody sat down cross-legged on the ground, and Amy sat on a low rock behind him, as close as she could get. She was sorry that these men had returned. She wished it could continue to be only her and Sam.

Sam seemed to sense her discomfort, for he wrapped his hand around her ankle and squeezed lightly. He rested his back against her legs. Amy smiled and ran a light hand across his hair. She loved to touch him, and she did so almost unconsciously, combing her fingers through his hair and smoothing it down, delicately massaging his scalp. Sam relaxed against her, luxuriating in her touch. It was Amy's nature to express her love in physical caresses, and that expression soothed and healed Sam in a way he'd never known.

Purdon watched them, and his mouth curled in contempt. "Damn. I never thought I'd see the day when Sam Brody'd be led around by the nose."

Amy's fingers stilled, and she glanced down at Sam. Had she embarrassed him in front of his men? Sam's eyes flew open, and they focused piercingly on Purdon. "What did you say?" His voice was low and soft, and it sent chills up Amy's spine.

"You heard me." Purdon crossed his arms in front of him, his expression defiant. "Used to be, no little split-tail coulda—"

Brody shot to his feet, his eyes blazing. "Shut up! You keep your mouth shut about her. Understand?"

The other men rose, too. Purdon faced Brody, his hands loose at his sides, and the other two men stepped back uncertainly, their eyes flickering from Purdon to Brody and back again.

"I got a right to say what I think."

"You got no rights where Amy's concerned except what I tell you."

"You think so? And who's goin' to stop me? You ain't man enough anymore. That little piece o' fluff's gelded you."

"Yeah? You want to test that? You want to go up against me, Purdon? See if I'm still man enough to spill your guts on the ground?"

Purdon's nostrils flared, and Amy saw fear flicker through his eyes, but he lifted his head. "Yeah. I would like to see that. 'Cause I don't think you can. She's made you soft."

"Amy, go inside."

Her stomach was a ball of ice. "Sam, no..."

"Don't argue. Just do what I tell you." Brody didn't look at her, and that scared her even more. His right hand went to the small of his back, where a flat leather holster was attached to his belt. He slipped the bowie knife from its sheath and brought it around in front of him. The firelight flickered on the metal, turning it red and gold.

Terror gripped Amy's throat, squeezing the breath out of her. She could envision Sam lying dead on the ground, blood oozing from his wounds. She clenched her hands together and brought them to her mouth.

"Amy, go."

She couldn't disobey him when he spoke like that. She turned and ran, stumbling, to the hut. She threw herself into the far corner and curled up in a ball, facing the wooden wall, her arms crossed over her head to block out all sound. *He would die! He would die!* Amy was frozen with terror.

But as she lay there, she realized that if Purdon did kill Sam, she would have done nothing to help him. She was too busy cowering in fear to try to save the man she loved. Amy forced herself to stand up and turn around. What was she to do? She tried to make her numb brain think. What would Victoria do in a situation like this? She would find a weapon with which to help Sam, that's what.

Amy glanced around the dark hut. She could see almost nothing. What was in here? Sam's rifle was outside. He had propped it up against a tree when he sat down at the fire. Then she remembered that Sam had unbuckled his gun belt and laid it on the table. She groped her way across the room and found the gun belt. Her hands shaking, she slid one of the revolvers out. She held it down by her side, hidden in the folds of her skirt, and walked outside.

The half-moon cast an eerie light over the scene. Jim and Grimes stood off to one side, watching Purdon and Brody fight, evidently awaiting the outcome rather than taking sides. The two antagonists circled one another, their arms out in front of them, the blades of their knives glittering in the pale light. Sweat dampened their shirts and hair and glistened on their faces. One of Sam's sleeves dangled from his arm, ripped from wrist to shoulder, and there was a red slash across his left forearm.

Amy swallowed. He'd been cut. Her fingers clenched on the butt of the gun, and for the first time in her life, she knew a desire to raise a gun and blast away at someone. At that moment she hated Purdon so fiercely that she could taste it.

But then she saw that if Sam had been hurt, he had hurt Purdon worse. Red stained Purdon's shirt and oozed from a cut on his cheek. Sam moved with a deadly grace, feinting, jabbing, retreating. Purdon was slower and clumsier, and he knew it. Amy saw the desperation on his face as he realized the mistake he'd made in challenging Brody. Sam moved in, faster than Amy could see, and danced back, leaving another slash of red across Purdon's chest. Amy sensed that Sam was goading him, as one might goad a bull until it was so enraged that it charged. He moved in and out, slicing each time, until Purdon lost control and lunged at him, throwing his all into one thrust. Sam stepped into it, dodging with his head and shoulders as his hand plunged toward Purdon's chest.

There was a sickening thud as his blade shoved into the other man's flesh. Purdon stopped, his hands flying open and his eyes widening in surprise. Brody stepped back, pulling out his long knife. Blood stained the blade and handle and splattered his hand. A red spot spread on Purdon's shirt. His hand came up to the wound, and he wavered, his mouth opening as if he would speak. He fell heavily to his knees, then pitched forward onto his face.

Sam stepped back, breathing hard. He bent over and wiped his knife clean on a clump of grass. He straightened. "Take him and get out." He spoke to the other two members of his gang. "Tonight."

For a moment the other men simply stared. Sam took a step toward them, and they hurried forward to lift the body and carry it away. Sam watched without expression as they saddled their horses and loaded Purdon's lifeless frame onto his horse. Then they picked up the lantern they had used earlier and disappeared into the black mouth of the cave. Sam turned away, starting toward the hut. He stopped abruptly when he saw Amy standing motionless in front of the shack, watching him.

She'd seen it. She had seen him kill a man.

"Amy..." He went to her, stretching out his hands to comfort her. He saw the wicked glitter of the knife blade in the moonlight and realized that he still held it. He realized, too, that there was blood on his hand. He stopped and hastily sheathed the knife. He tried to wipe the blood from his skin, but it was no good. She'd seen it. She must be horrified. Would she hate him now?

Amy sank slowly to the ground and sat back on her heels. Sam squatted down in front of her. "Honey, why'd you come out? I didn't mean for you to see that."

"He's dead." Her face was pale, and she looked sick. She shuddered. "Oh, Sam."

"I'm sorry." He felt helpless. He didn't know what to say. "He challenged me. It was him or me."

She nodded. "I know. He was a wicked man. But, oh, Sam, it was horrible. All that blood. I've never seen a man die before." Her lips trembled. "Please, you won't do it anymore, will you? Can't we go somewhere and—and not have men like him around?"

"Yes. We will. I promise. Tomorrow we'll ride out of here and never come back. We'll go someplace safe—Mexico. I'm not a wanted man in Mexico. I have some money, and we'll start a little ranch, live like normal people."

Amy looked up at him and smiled, her heart in her eyes. "You're good to me. Thank you."

He pulled her to him, wrapping his arms around her fiercely. "No, I'm not good at all. It's you who's good. But I promise

I'll protect you. I won't let anything bad happen to you. We'll stay away from men like Purdon and anything else that could hurt you. I swear to you."

"I love you, Sam. I love you." Amy's arms went around him. She was still holding the revolver in her hand, and it bumped against his back.

Sam reached back and took the gun from her hand. He held it out, looking at it. "What's this?" He gazed down into her face, his own expression softening into a kind of tender awe. "You were carrying my pistol? Why? To shoot Purdon?"

Amy nodded. "I was afraid he would hurt you. There were three of them. I didn't know what they'd do. I had to protect you somehow."

"Oh, sweetheart." He squeezed her even more tightly to his chest. It made him swell with pride and love to think that she loved him that much—that she, sweet, gentle creature that she was, would have fought to protect him. "I love you. And I swear to God, I'll make you happy. I'm going to make your life sweet from here on in."

Amy smiled and laid her head trustingly against his chest. "It will be, as long as you're with me."

It was too late that night to dig up the gold, and, anyway, Brody wasn't about to separate himself from Amy long enough to hunt for it. They went to bed in the hut and held each other throughout the night. Amy slept, comforted by his presence, but Brody lay awake much of the night, savoring the joy of holding her, and making plans.

The next morning, as soon as they had eaten, he dug up the small strongbox of gold and transferred the money into his saddlebags. Then, leading their horses, they scrambled up the incline and into the cave. Sam lit the lantern and led her through the tunnel. This time it didn't seem as long, and the heavy rock walls weren't as oppressive. She was leaving with Sam for a bright new life, and Amy doubted if anything could have weighed down her spirits. Even the killing last night had receded from her mind.

They neared the mouth of the tunnel, and Sam doused the lantern. He set it down near the entrance as he had always done, though now no one would be using it. But just as he was about to step out into the bright sunlight he heard the unmistakable sound of voices. He drew back instinctively, reaching for Amy's hand.

She looked at him, puzzled, and he raised a finger to his lips, signaling for quiet. He tapped his ear and pointed toward the entrance, and Amy went still, listening. Understanding dawned on her face. Very carefully, Brody led Amy and the horses down a separate offshoot of the cave until they were hidden by the darkness. He slid his Colt out of the holster and cocked it.

The voices grew louder and more distinct. He could separate them now into two different voices, one feminine and one masculine. A man stepped into the cave, followed by a woman in boots and a riding outfit. They stood in the daylight coming in from outside, and Amy and Sam could see them clearly. Sam stiffened. Slater—and Amy's cousin!

He glanced at Amy. Would she call out to her beloved cousin? He couldn't let her, but he hated the thought of clamping his hand over her mouth to stop her. Besides, he didn't have a hand free. His gun was in one, and he had his other on his horse's nose to keep it quiet.

It was too dark to see what Amy was doing, though he felt her move a little beside him. He waited tautly, the sweat trickling down his back, and watched Slater and Victoria. They moved around clumsily in the dim light near the entrance they disappeared into the darkness beyond. Slater lit a match and held it, and Brody saw him in the small glow.

"Slater, look, a lantern!" Victoria cried, holding up the lantern Brody had set down.

Slater lit it and held it up, looking around him. He turned all the way around. Brody and Amy stood beyond the circle of light the lantern cast. Slater peered down the tunnel that led to the valley. He knelt to examine the floor, and Brody suspected that he saw something to indicate the passage of a horse. Slater motioned Victoria to follow him, and they started off down the tunnel.

Brody relaxed. Elation poured through him. Amy hadn't called to her cousin. She had had a chance at freedom and returning to her family, but she had chosen him instead.

He waited for another nerve-stretching minute, letting Slater get far enough away that he wouldn't hear the sound of the horse's hooves. Then he started forward as quietly as he could, leading his mount. Amy followed him. He peered outside the cave, and when he was sure that there were no reinforcements lurking there, he waved Amy through. She went out into the bright sun, shielding her eyes. He followed her out, easing the hammer back down on his gun and reholstering it.

Slater's and Victoria's horses waited outside, reins tied to a mesquite bush. Brody untied both reins and took them in hand, then mounted his own horse. They walked their horses carefully through the jumbled rocks at the base of the hill. When they reached level ground, they broke into a trot. Amy glanced uneasily at the horses he was leading. He knew what she was thinking—that Slater and her cousin would die if they were left out here without their horses. He stopped, still in sight of the cave entrance, and looped the reins around another mesquite. They'd be able to get to their horses, but the journey would slow them down considerably.

Amy smiled at him, and Brody put his heels to his horse. They galloped off, laughing, giddy with the knowledge that they had escaped.

A lone rider, a long, thin man dressed in a vest of animal skins, sat his horse on the hill east of the cave, watching them. Then he tapped his heels to his horse's sides and started down the hill after them.

Chapter Fourteen

The tunnel made Victoria nervous. Even with the lantern to cast a light in front of them, she disliked walking into the dark unknown. She kept imagining a pit suddenly yawning at their feet, or Brody's gang waiting in ambush for them around the next bend. After they passed a pile of rubble that blocked half the passageway, she added a vision of the rock ceiling tumbling down on them.

Slater glanced back at her, and she could see the white flash of his grin in the lantern's light. "Don't tell me I finally found something that scares you," he whispered.

Victoria arched an eyebrow. "I notice you're the one whispering," she hissed back.

His grin grew wider, but he winked at her reassuringly. Once, a dark tunnel branched off from the one they were following, and, another time, they could have stepped out into a huge vault, the tops and sides of which the lantern didn't even reveal. But Slater stayed with the main tunnel, following instinct more than any kind of trail on the stony floor.

Victoria expected that they would eventually reach a larger cavern where the outlaws lived. She wouldn't have been surprised to have found Brody and his men waiting for them, guns ready. What she had not expected to see was a glow of light in the distance that grew in size and intensity until at last it became clear that it was another entrance to the cave.

"Have we gone around in a circle?" she whispered.

Slater shrugged in irritated puzzlement. They reached the opening, and Slater stuck his head out. The sunlight was dazzling, but he could see well enough to tell that they weren't back where they'd begun.

"It's not the same entrance."

"How could it not be?"

"This cave must honeycomb the inside of the hill. We've come out on the other side, or the back."

"Then we've missed them? They're in a different part of the caves?"

"I'm not sure." Slater crouched by the entrance, his eyes moving over the landscape. "There." Victoria heard the underlying excitement in his voice. "Victoria, look. There are a couple of shacks, and if I'm not mistaken, that looks like a camp fire site. I think this is their hideout."

Victoria joined him at the entrance and scanned the cliffs on either side. "You think this valley is boxed in? Sealed off from the outside?"

"Or close to it. That's my guess. Brody has a secret little valley to retreat to." He shook his head in admiration. "No wonder he can stay hidden."

"It doesn't look like anybody's around. Do you think they know we're here?"

"Let's give it a test. You cover me." He drew his pistol and crept out of the entrance and down the side of the hill. Victoria held her rifle to her shoulder and waited, her eyes searching the area for a glint that would tell of a gun hidden behind a rock or bush. She could see nothing, and she heard nothing except the call of a bird.

Slater reached the cover of a mesquite bush without incident, and Victoria started down the hill after him. They moved in this fashion across the valley floor, Slater darting from one spot of cover to another while Victoria covered him with the rifle, then Victoria following him. Slater reached one of the huts and ducked inside. He stuck his head back out the door and shrugged. He checked the other hut, and came back to Victoria.

"Looks like they're gone."

"But why?"

"I don't know. I haven't seen a sign of anything." He motioned toward the area at the base of the hill. "There have been a number of horses and people here lately. There are tracks all over the place. One of the prints is a woman's shoe. The rest are big, men's, I'd guess, and one of the boots looks like it has a notch in it—for all the good that does us." He drew closer to the cold ashes of the fire. "Look how many prints are around the fire, how scuffed and jumbled they are. Like an awful lot of people were here, or just a few people moving around a lot. And here's a large, smoother area, like something long was laid down here." He stopped, his attention riveted to the dirt.

The ground was a rocky shelf, lightly covered with dirt. The dirt was stained a dark color, and brown splotched the bare rock where it poked through the dirt. Slater knelt to examine it. "This is blood, I think." He glanced around. "Here's why." He reached over and picked up a long hunting knife from the ground. The edges were stained with brown. "These aren't old stains."

Victoria's lungs seemed to shut down. "Do you think he's killed Amy?"

"More likely Brody and one of his men got into a knife fight and one of them got killed. I'd bet money it wasn't Brody."

"But what's happened to them? Where have they gone?"

"I don't know. Unless Brody figured out they'd been followed. Maybe that's what caused the fight. The gang lit out, afraid we'd find the hideout."

"Whatever the reason, they must not be here, or they'd have shot us a long time ago. Right?"

"Yeah."

"Then let's find them. They can't be too far ahead of us."

"Just enough. Like they have been all along." Slater glanced up the narrow valley. "My guess is that that way it's a cul-de-sac, and the only way out is through the caves. Let's go back the way we came and search for prints leaving the area."

Victoria nodded, and followed Slater into the cave. They navigated it at a faster pace this time, driven by urgency and no longer afraid that their next step might pitch them into a chasm. They emerged from the front entrance, blinking in the blazing sun. Slater came to an abrupt halt, and Victoria, right behind him, ran into his back.

"Damn."

"What is it?"

"They got our horses."

"What?" Victoria stepped around him. Their horses were no longer tied to the mesquite bush in front of the entrance. She looked around frantically.

"There they are." Slater spotted them in the distance, grazing near another bush. "Come on, let's get them." He started walking toward the horses.

"Could they have wandered away?"

Slater shook his head emphatically. "That far? Not likely. Besides, I'm positive I tied the reins tightly. Didn't you?"

Victoria nodded. "That means someone was here when we went into the cave. They saw us, and while we were exploring the cave and the valley, they led the horses over there to give themselves more time to get away."

Slater nodded, his face grim. "I can't believe I was so careless. Damn! We must have been this close to Brody." He held up his fingers to form a space smaller than an inch. "If I'd just looked, I'd have had him!"

"You did look," Victoria pointed out resonably. "He must have been well hidden."

"Hell, we could have passed right by him in that cave. There were lots of dark places."

"But if it *was* Brody, and Amy was with him, why wouldn't she have called out to us?"

"Gagged, maybe. Or he put his hand over her mouth."

"But wouldn't she have made some noise—with her feet or something?"

"Don't go thinking she's dead, Victoria. Maybe she didn't think of making noise, or maybe she did, and we didn't hear it. Brody could have knocked her out to keep her from saying anything when he saw us. Or maybe she wasn't even there. There are a hundred reasons besides her being dead."

"I hope you're right."

When they reached the animals, they found that they had been tied to the bush. Victoria shook her head as she swung up into the saddle. "I don't understand. Why did he bother to tie the horses? Why not let them loose? We would have had a harder time catching them. In fact, why not take them with him and leave us stranded here?"

"Presumably he balked at murdering us." Slater tapped his heels to his horse's sides.

"I don't understand it. That doesn't seem like something a ruthless man would do."

"I never said he was ruthless. I said he's a lawbreaker."

"I know. But somehow—I don't know, it seems odd."

Slater nodded. "Maybe." He glanced over at Victoria; his thought had been that perhaps Victoria's cousin had mellowed the outlaw, but he decided it would be wiser not to say that. It would only remind her of the way in which Amy would have gentled Sam Brody.

He guessed there were women who could do that, even to a man like Brody. But, personally, he preferred his women with a touch of tartness, not as sweet and sticky as taffy candy. Again, involuntarily, he looked at Victoria. No one would claim she was cloying; she could be as astringent as vinegar. But her mouth was fire and delight; her body was everything a man could dream of.

Slater tore his eyes away from Victoria and kicked his horse into a gallop. He had sworn he wouldn't touch her. But why did his body have to make it so damn difficult?

It was a long, wearing day. Slater didn't stop until it was past dark. They were both exhausted, and he thought wryly that at least he wouldn't have trouble sleeping tonight.

After they finished supper, Victoria grinned slyly and brought out a small paper bag.

"What's that?"

"I brought a treat." She wiggled the bag enticingly. "Want some?"

"I don't know until you tell me what it is," he replied reasonably, but the corners of his mouth began to curve up.

Victoria made a pouty face. "You act as if I might feed you poison."

"Your idea of a treat and mine might differ, that's all."

"If you have so little faith in my judgment, I'll simply eat it all myself." She reached into the paper bag, pulled out a small orange circle and popped it into her mouth.

"What was that? A dried peach?"

"Apricot." Victoria smiled. "Dried apple slices, too."

"I'll take one."

"As I recall, I offered, and you didn't accept. I'd say the offer was rescinded."

"Rescinded, huh? We'll see about that." He lunged for the sack, startling her with his quickness. She jumped, but she was too late, and he plucked the small white bag from her hand.

He sat back down and reached inside it. Victoria laughed and grabbed for the bag. Slater held the sack out of her reach, twisting to elude her. He managed to keep it away from her long enough for him to pull out an apple slice and eat it, but then Victoria grasped his arm with both her hands and swung her full weight on it.

Slater threw his other arm around her waist and fell backward onto the ground, hauling her with him. They giggled and struggled like schoolchildren, the paper bag falling unheeded to the dirt. They rolled across the ground, and when they stopped, Victoria was underneath Slater and his arms were around her. Victoria looked up at him. Her heart was pounding, and she was panting for breath, but that condition had nothing to do with her physical exertion.

They looked at each other, the teasing and laughter gone. A strand of Victoria's hair had come loose from her braid and clung to her cheek. Slater brushed it aside, the callused tip of his finger lingering on Victoria's skin. Her lips parted. They were moist and soft. Slater knew exactly how it would feel to kiss them. He knew how her mouth would taste, and how her tongue would glide across his. His hand slid down her neck to the lush mound of her breast. His eyes darkened.

Victoria felt the telltale hardening of his body against her thigh. He wanted her. God knows, she wanted him. Why in the world did they stay apart? "Slater . . ." she began huskily.

He made a noise almost of pain and rolled off her. He jumped to his feet and walked away. Victoria sat up, watching his rigid back. She wished he would come back to her and take her in his arms. She was ready to fling aside all conventions and morality.

"Slater, come back."

"I can't."

"Don't you want me?"

He groaned. "Of course I want you. How could I not want you? You're beautiful and desirable. You're everything a man could want. But I'd be a blackguard to take you."

"No."

"Yes!" He picked up a stick and crashed it against the trunk of a tree. "I'm not the man you want, the man you need."

"Don't you think I should be the judge of that?" Victoria replied tartly.

"No. You don't know a damn thing about it. We're too different. We can't get through a whole day without arguing. We don't get along. It wouldn't work."

"Obviously you're deciding everything without asking me, as usual." Victoria got to her feet, her eyes flashing. "But, then, why should I have anything to say about what I should do? You, no doubt, are a better judge of that."

"Victoria, you're being unfair."

"No, it's you who's unfair—and pigheaded and bossy. Not to mention conceited!" She planted her hands on her hips and glared at him across the small clearing. "Frankly, I don't even want to sleep with you!"

With that she turned and whipped out her bedroll. Pointedly keeping her back toward him, she shook out the blanket and spread it on the ground. Then she lay down and wrapped it around her, turning on her side and facing away from Slater. She didn't even glance at him throughout the whole process.

Slater realized that he was grinding his teeth, and he forced his jaw to relax. He'd been doing a lot of that since he'd met Victoria. She was without a doubt the single most difficult person to deal with that he'd ever known. Here he was doing the decent thing, the gentlemanly thing, respecting her virtue despite the fact that he wanted her so badly that he had hardly slept the night before. And she acted as if he were a villain!

He was tempted to yank her out of the cocoon of her blanket and kiss her until she turned soft and yielding beneath his hands. What sweet revenge it would be to make her melt like syrup against him, to feel her tremble with hunger and press herself up into him, to conquer her with his lovemaking. He swallowed and clenched his fists at his sides. Damn, but she tempted him. Whether she was sweet or defiant, laughing or

spitting with anger, she tempted him. Keeping his hands off her
was turning out to be the hardest thing he'd ever done.

Slater spread out his own blanket and lay down, disgruntled
and feeling misused. You'd think that when he was practicing
such enormous self-restraint, the least Victoria could do was
not revile him for it. Other women would be grateful to him.
Other women would call him a gentleman for it.

The problem was, he didn't want other women. He wanted
Victoria, stubbornness, defiance and all.

Slater shut his eyes, willing sleep to come. But, of course, it
wouldn't. All he could think of was his anger—and how radiant her eyes were, how lustrous her hair, how soft and voluptuous her body. It would have given him some satisfaction
to know that on the other side of their camp, Victoria lay
equally wide awake and fuming.

Slater awoke the next morning feeling as though he had spent
the night on a bed of rocks. He vowed that he would leave Victoria behind as soon as they came to a town. Traveling with her
would kill him before Brody could. He glanced at her as they
silently made ready to leave. She was just as desirable this
morning as she had been last night.

He imagined putting Victoria up on his horse in front of him
and letting his hands roam over her body as they rode. Then she
would turn to straddle him, sinking down onto his stiffened
manhood, encasing him in her velvet fire as the horse gently
rocked below them.

Slater turned away, aware of how embarrassingly obvious the
direction of his mind must be. Why did she have this effect on
him?

They rode for the most of the morning without speaking
more than a few words. Slater couldn't rid his mind of the vision he had had of their riding together, and his sensitized flesh
was aware of every movement of the horse between his legs.
Doggedly he followed the tracks Brody and Amy had left, but
all the while he dreamed of hauling Victoria down from her
horse and ripping her clothes from her.

"There's something odd about these tracks," he commented, clearing his throat. He tried to concentrate on his job
instead of on Victoria.

"What?" Her tone was frosty, as it had been each time she'd had to speak to him. She wasn't really angry with Slater for not making love to her the night before. In the clear light of day she knew that he had been right. After all, she had decided long ago that there was no future for them. But she was nagged by the irritating thought that while she had been so far gone with desire that she was willing to toss all reason aside, Slater had apparently had no trouble conquering his desire for her.

"It looks like there are three people."

"Three?" His words surprised Victoria out of her iciness. "Do you think they have one of the gang with them now?"

"I don't know. But see these sets side by side? Over here, apart from them, I keep finding another set. Sometimes the two sets are messed up, as if the third one had ridden behind them."

"But why would there be only one of the gang with them?"

"I don't know. Maybe one of the men sided with Brody in the fight back at the hideout, and he left with them."

"Where do you think they're going?"

"We've been heading south. My guess is San Antonio."

"Why?"

"Brody has friends there. There's a woman who I know has hidden him before. She's a—" He stopped abruptly.

"She's a what?" Victoria gave him a hard stare. "Don't you dare tell me it's something I shouldn't hear."

"She's the madam of a brothel."

Victoria stared at him, fear dawning on her face. "You don't think—would he give Amy to that woman? Make her work for her?"

Slater shrugged. "It's possible he could sell her to Dorette. More likely they'll hide out with her. Where he'll go from there is anybody's guess. For some reason, I have this feeling . . ."

"What feeling?"

"That he's running for Mexico. His gang's broken up. His hideout's been breached. We're hot on his tail. I think he'll head for the border. Give himself a chance to recoup."

Victoria gnawed at her lower lip, disturbed. "And you couldn't chase him into Mexico?"

Slater shook his head.

"Then we have to be sure to catch him while he's still in Texas."

"We aren't far behind him. And if he goes to Dorette's place to lie low..." Slater grinned. "I think we've got him."

Victoria smiled back at him. Her smile hit him like a ton of bricks, and to cover it up, he looked away toward the horizon. He frowned. "That is, if a storm doesn't slow us down."

Victoria looked in the same direction as Slater. Dark, puffy storm clouds were piling up on the horizon. A few minutes ago, there hadn't been a cloud anywhere, but storms blew up quickly here, especially in the spring.

As they rode, Slater continued to glance toward the clouds massing ominously on the horizon. The storm moved closer and grew darker with every second. A cold wind blew up.

"Better find some shelter," Slater muttered.

"I can ride through the rain." But Victoria's face was uneasy. It looked like a hard thunderstorm was brewing. They kicked their horses into a trot.

Lightning forked through the dark clouds, which were now moving at a fast clip toward them, and thunder rumbled. They could see the sheets of rain pouring down in the distance. Then it was upon them. The rain fell so hard that it was like being pelted with tiny pieces of metal, and it was so thick and fast that within a minute they were drenched.

The sky blazed with light as lightning flashed directly overhead, and the clap of the thunder was deafening. Victoria's horse reared, and she had to fight to bring it back under control. Slater was right. They had to find shelter. She looked over at him. The rain was so thick that it blurred her vision. His hair and clothes were plastered to him, and she knew she must look the same.

They kept the horses moving forward despite the animals' skittishness. It was pointless to stop in the open. Nor was one of the large trees a good shelter, for while it would shelter them somewhat from the wind and rain, it would attract lightning. Victoria wished they could come upon a cave like the one yesterday, or at least a stone ledge under which they could huddle.

"Look!" Slater leaned forward, wiping the rain from his face in a vain attempt to see. "Isn't that a house?"

Victoria could see a dark, squat something in the distance. It could have been a formation of rocks for all she could tell. "Maybe."

They rode faster. Victoria's horse slipped a little in the mud, but caught itself and barreled on. As they grew closer, she could see that it was a small house—shack might have been a better description. She could also see that before they reached the house they would have to cross a river.

Slater pulled on his reins and stopped. He hopped off his horse and walked up to the edge of the water. It was a wide, shallow river. He could see the broad, flat rocks that covered the bottom. It couldn't have been deeper than half a foot. A few yards downriver, it deepened, but not more than a foot or two. In the normal course of events, Slater wouldn't have thought twice about crossing it, but in a heavy rainstorm like this there was the possibility of a flash flood. It happened swiftly, as its name implied, turning rock-strewn rivers like this into turbulent, rushing waters.

"It's still shallow!" Victoria called out. "Let's go."

Slater looked across the river. The house beckoned temptingly. If they crossed the river now, they could soon be warm and dry. But if they stayed here, the river would rise, and they would not only be cold and wet, they'd be trapped on the wrong side of it.

"All right. Let's go." He mounted his horse and started across the river, with Victoria right behind him.

They were halfway across when Victoria glanced upriver and saw a wall of water rushing straight at them. "Slater!" she screamed, spurring her horse forward. "Ride!"

Instinctively, Slater put his spurs to his horse at her words, even as he looked to see what was wrong. He saw the water rolling toward them, and he tensed, taking his reins in both hands and squeezing his legs around the horse's belly.

It hit them at the edge of the river bank. Victoria's horse stumbled under the force of the water, lost its footing and fell to its knees. Victoria clung to both the reins and her saddle horn. The water closed over her head, swirling around her, and pulled her from her saddle. Her horse floundered, trying to get its footing. It couldn't stand, but finally it broke the surface of the water, swimming with the strong flow. When it did, Victoria was no longer in her saddle, but beside the horse in the water, holding on for dear life to the saddle horn.

Water streamed down her face, and her wet hair was everywhere, obscuring her vision, but she didn't dare let go of the saddle with even one hand to brush it back. She shook her head to clear her face and breathed deeply, hanging on to the saddle and trying to swim with her mount.

"Victoria!"

She turned. Slater was still on his horse and reaching out for her. They were too far apart. Slater struggled to turn the animal, but Old Jack refused, swimming determinedly for safety. She heard Slater's vicious curses. Then a small tree rushed by her, and one of its branches struck her sharply in the back, knocking her loose from her horse, and she was swept down the river.

Slater saw what had happened, and he stopped his effort to turn his mount. Far lighter than he and his horse, Victoria would travel faster; he couldn't catch up with her in the water. He spurred Old Jack hard to the bank instead. Fortunately the horse found its footing and scrambled out of the rushing water. Slater turned Old Jack downriver and raced along the bank, searching for Victoria. He caught sight of her dark head in front of him, and he dug his heels in, leaning forward and calling encouragement to his mount, "Come on, Jack, come on, ole boy. Run, damn it!"

Victoria's horse lunged up the bank out of the water, and he had to swerve to avoid it, but Old Jack continued to run, closing the gap between them and Victoria.

At first Victoria could do nothing but roll and tumble helplessly in the water, struggling to the surface for a breath before she was pulled back under. She was dragged along the rocks, ripping her shirt and scraping her skin. But she barely noticed the pain. She was too busy fighting the rampaging water. Once, as she came up, she glimpsed Slater and his horse racing along the water's edge, and she was filled with hope. Slater would get her out. The panic receded, and she began to think. She had to get to the bank, where Slater could pull her out. She began to try to swim toward the side, but her waterlogged boots made her clumsy, and she made little progress. The boots were weighing her down, but they wouldn't come off, and she couldn't reach them to pull them off, with the water tumbling her about like a piece of deadwood.

A large branch whisked by her, and she had the presence of mind to grab it. She wrapped both her arms around it and pulled her head and shoulders up out of the water, resting on the log and letting it carry her. She gasped for air and looked for Slater. He was almost even with her. Holding on to her log, she kicked, trying to move toward the bank. It was no use.

A large rock jutted out of the water in front of her, and the branch rammed into it. The force of the impact snapped the branch and sent the piece Victoria held spinning off to one side. She grabbed frantically at a jumble of rocks at the edge of the river, letting go of the wood, but the stones were smooth and slick, and her fingers could find no purchase. She was swept onward with barely a pause. She was close to the bank now, and she clawed desperately at it, but her fingers found nothing but mud that gave way in her hands. The current was pulling her back out toward the center of the river. She grabbed blindly, and her fingers caught hold of a large root sticking out from a tree beside the shore.

Victoria curled her other hand around the root, too, and clung with all her strength. The water rushed around her, pulling at her. She could feel the tremendous suction around her hips and legs, dragging her down and out into the water. If her arms got tired, if her fingers gave out, she knew she'd be gone in an instant.

"Hang on, honey, I'm coming!" It was Slater's voice, just above her. It gave her renewed strength, and she tightened her grip. "I'm throwing you a rope. Look up."

She did so, and saw the loop of a lariat swooping through the air toward her. She held up one arm, and the rope settled neatly over both it and her head. It was just in time, for her other hand was pulled free of the log. She was sucked away by the water, but the loop tightened around her, stopping her.

Slater stood a few feet back from the bank, the rope wrapped around his waist for leverage. He held it with both hands, his heels planted firmly in the ground. With the last of her strength, Victoria began to kick. She had to help him, or the force of the water might carry both of them away. She held on to the rope with both hands and kicked through the water desperately.

Slater backed up, digging in his heels and pulling the rope with him, slipping in the mud, then regaining his footing over and over again, until he reached a large rock. He braced one leg against the rock so that he could hold firm and began to haul the rope in hand over hand.

It was a slow, agonizing process, for the water's pull was strong. But at last, as Victoria neared the bank, she was able to find her footing and climb up onto the bank as Slater pulled. When she came out of the water, the release was so sudden and great that Slater stumbled backward and went down in the mud. Victoria crawled across to him, too exhausted to stand. He reached out and jerked her to him, wrapping his arms tightly around her.

Heedless of the rain and the mud, they lay there, Slater gently rocking Victoria in his arms. "Victoria, Tory, oh, God, you scared me to death." He punctuated his words with brief, hard kisses all over her hair and face. "I thought I'd lost you."

His heart was pounding so hard that it seemed it might leap out of his chest, and his stomach was a solid block of ice. He'd never been as scared in his life as he had been during the past few minutes—not even in the midst of battle, when men were falling all around him.

Victoria said nothing. She couldn't. She could only shudder and cling to him.

Slater kissed her forehead, her eyes, her cheeks. He took her chin in his hand and tilted her face up, and he kissed her on the mouth. It was a deep, driving kiss, a kiss born of fear and the need to reassure himself that they were both alive. Victoria's arms flew up around his neck, and she answered him with the same fervor. She strained against him, and his arms tightened around her. The life force pulsed inside them, fierce and strong, routing the fear of death. He worked his mouth against hers with no regard for gentleness, restraint or reason. His legs wrapped around hers, pressing her into him so that she felt the hard bulge of his masculinity. But Victoria didn't recoil from his ardor; she savored the unmistakable proof of his desire, moving her hips so that her body rubbed against his.

Slater groaned. He kissed her again and again. He wanted to be inside her; he yearned to fill her and feel her close tightly around him. It was almost a physical pain not to be part of her.

He rolled over on top of her, grinding his pelvis into her. He felt strong and primitive and hungry. He had almost lost her, and now he was desperate to have her. He wanted to make Victoria part of him, as if that would ensure that he wouldn't lose her again.

But the cold wind and the hard, drenching rain on his back finally penetrated the thick haze of his desire. This was neither the time nor the place, and he had to overcome the savage masculinity that was pumping through him now. He couldn't take Victoria here in the mud and the rain, stealing her virginity while she was filled with gratitude for him. He broke off their kiss and buried his face in her neck, willing the storm in him to subside enough that he could let go of her.

"We need," he panted at last, "to find shelter. We have to get you dry and warm."

His arms eased around her, but for an instant Victoria held on stubbornly. She didn't want him to stop, didn't want to release him. But she was also shivering in the cold and from the shock of her experience, and she knew he was right. Reluctantly she dropped her arms.

He helped her up. Both horses were standing nearby, their backs to the wind, miserably wet. Slater mounted and took Victoria up in front of him, cradling her against his chest. He refused to let her out of the protection of his arms. Victoria leaned against him, happy to be coddled for once. She was exhausted and cold, and she wanted nothing but to be close to Slater.

When he had pulled her from the water and taken her in his arms, she had gone to him as if he were her home, her life. She had known then, in that moment of utter, raw honesty, that she loved him.

She wondered how she could have been so blind as not to have seen it before this. He had maddened and provoked her precisely because he was the man for her. He was the first man she had ever met who was strong enough for her, who had the kind of courage, honor and grit she needed. Because of that, they had clashed titanically. He was the only man who had threatened her heart and her peace of mind, and because of that he had frightened her.

She loved Slater, and she always would. Victoria was not a woman who wavered, nor one to give her heart lightly. She had always known that when she loved, it would be forever. However much or little Slater felt for her would not change that fact. And she wanted that love physically; she wanted to belong to him and know that he belonged to her. She wanted his body, his lips, his heart—even if it was for no more than today. For whatever she had of him would be all that she had of love for the rest of her life.

Chapter Fifteen

They rode back to the dilapidated house that Slater had spotted earlier. There was a small lean-to behind it that was adequate shelter for the horses. Slater unsaddled the animals and left them tied in the lean-to, then carried Victoria into the house. She made no protest that she could walk, just laid her head upon his shoulder. She had no desire right now to be either strong or independent.

Her acquiescent manner frightened Slater a little. He thought she might have been hurt somewhere that he hadn't seen, or that she was going into shock. He knew he had to get her warm and dry immediately.

The inside of the cabin was bare except for one broken-down cupboard. A rock fireplace stood on one wall, but there was no dry wood for miles around. Slater broke up the doors and shelves of the cupboard and stacked them in the fireplace. It was a difficult fire to light, but he finally did it.

He had brought in their saddlebags and bedrolls, and now he dug through them for something dry that Victoria could put on. The blankets were soaked, but he had stuck an extra shirt in one of the saddlebags, and it had remained dry.

"Here. This will have to do," he said, taking the shirt to Victoria. "We have to get these wet things off you."

He knelt and took off her boots, then stood and began to unbutton her blouse. His intent wasn't sexual, even though his body still throbbed from the passion of their earlier kisses. He simply wanted to take care of her. He was filled with a deep, primitive feeling that he didn't stop to analyze, an awareness that she was his and infinitely precious, that he had almost lost her and now must take doubly good care of her.

He unfastened her blouse quickly and peeled it back off her shoulders, letting it drop to the floor in a sodden heap. His breath caught in his throat, and suddenly the sexual provocation of what he was doing slammed into him. Victoria's wet chemise was molded to her like a second skin and almost completely transparent. It cupped her breasts, revealing the rose circles of her areolae, ringing the darker, pointing buds of her nipples.

Desire surged in Slater, swift and elemental. He had never wanted a woman as he wanted Victoria now, with a deep, primitive sense of possession. He looked at Victoria, and she gazed back at him, her eyes soft and radiant, without saying a word. He knew, as he had known by the riverbank, that he would have her, that there was no other course for either of them.

Victoria's cheeks were tinged with pink. She knew how clearly the wet garment revealed her breasts; she might as well have been naked before him. But what she felt when his hungry eyes touched her was only partly embarrassment. There was a wild sort of excitement in her, too, and pride in her beauty and desirability. It made her breathless to see him look at her and watch his lips and eyes turn heavy with passion. A heavy, warm ache started deep inside her, and it grew as he gazed at her.

Slater unhooked the top fastening of Victoria's chemise. His hands slid down, his knuckles grazing the supremely soft flesh of her breasts, to the next hook and eye. By the time he finished undoing the chemise, his hands were trembling. He opened the scanty garment and slid it off her. He stared at her, his lips parted. Her breasts were luscious and full, the pebbled nipples like little raspberries. His manhood swelled, straining against his trousers.

Slater unbuckled the wide leather belt around her waist, then unbuttoned her skirt and let it fall to the floor. Victoria was left in nothing but her long cotton underpants and stockings, both as transparent and clinging as her chemise had been. He could not look away from the smooth swell of her hips and the wide, flat plane of her abdomen, or the thicket of dark hair beneath.

Her legs were long and slender, finely shaped. Dainty blue satin and white lace garters encircled her thighs to hold up her stockings, and he found the sight of them unbelievably erotic.

Slater slid off each garter and crushed it in his hand, struggling to control his lust. He rolled down the wet stockings, his hands gliding over her skin. He untied the ribbon at the waist of her underpants, but they were too wet to slide to the floor, and he had to roll them down as he had the stockings, touching the sleek skin of her hips and thighs. He longed to sink his fingertips into her and pull her forward for his mouth to devour.

At last he was done, and he stood up, his eyes roaming over her. She was lovely, perfect. He wanted to explore every curve and valley of her flesh, to caress her breasts and slip into the warm, feminine, secret place between her legs and find the dew of passion there.

He would make love to her this afternoon. The life force surging in him demanded it. There was no longer any thought in him of what was wrong or right, of how he ought to act with a young lady like Victoria. There was only the driving need to make her his. But he must go more slowly than his throbbing desire demanded. Victoria was untouched, and no matter how fiercely, how blindly, he wanted her, he had to bring her to the act of love with care and tenderness.

Slater picked up his flannel shirt and dried her skin. The flannel was soft against her flesh, creating a delightful friction. Victoria let out a breathy sigh, and her eyes fluttered closed. Slater circled her breasts with the cloth, lingering on her nipples, moving the material around and around each one until they puckered, thrusting out boldly. His hand moved down her stomach and abdomen, stopping short of the thatch of hair where her legs joined. He moved the shirt over the curve of her buttocks and down her thighs. He knelt to dry her calves and feet. He stood up. His heart was racing, his nerves humming with desire.

He wanted to grab her and take her down to the floor with him. Instead he laid the shirt around her shoulders to cover her and stepped back.

Victoria's eyes opened, and she looked at him, bewildered. Why had he stopped? Slater stood across from her, his chest rising and falling in short, rapid breaths. There was no mistaking his desire; it pushed crudely against his trousers. But he had wanted her before and had stopped then. "Slater?"

"I want you, Victoria." His voice was husky. "But I don't want to rush you. I don't want to push you into anything you might regret."

She smiled, a slow, secret, sensuous smile. "I won't regret it."

Her words twisted a trail of fire through him. Slater knew he had expended what gentlemanly conduct he had left in him. He began to undress, his fingers clumsy and slow on his buttons. All the while, Victoria simply stood, waiting and watching. She didn't put her arms into his shirt and button it, or even pull it closed around her. She left it hanging on her shoulders, open down the front so that a tantalizing stretch of her naked skin showed from her neck to her legs. The shirt stopped partway down her thighs, leaving her long, well-curved legs exposed to his gaze. In a way, it was more titillating than if she had stood before him completely naked.

Slater yanked off his shirt, hampered by its wetness, and dumped it on the floor. Victoria sucked in her breath sharply at the sight of his bare chest. She had seen it before when he was sick, but this was different. Now he was well and undressing for her. In a few minutes she would be in his arms, and he would make her a woman, his woman. She felt equal parts of anxiety and excitement, and seeing Slater's naked, powerful chest only increased both feelings. He was so strong, so utterly masculine, that it was scary. He could overpower her—not just physically, but emotionally, as well. She loved him; she wanted him. How easy it would be for him to rule her with her own emotions. As easy as it had been for him to lift her in his arms and carry her into the house.

The smooth, sleek muscles of his chest and arms invited her touch. She remembered the feel of his skin as she had bathed away his fever. She wondered how different it would be to rub her hand across it without the cloth in between, when the heat in his skin was from desire, not fever. Light brown hair grew in a V across his chest, narrowing into a line down to his navel. Victoria thought about twining her fingers through the curls;

she wondered if the hair was stiff or soft. She wanted to touch his masculine nipples. Would they harden as hers did now?

Slater pulled off his boots and socks and peeled down the soaked, clinging trousers. Victoria's eyes widened as his full, distended manhood came into view. The heat between her legs increased. He was too big; he would hurt her—and yet she ached to feel him inside her. She wanted to take him into her; she yearned to feel the full extent of his power.

Slater saw the mingled apprehension and desire on her face. It was rare to see uncertainty on Victoria's face; he looked forward to teaching her what she did not know. "Don't worry, sweetheart." His voice was low and reassuring. "I'll be gentle with you. I won't hurt you."

Victoria summoned up a small smile. "I'm not sure you can help that. But I know that you'll do your best not to. And I—I want to, anyway."

He came toward her. He was narrow-hipped, his legs long and lean, lightly covered with curling hair. Victoria had never seen a naked man before, and though she felt a blush of embarrassment rising in her cheeks, she was too curious to look away. Excitement rose in her throat.

Slater took her hand and raised it to his lips. His mustache tickled her skin. "I promise, it's not as fearsome as it looks." He brought her hand down to brush his thickened staff. "Here, touch it. It won't harm you."

When her fingers grazed it, his manhood leaped, startling her, and she drew her hand back with a soft gasp. But she brought it back, brushing her fingertips down him in tentative curiosity. Again his staff pulsed at her touch, but Victoria wasn't surprised this time, and she curled her fingers around him softly. Slater drew in his breath.

"What? I'm sorry. Did I do something wrong? Did I hurt you?"

"No." His voice was low and thick with restraint. "Far from it. You give me too much pleasure. I'm afraid I'll get too excited and rush you."

Victoria's hand circled gently around him, then stroked back up the underside. Her fingers delved curiously into the nest of hair out of which his manhood sprang, then roamed lower. Slater groaned, and his teeth bit into his lower lip. She glanced up at his face. Sweat glistened on his forehead, and his face was drawn tight. His lids drooped down over his eyes, heavy with passion, and his mouth was fuller and softer than before. The sensuality of his expression sent tendrils of desire down into Victoria's abdomen, where they tangled and knotted in an ever-growing ache of desire.

"Now you must give me my turn," Slater whispered, and his hands came up to rest on the center of her chest. He slid his fingers beneath the sides of the shirt and pushed it back off her shoulders. His hands moved down to the heavy globes of her breasts, and he squeezed gently. The soft flesh quivered beneath his touch. He cupped her breasts, luxuriating in their weight and texture. His thumbs traced ever-narrowing circles until they touched her areolae and then the nipples themselves. The soft, fleshy buds tightened and puckered. Slater watched their transformation with a hot, heavy-lidded gaze.

When he touched her nipples, Victoria began to throb between her legs, and she realized that she was damp there. As his thumbs continued to play with her nipples, the throbbing grew more insistent, and she became wetter and wetter. The moisture embarrassed her; she didn't understand it, but she thought it probably shouldn't happen. Still, she could not will it to stop.

He left her breasts and slid down her stomach, his hands teasing at the circle of her navel and spreading out over her abdomen. Down he traveled, and she moved a little nervously.

"There, now," he said soothingly, as he would calm a skittish horse. "It's all right. I won't hurt you."

"I know," Victoria replied breathlessly. "It's just that I've never been—oh!"

His hands slid around to curve over her tight, rounded buttocks and down to her thighs, startling her. His smile was slow, and so sensual that her stomach flip-flopped. "I know you haven't. But I'll teach you."

Slater's hand glided around her thighs and up to her abdomen. Then, to her astonishment, one hand went to the curling V of hair where her legs joined. Victoria had never imagined a man touching her in so private a place, and she moved a little, but his other hand on her hip held her firmly where she was. His fingers slid down and in between her legs, touching the satin-soft flesh. He would feel that strange dampness there!

"Ah." His eyes closed briefly, and his nostrils flared. His fingers gently caressed the secret feminine folds, slick with the liquid of her desire. "Sweet. You're ready for me."

She looked at him. His face was flushed, his mouth stretched wide. His eyes were piercing, almost silvery. He leaned closer, his hand remaining where it was, and kissed her. Victoria moaned softly, her head falling back, surrendering to his kiss. His lips moved over hers, angling one way and then the other, insistent and searing. His tongue delved into her mouth, coaxing her own tongue out in a slow, simmering dance. All the while, his fingers rubbed and teased and opened her. His finger slid up into her, imitating the penetration of his tongue into her mouth.

Victoria whimpered. She felt invaded, but deliciously so. Unconsciously her hips moved against his hand, circling in invitation. She felt the blast of his heated breath against her cheek, and his mouth dug into her as if he would consume her.

He trailed kisses across her cheek to her ear and worried it between his teeth, shooting wild sparks through her. His tongue explored the curves of her ear; then his mouth went lower, feasting on her neck. He pulled her down to the floor with him as he kissed the long column of her throat and moved onto her chest. His lips touched the trembling top of one breast. He stopped, and his tongue began to trace looping circles down her breast, going lower and lower until it reached her nipple.

Victoria shivered, her nipple pointing in response, and at that moment, his finger slid up to find the small fleshy nub among the slick folds of her femininity. She was bombarded with wildly exciting sensations, both from that small pleasure point and from her engorged nipple. Her breasts seemed to swell, and her whole body grew hot. She had never felt anything like this, never even imagined it. She was lost in a haze of pleasure, hardly knowing who or where she was, aware only of the places where Slater touched her and the ever-increasing throbbing between her legs.

Slater's mouth was wet and hot on her breast. His tongue lashed her nipple, then laved it slowly and soothingly, then circled it tauntingly. Victoria arched up toward his mouth, seeking more, although she wasn't sure what she sought. At last he gave it to her, his whole mouth closing down on her nipple and pulling at the hard bud. He suckled her, his tongue all the while moving over her nipple, while between her legs his finger brushed lightly and rhythmically over the pulsing center of her passion.

Victoria groaned, writhing beneath him, begging him with her body to bring her satisfaction. Slater could take no more of his love play. He was on fire from her eager, inexperienced responses, and he thought that if he waited a moment longer he would explode, or go mad. He moved between her legs, his stiff manhood prodding at the tender flesh his fingers had just loved. Slowly he slid into her, sinking inch by inch into her tight flesh. It was his single, last coherent thought that he would not breach her quickly and cause her pain, but would ease her maidenhead from her.

But Victoria was too inflamed, too eager, to wait, and she pushed up against him, hardly noticing the spurt of pain in her longing to ease the throbbing ache inside her. Slater thrust home then, his passion soaring out of control as she stretched to accommodate him, her tight, virginal body taking him into her. He began to move in long, steady thrusts, shoving into her as though he would touch the very center of her being. He was aching and wild, mindless in his need to possess her. They went higher and higher, beyond all limits, until at last they exploded together, shuddering in spasms of release. Victoria gasped, clutching at his back, and Slater groaned out her name, his fingers digging into her hips.

They clung together, riding the waves of their passion, until at last they reached the other side, exhausted, trembling and sated.

Brody and Amy rode hard and fast for San Antonio. He wasted no time trying to cover their tracks. He was sure that Slater would guess his destination, anyway. From here on in, he thought, it would simply be a race to Mexico. He figured that between Slater's exploring the cave and having to walk to the horses, he and Amy would have at least a couple of hours' head start. He knew their horses were tough, and he would push them to the limit. In San Antonio, he could purchase fresh mounts for the rest of the trip.

With luck, he would be able to throw Slater off their trail in the city. Slater couldn't follow their tracks on the heavily traveled streets, and Brody was sure that no one at Dorette's would betray him. He and Amy could rest for the night, get new horses and supplies, then head for Mexico.

It looked as if the odds were with him the next afternoon when the skies opened and torrential rains poured down. He and Amy had already crossed the Guadalupe River, and there were only creeks between them and San Antonio. But Slater would be trapped for at least another day on the other side when the rains swelled the river.

Sam put the yellow slicker he'd brought with him from the hideout over Amy, and they rode through the rain. There was no good place to stop for shelter, anyway. They continued through the afternoon, and even risked the last few miles into San Antonio in the dark. Once in the city, Brody made his way to a large house, which sat next to a saloon.

As Amy dismounted, she glanced around her in surprise. People here seemed not to notice the lateness of the hour. There were lights on in many establishments up and down the street. She could hear laughter and loud talking from the saloon. The door to the house stood open, only its screen door closed, and from inside came the noise of people enjoying themselves, as well as the tinkling of a piano.

"Are they having a party?" she asked Sam innocently as he led her toward the front door.

He gave a short bark of laughter. "No. Not exactly."

"They sound as if they're having a good time."

"They always have a good time at Dorette's." Sam put his arm around her shoulders, pulling her close. "You stay right with me in here, understand? Don't wander off."

"I understand."

Sam opened the screen door, and they stepped inside. Sam glanced around the two large rooms on either side of the hallway, looking for someone. Amy simply stared. She had never seen anything like this place.

The furniture was heavy and ornate, much like the fancier pieces in her own home, but the couches and chairs were of red velvet, with none of the darker colors or leathers she was used to. The curtains, too, were heavy velvet of a dark red color, draped back and tied with thick golden ropes. In the corner of one of the rooms, a thin black man played a piano. Against one wall of the other room was a large bar, well stocked, with another black man behind it, serving drinks.

But it wasn't the furniture or the bar that caused Amy to gape. It was the occupants of the rooms. Over half of them were men, all sorts of men in dress ranging from the rough clothes of a ranch hand to elegant evening wear. They sat and stood around the room, drinking and smoking cigars. And chatting with them, perched on couches, or the arms of chairs, or even in the laps of some of the men, were women in the scantiest clothes Amy had ever seen. Some wore satin dresses, cut so low at the neckline that half their bosom showed. Others wore sheer nightgowns and robes that anyone could see right through. Some were even dressed in only their underwear—lacy chemises and ruffled corsets, with black patterned stockings and garters. Their cheeks and lips were abnormally red, and their eyelids were colored and lined with black. Hanging over the fireplace in each room was a large oil painting of a woman, nude except for a diaphanous cloth draped strategically across her lower abdomen.

Amy turned slowly around, her jaw dropping open, staring. Beside her, Brody shifted uneasily. He had forgotten what the inside of Dorette's house looked like. The truth was, he'd never really noticed it until he had Amy with him.

"Sam?" Amy turned and looked up at him in amazement. "Who are these people? Why are the women dressed like that?"

"Well, uh . . ." He was saved from having to answer by the arrival of a well-endowed woman whose hair was a startling shade of red. She wore a dark green velvet dress cut to show off her magnificent breasts. A black feather was stuck in her hair and curled down to brush her cheek.

"Brody!" she cried in a husky, appealing voice. "You ole devil. Where the hell did you spring from?"

She threw her arms around him and hugged him, then kissed him soundly on the mouth. Amy was aware of a distinctly unpleasant emotion rising in her chest; she was too inexperienced to recognize it as jealousy.

"Hello, Dorette." Sam returned the hug, but he broke off the kiss quickly. Dorette glanced from him to Amy, and her eyes narrowed shrewdly.

"My, my, my, what have we here? What is going on? Last I heard you broke outta jail in Santa Clara and hightailed it north, and now here you are on my doorstep with a Sunday-school teacher on your arm."

"It's a long story. We need a place to stay for the night. And quickly. Folks are starting to stare."

Amy couldn't imagine why anyone would stare at them, considering all the oddly dressed women in the house, but several curious glances had been sent their way.

"Sure thing." Dorette led them down the hall, away from the crowd. They passed through the kitchen and up a back staircase to the floor above. They walked along two hallways that crossed in a T, and Dorette opened the door of one of the rooms. Sam and Amy walked past her into the room.

"Anything I can get you?"

"Yeah. Food. Something to drink." Amy tugged at his shirtsleeve and whispered something to him. He smiled down at her fondly. "Sure." He turned back to Dorette. "And a bath?"

"Coming right up." Dorette studied his face for a moment. She'd known Sam Brody a lot of years, and she'd never seen him look at a woman the way he'd just looked at this one. Come to think of it, there was something altogether different about his face, something peaceful and relaxed, the fierceness and sharp edges smoothed away. Dorette was more curious than ever about Amy. But she knew better than to ask. Brody only told you what he wanted, and in his own time. Dorette left, closing the door behind her.

Amy walked into the middle of the room, staring around her with openmouthed wonderment. Sam watched her, a smile hovering about his lips. He could imagine what kind of questions she was going to ask in a minute.

A huge bed, covered with a rich red-and-gold spread, dominated the room. There was also a small red velvet love seat, an ornate marble-topped washstand, and a vanity with a low, red velvet chair. A floor-length mirror hung on one wall, and another wide mirror covered the ceiling above the bed. Amy craned her neck to look up at it.

"Why on earth is there a mirror on the ceiling?" she asked, turning to Sam. "What are you grinning about?"

"You. You look adorable when you wrinkle your nose like that." He walked over to her. "It makes me want to kiss you."

Amy happily turned up her face to oblige him. But when he finally pulled away from her, she continued with her questions. "Isn't this the oddest room you've ever seen? And why are those women downstairs dressed like that?"

Sam sighed. He touched her cheek. "I shouldn't have brought you to a place like this. But I've frequently hidden out here. Dorette's a good friend. She'd never give me away. She's a madam, Amy. This house is like the one I was born in, the one where my mother worked. It's a house of ill repute."

"Oh." Amy looked at him. "Then you mean the women down there sell themselves to men, like you talked about?"

He nodded.

"Dorette, too?"

"Not anymore, unless she happens to want to. She runs the place, so she can do as she pleases."

She paused, digesting the information. "Did you and Dorette ever... I mean..."

He grinned. Amy looked jealous. He found the idea rather pleasing. "No. We've just been friends for a long, long time. I helped her out once, and I loaned her the money when she started this place. She's somebody I can count on."

"Like Raul."

"Yeah. Like Raul."

"I'm glad," Amy admitted candidly. "I didn't like thinking you'd done the same thing with her that you'd and I do."

"I've never had that with any woman, not like you and I." His face was suddenly serious.

A smile glowed on Amy's face. "That makes me even gladder." She paused, then said very seriously, "But why are those mirrors there?"

He chuckled, shaking his head. "This is Dorette's fanciest room. It's where some of the women come with the men who hire them. And the mirrors are so you can look up and see yourself and the person you're with."

Amy's eyes widened, and she stared at the bed, then up at the mirror over it. "You mean you look in it while you're loving?"

She gazed at Brody in amazement.

Sam smiled. "Yeah." Just talking to Amy about such things and seeing her in this blatantly sexual room started a familiar heavy ache in his loins. She was dressed in the outfit she wore for riding, the boy's trousers and shirts, and she looked incongruous in the midst of the richness and decadence of the room, but somehow that made her all the more alluring.

Amy glanced at the mirror, then cast a sideways look at Sam. A faint blush tinged her cheeks, and Sam knew what she was thinking: she was wondering if they would use it tonight. His blood began to thrum in his veins, rushing down to pool in his loins and build the heat there.

Sam drew a long breath. There were things he had to do. He couldn't let his passion lead him into ignoring them. "I must go now, Amy. I have to buy new horses and supplies for tomorrow. We can't afford to lose any time in the morning."

"At this hour? How can you look at horses?"

"The horse trader won't object. He's seen me before at odd hours. I trust him to give me his best mounts. He knows what will happen to him if I discover they're duds by the light of day. I can probably get the supplies from Dorette. I'll be back as fast as I can. In the meantime, Dorette and the girls will take good care of you. I promise."

"All right. But, Sam . . . hurry back. Please?"

He would have done anything when she asked him like that, let alone something he wanted to do anyway. "I will."

It didn't take Sam long to transact his business. He kept thinking about Amy back in that room, with the soft bed waiting for them. When he returned to Dorette's, he decided he could discuss the supplies with her later. He hurried up the stairs to his room, his mind so centered on Amy that he didn't notice that a thin man had followed him to Dorette's house and up the stairs. The man tiptoed down the hall, pausing outside each room until he heard the voices he sought. He listened for a few minutes, a sly smile spreading across his face, then went quietly back down the stairs and out into the street to wait.

When Sam stepped into the room, he stopped abruptly, stunned. Mechanically, he reached behind him to close the door, all the while staring at Amy. She smiled at him, turning around slowly for his approval.

She wore a pink satin gown that had obviously been lent to her by Dorette. The bodice was held up by two narrow straps across her shoulders, decorated with pink velvet bows, and the neck was scooped out in a heart shape that left most of her white chest and shoulders bare, as well as the quivering tops of her breasts. The tight boning of the dress pushed her breasts up and together, and the neckline dipped down in the center to give an ample view of the cleavage the garment had created. A tiny pink rosebud nestled at the lowest point of the neckline, snug between her breasts. The waist was impossibly small; then the dress swelled out again around her hips. It was drawn into a small bustle in the back, and the skirt was tighter than what women normally wore, so that it stretched across her abdomen and thighs, delineating their curves.

Amy's skin was soft and pink from the hot bath she had taken, and the lilac perfume with which she had scented the water hung enticingly in the air. Her hair, clean and shining silver-gold, had been done up atop her head, leaving her slender white throat naked and heart-stoppingly vulnerable.

Sam had never seen anything as beautiful. Or as desirable. Blood rushed into his head, pounding and violent, and for a moment he could not speak.

"Well, do you like it?" Amy asked, not content with the expression of stunned wonder on his face. She wanted to hear his voice, husky with passion, telling her that she was beautiful.

"Don't go downstairs like that, or you'll cause a riot." He walked toward her. "God, you're gorgeous." He knew there must have been a mistake made somewhere. There was no way he should have a woman as lovely and loving as this.

A smile burst across Amy's face like sunshine. "Thank you." She looked back at herself in the mirror. "I found this dress in the closet, and Dorette let me wear it. Wasn't that sweet of her?"

"Um-hmm."

He stopped behind her and ran his hands lightly up her arms and rested them on her shoulders. He gazed at their joint reflection in the mirror. Amy was shimmering and beautiful, a vision in that dress. He looked dark, hard and dirty beside her.

"I shouldn't even touch you. I'm still dirty from the trail."

"You shouldn't be dirty," Amy teased. "As I remember, we had quite a bath this afternoon."

"Not exactly the kind I had in mind." He stepped away. "I'd better wash up and shave."

She took his hand to pull him to the washstand. "Look, a maid brought this razor and soap for you. There's even warm water." She smiled in a low, warm way that made his nerves sizzle. "I like to watch you shave."

He looked at her in surprise. "You do?"

She nodded. "Yes. It's—I don't know—it makes me feel that you belong to me. I get all hot inside. Is that silly?"

Sam swallowed. "No. No, it's not silly." But it made him want to throw her back on the bed and rip apart the bodice of her dress with his hands.

Amy dipped a cloth in the steaming water for him. She wrung it out and cupped his face with it, stretching up on tiptoe.

"Better let me do that." He reached for the cloth.

"No. I like to care for you. Please?"

His breath became a little more ragged. "All right. I'll sit down, then, so you won't have to reach." He sat on the edge of the bed. That was a mistake; he kept thinking how easy it would be to lie back and pull Amy down on top of him. But he sat still. She stood in front of him, her hands holding the cloth in place on his face. She was so close that he could smell the scent of lilacs on her skin, and his eyes were at the level of her bosom, only inches away. He longed to bury his face between her milky breasts. It was sweet torture to remain where he was, letting her minister to him.

When his beard was softened, Amy whisked up a lather with the shaving soap and brushed it across his cheeks and jaw and neck, then handed him the razor.

Sam moved to the mirror above the washstand. Amy took his seat on the bed, curling her legs up under her, and watched him. There was a warm glow in her eyes that made his hands unsteady on the blade. He nicked himself twice.

When he had finished shaving, Amy showed him the ivory-and-gold slipper tub sitting by the fireplace, which the maid had filled with water for his bath. She went to the fireplace and picked up the kettle of water heating over the fire.

Sam stripped off his vest and began to unbutton his shirt. "You going to watch me do that, too?" His voice was teasing, but the thought turned him pulsing and hard.

Amy poured the kettle of steaming water into the tub and looked back over her shoulder at him, her expression arch. "Actually, I was going to help you."

His fingers stilled on the buttons. "What?"

A hot blush rose in her face. "You know, wash your back and all. That is, if you don't mind."

Sam's mind was so focused on the erotic picture she evoked that it took him a moment to speak. "No. I don't mind." His mouth widened sensually, and his lids drooped down to hide the fierce desire in his eyes. "I don't mind at all."

Sam skinned out of his clothes as fast as he ever remembered doing, kicking off his boots and tossing aside his clothes with no regard to where they fell. He was done almost as soon as Amy turned around from emptying the kettle into the tub. He walked across the room and stepped into the tub. He saw Amy's eyes drop down to the evidence of how just the sight of her had aroused him. Seeing her look at him only made his manhood swell anew.

Sam lowered himself into the tub. It was too short, and he had to sit with his knees bent, but he didn't mind. Amy picked up a rag, soaped it and began to lazily circle his chest. Sam leaned back against the rim of the tub, closing his eyes. The hot water was soothing to his tired muscles, but the feel of Amy's hand on him was anything but relaxing. Everywhere she touched him, his nerves caught on fire, the flames racing down to his groin, where they simmered and grew.

"You should see the things in this room," Amy told him as she rinsed off his chest and started on his arms. "I've never seen anything like them. I looked through the drawers and closet for something to wear after I took my bath, and I found underthings made out of lace and just nothing. Well, you'll see when I take off this dress."

Sam's eyes popped open. Sweat gathered on his upper lip. "You put some on?" he croaked.

"Well, yes. I didn't have anything else, and I had to wear something underneath my dress." That evoked an even more tantalizing image, and Sam groaned. "And the nightgowns—well, you can see right through them, and they're cut down to here in the front." She pointed to a spot almost to her waist. "One of them was slit up the side, too. But, Sam, that wasn't the strangest thing. Lean forward and let me wash your back."

He obeyed her, unable to keep from asking, "What was the strangest thing?"

"There were fancy ropes in one of the drawers, red and gold, and they looked as if they were made out of silk. And there was this corset, or at least I guess it was a corset, but it was made out of leather. What is that? Do they wear them?"

"I suspect so," he replied in a muffled voice, torn between laughter and lust at her innocent descriptions of the prostitutes' clothes and appurtenances.

She washed his legs and feet, then shampooed and rinsed his hair, all the while continuing to describe the variety of sexual devices she had uncovered. It was almost more than he could bear to feel her fingertips massaging his scalp while her sweet voice talked of velvet gloves and black lace corsets. Worst of all was that she asked him for explanations. It seemed as if the more he tried to explain them without offending her sensibilities, the harder he grew.

Finally he growled, "Hush, or I'll have you wear one of those costumes." He looped his arm around her shoulders and pulled her close to nuzzle her neck.

"Really?" Amy asked, wide-eyed and breathless. "Would you like to see me in one?"

He groaned and kissed her, his tongue filling her mouth. He pulled back slightly. "I'd love to see you in anything. Or nothing." He kissed her again, and his hand brushed her breast where it was pushed up out of her dress, trembling and full and soft. "I'm getting you wet," he whispered finally, breaking their kiss and leaning his forehead against hers, struggling for breath.

"I don't mind." Amy slid out of his grasp and stood up. "I'll take it off, and that way we won't have to worry."

Sam watched, his face falling into the heavy lines of sexual excitement, as she unhooked her dress down the front and stepped out of it.

"These clothes are nice," Amy remarked with a little giggle, "'cause they're easy to get out of."

She stood before him clad in white satin and lace underclothes. They clung to her body softly, outlining each curve. The top of the chemise that cupped her breasts was made of lace, revealing glimpses of her white skin and rosy nipples. Her nipples prickled and pushed against the webs of lace under Sam's gaze. He stood up, unable just to watch her anymore. He curved his hands over her breasts, and the lace got wet; it clung even more closely to her skin. He rubbed the lace gently across her nipples, stimulating them with its delicate friction. He loved to watch her nipples harden and elongate beneath his fingers, visible proof that he could arouse in her the same swirling excitement that she caused in him.

Amy's eyes fluttered closed, and she breathed his name. The sight of her lost in passion stirred Sam even more than the provocative garments she wore. He stepped out of the tub and pulled her up into his arms, lifting her so that their faces were level. He kissed her, his mouth grinding into hers. Amy twined her arms around his neck and clung to him, uncaring that her feet dangled off the floor or that he was getting her wet. All she cared about was Sam; all she wanted was his lovemaking.

Sam walked with her across the room to the bed and fell down on it, never ceasing his hot, hungry kisses. They rolled across the bed, tearing off Amy's few remaining garments, kissing and stroking as if they would consume each other. He kissed her everywhere, his mouth sliding lower and lower until it found the hot center of her desire and teased it into pulsating life. His hands dug into her hips, holding her captive beneath his questing mouth. Amy writhed, digging her fingers into his hair, and whimpered for release. But he did not bring her to it yet, holding her tantalizingly just short of the summit. His tongue teased with infinite slowness, building the searing knot inside her until it was so huge and fiery that it consumed her. Then, at last, he thrust into her, filling her powerfully.

Amy groaned and clutched at his back, her fingernails digging into him. "Sam, oh, please."

He paused, fighting for the control to prolong their pleasure. Amy's hands skimmed over his back and buttocks with the shaking, erratic movements of a person on the edge of losing all reason and control. His skin was slick with sweat. Sam pulled back, almost leaving her, causing her to cry out and cling to him, then thrust back in, groaning as she closed around him, slick and tight. It was heaven; it was madness. He thrust in a primal rhythm, lost in the almost unbearable pleasure. Amy sobbed, moving her hips with him, her legs locked around his back, loving the feel of him inside her, so huge and hard, and yet wanting more, more.

She teetered on the edge and finally fell into the dark abyss of pleasure, flying free and wild. She shuddered, and her teeth sank into Sam's shoulder. The sharp prick of sensual pain as she bit him, the feeling of her tightening, then melting, around him, spurred Sam into his own explosive release. He cried out, digging his fingers into the sheets, and poured his seed into her. For an instant they hung suspended together, joined in every way. Then the moment was over, leaving behind the sweet taste of fulfillment. Sam held her, rolling onto his back and taking her weight on him, and they lay cuddled together, quietly slipping into sleep.

It was some hours later that Sam awakened, his body growing cool. He edged out of Amy's arms and pulled the sheet over her so that she would not be chilled. He stood for a moment, looking down at her. For the hundredth time, he wondered where his luck had come from that she should love him, that she would willingly follow him into exile.

He bent and brushed a kiss across her forehead, and she smiled in her sleep, snuggling into her pillow. Sam went to the closet and pulled down a box. Inside were a folded set of his clothes and a small box of money. He dressed and stuck most of the money into his saddlebag. The rest he put in his pocket and went downstairs, looking for Dorette.

He found her in her office, where she usually was this late at night, totting up the evening's receipts. When he stuck his head inside the door, she smiled and waved him inside. "Want a drink?'' she asked, opening the bottom doors of a narrow mahogany cabinet, where she kept only the best Irish whiskey.

"Of your stock? Sure. It's like drinking gold."

Dorette poured a healthy shot for Sam and another one for herself. She handed him his drink, and they sat down, facing each other. Sam took a sip and sighed with satisfaction. They sat together for a moment in the comfortable silence of old friends.

"We're starting early tomorrow. That Ranger, Slater, is on my tail. I need some supplies. Can I get them from you, so I won't have to wait for the stores to open?"

"Sure. What do you need?"

"Ammunition, food, a couple of extra canteens. We're going to Mexico."

"Is it that bad?"

"The hideout's been discovered. But I was leaving anyway. I'm giving it up, Dorette."

"You're taking her with you?"

"Yeah. She's the reason I'm going."

"I've never seen you this way about a woman."

"I've never been this way." He smiled. "She's different."

"I know. How'd you find her?"

He shrugged. "I grabbed her and took her with me when I escaped in Santa Clara."

"You kidnapped her?" Dorette's eyebrows rose. "But she acts like—"

"Oh, she's going with me willingly. It's the strangest thing in the world, Dory. She loves me."

"That's not so strange." A wistful smile curved her lips. "Maybe I should be jealous."

He grunted his disbelief. "Come on, Dory. Don't try to kid me. You know you've got no use for a broken-down old bank robber."

"Right. Long as I got my gold to keep me warm at night." Dorette had loved Brody for years, ever since she'd known him, she guessed, but she was a realist. There had never been a chance for anything between her and him. She could take no pleasure in a man, and Brody could never love a woman who lived as his mother had. "I'm happy for you. I talked to Amy. She's a sweet girl."

Sam smiled, his whole face softening as he thought about her. "I love her."

Dorette sighed. "Have you thought of what you're taking her into? She's never lived hard. I can see that."

"She's tougher than you think. She's ridden hard and slept out on the ground, gone without any of the fine things she's used to."

"But that's been for only a few days. Do you want her to do it the rest of her life?"

"She won't have to. I have some money. I'll buy land down in Mexico. She'll have a house and furniture, nice clothes, whatever she wants."

"She'll be stranded in a country where she can't even speak the language. She'll be surrounded by strangers. She'll never see her family again."

"She'll have me."

"I know. But it's a hard life. Besides, maybe the law won't get you in Mexico, but do you think that'll stop the bounty hunters? If they hear you've settled down in Mexico, they'll come gunning for you. You know it."

Sam frowned. He'd tried not to think about that. "I'll make sure I get them first."

"More killing. Do you think she can live with that kind of violence, that kind of threat? What are you going to do? Keep on running? Kill every bounty hunter that comes along until one kills you? Then Amy will be left there all alone."

"Stop it!" Sam slammed his drink down on the desk. "Damn it, Dorette, what are you trying to do?"

She shook her head. "I don't know. A fool's errand, I guess. I don't wish you harm, Sam, you know that. I want you to be happy. I'd like for you to have that little girl. But I wonder if you're doing right by her."

"Let me worry about that, all right?"

Dorette shrugged. "Sure, honey. I got no stake in it. Just let me hear from you every now and then. Somebody's heading for San Antonio, tell him he's got a free night here if he'll bring me word of you."

He chuckled. "I'll have every drifter in the country knocking on my door, finding out how I am."

She smiled. They finished their drinks, and Dorette assured him that she would have his supplies ready the next morning. Sam walked back up to his room.

He went to the bed and stood looking down at Amy. How young and fragile she looked lying there. He thought of what Dorette had said, and he was assailed by doubts. Could Amy really be happy separated from everything she knew, living among foreigners, never seeing her family again? It wouldn't be that bad for him; he had always been an outcast. But wouldn't Amy come to miss her family? To long to see familiar faces and hear English again?

Dorette was right, damn her; the bounty hunters would follow him into Mexico. They'd figure he was easy pickings once he'd settled down on a ranch. He would be. He wouldn't be able to run. He'd have to kill them. Amy would be subjected over and over to the very violence and uncertainty that he was trying to avoid. He remembered her reaction to Purdon's death. She abhorred violence. It would shock and horrify her every time. Would she come to abhor him, too?

Or maybe one of the hunters would get him. Then she'd be left alone in a strange country, defenseless, prey to anyone who happened along. Even worse, what if, in trying to get him, one of the bounty hunters hit Amy instead?

Sam sighed and walked over to the window. He stared blindly out at the dark street below. Dorette was right. He'd known it, but he had refused to think about it. He'd been selfish, wanting Amy with him so much that he wasn't doing what was best for her. He'd been nothing but selfish from the moment he met her, stealing her away from her family and forcing her to endure the hardships of running from the law, taking her virginity, taking her love. She was too innocent to know what she was doing; she had no idea what her life would be like with him, or how much she would be giving up.

If she remained behind, she would meet another man someday, a man who was good and honest, who might be worthy of her, who would give her a decent home and a settled life. She was the only woman Sam had ever loved, but it was foolish to think that she loved him in the same way. She had never had another man; perhaps she mistook desire for love. She was just so inexperienced that she didn't know that she could love another man and have a better life.

He was taking advantage of her sweetness and her innocence, selfishly using her, taking her love and warmth. A man who really loved her would not harm her just so he could have the pleasure of her presence. A man who loved her would do what was best for her.

Sam walked slowly back to the bed. He stared at Amy, as though to burn the image of her into his mind. He had known all along that he wasn't good enough for her. She was an angel, whereas he was lucky his head hadn't already been put in a noose. If he took her to Mexico with him, he'd pull her down into his way of life. He'd taken her with him at first because he always took what he wanted, selfishly, wickedly. But Amy had changed him; she had given him enough of her own goodness that he knew he couldn't do that again. He couldn't wrong her, couldn't hurt her, just to please himself. He had to do what was best for her.

He bent down and kissed her forehead, her lips. Then he gathered up his belongings and left the room quietly. He went down to Dorette's office and walked in without bothering to knock. She looked up from her account books, her face registering surprise.

"I need the supplies right away," he told her. "I'm leaving now, and I'm going alone."

Chapter Sixteen

Amy awoke slowly. The room was dim, the windows blocked by the heavy curtains. She sat up, yawning and stretching. She wondered where Sam was. Probably down seeing about the horses and supplies. He had wanted to get an early start this morning. Amy slipped out of bed and padded over to a chair, where her boy's clothes lay cleaned and neatly folded. She dressed and picked up the hairbrush. As she brushed her hair, she wandered over to the window and pushed aside the curtain to look out.

What she saw made her frown. It was full daylight outside, and there were people on the streets. She would have said it was mid-morning, if not later. Why had Sam waited so long to get started? Perhaps he had overslept, too. Quickly, she finished brushing and began to braid her hair. She wanted to be ready to leave as soon as Sam returned; they couldn't afford to waste any time.

The door opened, and Dorette entered, carrying a tray. "Hello. Jewel said she heard you up and moving around in here. I brought you some breakfast."

"Thank you." Amy smiled. Dorette set the tray down on the low table and poured two cups of coffee. Amy picked up a slice of bacon from the plate. "Where's Sam? Has he eaten?"

"Yes, I'm sure he has." Dorette put down the coffeepot. "Amy, there's something I need to talk to you about."

"Oh? What?" She finished the bacon and reached for a piece of toast.

"Sam's gone."

Amy froze. Slowly she straightened, her hand falling back to her side. "What?"

"Sam is gone. He left in the middle of the night."

"But why? Where?"

"Sit down. He asked me to tell you."

"Tell me what? I don't understand." Amy's face began to crumple. "Was it a lie? Didn't he want me, after all?"

"No! Oh, no, it wasn't a lie. I've never seen Brody taken like that with any woman. He loves you. But he could see that going to Mexico won't be any kind of life for a woman like you. There'll be bounty hunters chasing him for the rest of his life. He won't be safe from them in Mexico."

"Then he'll need me more than ever," Amy protested. "I could help him." She sighed and looked away. Tears glittered in her eyes. "No. I guess I wouldn't be much help to Sam, would I? I'm not smart enough."

"It's not that," Dorette said earnestly. She was beginning to wonder guiltily if she had done both Sam and Amy a disservice by advising him not to take the girl. Knowing that Amy was a lady and that Sam had kidnapped her, Dorette had assumed that Amy's feelings for Sam were lukewarm at best. She would not have dreamed that Amy would react with such pain to Sam's leaving. "Sam loves you. He wanted you with him. But you shouldn't have to live like that. Sam wanted what was best for you."

"Best for me!" Amy cried out, tears running down her cheeks. "Best for me! All I want is to be with him! That's what's best for me! Oh, God, what am I going to do? How can I live without him?"

"Amy..." Dorette rose and went to her, touched by the girl's grief. "Believe me, he didn't do it to hurt you."

"Then why did he go?" Amy lashed out, twisting away from Dorette. "Why did he leave me?"

Amy sank down to her knees on the floor, wrapping her arms around herself, and giving way to sobs of anguish.

The first pale rays of the sun slanting through the broken windows brought Victoria awake. She lay there for a moment, luxuriating in the peace and contentment of being in Slater's arms. Her head was pillowed on his chest. One of his arms lay across her back; his other hand rested on her hip. Victoria smiled and nuzzled into his bare chest.

Last night had been the most wonderful night of her life. She had never dreamed that the kind of joy Slater had given her even existed. After they had made love, they had lain together in happy exhaustion. Slater had lazily stroked her body and whispered to her of her beauty, and of his delight in her. She had never before heard his voice sound so young and peaceful.

After a long while they had found the energy to rise and wring out their wet clothes and blankets and hang them before the fire to dry. While their clothes dried, they had remained naked, and it wasn't long before their glances had turned long and hungry, then had changed to kisses and caresses. They had made love again, slowly and tenderly this time, and the conclusion, if less shattering, was just as satisfying.

They had eaten, and when the blankets were finally dry, they had lain down and slept, but Victoria had had little need for either food or sleep. She felt as if she could live on love itself, so great was the emotion bubbling within her. Slater said no words of love, and Victoria, strangely shy, could not bring herself to speak first. But she showed her love with her hands and mouth, and she felt the love that Slater gave her in return. She knew that whatever obstacles lay between them and a happy future they would be able to overcome them.

She kissed Slater's skin, tasting the salt, and breathed in the arousing scent that was his alone. She drew tiny circles on his chest with the tip of her tongue, and his eyes snapped open. He stared at her blankly for an instant; then his eyes cleared, and he let out a breath. "Victoria."

"Yes." She smiled.

Slater's face softened. "Good morning."

"Good morning."

He cupped the back of her neck with his hand and pulled her down to him for a long, melting kiss. He thought of rolling over and pulling her beneath him, of nuzzling his way down her throat and chest to her breasts. But then he remembered what he was supposed to be doing, the duty that he had conveniently ignored yesterday. He thought of what he had done to

Victoria. Suddenly he was flooded with guilt. He released her abruptly and sat up.

Victoria stared at him in surprise. Slater rubbed his hands over his face. "What time is it? We have to get going."

Victoria blinked. She hadn't expected Slater to spend the morning cuddling her and talking sweetly, but she had thought he would at least mention what had happened between them the night before.

"It's still early. The sun's just up."

"We can't waste any time." He stood up, reaching for his clothes and pulling them on. "We've already lost too much as it is."

Wasted? Lost? Was that how Slater thought of the time they had spent making love? Didn't he have a single gentle, loving word for her after the way their bodies had melted together in perfect union last night?

Amazed and confused, Victoria stood up, too, reaching for her own garments. Suddenly she felt very naked. She turned her back to him and began to dress.

"Victoria." Slater glanced at her hesitantly. "I—I'm sorry."

"What?" She turned, astonished. "Sorry? For what?"

"For what?" Now it was his turn to look amazed. "For what I did last night."

Pain sliced through Victoria's chest. In the cool light of day, he regretted what they'd done. "Oh."

"I seduced you. It was—wrong of me. I should be protecting you, but instead I took advantage of you. I've done a lot of things in my life that I'm not very proud of, but I haven't ever abused someone's trust. I haven't seduced an innocent girl."

For a moment, Victoria could only stare, her jaw dropping open. "You *seduced* me?" she said finally, in a strangled voice.

He looked at her oddly. "Yes."

Victoria planted her hands on her hips. The pain and doubt his words had first aroused in her were gone; she felt like laughing with relief. But she didn't. She wasn't about to let Slater get away with this. "And now you're feeling guilty."

"Of course. Any decent man would."

Victoria assumed a mockingly sweet expression and gazed up at him through her lashes. "Imagine, taking a poor, sweet little girl like me. Defenseless. Timid. Reluctant. Shy."

Slater frowned. "Victoria, I'm serious."

She raised her head, the sweet expression turning into one of square-jawed determination, high color and flashing eyes. "So am I. Of all the gall! You have to be the most pigheaded, blind, *egotistical* man I ever met! Seduced me! You didn't seduce me! I was willing. I was eager. Or have you forgotten?"

Looking at her, hearing her words, desire and anger stirred in him in equal parts. "No, I haven't forgotten."

"Do you honestly think that you could make me do anything I didn't want, that you could persuade or cajole or trick me into anything?"

"No. But I'm years older than you. I have experience. I should have better control over myself than that."

"That's what you feel guilty about." Victoria stabbed her forefinger at him. "Not about seducing me, but about losing control over yourself. About wanting me so much you forgot your logic and your duty and just did what you've been aching to do since Austin!"

Slater straightened, clenching his fists at his sides. His eyes were steely. "Damn it, Victoria! Stop twisting everything to suit yourself. You didn't know what you were getting into. Sure, maybe you wanted to make love, but you didn't know the consequences. You didn't have any experience."

"Now you're complaining about my lack of experience?" Her tone was frosty. "Wasn't I competent enough for you? Perhaps I should find another teacher, so I can acquire some experience."

She whirled away, but Slater's hand lashed out and grabbed her wrist. He made a low sound in his throat that was suspiciously like a growl. "Damn it, you do, and I'll—"

Victoria lifted her chin, her eyes challenging him. "You'll what?"

"I'll take him apart piece by piece." He pulled her to him and grasped a handful of her hair. He twisted his hand, winding her hair around his wrist and tightening his hold until she couldn't move her head.

Victoria said nothing, just gazed at him, her lips parted slightly, waiting. Slowly, Slater lowered his head. His lips met hers. They kissed as though it was a battle, tongues sparring and clashing. But when at last they parted, their faces flushed, panting for breath, it would have been hard to tell who had won.

Victoria smiled, and Slater knew he had done exactly what she wanted him to. His eyes narrowed, and he started to say something, but he stopped. He looked upward and sighed, then began to chuckle. "You are the most beautiful—and the most infuriating—woman I have ever known." He kissed her again, briefly and hard. "All right. I'm not sorry—as long as you're not."

"I'm not sorry."

"Then let's ride out of here before it gets any later."

It wasn't exactly a declaration of love, but Victoria was content with it—for the moment. She didn't doubt that the declarations would come eventually.

They saddled up and rode for San Antonio. The rain had washed away Brody's tracks, but Slater was certain that the city was his destination. They rode fast, neither of them saying much. Victoria was too happy to care whether they talked or not. She enjoyed the opportunity to simply explore all the facets of the joy inside her.

Slater, on the other hand, was deep in thought. He had been stunned by their lovemaking far more than Victoria had, for he knew how greatly it had exceeded the limits of the usual sexual congress. He had been amazed, awed, astonished; there weren't words strong enough to describe his reaction. He hadn't known anything like the power and beauty of their joining before. It was as if, for an instant—and an eternity—their souls had merged. Victoria was inside him now, and he in her. They belonged to each other in the most basic, elemental way.

The thought scared him. Was he to be bound to Victoria for the rest of his life? Was he to carry her in his heart and his mind wherever he went? Could he actually be in love with her? The thought of such a commitment to any other person after his long years of responsibility only to himself and his job was enough to make a man nervous. And the thought of a commitment to Victoria Stafford was soul-shaking.

It would never be easy with this woman. There would be tremendous heights and unbelievable depths. Angry struggles and nights of wild passion and moments of such tenderness they would make a man weep. She would tease him, torment him, infuriate him, rouse him to rage. He knew because she had already done so many times. He would want to shake her, leave her, force her to accept his will. He would know the deep, chilling terror he had felt yesterday when he saw her swept away by the river. She would embarrass him; she would frustrate him; she would all too often *win*.

What little thought Slater had ever given to marrying had not included a woman like this. How could it? He had never seen a woman like Victoria, never even imagined one. She would grind most men into dust.

The excitement of a challenge coiled in his gut. He had never hungered for safety; he'd never run from danger. He thought of standing toe to toe with Victoria in argument, and his loins began to throb. God, she was beautiful. She was wild and passionate. She was strong.

And he loved her.

But what in the blazing hell was he supposed to do about that? Ask her to marry him? He had nothing to offer her. A ranch he'd let go to seed. The life of a Ranger's wife, living alone half the time, never knowing when he'd come back, or if he'd come back at all.

He wasn't any kind of husband for her. He was too rough, too hard. He'd lived too long with danger and death. He knew more criminals than he did decent folks. A woman like Victoria, lovely and passionate, deserved something better than that.

The best thing for both of them would be for him to walk away from her. Set her free to find a better man. But the thought of doing that filled him with jealousy and pain. He wanted her. He thought he had some notion of how Brody must have felt when he took Victoria's cousin without regard for the world or her wishes.

Slater had arrived at no solution to his dilemma by the time they reached San Antonio. He was glad of the excuse to drop his viciously circling thoughts and concentrate on something else. He rode through town to the red light district and pulled up in front of an innocuous-looking house next to a saloon. He dismounted and started toward the house, then stopped and cast an uneasy glance at Victoria. He had become so used to having her with him that he hadn't thought until this moment how improper it was for her to go into Dorette's place. "Uh, maybe you better wait for me out here."

"In front of a bawdy house?" Victoria asked, her eyes dancing. "Why, Slater, how damaging to my reputation."

"It could be dangerous."

Victoria responded by holding up her rifle.

"Damn it, if there's shooting, you'd better take cover fast. If you get yourself shot, I'll—" He stopped, realizing the absurdity of his threat. "Oh, hell, come on." He walked up to the front door and knocked loudly. The door was opened by a large black woman. Her eyes slid from Slater's face to the star on his chest, then behind him to Victoria. She frowned and crossed her arms defensively.

"What you want here?"

"I want to come inside. Now," Slater said in a deceptively quiet voice, placing his hand on the door and shoving it wide open.

"Here, now, you can't jus' walk in like that," she protested, moving her bulk to block him.

"No?" Slater slid his revolver from its holster. Victoria stepped up beside him, her rifle raised.

The woman's eyes widened, and she stepped back, calling, "Miss Dorette, you better get in here. Quick."

"Where's Brody?" Slater asked.

"I don't know no Brody."

He walked past her, Victoria on his heels. Victoria couldn't keep from glancing around her, amazed by the lush surroundings. She stared at the large painting of a nude over the fireplace.

"Victoria . . ." Slater said impatiently.

"Yes, I'm coming."

They started up the stairs, their footsteps muffled by the runner. There was the sound of a woman's heels on the hard wood floor above them, and seconds later she appeared on the stairs. Her hair was a flaming red color and hung loose around her shoulders. She was dressed in a satin robe trimmed with white feathers, cut low enough in the front that Victoria could see her cleavage.

"I'm Dorette. This is my place. If you have any problem with us, I suggest you see the sheriff."

"I'm not interested in the sheriff. I want Brody. Where is he?"

"Brody? I'm afraid I don't know the name. But I can tell you he's not here. There aren't any men in this house." A provocative smile curved her lips. "Except for you, of course."

Victoria gritted her teeth. She didn't like the way this woman was looking at Slater.

"You won't mind if I take a look, then." Slater brushed past her and continued down the hall.

"My girls are asleep. I don't want you to wake them up."

"I'm sure it won't be the first time."

"There was a man who come through here. Maybe he's the one you're looking for. But he's gone. He had a woman with him, and he left her here. Said there'd be people coming to town looking for her."

"Amy!" Victoria brushed past Slater and seized the woman's arm. "Where is she?"

"Third door on the right."

Victoria started down the hall.

"Wait!" Slater caught her arm. "Maybe it's a trap. She's too free and easy with the information."

Dorette shrugged. "I got no reason to hide that girl. I don't want her. If you take her, it's easier on me. Look, if it's worrying you, I'll open the door myself."

Dorette went to the door in question, knocked and swung it open wide. "I think somebody's here to see you."

Victoria hurried after Dorette. She stopped in the doorway, her heart tightening in her chest. Amy sat inside the room on a red velvet chair. Her hair hung in a braid down her back, and she was dressed in men's clothing. She had been crying, and she looked up uninterestedly at their entrance.

"Amy!" Victoria ran to her, holding out her arms.

Amy rose, smiling weakly, and came into Victoria's arms. "Hello, Tory."

It seemed to Slater a curiously restrained greeting from a woman who'd just been released by her kidnapper. He went through the room carefully, opening the wardrobe doors and peering inside, even looking under the bed. There was a small door in the far wall, and he opened it. A narrow set of stairs led downward.

"He must have gone out this way. Damn it, he probably slipped out while we were talking to the madam."

Slater ran down the stairs. It was some time before he came back up, and he wore a look of disgust. "No sign of him anywhere."

"He left hours ago," Amy said quietly. "There's no point in looking. He went last night."

Slater sighed and shoved his gun back into his holster. "Come on. I'm going to take you girls to the Menger. Then I'll go after him."

"Why?" Amy asked. "He's far away by now. I don't even know where he's going."

"He's headed for Mexico."

"No," Amy replied quickly. "No, he's not. I think he went back north."

"You just said you don't know where he's going." Slater regarded her thoughtfully.

Amy shrugged. "I mean, I don't know exactly. But I know he wasn't going to Mexico."

"Why are you covering for him?"

"Covering? I'm not. Why should I do that?"

"Don't be absurd, Slater," Victoria snapped. "Come on, let's take Amy to the hotel."

Amy was acting strangely. Victoria couldn't figure it out. Of course, she hadn't expected Amy to act normal after the ordeal she'd been through. But that was the odd part. She seemed too normal. She was obviously unhappy, but there was none of the terror or the relief that Victoria had expected to find. The only explanation Victoria could think of was that Amy had blanked out her memories of the kidnapping just as she had done as a child, blocking out the memories of her parents' deaths. If that was the case, Victoria didn't want Slater asking her questions and dredging up the painful past.

Slater sighed. "All right." He was positive Amy wasn't telling the truth, and he thought he knew why. For some reason, she harbored a liking for her captor, and she wanted him to escape. Slater was sure from how quickly and firmly she had denied that Brody had gone to Mexico that that was exactly where he *had* gone. There was no need to question her further. Brody wouldn't have been so foolish as to tell the girl exactly where he was going. The thing to do now was make sure the two women were safely ensconced in their hotel, then set out after Brody.

They left the room. Amy insisted on taking the Mexican blouse, skirt and sandals that lay on the dresser, despite Victoria's assurances that they would find her something better to wear. They walked out of the house, and, to Victoria's amazement, Amy hugged Dorette goodbye at the door.

Amy saw Victoria's surprise, and she explained softly, "She was kind to me."

"Yes, but—well, of course you don't know what she is."

"Yes, I do," Amy assured her. "She owns that place. It's called a brothel, and the women in it sell their bodies to men. But not Dorette. She used to, but now she doesn't have to."

Victoria gaped, and Slater had to hide a smile. Obviously Victoria's cousin had learned a few things during the last couple of weeks.

They mounted their horses and rode away, Victoria and Amy riding double. None of the group glanced across the street, so they did not see the thin man who stood there, staring at them in dismay.

Cam McBride had been positive that he finally had Brody cornered. He had followed Brody and the girl from the hideout, planning to ambush them before they reached San Antonio. But then he had lost them in the rainstorm. He had ridden into San Antonio, cursing himself for not jumping them earlier. He was essentially a cowardly man, and he was particularly scared of Brody. So he had hesitated, delaying the moment of truth. The result had been that he'd lost him again.

He had gone to a saloon to drown his sorrows, and as he had come out of it, he had glanced across the street. And there, miraculously, had been Sam Brody. Cam realized that his luck had finally changed. He had followed Brody, but there hadn't been a good opportunity to ambush him. Cam wasn't about to go after Brody in a face-to-face fight. When Brody returned to the whorehouse, he'd followed him inside and listened outside the door. It was obvious that Brody was there for the night, so Cam had slipped away to catch some sleep, returning to stand watch at the crack of dawn.

He wasn't going to charge into the house, shooting. There was too great a possibility that he would get shot himself. He would wait for Brody and the girl to leave and follow them. This time, he would make sure he killed the other man at the first opportunity. The girl, too. She would be too much of a nuisance to travel with, and besides, she might kick up a fuss with the authorities about the way he killed Brody. Cam intended to make sure Brody suffered for what he'd done to Cam's face before he let him die.

But now, here were Slater and that damn woman, walking out of the whorehouse with Brody's woman between them. That could mean only one thing—Brody had slipped out of the house during the night, leaving the girl behind. He had lost Brody again!

McBride wanted to throw his gun down and howl in rage. After all this, he'd lost him! He seethed with frustration. He hadn't suspected that Brody would slip out in the night. The things he'd heard Brody saying to the girl in the room last night hadn't sounded like the words of a man who was about to leave. He'd sounded like a man so far gone on a woman he didn't know which way was up. But Brody must have worked up some trick to evade Slater. Maybe he would come back for the girl later, or. . .

McBride straightened, a grin spreading over his face. Luck was on his side, after all. He'd thought of a way to get Brody back and in his power, without a lick of danger to himself.

He hurried off down the street after Slater and the women.

Slater checked Victoria and Amy into the Menger Hotel. Victoria was relieved to have him handle things for her after her experience with the hotel in Austin. She could have done it herself, of course, but it was far easier this way—and she had to admit that there was something nice about having Slater take care of her. He escorted them to their room, then pulled Victoria out into the hall to talk privately.

"Will you and Amy be able to take care of yourselves?"

For a moment Victoria gazed at him blankly. "Yes, of course. Why?"

"Good. Wire your father to come and get you, and, please, for once, stay put in the hotel. I'm going after Brody."

"Oh." Of course. She had gotten Amy back, which was all she had been interested in, but Slater had sworn to bring Brody back. She should have known he would continue chasing him. "I see. But—how will you find him?"

"He's going to Mexico, so I'll take the south road. I'll ask about him, try to find someone who's seen him. He'll have to stick to a route where there's good water. That will limit his possibilities."

Victoria frowned. "But Amy said he'd gone the other way."

"She wasn't telling the truth. She denied it too fast and too vehemently, right after she said she didn't have any idea where he was going."

"Amy never lies. She doesn't know how."

"Then Brody taught her something."

Victoria's eyes flashed. "How dare you—"

Slater grimaced. "Don't get all fired up about it. I'm not saying your cousin's a liar. But for some reason she wanted to mislead me. Maybe she's scared of him, thinks he'll come back and get her if she tells me where he went. I don't know. But I'm positive Brody headed for Mexico."

Victoria sighed. She reached out and took his hands and squeezed them. "When—when will you be back?"

He shook his head. "I don't know." He paused. "Your father will come to get you."

"Yes. I'll send him a telegram. I'm sure he'll take us home." She looked away. Suddenly she realized that Slater would go one way and she would go another. Their lives would split unless they did something to change that. This was where it would end unless Slater chose to return to her. She wanted to tell him that she loved him, wanted to beg him to return to her, but even Victoria's nerve failed at that. She couldn't make a man love her by begging.

Slater stood for a moment, gazing down at her. He hated the idea of her leaving San Antonio and going home with her father, slipping back into the family and life she'd known before him. It surprised him how much he wished she would be waiting here for him. It was hard as hell not to ask her to. He wanted to tell her that he'd be back for her in a few weeks. He wanted to ask her to be his wife.

But he knew how unfair that would be. They had just gone through an exciting, dangerous time together; they were still filled with wild emotions. What Victoria felt might not be love at all, but only the desire and closeness of the moment. It would be wrong to ask her to commit herself to him now. She needed time to discover her true feelings.

And he had to finish this thing with Brody. He had to find him and bring him in, or he'd never be able to rest. It could be a matter of weeks. It could be months. Hell, he'd been after him now for years. When he finally did catch up with Brody, there was always the possibility that it would be Brody who walked away from the confrontation, not him. It would be cruel to ask Victoria to give her heart and her word, knowing how uncertain his future was.

Everything was against it. But, Lord, it was hard not to take her in his arms and pour out his love to her.

A door opened down the hall, and a man emerged. He walked down the hall past them, tipping his hat. They nodded, and Slater stepped back, letting go of Victoria's hands. He couldn't even kiss her goodbye, couldn't even lay claim to her with his mouth or press her body against his one more time. This was too public a place.

Slater moved back another step. "I'd better not waste any time."

Victoria's hands clenched in the folds of her skirt. "All right. Good luck." Wasn't he even going to hug her? Kiss her? Was this to be all she would ever have of Slater? "I—be careful. Don't get yourself hurt."

He smiled. "I won't." He paused, then turned abruptly and walked away.

Victoria watched him until he was out of sight. Tears blurred her vision. She leaned back against the door. She had to go inside now and take care of Amy. But all she wanted to do was burst into tears. Slater was gone, and without a word of love to her!

Chapter Seventeen

Numbly, Victoria walked back into her room. Amy was sitting by the window, gazing out. She glanced at Victoria as she came in, then turned her face back to the window.

Victoria sat down heavily on the bed, suddenly weary. She remembered her elation this morning. It seemed strange to think that it had been only hours ago. It was too soon and too far to fall.

Slater was gone from her for good. He had said nothing about seeing her again. He had said nothing about love. Was it possible that he felt nothing for her? Had his moans of passion and sweet words been born only of desire?

Victoria remembered what he had said one night when they were camped out. They were too different, he had told her. They couldn't get along; they were always fighting. He must have been trying to make her understand then that he didn't love her, would never love her, that what he felt for her was only lust. She had simply been too stubborn and blind to accept it.

Victoria had gotten what she wanted all her life, with very few exceptions. She did as she pleased, and when she desired something, she pursued it until she had it, whether it was a horse, or a piece of knowledge, or going with Slater to catch Sam Brody. Because she wanted Slater to love her, she had believed that it would happen. Even though yesterday she had told herself that she wanted Slater no matter how he felt about her, she knew that in the back of her mind she had believed that somehow, some way, she would make him love her.

Now she saw how foolish and wrong she had been. No matter how much she could usually bend people to her will, Slater was one person she could not dominate. And love was something that could not be forced on a person. It came freely or not at all. Victoria swallowed hard, blinking away her tears. Well, she had asked for this. She had wanted to make love to Slater, no matter what, and she had gotten her wish. She refused to regret it or sorrow over it. It had been beautiful, and she would treasure it always. Slater's lack of interest in her didn't change the way she felt about him, or about the lovemaking they had shared. She would not cry because she hadn't gotten everything she wanted.

She was a strong person. She would go on with her life. She could live without the love of a man; she'd done it for years without any problem. She had Amy and her father and the ranch. They would have to be enough for her. She would make them be enough.

Victoria burst into tears. She stretched out on the bed and buried her face in the pillow, trying to muffle her sobs.

"Victoria!" She heard Amy's shocked voice, and then Amy was beside her, bending over to lay her head against Victoria's. "Tory, love, what's the matter?"

Victoria shook her head, digging her fingers into the bed cover, trying to choke back her tears. But she could not. Amy's kind, concerned voice was too much for her, and she turned over and reached blindly for her cousin. Amy wrapped her arms around Victoria and held her, rocking gently and patting her on the back, until finally Victoria's tears subsided.

"Oh, Amy, I'm sorry." Victoria pulled back, wiping away her tears. "I'm so ashamed. I should be the one giving you comfort, after all you've gone through—being kidnapped by that awful man and forced to—"

"No! Don't say that. He's not an awful man."

Victoria stared. "What? How can you say that after he grabbed you off the street and carried you away? After he—he—had his way with you!"

To Victoria's astonishment, Amy giggled. Amy covered her mouth and tried to draw her face back into sober lines. "I'm sorry. I shouldn't have laughed. I know you were concerned about me. But I—what you said sounded just like something

Aunt Margaret would say. And it's so silly, you know, compared to what it's really like.''

"Compared to what it's really like!'' Victoria's voice rose. "What are you saying, Amy?''

"Oh, Tory, it was wonderful, magnificent. I wanted to, I participated. We made love. It wasn't Sam 'having his way with me.' ''

Victoria stared at Amy, too stunned to speak.

"I know you were worried about me, and I'm sorry. I wish I could have let you know that I was all right. But when we saw you in the cave, you had that lawman with you, the one who wants to capture Sam, and I couldn't call out. He would have hurt Sam, and I couldn't risk that.''

"In the cave? You were in the cave that day? You saw me, and you didn't say anything!''

"I told you, I couldn't, or that man would—''

"Amy, how could you! How could you help that criminal get away! Slater was right. I didn't believe him when he said you were lying. But he was right, wasn't he? You knew Brody was headed for Mexico, and you tried to make Slater think he wasn't.''

Amy nodded and sighed. "I only wish I'd done a better job. I'm not any good at lying.''

"Amy! This is crazy! Brody is an outlaw. He's a bank robber. He's killed people. He kidnapped you and held you prisoner for days and days. He—he raped you.''

Amy shook her head vehemently, and her eyes flashed. "He did not! You're wrong, Tory. He's not a bad man. He was never anything but gentle and kind to me. Some of his men were bad, but not Sam. He never killed anybody unless he had to. He didn't rape me. I had to persuade him to make love to me.''

"I can't believe this.''

"I love him.''

"Amy!''

"I do. The reason I was crying when you found me wasn't because of what I'd 'been through.' It was because he'd left me behind.'' Her lips wobbled on the words, and tears filled her eyes. "Dorette says he did it for my own good, that he doesn't think the life he has to lead is fit for me. But I don't care! I wanted to go."

"I don't understand," Victoria said weakly. She felt as if the world had suddenly gone mad. The last person she would have thought her sweet, gentle cousin would fall in love with was an outlaw!

"He was good to me, Tory. He treated me differently from anyone else. He didn't act as if I was stupid, or crazy, or a child who couldn't do anything. He treated me like a woman. He loved me. He listened to me. He taught me how to do things, and answered anything I asked him, and he never told me that it was something I shouldn't do, or that it was too hard for me, or that I didn't need to know it."

Remorse swept through Victoria. "Oh, Amy, have we treated you so badly? Have I told you those things?"

"No, of course you didn't treat me badly. I love you and Uncle Edward, and I know you love me. I was happy with you. But with you, I was a child. You were good at everything and took care of things far better than I could. There was never any reason for me to do anything. Besides, however much you and your father love me, it's just not the same as a man loving you."

"I see." Victoria thought about the way she felt in Slater's arms, the wild passion that erupted inside her when he made love to her. She thought about how much she loved him. Was that the way Amy felt about Brody? Her sweet, innocent Amy? It seemed impossible, yet apparently it was true.

Suddenly Victoria giggled. "Oh, Amy! Isn't it crazy? We've both fallen in love with men that nobody would believe we'd love." Tears filled her eyes, and her giggles turned watery. "And we've lost them."

Amy held out her arms, and the two girls clung to each other, crying.

They spent the afternoon talking, trying to describe their adventures to each other and to explain the men they had fallen in love with. Victoria knew she should send a telegram to her father, to let him know where they were, but she held back. She told herself that she was too tired, that one more day wouldn't matter, but the truth was simply that she couldn't bring herself to face her father yet.

They ate their dinner in their room, neither of them wanting to face the other diners in the hotel restaurant. Late in the evening, when they were about to get ready for bed, there was a knock at the door.

Victoria jumped up and rushed to the door, her heart leaping. Maybe it was Slater, come back for her. She flung open the door, and her face fell. "Oh. It's you. What are you doing here, McBride?"

Cam McBride walked into the room, shutting the door behind him. Victoria gasped, indignant, and opened her mouth to tell him what she thought of his rude behavior. But McBride pulled a revolver from his holster and leveled it at her, and the words died in her throat.

The two women stared at him. Victoria thought with regret of the pistol wrapped up inside her bedroll. It had never occurred to her to take it out before she answered the door. She hadn't even thought about anything happening to them inside the hotel!

Cam slid over to Amy, keeping his gun trained on Victoria. When he reached the other girl, he grabbed her braid and jerked her closer. "Well, Brody's woman." He held the pistol to Amy's temple. "Can't see what he sees in you. Now this other one—" He cast a leering glance toward Victoria. "She'd be an armful, I reckon. But you—I don't 'magine I'll get any pleasure outta you. 'Cept, of course, for lettin' Brody watch me take you while he's dyin' slow."

Amy gasped, and the blood drained from her face. "No!"

He chuckled. "That's right. I'm gonna bring Brody in this time. An' you're the bait." He pulled her roughly across the room. "All right, girls, let's go. The three of us are takin' a little trip."

Slater took a last swig of water from his canteen and capped it. He stretched out on the ground, wrapping his blanket around him, and closed his eyes. He was dead tired. Maybe he'd be able to get some sleep tonight. God knows, he hadn't last night. He'd lain awake for what seemed like half the night, thinking about Victoria.

He had been chasing Brody for two days now, and he still wasn't sure he was headed in the right direction. But that wasn't the worst thing. The hell of it was how much he missed Victoria. He'd ridden alone for years and liked it that way, but now he was lonely by himself. All day long he kept thinking about how they had talked while they rode or laughed or just been companionably silent. He missed her presence; he missed her voice; he missed the way she always kept him on his toes. And at night he lay there, remembering the night they had made love, picturing her soft, sweet body, her face tender and slack with passion, that black hair spreading out like a cloud around her. It wasn't long before he was so sweating and hard that he couldn't sleep.

Not tonight, he told himself. Tonight he was determined not to think of her. But he did. It seemed as if there was no way he could keep her out of his mind.

Eventually, however, he must have slept, for the next thing he knew, something was prodding the bottom of his foot. His eyes flew open. He found himself staring into the barrel of a Winchester repeating rifle. There was no hope of reaching his revolver.

"Don't even think about going for your gun," Sam Brody said.

"So I was headed in the right direction. I knew Amy was lying."

"Amy? She told you I went the other way?" There was an odd tone to Brody's voice.

"Yeah. But she's no good at lying. I knew she was covering for you."

"She would."

"You planning to shoot me?"

"Not unless I have to. I'm here to ask for your help."

"What?"

"Sit up." Brody moved the gun back, allowing Slater to rise to a seated position. Brody sat down across from him, cross-legged, his rifle still trained on Slater.

"I have a little trouble carrying on a conversation when somebody has a rifle aimed at my chest."

Brody's lips moved in what might have been a smile. "You'll have to. I know how quick you are, and I don't plan to give you an opportunity to grab that Colt."

Slater shrugged. "What's on your mind, Brody?"

"Dorette knew where I was going. She sent me a telegram. It was waiting for me this afternoon."

"To tell you I was following you?"

"Yeah, she mentioned that. But there was something more important. Cam McBride's got Amy."

"What?" Slater leaped to his feet.

Brody jumped up, too. "Damn it, man! What are you doing? I almost shot you."

Slater made an impatient gesture. "Forget your damn gun. Does he have Victoria, too?"

"Amy's cousin? I don't know. He told Dorette he had Amy. He didn't say anything about anyone else."

Slater ran his hand through his hair, willing himself to think straight. His heart was pumping like a steam engine, and his brain screamed that Victoria was in danger, maybe even hurt. "She'd be with Amy. Victoria wouldn't have left Amy by herself, even for a second. McBride couldn't have gotten Amy without taking Victoria, too—unless he killed her."

Slater reached down and picked up his holster and strapped it on. "I'm going to kill that son of a bitch."

Brody reached out to grab Slater's arm. "Damn it, would you listen to me? What the hell's the matter with you?"

Slater turned to him, and Brody saw in his eyes the same cold glitter that he knew had been in his own from the moment he'd learned that McBride had Amy. "He has Victoria," Slater said simply. "And I'm going to get her back."

"I see." Brody's smile was feral. "Good. Then I reckon I won't have to beg for your help."

Slater showed surprise. "You're going, too?"

"Of course. I'm the one he wants. That's why he took Amy. He told Dorette to let me know that he'll trade Amy for me. If I don't surrender to him, Amy's dead."

"He'll shoot you as soon as you show your face. McBride doesn't take anyone alive."

"You don't have to tell me how McBride works."

"So you plan to walk in and let him kill you?"

"I can't let him kill Amy."

"He'll probably kill her anyway. And Victoria. They'll have seen him gun you down in cold blood, and he won't want them talking." A faint smile, half rueful, half proud, touched his lips. "And there's no other way to keep Victoria quiet."

"That's why I came for you. If he kills me, I want you there to make sure he doesn't hurt Amy."

"What are we standing around here for? Let's ride."

Slater glanced over his shoulder. The sun had just set in a splash of crimson, gold and purple, and a golden glow still edged the horizon. It would soon be dark, but they weren't far from their destination now. The telegram had directed Brody to go to the old Cofield farmhouse, two miles from Schmidt's Creek, a tiny settlement southwest of San Antonio, and they were almost there. They had made good time, despite having to accomplish the first portion of their journey in the dark last night.

Slater turned his eyes to his companion. Brody had been traveling even longer and had gotten less sleep than he, but he showed no signs of slowing down. He was tough. But that was no surprise to Slater. What had surprised him was Brody's coming back at all, knowing that he faced certain death at McBride's hands. Slater had known Brody didn't lack for courage, but he had never suspected him of such emotional depths. He could see in Brody's eyes the same cold combination of hatred, determination and fear for his woman that lay inside Slater himself.

If McBride had hurt Victoria, if he had dared to lay a hand on her, he would kill him. It was no idle threat; he would see McBride dead at his feet. If Slater had needed anything to convince him of his feelings for Victoria, this had. He'd never before felt this kind of murderous rage or heart-stopping fear. He loved her. Once he got her back, he would never let her out of his sight again. If the only way he could save Victoria from McBride was to give his own life in exchange, he would do it, just as Brody was willing to give his in exchange for Amy's.

Slater couldn't help but admire the man for it.

"Why are you giving yourself up to save her?" Slater asked.

Brody glanced at him in surprise. They hadn't talked except for a few necessary exchanges. "That's a damn fool question."

"Humor me."

Brody grimaced and looked away again. "Because I lov
her."

"I had begun to think you did. But then you left her behin
in San Antonio. I figured I'd been wrong."

"You think it would be love to make her live on the run?" H
let out a short, mirthless laugh. "I didn't want her exposed t
people like Cam McBride. I didn't want her to have to watch m
die, or kill people."

"But you were running to Mexico. You could have gon
straight."

"Bounty hunters don't respect national boundaries. Yo
know that. As long as I was alive, wherever I was they'd hav
been after me."

They reached Schmidt's Creek, and Slater dismounted an
knocked on a door to ask the way to the old Cofield place. The
started off again. It wouldn't be long now.

"You know," Slater commented as they rode, "there migh
be a way to stop McBride without your getting killed."

Brody searched Slater's face in the ever-increasing gloom
"Why? So you can take me back to prison?"

"It would be better than dying."

"I can tell you haven't been in prison."

"You want Amy to live with knowing you died for her?"

"No. Of course I'd rather come out of it alive. But I don't se
how."

"I've been thinking. I have a plan. You might come out o
it with a whole skin."

"You're a strange one, Slater. You've been after me like
dog with a bone for two years. I wouldn't think you'd car
whether you brought me in breathing or cold."

"Maybe I've killed too many men in my life. Do you want t
try this my way or not?"

Brody shrugged. "Sure. Let's hear it."

Victoria tugged uselessly against the ropes that bound he
hands behind the chair. She had never felt so helpless in her life
With McBride holding a gun on Amy, she had had no choice bu
to walk out of the hotel, saddle her horse and ride out with him
McBride had taken Amy up on his horse in front of him and ha
kept the gun jammed in her side, so Victoria had still been un

able to escape, even in the dark and on horseback. Once they'd reached this old, dilapidated house, he had tied her up.

At first he had underestimated Victoria and had tied her hands in front of her, but after she'd tried for his gun and almost gotten it, he'd tied her hands behind the chair. It had been two days now, and he hadn't untied her except to let her eat or answer the call of nature, and then he'd kept a gun to Amy's head the whole time.

Amy, of course, had been scared out of her mind by the abduction. She had shivered and cried all the way out to the farmhouse, and, ever since, she'd sat like a stone, staring at the floor. McBride had untied her to make her cook their meals, and the last time, he'd let her stay untied, realizing that Amy was no threat to him.

Victoria ached for Amy's fear, but she couldn't help but wish her cousin could remain calm in a crisis. If only McBride would leave them alone, maybe Victoria could at least get Amy to untie her bonds. But McBride hadn't given them a second by themselves. He'd even crudely relieved himself right in front of them.

She glanced over at McBride. He was watching her. When he saw her looking at him, he gave her a leering smile. Victoria wondered how long it would be before he made good on his threats to rape her. He obviously enjoyed building up her fear; she was sure that was why he had waited as long as he had. He found it fun to touch her breasts and make her flinch, or to describe what he planned to do to her and watch the revulsion and fear she couldn't keep out of her face. But he was also getting bored, waiting for Brody. If much more time passed without Brody showing up, Victoria was afraid that McBride would take his impatience and irritation out on her.

Now she put on her coolest, haughtiest face to show him that he didn't scare her, staring him down instead of turning away in terror. As she watched him, she noticed Amy behind him in the kitchen, making their supper. It took a moment for her to register how odd her cousin's movements were. Instead of slowly, listlessly preparing the food, as she had been doing minutes before, Amy was tiptoeing all over the room, silently opening the cabinets and peering inside. Now and then she glanced back over her shoulder at McBride.

Suddenly it occurred to Victoria that Amy had been playac ing. Why, that crafty girl! She wasn't numb with fear; she ha tricked McBride into thinking she was, and she was using th freedom she'd gained to search the place. No doubt she wa looking for a knife or some other weapon.

Victoria was glad that she had rigidly schooled her face int a cold, haughty mask. Otherwise she might have given away th fact that something was going on with Amy. Now that she ha caught on, she would keep McBride's attention on herself, t give Amy more time to search.

"He's not coming, you know," she said, saying the firs thing she could think of that would irritate her captor. "Wh should Brody risk his life to save us?"

McBride grinned. "'Cause he's hot for your little cousir that's why. I heard him talking to her. He don't want to see he dead."

"You're talking romantic nonsense. Men like Brody don sacrifice themselves for a woman."

Behind them in the kitchen, Amy heard her cousin's word: She could have told Victoria that she was wrong. Brody woul come for her. However unhappy she had been because he'd le her, Amy knew Sam had done it out of love. She had seen th love shining in his eyes, heard it in his voice, felt it in his touch Brody would never let McBride harm her. It was that know edge that had shaken her out of her quivering fear last nigh McBride would kill Sam as soon as he showed up—unless sh did something to stop him.

She had pretended to continue to be numb with fear, hopin to make McBride relax his guard around her. It had been ob vious from the first that he was far less careful with her than h was with Victoria. The last time he'd untied her, he hadn bothered to tie her up again. He had hardly looked at her whil she fixed supper, which had given her the opportunity to searc the kitchen for a knife. But she had discovered that the peop who had lived here had left no knives behind. The only thin she had found to use against McBride was the cast-iron skill in which she was cooking. She guessed that would have to d If she could sneak up on him and knock him over the head wit it, the skillet would do fine. The only problem was she wa afraid she couldn't get close enough to him without him hea ing or sensing she was there. If she tried and failed, he'd be on to her scheme, and she'd never have another chance.

Amy set to work on supper, all the while worrying about what she should do. If only that monster would leave her and Victoria alone for a few minutes! She could ask Victoria for advice. She could even untie her hands, and the two of them could jump McBride when he returned. But she was beginning to think that he never would.

"McBride!" a man's voice called from outside in the dark.

McBride and Victoria jumped, surprised, and Amy went utterly still. Sam! Oh, no, Sam was here! Amy dumped the meat from the skillet and curled her hand around the handle. She started forward quietly, holding the pan behind her back.

McBride jumped up from where he was sitting and grabbed his shotgun. He hurried to the window and peered out. The moonlight revealed a man standing in the distance, far out of shotgun range. McBride waited, his palms sweating. Brody came forward slowly.

"McBride! This is Brody. I'm here. Let Amy go."

"Not till I've got you tied up. You come in, then I'll let her go."

"I'm not coming any farther until I see that she's all right. Show her to me."

"You ain't calling the shots here, Brody. I am. You'll see her when you get here."

Brody stopped. "No. Now. I want to see her now."

McBride laughed. "You ain't seeing her. I'm not setting foot outside this house where you can see me."

"Then let Amy out by herself."

"You must think I'm a fool. Well, I ain't. You come in, or you'll hear a gunshot, and you'll know that's Amy."

The attention of all three occupants of the room was riveted on the front window and Brody's voice. None of them noticed the man who slipped like a shadow through the kitchen window behind them.

Outside, Brody started forward again. McBride sighted down his gun, tensing.

"Drop it, McBride." Slater's voice was deadly in the quiet room.

Amy and McBride both whirled around at his words, and Victoria twisted in her chair. "Slater!"

McBride pointed his gun at Victoria. "No. You drop it. Unless you'd like to see this little lady splattered all over the room."

Slater's mouth twisted. He dropped the gun.

Amy raised her skillet and brought it down as hard as she could on McBride's arm. His gun dropped, going off as it hit the floor and blasting a hole in the side wall. Slater was across the room in an instant, leaping at McBride. He knocked him to the floor, and the two men rolled across it, struggling.

"Slater's gun!" Victoria screamed to Amy. "Get his gun!"

Amy darted across the room and picked up the gun, but the two men were too close together for her to get a clear shot. They lurched to their feet, and Slater landed a blow to McBride's chin. The bounty hunter staggered back, crashing into the table. The kerosene lamp atop the table fell to the floor and broke, and suddenly there was fire running up the legs of the table and across the wooden planks of the floor. Amy and Victoria screamed. McBride came back at Slater, punching wildly.

The door burst open, and Brody charged into the room, his revolver in his hand. He couldn't get a clear shot, either, and he cursed briefly, then ran across the room. Coming up behind the two men locked in combat, he brought his pistol down hard on McBride's head, and the bounty hunter sagged to the floor.

"Sam!" Amy ran across the room to him and threw herself against his chest. He wrapped his arms around her and held her close. He buried his face in her hair.

"Amy. Oh, God, Amy."

"Please don't leave me, Sam. Please don't leave me again."

"I won't. Ever." He knew he couldn't, not now. He'd done it once, and that had used up all the nobility in him. He didn't have the willpower to do it again. "I won't let you out of my sight."

He looked up. Slater was across the room, pulling out his knife and slicing through Victoria's bonds. The fire was spreading rapidly, already racing up the walls.

"Come on, let's get out of here." Brody took Amy's hand, and they ran out of the house. He hadn't thought there would be a chance to escape from Slater, if he managed to survive

McBride, but now he saw it. While Slater was busy setting Victoria free, he had a few precious moments to spare. "Where are the horses?"

"Over there." She pointed to a stand of trees.

Brody had never put a bridle and saddle on a horse so fast in his life. He threw Amy into the saddle and jumped up behind her to ride to where his own animal was tied. He glanced toward the house. It was burning rapidly now, the flames bright against the black night sky. Victoria stood in front of the house, her hands to her mouth, staring at the front door. Where the hell was Slater? Brody touched his heels to the horse, and it started off. At that moment fire burst through the roof, and it collapsed.

"Slater!" Victoria screamed, and started running back to the house.

Brody hesitated, then turned the horse and ran toward Victoria. He jumped to the ground and grabbed her arm before she could reach the door. "Hold it! What the hell are you doing? You'll kill yourself."

Victoria struggled against his grasp. "Let me go! Slater's inside there! He said he couldn't let McBride burn to death like that, and he stayed to pull him out. Then the roof collapsed. He's trapped! Let me go!"

"That damn noble son of a bitch." He looked at the house, then back at Amy, sitting on the horse. All he had to do was ride away, and he'd be free. His face contorted, and he shoved Victoria toward Amy. "You stay here. I'll get the fool."

He loped toward the house and through the front door.

The heat hit him like a blow. The air was filled with smoke, and he couldn't see. He crouched over to get below the smoke and ran toward the place where McBride had fallen. "Slater?"

"Brody?"

The surprise in Slater's voice would have made him laugh if he'd been in the mood for humor. He wasn't.

Brody crouched even lower, almost crawling, and hurried toward the voice. The heat seared his lungs. A stray flame jumped out and lit his sleeve, and he beat it out. He almost stumbled over Slater's boots before he saw him. A beam had fallen, and lay across Slater's legs. At first he thought Slater's legs had been crushed, but then he saw that the beam had caught on something, keeping its full weight off the other man.

"Can you move your feet?"

"Yeah. My legs aren't broken." Slater coughed. "It's just too heavy. No leverage."

Brody went to the side of the beam that slanted upward. He followed it up until he could squat down and get his shoulder under it. "When I lift up, get the hell out. All right?"

"Yeah."

Brody tried to stand, shoving with all his strength. The beam moved up by inches. The smoke was all around him, and he held his breath against it. He closed his eyes, straining upward. There was a hand on his shoulder. He opened his eyes. Slater was on his feet beside him.

"Come on."

Brody dropped the beam, and the two of them ran, bending over to escape the worst of the smoke. They stumbled out the door. The air outside was cleaner, and they sucked it in gratefully, coughing. Victoria and Amy led them away from the burning house. Brody collapsed on the grass, gasping and struggling for breath. Amy fussed over him, wiping the soot from his face and exclaiming over the hole burned in his sleeve.

When he had recovered his breath, he looked over at Slater. Slater sat with his arms around Victoria and his head resting against hers, eyes closed. Brody thought of grabbing Amy's hand and running for her horse, but he knew he wouldn't make it before Slater could draw his pistol and fire. Anyway, he no longer had the strength to run.

Slater opened his eyes, and the two men looked at each other for a long moment. Slater said, "I reckon if Amy chose to ride off with Cam McBride to some other state, nobody'd think a thing about it."

"What?" Victoria stared at him as if he'd lost his mind. "What are you talking about? Cam McBride's dead—in there." She pointed toward the house.

"No. Sam Brody's dead in there. McBride shot him. Rescued Amy. And I think they fell in love and left the state together." He continued to look at Brody.

Something squeezed up tight in Brody's chest. Amy blinked, and a giggle bubbled up out of her throat. "Oh, Sam. Thank you, Mr. Slater."

Brody nodded once at Slater. He turned back to Amy. "You ready?"

Amy nodded, and Brody walked away to untie his horse.

Victoria slipped out of Slater's arms and stood up. "Amy? You're going with him?"

Amy's face glowed. "Yes. Oh, yes."

Victoria looked at Brody. She didn't understand it. She couldn't imagine Amy with this man. But Amy was happy. She couldn't ask for any more than that. She went to her cousin and hugged her. "I'll miss you."

"I'll miss you, too. Maybe someday I'll come for a visit." She smiled. "And bring my children."

"I hope so." Victoria swallowed the enormous lump in her throat.

Brody rejoined them, leading his own horse. As he and Amy mounted and started off toward the road, Amy twisted around in her saddle to wave, and Victoria waved back. Slater put his arm around Victoria's shoulders, and they watched the other couple until the darkness swallowed them up.

"She's gone." Tears shimmered in Victoria's voice.

"It's what she wanted."

"I know."

Slater turned and looked back at the house. It was consumed by flames, half fallen in, and the fire was beginning to die down. He sighed. "I guess we'd better ride, too. Where's your horse?"

"Amy took it. McBride put Amy on his horse, so he could keep his gun in her ribs."

Slater's eyes darkened, and the hard line of his mouth was suddenly softer. "Then we'll have to ride double, won't we?"

Victoria nodded, the familiar melting warmth starting in her abdomen at the thought of being so close to him. They set McBride's horse free; it wouldn't do to ride it back into town when they were claiming McBride had left the state. Then they got up on Slater's horse, Victoria sitting crosswise on Slater's lap, snug between the saddle horn and his chest. She shifted her bottom, and Slater felt himself harden in response. His arms went around her to handle the reins.

"I'm glad we only have one horse," he murmured, bending his head close to her. "I don't want to let you go long enough to ride back to town."

Victoria leaned against his chest, sighing contentedly. "I'm glad, too." She felt warm and protected in his arms. Frankly, she didn't want to be anyplace else, ever again. She could feel the rigid line of his desire beneath her, and she liked that, too. After all he'd been through and tired as he was, he still wanted her. She squirmed a little just to feel his immediate, firm response. A smile curved her lips.

"Witch." He pressed his lips against her hair, his voice amused. "You're determined to drive me crazy, aren't you?"

"Not completely crazy..." she demurred, stretching up to kiss the tender skin of his throat.

He made a noise, and his arms tightened around her. His free hand came up to cup her breast, caressing her nipple through the cloth of her blouse.

"I thought you didn't want me anymore," Victoria admitted, her fingers working at the buttons of his shirt. "When you left like that, without a word about coming back, or how you felt..."

"Not want you!" Slater nuzzled her ear, his breath searing her skin. "How could you think that? I want you all the time. I can't think of anything else."

"Then why didn't you say anything? Why didn't you ask me to wait?"

"How could I? I didn't know when I'd be back—or if I'd even be coming back. It might have turned out that I'd wind up dead instead of Brody."

"Don't say things like that."

"It's the truth." He sucked in his breath sharply as Victoria finished with his buttons and slipped her hand inside his opened shirt. "I didn't have anything to offer you. I still don't."

"Yourself. That's all I want."

She pulled the sides of his shirt apart and kissed his chest. Her lips moved over him slowly. He shuddered, and his hand came up to wind through her hair, pulling her head away.

"No, wait. Stop. I can't think when you're doing that, and there's something I have to say."

Victoria gazed up at him. Her lips were damp and slightly parted, her face soft with desire. Her eyes shone up at him with trust and love and a deep hunger. The sight shook him even more than the exquisite pleasure of her lips on his skin.

"Oh, Victoria. God, I love you." He swallowed, trying to collect his scattered thoughts.

"Good. 'Cause I love you, too. And this time I won't let you escape."

"I'm not planning to go anywhere. That's what I want to say. I don't want to be without you. I want—well, would you consider marrying me? I know I don't have much to offer. But I've been thinking. I could quit the Rangers. I'm getting tired of being rootless and alone, chasing crooks. We could settle down at my ranch, but it's been neglected for three years. We'd have to build a herd. It's nothing like what you're used to."

Victoria placed her hand across his mouth to stop the flow of words. "Hush. I'm not looking for money or comfort. I told you, all I want is you. I love you, Slater, and I'd marry you if you had nothing. I can't think of anything I'd like better than spending the rest of my life with you, building a herd and a ranch that will be better than anything I grew up with. Yes." She moved her hand away and kissed him firmly. "Yes, I'll marry you."

She kissed him again. His hand came up behind her head, and he held her there, kissing her thoroughly. When at last they separated, Slater's eyes were glittering, and his skin felt like fire.

He looped the reins around the saddle horn, then lifted his hand to the fastenings of her skirt. "Slater! What are you doing?"

He grinned wickedly, swinging her around to face him.

"There's something I've been thinking about for days. I think it's time you really learned how to ride double."

Victoria's eyes widened, and she wrapped her arms around his neck. "Anything you have to teach, I'm ready to learn."

His mouth came down to take hers in a kiss that seemed to last forever. There wasn't going to be any more chasing and hurrying. From now on, they had all the time in the world.

* * * * *